THE SAND BRIDE

-- Book 2 --

CYANA GAFFNEY

This is a work of fiction. Names, characters, businesses, places, and incidents either are the product of the author's imagination or are used fictitiously. Any resemblance to actual persons, living or dead, events or locales is entirely coincidental.

Copyright © 2017 Cyana Gaffney

Published by Blue Sky Publishing

All rights reserved.

ISBN-13: 978-1981291991
ISBN-10: 1981291997

TO MY SISTER
&
TO HE, WHO GAVE ME THIS DREAM

CHAPTER 1

With the death toll now over three hundred, this new frustration he felt seemed to be shrinking his skin, as if it was trying to constrict him. He hated the sensation. He shifted in his seat. It didn't help.

Ehsan couldn't believe that a bombing had happened so close to home. He didn't agree with many of the radicals' politics, and now with this foolish act of theirs, they had added to his workload and he resented it. He resented them.

What were they thinking?

Tensing his jaw, his teeth started grinding against each other.

Bombing one of the westerner compounds? It's… it's so incredibly reckless. No, it's stupid and idiotic.

He glared out the window. The scenery whipped by.

At least I get a short break. Who knows what will be required to smooth this all over and clean up their mess?

The car rounded the last corner. Ehsan rubbed his temples in hopes to dislodge the headache starting to build behind his eyes. The four-day trip to Dammam had taken more out of him than he realized. He yawned again and rubbed the back of his neck. Despite all the stress rising up in him, a thought crept in. It infused him with anticipation and succeeded in pushing his ill emotions away.

Seeing his new bride again couldn't come fast enough. The last time he had seen Hailey, that beautiful American treasure, she had displeased him. He hoped she was starting to settle in and that maybe the time alone had helped her to accept her fate as his third wife. Regardless, he knew, as time went on, things would be much more fruitful between them. The thought pulled at the corners of his mouth.

His shoulders slumped as the car drove through the front gate of his estate. Hailey wasn't on the front steps with the others. His other two wives were there with the house staff and his sons, but where was Hailey?

Maya stood proud and strong, smiling at him, proving to him yet again that she was an excellent choice for his first wife. Ghada, his tender soul, stood fidgeting beside Maya, keeping her eyes on the ground. He pursed his lips. Ghada, on the other hand, would still take more grooming.

"Where is Hailey?" Ehsan asked as he climbed out of the car.

"She's gone to the market *again* with Daib."

At Maya's emphasis on the word again, a silent alarm sounded in his head. He took a breath to keep his cool.

"Again? Has she been going out a lot?" Ehsan looked suspiciously at Ghada as he spoke.

Ghada lowered her head, avoiding eye contact with him.

"Nothing to concern yourself with. She's planned to cook us a great dinner once you returned. I can call Daib and have him bring her back now if you wish for the dinner to be tonight."

Ehsan would never tire of her respect for him. *I wish Ghada would express it as naturally.*

"No, that won't be necessary. Leave her be."

After instructing his staff to take care of his bags, he greeted each of his five sons, then dismissed them along with his wives. Too tired to take the stairs, he entered the elevator.

Collapsing into the padded, oak chair behind his desk, he let out a deep sigh.

Actually, a nice meal might be just the thing to perk me up. I think I will call Daib... soon. The house bank accounts would need his attention first.

Warmth spread over him as he thought about how Hailey showed ambition to add to the household. He scooted the chair closer to the desk.

I bet she's enjoying the expense account I left for her. Money is such a helpful persuader. He didn't know much about her life back in the US, but he knew it was nowhere near as luxurious as she would soon get used to by being with him. His chest puffed out as he smirked to himself.

He opened his laptop, and after a few clicks, his eyes met the balance in her account. Both hands curled into fists. Ehsan tried to shake it off and think of what possible justifications there could be for it being so low. It didn't work. Something wasn't right.

He stood abruptly as the concern erupted, causing his chair to roll back and strike the wall behind him. He stormed out of the office and thundered downstairs. He could hear Maya's voice before she came into view.

Seeing her at the bottom of the stairs in a conversation with one of the maids, Ehsan didn't bother to try and hold in the anger.

"Where is Ghada?" he screamed.

"Ah, ah... she's in the library. What's wrong?"

Ehsan ignored her and continued his pace to the library. Bursting through the doors, he saw Ghada standing with her back to him, phone in hand.

"Who is that?" Ehsan yelled as he spun her around to face him.

Ghada's face paled. "It's... it's..."

Ehsan grabbed the phone but didn't put it up to his ear. With his free hand, he grabbed Ghada's arm and squeezed, causing her to yelp.

"You better not have been planning another escape with Hailey."

"No, I-I wasn't going to go with her. She..." Ghada's face filled with fear and she clamped her hand over her mouth and started to cry.

"So... Hailey is planning something? Get to your room." Ehsan shoved her towards the door. "I'll deal with you later."

As soon as Ghada had run out, Ehsan put the phone up to his ear.

"Daib, I'm guessing?"

"Y-y-yes?"

Daib's voice sounded pitiful and it added to Ehsan's anger.

"Where are you? Are you with Hailey?" he demanded.

"We're... we're... at the market by Deera Square."

"Don't move!"

Ehsan got the details as to their exact location, then slammed the phone down and stormed out of the library. Every inch of him seethed from not knowing who to direct his anger at first.

- - - - - - -

Ehsan paced around the room as the frustration turned violently inside his core. His hands were clammy, and his throat hurt from the lack of moisture. It had been hours since Hailey had run from him in the square. He still couldn't believe she had been bold enough to try, and even more shocked she so easily got away.

Ehsan stopped pacing and leaned on the edge of his desk.

"So... what you're telling me is that you still have no clue where she is. How can that be?" Ehsan pounded his fist on the desk, his bellow echoing off the walls of his office.

"My apologies, Councilman. But we have tracked down most of her movements after she left the square. Two officers had pursued her after they left the market. I personally, and discreetly, talked with them. They don't know the details of your..." Taavi paused, seeming to search for the correct word, "arrangement."

Ehsan breathed out a frustrated sigh. "I appreciate your discretion, Taavi. However, I'm more interested in what happened to my bride, so please stop wasting time by trying to appease me with frivolous tact."

"Of course." Taavi cleared his throat. "From the intel we have, she ran into a man as she left the market. For whatever reason, he held her for a moment which caught the attention of one of the religious police."

Tension gripped every muscle as he thought about another man touching Hailey, but he managed to remain silent.

"It was strange," Taavi continued, "but the man then ran with her when the Mutawa called to them. The Mutawa alerted some officers to assist. But even after the officers got involved, the man continued to run with her."

"Was he Saudi?"

"No, a Westerner."

Ehsan was shaking now from the contempt. His hands desperately desired to be around the man's throat.

"Who was he?" Ehsan demanded.

"No one knows. As the officers were gaining on them, they jumped into a vehicle and drove off."

"Tell me they were able to track down that vehicle."

"We are still looking into that. But we did put up wanted posters for them at all the stations, and alerted all the officers."

"Hmmm... that's not enough. I want roadblocks set up within the hour at all the major roads out of Riyadh, as well as alerting the border crossings into the United Arab Emirates."

"And at the Riyadh airport?" Taavi suggested.

"No, Hailey's smart. She wouldn't chance to try to fly out of Riyadh without papers, and she'd probably expect that I would send people there." Ehsan paused, he didn't want to be hasty and miss something and have her slip through their fingers. "Actually, send out notices to the airport... and to all of the other major border crossings out of Saudi. My guess is she'd head for Dubai. I doubt she'd go south. But I don't want to assume anything, so get as many blocks set as you can manage. You can get Hailey's photo off of the security cameras. There should be a decent shot of her when she first arrived."

"Of course, Councilman. I will see to it right away."

Taavi shifted while he wrote some notes. The movement annoyed Ehsan. When he didn't move toward the door but continued to look down at his notepad, pen still poised over the paper, Ehsan's irritation grew.

"What is it?"

"What... um, would you like me to tell them when I send out her photo?"

"Oh right. Good question." Ehsan bit his lip as he searched for an idea in his mind, but nothing came to him.

"If I may offer a suggestion, Councilman?"

Ehsan nodded his head.

"We could send a report along that explains you had sponsored her to tutor your sons in their English studies, but that she had stolen from you and is now on the run."

Ehsan's eyes squinted. His lips curled as the story sunk in.

"Yes, Taavi, I think that will do quite nicely. Get it done at once."

Ehsan watched as Taavi left the room, but his mind was already elsewhere.

Now to deal with my family.

CHAPTER 2

Taavi had left some time ago, but Ehsan remained at his desk. He knew he needed to go and talk with Ghada and Daib to find out what they knew, but his anger just wouldn't subside.

He rubbed his temples.

You need to calm down, Ehsan. You need to think this through.

His cell phone rang.

Taking a deep breath, he looked at the number.

Damn!!

It was work.

"Hello?"

"I'm sorry to bother you so soon, Councilman. I know you haven't been home long. But we received a call from the defense minister's office. They are requesting your attendance at a meeting tomorrow. Can you arrange that?"

Ehsan could taste the bile rising up his throat. It couldn't be a worse time to be away from home. *I couldn't possibly leave Taavi to deal with all this. I can't let Hailey get away.*

"Councilman?"

"Yes, of course." Ehsan shook his head to focus. "What time?"

"7:00 a.m."

When the phone clicked off, Ehsan checked his watch.

Probably too late to question them. Ghada's probably already asleep.

He pushed his chair back from the desk and stood. Pacing the room. Everything seemed to be slipping away from him, and he couldn't act fast enough to catch up.

I should go and wake them. He moved towards the door. He paused. *What good would it do? Maybe I should leave that to Taavi.*

Ehsan stroked his beard. He should talk to Taavi. He walked over to his desk, leaned over, and pushed the small red button tucked under the beveled edge. He held it for a few moments, then released it.

Ehsan did another two laps around the room. It did little to ease the tension.

A knock sounded. He rounded the desk and sat.

"Come!"

Taavi entered and stood at attention with his arms behind his back. "Is everything alright?"

"Yes, Taavi, but I have some unfortunate news. I have been summoned to speak with the defense minister tomorrow morning. Are you able to handle things from here?" Ehsan didn't wait for a reply. "First, I need you to succeed in tracking down that vehicle. My guess is that my surprise arrival might have derailed Hailey's plans, so that vehicle might still be our best lead."

Taavi nodded his agreement.

"I also need you to question Ghada and Daib while I'm gone. I'm wary of the odds that Hailey confided in them. But if she did stick to her plan, those two are the only ones who might know what that plan was."

"Is there anything else?"

Ehsan thought for a moment. "No, but if I think of something,

I'll let you know. I'm not sure how much I will be available tomorrow or even when I'll be back." Ehsan leaned forward and rested his elbows on the desk, narrowing his eyes. "So you need to understand how much trust I'm putting in you with this."

"Of course, Councilman. I am honored to be charged with such an important task. And if you will permit me, I will put my second in charge of your detail tomorrow."

"Very well. But don't let me down!"

- - - - - - -

A rush of activity filled the morning as Ehsan left the house early and made his way to the heart of the city. He made sure to arrive an hour early and now sat waiting for someone to direct him. A few people walked past him, but clearly, none of them were sent for him. The sound of the clock on the wall in front of him stole an inch of his peace with each tick.

He'd never admit it, but his nerves were getting the best of him. His sweaty hands were the only proof. He dried them on his robe and tried to watch the bustle of the office to distract him.

Taavi is the best head of security you've ever had, Ehsan tried to reassure himself. *He will find her. Relax!*

He needed to get to work if he couldn't be home. Sitting still was becoming unbearable.

"Please, follow me, Councilman. The minister is ready for you now."

Ehsan stood and eagerly followed the man down the hallway and into a large office.

Rich furnishings decorated the room. A long conference table sat in the center of the room. Numerous men already were seated around it, but Ehsan only recognized a few of them. After a few others had joined them, the minister entered.

"Please, take your seats. I won't bother with introductions. Time is sensitive today." The minister stopped to look up from his notes. After seeing them all nod, he looked back down.

"Has it been confirmed yet who is responsible for the bombing?" the minister said, addressing the two men who sat opposite of Ehsan.

"The reports are coming in as we speak, Minister." the man on the left confirmed. "You will have them on your desk by the time you leave here."

"Good."

The minister addressed a few others with more questions, but Ehsan's mind started to wander. He usually loved being in such a room. It gave him an intoxicating sense of power and importance. However, his mind kept pulling his attention away.

I wonder where she is?

He quickly squeezed his eyes shut to summon some focus.

"I have asked Ehsan Al-Ma'mar to join us today," the minister informed the room as he looked at Ehsan. "I have been told that you have been on the ground at Dammam for the last few days and have just recently returned home. Is that correct?"

Ehsan sat up straight and cleared his throat. "Yes, sir."

"Good to hear. It has been decided that you will be our liaison with the oil companies. Entrata has already pulled out most of their foreign workers, and there are others who are threatening to do the same. You are tasked with aiding in helping with the arrangements of those who wish to leave. You are not in any way permitted to try and negotiate with them to get them to stay. That will be done at a later date when we can offer them answers and more assurances. Do you understand?"

"Yes, I fully understand. I know how delicate this situation is and I, in no way, wish to threaten any of our foreign oil relations." Ehsan's resolve wavered for a moment, and he stole a quick breath. "And in light of that. I think I must disclose that I am in the midst of a family crisis. So I graciously and most humbly ask, if possible, that someone else is to be given this honor at this time."

Ehsan held his breath. The minister's eyes bore into him. Ehsan instantly regretted the request, but it was too late to recant it. The minister stood, everyone else in the room did the same. Ehsan forced his head to stay tall to portray confidence and respect.

"Ehsan, the country's crisis outranks yours. You will do this job, and you will do it well."

"Of course, Minister. It will be my honor," Ehsan lied as he bowed his head.

"Everyone is dismissed. Ehsan, stay here. Someone will be in shortly to brief you on what you need to know."

- - - - - - -

There was not one moment where Ehsan wasn't in a meeting that he could call and check in with Taavi. With all the time differences between Riyadh and the other cities, the calls with the delegates or presidents of the oil companies happened sporadically throughout the day and late into the evening. Then meetings and debriefing sessions interspersed each of those calls with representatives from different government departments. Ehsan stifled a yawn as he stared at the computer screen.

He discreetly looked down at his watch as the president from one of the Canadian oil companies expressed his concern over the video chat. It was two o'clock in the morning, which meant that Hailey had been gone for more than thirty-six hours. The lack of knowledge about any developments drove Ehsan insane. He shifted uncomfortably in his chair.

"I can assure you, we will aid you in any way you need, regardless of your decision." Ehsan forced his attention back to the screen. "Yes, we are all shaken by this tragedy. On behalf of all the Saudi officials, we wish to convey to you that we are committed to helping you and your workers feel safe until the issue is resolved. I want to thank you for your time and will wait for your instructions."

After saying goodbye, he clicked off the call. Ehsan yawned and looked around the room. After the briefing that morning, they had set him up in a small office a few doors away from the boardroom. The room felt stuffy and confining compared to his office at work and even more so compared to his grand home office. But he didn't dare complain again, he just got to work.

He yawned again. It was unfortunate it was so late. His mind was shot, and he doubted he would process any updates from Taavi very well. He picked up his cell from the desk.

Maybe it's best that I get a few hours of sleep before talking to Taavi. If he had any important or time-sensitive news, he would have tried to call.

Ehsan stretched in his seat. His body ached. He couldn't wait to get home. As he waited for his new security detail to answer, the ringing seemed louder than usual, and it exasperated his impatience.

Taavi better have some good news.

CHAPTER 3

Taavi barely got a wink of sleep after his second in command called to inform him that they were on their way back to the house. He had hoped he would have another day before he needed to report his findings, but now that wouldn't be possible.

He plodded around the room with nervous steps. Ehsan was still asleep but could wake at any moment. Likely demanding a report immediately.

I hope I don't lose my job over this.

Something moved over by the door. Taavi stopped pacing.

Ehsan entered the room slowly, looking him up and down as he closed the door behind him.

"Please, tell me you know something," Ehsan said yawning. "Did you track down the car?"

Taavi decided a direct, confident tone would be the best course. "No, Councilman. That lead ran cold. But we have set up secure roadblocks as you requested. The lead officers at each site have been instructed to report anything even remotely suspicious."

"I guess that means there has been no news from any of them then?"

Ehsan's tone turned Taavi's stomach into knots, but Taavi

didn't let it show. He kept staring straight ahead.

"No, Councilman, not yet. But it is still early."

"What about Ghada and Daib? Did they give you anything useful?"

"I have men searching for Daib as we speak."

"What? Why?"

"The coward never returned to the house and isn't answering his phone."

Taavi hoped that the insult would redirect Ehsan's anger away from him. Ehsan walked over to the sitting area and sat on one of the pillows. He put his head in his hands and pushed a forceful breath out of his lungs.

"What about Ghada?"

"She refused to talk to me. I tried multiple times and told her that I was tasked, by you, to find out what she knew. But she stonewalled me each time."

Ehsan raised his head and glared at Taavi.

"I didn't know how forceful you wished for me to be with her. She is your wife, and I would never dream of overstepping and dishonoring you like that."

Taavi hoped the flattery would dull Ehsan's disappointment. He held his breath.

"Yes, of course. You made the right call. If Ghada isn't cooperating, then it is my job to deal with it."

"Thank you, Councilman."

"Taavi, I need you to visit each of the roadblocks in the city. I want the officers in charge to confirm with you personally, that there have been no American's going through. If you find anything, you need to report it to me immediately. We can't waste any time by just waiting around hoping to hear something."

"Of course, Ehsan. I'll leave immediately. Are you going to talk to Ghada now?"

Ehsan looked at his watch. "Damn it. No, I have a meeting this morning with the defense minister. I'll talk to her when I'm back."

Ehsan rose and headed for the door.

"Let me know if she tells you anything of use, and I'll adjust my course as needed."

"I will. Now get going. I'm already fearful that it's been too long and, as such, Hailey's already made it through. But at least she doesn't have papers, so that's something." Ehsan looked exhausted and achingly sad as he spoke.

"Councilman, I won't rest until she is returned to you."

Taavi decided to head out the east side of the city. If Ehsan's guess was right and Hailey had decided to try and get to Dubai, then the roadblock at Highway 40 would be the best place to start. If nothing came from that, he would head north and around to the west, leaving the south for last.

Two and a half hours and three roadblocks later, Taavi still had nothing of worth to call Ehsan about.

Maybe she's still in Riyadh, Taavi reasoned. *If she's not, then I don't understand why she wouldn't have chosen to get to somewhere like Bahrain or over to Dubai. They're the closest.*

Taavi currently headed north, near the west side of the city, and up Highway 65. As the next roadblock came into view, he hoped that Hailey might have decided to try to make it to Buraydah and that these officers would have something to tell him.

He parked the car and exited the vehicle. As Taavi approached, he withdrew his credentials and handed them to the closest guard.

"I need to speak with the officer in charge immediately!"

"Of course. That would be the officer over there. The one with the clipboard."

Taavi looked in the direction the man pointed. He spotted the officer - a large man stroking his beard, deep in conversation with a young officer. Taavi started off towards him, careful to dodge the approaching vehicles as he went.

"Are you in charge?"

"Yes. Who are you?" The man's voice was a bit too obnoxious for Taavi's taste.

"My name is Taavi. I set up these roadblocks so I would advise you to show more respect."

The officer straightened and apologized. It was a sad attempt, but he let it slide.

"I need your report," Taavi ordered.

"As requested we searched for any American that resembled the description that was sent over and the-"

Taavi didn't have time for redundant play-by-plays, "Yes, and the photograph. Get on with it."

"No... there was no photograph. We were only given this description." The officer flipped the clipboard around so it faced Taavi.

Taavi scanned it quickly.

"So you never received the photo of her? One should have been sent along with this description."

"No. Just what's there."

Oooh, someone's going to get it, Taavi seethed silently to himself.

"I'll get you her picture. Did you have any, and I mean any, Americans come through? Or anyone that matched the description?"

The officer switched his weight from one foot to the other. The younger officer, to his right, excused himself and joined the team searching vehicles a few yards away.

"We did have one of the tour buses come through a few hours ago. It had someone who might have... ah... matched the description..."

Taavi's pulse quickened.

"... but she was from Australia, and her passport checked out."

Taavi's momentary hope deflated. "So... no Americans?"

"There were two. A woman and a man. But she didn't match the description at all."

"Where did her passport say she was from?" It was a redundant question, Hailey didn't have a passport, but it would reveal how thorough these men were at their job.

The officer hesitated and flipped through a few sheets on his clipboard.

"Now, don't tell me you aren't taking good records here," Taavi said cockily.

"No, sir. It's not that. We take detailed notes. It's just that..." The officer paused again and nervously looked over towards the group searching vehicles.

"Well, what is it then?"

"We didn't actually check her passport." The officer looked back at Taavi and swallowed hard.

"What!?!"

"Her papers were under the bus, and the line of vehicles was growing. We had to keep traffic moving."

The excuses from the officer infuriated Taavi. His hands balled into tight fists. His chest started to rise and fall dramatically with the increase of his breathing.

"Trust me, it wasn't her."

The officer's attempt to assure him did nothing to deflate even an ounce of his anger.

"She was traveling with a man, but the woman had short red hair, and her eyes weren't green. Oh, and then there was the Australian couple."

"What about them?"

"They vouched for them and said that they had been traveling together for weeks. There was no reason to suspect that it was the woman you're looking for."

"Yes, but you can't guarantee it wasn't, can you?" Taavi glared at the man. "She could have changed her appearance, you fool. We knew she didn't have papers, which is why it was paramount that you were to check every - single - one." The volume of Taavi's voice rose so dramatically that it caused everyone around them to stare. He didn't care. This man might be the reason Ehsan lost Hailey.

Taavi wiped his hand over his face. He had to calm down to keep from punching this man.

"This is ridiculous. Give me the name of the tour company!"

"Um..." the officer diverted his eyes to the clipboard again but didn't flip any pages.

"You've got to be kidding me. What's your name?"

The man complied and Taavi made a note of it.

"Now get back to work. And do better at your job this time. But trust me, you probably won't have it for very long."

Taavi turned and stormed off towards his car. Ehsan needed

to be updated. If they hurried, they might still have a chance to catch up to the bus. This all seemed too much of a coincidence not to be Hailey, and he was going to assume it was her until he knew otherwise.

=======

The meeting with the minister only lasted a couple minutes, and Ehsan was now thirty thousand feet in the air, flying back to Dammam. The small jet wasn't spacious, but it made up for it in luxury. The white-leather seats were comfortable. Gold-encased, recessed lighting lined the mahogany aisle, and a lovely lavender scent filled the cabin.

Ehsan thanked the flight attendant who handed him a drink, as he finished reclining his seat at a pleasant angle. He leaned back to look out the window. Clouds sprawled out a few feet below the plane, leaving the rest of the crystal-blue sky completely clear.

After taking a few more moments to enjoy the sight beyond the window, Ehsan set his drink down on the small table just past his knees. He reached for the dossier sitting on the seat beside him. He needed to study. Opening the front cover, he looked at the first profile. Liam Pratt, fifty years old, based out of Europe, a wife, no kids, working for Herche Oil, been in Saudi for two years, and was recovering from an amputated leg.

Ehsan cringed. *Poor bastard.*

He quickly flipped through the other profiles before closing the dossier and returning it to its seat. Being tasked with speaking to each of the compound survivors personally seemed like a waste of resources to him. But after setting the defense minister off when he had requested a replacement the first time,

Ehsan wouldn't dare to even hint at his opposing opinion.

Ehsan cringed as the memory of the conversation with the defense minister from yesterday morning replayed in his mind. He felt so stupid for even attempting it. It rolled over in his mind again and brought a feeling of nausea with it. He shifted in his seat as he tried to force his mind to think about something else. It didn't help. The conversation played once more. He chided himself for his foolishness.

- - - - - - -

"Liam Pratt?"

"Yes?" a raspy reply came.

Ehsan looked up from his file. The sight before him stopped him in his tracks. His words caught in his throat. The man laid flat, most of him wrapped in bandages. Scratches, bruises, and stitches covered everything else. Ehsan tried not to look at the stump, but the sight pulled at his eyes, making it hard to look away. He forced himself to recover quickly, hoping his response hadn't been noticed.

"I'm sorry to bother you, Mr. Pratt, but the defense minister requested that I come to hear your account of what happened. Do you mind speaking with me?"

Painful sadness flashed in the man's eyes. Ehsan diverted his attention to the chair near the end of the bed. He only looked at the man again once he was seated.

"Yes, alright."

Ehsan took out a pen and flipped to the blank page at the back of the man's file. "Please start at the beginning, but feel free to take your time," Ehsan lied, he wanted nothing more than for this man to be concise so he could get back to Riyadh as soon as possible.

The man started to shift but winced and laid back down. He laid still and silent. Ehsan tapped his foot under the bed in an attempt to keep his impatience hidden. The man took a slow breath.

"Everything seemed so... so normal that day. We got up, made breakfast, and–"

"I'm sorry. We?"

"My wife and I."

Ehsan made a note in the file.

"I was getting ready to head into the office when I heard the first explosion. I've never heard anything like it. It shook the whole house. As soon as I heard people screaming, I knew something awful had happened. I ran back to the kitchen to get Ellie. But I didn't make it there. The next explosion must have been closer to our house. Everything went black. The next thing I remember, I was waking up in an ambulance and seeing that my... my leg was gone, and everything hurt. It hurt more than I even thought was possible. And the blood. There was so much blood. I'm not sure if they gave me something or if I passed out from the pain, but everything went black again. Then I woke up here. I-I've been here ever since."

"And... your wife?"

"Dead. She's... she's dead."

"I'm truly sorry for your loss."

He gave the man an empathetic smile. Seeing tears starting to gather in the man's eyes, Ehsan dropped his head to make more notes. He couldn't imagine losing any of his wives like that. Memories of Fareeta drifted in.

But that was different, wasn't it? Ehsan debated with himself as he wrote. *Yes, definitely different. Losing my wife by my own hand is surely better than having her taken from me by foolish men. This poor man.*

"Have you been informed of the details of what happened?"

"Yes, the doctors have been to speak with me a few times. They said some suicide bombers drove into the compound and everything was destroyed. But no one will tell me anything about what to do now. I've lost everything, but I can't very well stay here forever."

"Certainly, no. Please be reassured, Mr. Pratt, we are working diligently with your government and with your employer to take the very best care of you. Everything will be taken care of, and you will be kept apprised of the situation. I'll make sure of it."

"Thank you."

"It is the least I can do."

Ehsan moved to finish off the notes, but not before his eyes betrayed him and glanced back to where the missing limb should have been. Bile rose in his throat.

- - - - - - -

By the time he had finished interviewing the seventh patient, exhaustion had set in. His hand cramped as he made the last of his notes.

He said goodbye to the man in room 319 and now only had one more person to talk to, but he needed a break. Walking up to the counter, just outside one of the patient's room, he caught the eye of one of the nurses to get directions to the cafe. With his security team in tow, Ehsan snaked through the long halls.

He slumped into a hard-plastic chair after he tasked one of his men to go put in his order. After tossing his files on the table,

Ehsan rubbed both his temples. A throbbing headache gripped deeply into his head.

He grabbed his phone to see if there were any messages from Taavi. There wasn't. He glanced at the time. The morning was almost entirely shot, and he still had that other patient to see, not to mention the flight back home.

At least I should still have time to talk to Ghada today, he tried to console himself. *I need to see if we can, by any chance, get ahead of this. Worse case, if she doesn't know anything, Taavi should be able to come up with something.*

Ignoring the smell of disinfectant, Ehsan tried to enjoy the items brought to him. After drinking his coffee and eating the small snack, he dusted off the crumbs in his beard, then rose slowly, allowing his knees to crack back into place. Resenting the fact that his age was starting to catch up with him, he stretched his arms. First in one direction then the other before grabbing the file. Yawning as he went, Ehsan made his way back to the nurse's station and asked for directions to the last patient's room: a young girl named Anna, from America.

CHAPTER 4

As the tour bus jerked and jolted along the desert road, Hailey braced her arm against the back of her seat to stay upright. Her eyes scanned Ryan's face to try and pick up the smallest indication of who might be on the phone.

Hailey's heart sank as she saw his face drain of all color. He leaned forward in his seat.

"Is this a joke?"

Ryan's voice sounded mad.

"Who is it?" Hailey whispered to him.

Ryan ignored her.

Was it Ehsan? Had he found them? The questions in her mind made her skin grow cold. Hailey's stomach lurched. They hadn't made it very far from the city, and the long fingers of her fear were reaching out to her.

"How? I mean, how can you be alive?"

After a few moments, Ryan looked at her with a small, confused smile. His eyes wide with, what seemed to be, a mix of disbelief and shock.

"It's Anna," Ryan said, shaking his head.

Anna? It was Anna! She's alive? But how? Hailey's mind couldn't accept what Ryan was saying. Her body flooded with so many competing emotions. She felt ill. Hailey pushed the feelings aside and lunged for the phone. Prying it out of Ryan's reluctant hands, she fumbled with it until it rested securely against her ear.

"Anna? Anna?"

"Hailey! Are you're OK? I can't believe Ryan found you. Are you still in Saudi?" Anna's voice sounded weak.

"How are you still alive? Ryan said the bombs destroyed everything. Where are you? Wait, how did you get this number?"

"I called Thomas, and he gave it to me." Anna chuckled. "Thomas said you were OK, but I still can't believe it. I can't believe I'm talking to you."

"It's kind of hard to believe it myself, but yeah, I'm OK. But, Anna, how are you alive?"

"You won't believe it. I don't know if Ryan told you, but my plan was going to be to call the train station in Riyadh to see if anyone had seen you. My dad…" Anna paused briefly.

Hailey could hear the sadness in her voice.

"Well… he was going to go to the Dammam train station to show your picture to everyone there, just in case you had missed your connecting flight and caught the train instead."

"Yeah, he told me."

"Well, just after Ryan left for the airport, I had switched with…my dad. His Arabic is better than mine, so I thought it would be better if he called the Riyadh train station. So, I grabbed a picture of you and headed out for the Dammam train station." There was a slight pause. "I shouldn't have…" Anna's resolve broke and she started to cry.

"Anna, I'm so sorry."

"Hailey… my parents… are dead. My friends at the

compound they're all... dead."

"I'm so sorry." Hailey felt helpless not being able to hold her. "I know what you must be feeling right now, and I wish with everything in me that I could take it from you." Hailey had to pause to stifle her tears and push back the memories of her own family. She needed to be here for Anna. "Where are you? You shouldn't be alone."

As Hailey finished the question, she could see Ryan going absolutely crazy by not being able to hear what was going on. She leaned towards his seat and tipped the phone towards him so he could hear. Ryan leaned in.

"Well, I had just gotten to the front gate when the explosions started. I wasn't quite far enough away from the blasts though. I'm pretty banged up."

"Anna?" Ryan interjected.

"Yeah?"

"I saw the gate. It was completely mangled. I can't believe you're still alive. Oh no!"

"What is it?" Hailey pulled back and looked at Ryan confused.

He grabbed her arm and pulled her back so Anna could still hear him.

"Anna, you must have still been there when I came back. The cab driver brought me back to the compound after he heard about the explosion. When I got there... Ah, I'm so stupid... I ran towards the compound and ignored all the officers yelling at me to stop. They thought I was a threat, so they took me down and handcuffed me. They let me go after things were cleared up, but I was so in shock that I just sat there for the longest time... not doing anything. Oh, Anna, I'm so sorry. I could have been there for you." Ryan raised his hand to wipe his eyes.

Hailey's heart broke. She reached out her hand to hold his shoulder, hoping the act offered a bit of comfort.

"Ryan, really it's OK. I'm OK. I was unconscious anyway so I wouldn't have even known you were there. And hey, I'm safe now."

"So, where are you?" Hailey asked.

"At a hospital in Dammam." Anna paused to cough. "I have some pretty nasty cuts and bruises, but I'm OK. Can you come here? Where are you g…"

Anna's voice trailed off.

"Anna?" Hailey said after a moment of silence.

"Just a sec."

Silence again and a few muffled voices.

"Sorry, I have to go, there's someone from the government here. I'll call you back as soon as I can."

"OK," Hailey said reluctantly. "Anna… love you."

"Love you too. We'll talk soon. Bye."

Then she was gone. Hailey hung up the phone and beamed at Ryan.

"She's alive! I can't believe it."

Hailey's heart felt like it would explode with the gratefulness that pulsed through every part of her. Her cheeks started to hurt from the force of the smile on her face.

"I know… it's crazy," Ryan said shaking his head. "Hailey, you should have seen the front gate. Here this huge piece of metal was ripped from its hinges. It was a twisted mess. But tiny Anna is alive? It's unbelievable." Ryan's tone matched Hailey's own shock.

Hailey leaned back in her seat, cradling the phone in her lap. She raised her eyes to the compartment above her head. From the shock of it all, three things kept repeating themselves in her

mind over and over again:
She's OK.
She's alive.
Thank you.

=======

Anna didn't want to hang up the phone. Hearing Hailey's voice brought her comfort. However, seeing that the man in the doorway didn't seem to have a lot of patience, she leaned over and put the receiver back on the base.

She wasn't the best at guessing ages, but he looked to be in his fifties, maybe sixties. Anna moved to readjust herself in the bed. The movement caused pain to shoot through her, and her body chided her for forgetting again. She moved slower and pushed through the discomfort, then fixed the blankets around her tummy.

The man walked over. "Again, I'm sorry to interrupt. You are actually the last patient I have to see today, so I appreciate you taking the time to speak with me now." He had a manner to him.

Anna smiled. "No problem. You said you were from the government?"

"Yes."

Anna continued to watch silently as he pulled the tray table over to him and sat down. He placed a large file in front of him and flipped it open. Seemingly finding the spot he was looking for, he raised his eyes back to look at her.

"The defense minister has asked me personally to talk to each of the survivors to see if–"

"Wait! There are others?"

"Why, yes. Eight actually, including you."

Anna's voice caught in her throat. She bit her lip. "My parents, Chuck and Linda Harington, are they..."

The man's face fell, pulling Anna's heart with it.

"No, I'm sorry... those names aren't on my list."

Anna sniffed and clenched her fists, causing her fingernails to press into her palms. The slight pain from it helped to push back the emotions that fought to burst from her. She had already spent much of the last few days mourning her parents. Now wasn't the time to allow for more.

"It's OK," Anna lied. "It was silly of me to hope."

The man shifted uncomfortably in his seat. She gave an awkward laugh to hide the embarrassment she felt.

"So, what was it you needed to ask me?" Anna asked, trying to change the subject.

"Yes, well..." The man reshuffled his papers. "I am here to see if you would like to remain in Saudi or be transferred immediately back home. I see here in your file that you have a concussion and some fairly significant cuts, but that the doctors are planning to release you tomorrow. Barring any further complications from the concussion of course."

The man looked up at her and smiled.

"The minister sends his deepest apologies for this ordeal you've been through. And, although we would love for you to remain in our country if you wish to do so, he understands if you would like to return home."

"Actually, I'm not quite sure."

Her answer prompted a confused look on the man's face.

"Yeah, it is a long story. And actually, I... I don't know it all myself just yet," Anna said, realizing that Hailey hadn't told her any details. "You see I was waiting for a friend from the States to come visit me, but she never made it. I actually just got off the phone with her, and it turns out she's still in Saudi. I have no idea what happened to her. But now that I don't really have," Anna had to steal a hard swallow to keep her voice level, "a home to go back to, I'd like to meet up with her first. But yes, I do want to go back to New York as soon as we can."

"Really?" the man said.

"I know, crazy right?"

The man raised his eyebrows. "Actually, that's unbelievable. I mean, ah, you won't be alone, and that's marvelous. Just curious, what's your friend's name? I'd like to keep my records as up to date as I can."

"Hailey. Hailey Pearson. Do you think I can have some time to talk with her before deciding about my plans?"

"Certainly. And I can do more than that. I can even help you meet up with her, and we would be happy to cover the cost to fly you both home. It is the least we can do."

"Wow, that's fantastic. Thank you."

The act of kindness caused tears to fill Anna's eyes. She couldn't believe she was so close to having Hailey back with her. Yet, it was a bittersweet moment. Hailey was now the closest thing she had to any family.

"Sorry," Anna said as she wiped her eyes.

"It's quite alright, miss. Although, before we can move forward, I will need a phone number for your friend. And I'm curious, do you happen to know where she-"

Before the man had a chance to finish his question, the door to the room opened. In walked one of the doctors from earlier in the week. He jumped when he noticed she wasn't alone.

"Oh, my apologies. I didn't realize you were still here."

The government man rose and stepped towards the doctor. "Quite alright. But we will need more time. So if you will excuse us, this won't take much longer."

"I'm sorry, I can't do that." The doctor seemed annoyed at being ordered about and it spilled over his tone. "Anna needs to go for her MRI and then she'll need her rest if she is to be released tomorrow."

The doctor looked over at her and smiled. Anna returned the smile. Getting out of this place sounded so wonderful. Being in this room alone any longer than absolutely necessary when she knew Hailey was so close, would drive her nuts.

"Doctor, I understand. Although, it is paramount that I finish my interview with her. So I'm sure you can make an exception."

"No, I can't," the doctor shot back. "Look, you have been here for hours, and we have made allowances for it because we understand that you have a job to do. But now you have to understand that I have a job to do as well. And my job right now is to get Anna to her exam and ensure that her release isn't delayed because her care was hindered. You need to leave now. You can return tomorrow."

"Tomorrow?"

"That's right. You may finish your interview tomorrow when she is released."

The man didn't respond but stood staring down the doctor with his mouth agape. For a few moments, the only sound in the room was the occasional beeping of the machine beside Anna's bed. The whole interaction was uncomfortable to watch. Anna stayed silent.

"Alright, fine." The man turned to look at her, his countenance softening. He smiled. "I agree, we can't delay your recovery now, can we. I will return tomorrow."

"Yeah, that's probably best."

The man walked back to retrieve his file from the tray table.

After he had it safely tucked under his arm, he looked at her and grinned.

"I am going to leave one of my men just outside your door, so if you need anything don't hesitate to ask him."

"Thank you, that's very kind."

With a quick sneer at the doctor as he passed, the man left the room. Anna stifled the laugh.

The doctor moved to her and started taking her vitals. Anna could hear muffled voices in the hall but couldn't make out any words. It must be the man giving instructions to whoever he was leaving behind for her. The sounds soon dwindled down to silence.

"Oh, shoot! I never got his name."

"I believe it's Councilman Ehsan. Can you lean forward?"

Anna sat up so the doctor could listen to her lungs.

"Hmm... he seems nice."

"Nice? That seems a bit of a stretch to me."

"He's going to help me find my friend."

"Well, I guess that's something. Deep breath. I'm glad you will have your friend. Recovery will go better with support."

"Oh, it's OK, my head doesn't hurt anymore."

"I'm not talking about physically. One more deep breath."

Anna took the breath but didn't respond. She didn't want to talk about any of it yet. Thankfully he didn't say anything else and only made a few notes on her chart.

"Oh, I need to call my friend back." She leaned over to retrieve the phone.

He pulled her arm away. "Sorry, no more calls today I'm afraid."

"But–"

"Anna, I stood up to the councilman, do you really think *you* will get me to relent?" He eyed her for a moment, then walked around her bed. "I don't mean to be rude, but I don't trust you to make your rest a priority."

The doctor unhooked the phone and left the room with it, ignoring her protests. Anna slumped back against the pillows, feeling degraded. But she couldn't blame him, she totally would have called if he had left it.

Moments later three nurses came and wheeled her out of the room towards the MRI room. She forgot to look back to see who waited for her in the hall.

CHAPTER 5

It felt excruciating to leave the hospital, but Ehsan had to get back to Riyadh. Although, knowing that his man was posted at the girl's door brought him a bit of comfort. With explicit instructions not to give Ehsan's full name, and that he needed to listen in on all phone calls, Ehsan hoped that his man would be able to handle things until he could return tomorrow.

There was still no word from Taavi, but with this new lead from the girl at the Dammam hospital, Ehsan wasn't concerned. And even though he had yet to see if she would lead him to Hailey or at least reveal her whereabouts, the thrill of having Hailey's friend in his grasp exhilarated him. A feeling of power flowed through him.

Looking below the jet as it neared Riyadh, Ehsan watched the city come into focus. He loved living here, working here. The city had this energy, a buzz that pleased his ego. In the midst of admiring the city, a sinking thought occurred to him.

If somehow my cover is blown with Anna, or if Hailey finds out I've found her, or if Taavi doesn't find anything at the roadblocks, there is still a chance I could lose her.

The thought decimated his peace. He knew then that he shouldn't bank on anything.

Ehsan grabbed a blank sheet of paper from the file and jotted down a quick letter. Motioning to the flight attendant, Ehsan inserted the note into the file as he waited for the man to walk down the aisle.

"Scan and send this directly to my office immediately."

Submitting the survivor report was the last task for the day, and that could be done digitally. He needed to get back home. Whatever Ghada knew required his attention.

The concoction that came from having Hailey's fate out of his control and from remembering Ghada had betrayed him yet again, stirred up his anger.

Ehsan's jaw seethed, and his eyes narrowed.

Ghada, you better know something of use.

- - - - - - -

Ehsan's hand slid over the dark cherry-wood banister as he slowly ascended the stairs towards Ghada's room. Each time he rose a foot to take another step, his anger swelled. He turned his head to look towards the top of the next flight of stairs. There was no one in sight. Nothing stood between him and her door.

How much does she know? Did Ghada and Daib help Hailey to do all this? Did they know what she had been planning? Did they even try and stop her? Each questioned increased the possibility of their collaboration in Hailey's plans, further enraging him.

As Ehsan's foot settled on the landing of the third floor, he saw the girl who had helped with Hailey's injuries after her first escape attempt. She was polishing one of the three silver mirrors in the east wing.

Why can't I ever remember her damn name?

He signaled for her to come over when she had caught sight

of him.

"Has there been any sign of Daib yet?" Ehsan whispered as she approached.

The girl said nothing, just shook her head and quickly hurried off.

Ehsan huffed, amused at the girl's obvious fear of him. He turned once she was out of sight and made his way over to Ghada's room. The metal handle of her door felt cold in his hand. Taking one last deep breath, he turned it and entered.

=======

Ghada sat in her favorite armchair by the window. Her knees tucked up to her chest, and she rested her chin on top. As she looked out over the garden below her, her mind raced with scenarios of what might be coming. None of them were pleasant, and each caused her to tremble.

The click of the door snapped her head around. She jumped off the chair as soon as she saw him.

"Ehsan..."

"Sit down, Ghada!" Ehsan ordered.

Fear started to strangle her. His anger sounded under control, but with past experience, Ghada knew it was the unpredictable kind, the worse kind. She lowered herself back into her chair.

"Now, I'm only going to ask you this once." He turned to close the door behind him. "If you tell me everything in detail and in its entirety, I promise you that I will show you mercy. Do you understand?"

"Y-y-yes, Ehsan." She wished her voice hadn't sounded so pitiful.

"This is the second time you have made me a fool in my own

house."

Ehsan paced along the edge of the rug that laid in front of her chair. He clasped his hands behind his back and he kept his chin down to his chest as he walked. In silence, he walked one full length of the rug, turned and walked back, then stopped. He looked up at Ghada.

"Do I not provide you with everything you and our children need?"

"Yes, Ehsan, you do. I never meant–"

Ehsan held up his hand. She clamped her mouth shut.

"I'd like for you to not waste my time with your feeble apologies or justifications, please." He started pacing again. "What I do want is for you to start, from the beginning, and explain to me why my new wife is no longer in my house. And Ghada… I would advise you not to leave anything out."

Ehsan came to a stop and stood right in front of Ghada as the last word rolled over his lips. Crossing his arms, he waited for her reply.

"And it will do you well, my love, not to defy me further."

Ghada's throat constricted at the sound of his icy tone. It was hard to swallow. She dropped her head and quickly worked up some more saliva and forced it down.

"W-when you had left for Dammam and I was still away visiting Parvina, Hailey started making plans for her escape." Ghada couldn't look at him as she spoke. She could only sit and look at her wringing hands. "Hailey had told the household that she wanted to surprise you by cooking us a nice dinner. This is how she made so many trips out of the house and didn't raise any suspicion. During each trip, she picked up her supplies: clothes, hair dye, a bag. I'm not sure what all else. It should all still be in her room."

"So how did Hailey plan on getting out of Saudi? Was she going to head to the airport or drive out of the city?"

The annoyance in his tone grew. She had to talk faster.

"She found a tour company that was going to get her out on one of their buses. I don't know any of the details or the name of it."

"When did you know about all of this?"

The question felt bitter in her ears. It was the one question she knew he would ask but the one she dreaded the most. Ghada looked up at him. Tears pooled in her eyes.

"She told me as soon as I returned home. Hailey had intended for me to go with her. But... but I knew I couldn't leave you again. And Daib isn't to blame for any of this." She hated the fact that she was panicking, but the more she fought to keep control the worse it got. "It was my fault that he was involved."

Ehsan put up his hand again, but the words continued to tumble out of her.

"I see now that I should have contacted you as soon as I knew of her plans."

Ghada stopped to swallow, she had to get a grip. Maybe her idea would work. She had to try. She switched gears.

"But if I'm honest... I was jealous of her being here."

"What?" Ehsan's face contorted with confusion. It was clear that the admission was the last thing he expected.

So far, so good. At least he is derailed from his anger. At least for now. Ghada slowly raised off her chair and moved closer towards him. She kept her eyes on the floor as she advanced forward. At a mere foot away, she kept her head down but raised her eyes.

"You see, I was used to being the newest wife. When you brought Hailey here, I was hurt, and I wanted to get away from you. But after visiting our daughter, my head was set straight. Parvina misses you, and when I saw her love for you, it reminded me of how things were before Fareefta came."

Ghada raised her hand and stroked the side of his face, being sure to linger by his earlobe before moving her fingers down to his chin. Touching his favorite spot seemed to erase more of his anger. Her plan was working. She ran her hand back up to take another pass.

"So, when I returned home, I saw how foolish I was and I knew I wanted to stay. But I still wanted Hailey to leave... so I helped her."

Ghada barely noticed the movement of his hand as it flew up and grabbed her wrist. The initial tension of his grip startled her. Looking for an explanation, her eyes snapped to meet his. Anger blazed in his eyes.

"Well now. That is the problem isn't it, you bitch. You were just thinking of yourself. There was no regard for me in any of your actions. This greatly displeases me, Ghada."

Ehsan's grip tightened even further. Ghada bit her lip, expecting that he would stop any moment. She didn't want to cry out. He didn't stop and the pain increased. As a yelp shot out from her, Ehsan whipped her around, pinning her arm behind her back. Ghada felt the strain on her shoulder as he pulled her arm higher and higher.

"Ehsan, please stop. You're hurting me."

He raised her arm higher and stopped. His hot breath brushed against her cheek as Ehsan lowered his mouth down to her ear. She squeezed her eyes closed to try and clear away the nausea building from the stench of his stale breath. She had to keep still.

Ehsan reached his other arm across her chest and pulled her

against himself without releasing her pinned arm.

"I will forgive you... on one condition," he said as he jerked her arm up farther.

Ghada felt each tendon strain under the pressure. She feared that if he kept going, her shoulder would dislocate at any moment. She gritted her teeth to remain silent, but a small whimper escaped.

"Does Daib know anything about the tour?" he hissed in her ear.

"I don't know. Maybe. But please remember, Daib only helped her at my request. He isn't at fault."

Ehsan squeezed her wrist as he released a hot sigh against her neck.

"I will be the judge of that. But if you call Daib and talk him into coming back to the house, I will–"

"What do you mean? Where is he? Is he OK?" The concern left her mouth before she had a chance to shop it.

Ehsan dropped her arm, it tingled as the blood flowed back in. She moved to massage her throbbing wrist, but he spun her around to face him. Grabbing both of her shoulders, he gave her a vigorous shake.

"I'm getting sick of hearing how you seem to care so much about Daib. And yet have such little concern for me."

Ghada's heart covered in dread. Her words and tone had betrayed her. Could Ehsan see her true feelings for Daib? Or was he just jealous? She tried to quickly think of a way to recover. But with the look of rage building on Ehsan's face, her mind wasn't working quick enough.

Ehsan slid his hands over her shoulders, along her collarbone, and up to her neck.

It started slow, and she could barely feel his touch at first. But as the tension built, she became alarmingly aware of what was happening. Instantly her hands flew up and she gripped his wrists. She tried to pull them apart, but his strength significantly outmatched hers.

Ghada's lip quivered as his grip tightened around her throat. "Ehsan, please, no. Don't do this."

His lips formed into an eerie smile. He said nothing as he increased the pressure. She tried to plead with him again, but she was too late. His thumbs were compressing her larynx. Ghada tried to gulp for air, nothing happened. Her head throbbed from the building pressure of blood and it felt like it might explode. Pain covered her whole body, and it jolted into a panicked frenzy.

She hit his arms, but they didn't budge.

She tried to reach out to strike his face, but his arms kept her too far away.

Her legs tried to pull her away, but he held her in place.

Her only resort was to claw at his hands. The act was feeble. He barely seemed to notice as her nails raked across his skin.

The panic started to wane as a sliver of calm eased its way over her.

What's happening?

Ghada's head felt fuzzy. Her eyes were struggling to focus. Her body wasn't responding as quickly to her commands to keep fighting. When blackness started to overtake her vision, her knees buckled. Ehsan let go and she fell to the floor.

She gasped for breath. Her throat stung as her lungs pulled in the air. It felt raw. She coughed, causing further pain. Ghada gingerly touched her neck.

"Daib is a coward!" Ehsan's voice boomed above her. "He never returned to the house after Hailey ran away. My guess is that he is more culpable than you want to let on. But something tells me you can talk him into coming back, especially after what I just heard. If you succeed, then I will relent... for now at least."

Tears gathered in her eyes. Ghada hadn't felt free since coming to this house, but she had never felt as trapped as she did at this moment.

What am I going to do?

"I will need an answer, Ghada." He nudged her with his foot. "Do you concede or should I resume your punishment?"

Her shoulders slumped in defeat.

"Alright," she said, barely able to speak above a whisper.

"Good. Now get cleaned up, then go call Daib. I have some calls to make in case you fail me... or if Daib does."

Ehsan's feet walked out of her view. She didn't bother to raise her head to watch him leave. Soon the sound of the door creaking open filled the room. Once she heard the click of it being closed, she looked to ensure he had left. He had. She let out a slow breath.

Her body threatened to break down, but she shut her eyes and willed herself to relax. Anything other than a slow, even breath hurt her throat, and she couldn't handle the pain from sobbing.

Ghada struggled to win the battle for control. The ache in her chest grew. She was about to betray the only two friends she had in this world.

CHAPTER 6

As Ehsan reached the first landing, he went to pull his phone out of his pocket. His body trembled with anger, which made the task difficult when the cell caught on the hem of his pocket. He took a few deep breaths to shake off some of the hostility running through him. He removed the phone and held it as he jogged down the next flight of stairs.

He shook his head in frustration.

How could she do this to me?

His anger had been much simpler on his way to her room. But now? Now it was getting harder to ignore that Ghada had feelings for Daib. His jaw tightened. Not to mention that it seemed like Ghada had tried to play him. Replaying the moments with her, thinking about her flirting with him, erased the work the deep breaths had done.

Ehsan's anger returned and boiled over as he reached the foyer. He released a long, throaty yell as he swung at the blue vase that sat on the pedestal at the bottom of the stairs. It crashed to the floor. Hundreds of ceramic shards slid across the tile. Satisfied from the action, his body relaxed.

"Is everything alright, Ehsan?" Maya asked, startling him. "Sorry, I thought you saw me. Is everything alright?"

He ignored her questions and moved to make his way to the library. He needed privacy. The sound of the broken pottery crunched under his feet as he raised the phone. He went to access the contact list. It rang in his hand. Taavi's number flashed on the screen. Excited, Ehsan answered as he swung the library door shut behind him.

"You can't be finished with all the roadblocks yet, so please tell me you have good news."

"Councilman, I just might. I'm at the roadblock at Highway 65 at the north side of the city. The lead officer here is an idiot, but we may have found Hailey."

"Tell me," Ehsan urged. "Did you find the tour bus?"

"Wait, how did you know about the bus?"

"I just talked with Ghada. What do you mean that you *may* have found her?" Ehsan's impatience brimmed over.

"The officer said a tour bus passed through a few hours ago and confirmed there was an American man and woman on board."

"That has to be them. So why weren't they stopped?"

"That's where the officer's idiocy comes in. This roadblock, for some reason, never received her photo, just the description. And seeing how the woman didn't match the description, and that there were–"

"Damn, Ghada said that Hailey had purchased hair dye. So it makes sense that she looks different. What about papers?"

"The officer said that they didn't bother getting them to show their passports because there was a long line and that another couple on the bus vouched for them."

"You've got to be kidding."

"I wish I was, Councilman."

"After this is all over, I want that man fired," Ehsan

demanded between clenched teeth. "But if I lose her because of this moron's mistake, he will lose more than his job."

"I will deal with it personally, Councilman, I can assure you."

"Did the man at least get the name of the tour company?"

"Sadly, no. Was Ghada any help with that?"

"No."

Taavi sighed "So it seems like we both have the same intel."

"Well, not necessarily. We still have two good leads. Ghada might be able to get Daib to come back, and I'm hoping he will know more. And get this, I also spoke with a survivor of the bombing a couple of hours ago. It turns out she may be able to lead me to Hailey. I don't want to get into it all now. We'll just have to wait and see which lead pans out first."

"This waiting must be driving you mad, Councilman."

"Taavi, you have no idea."

=======

The silence continued between them as the bus moved farther and farther away from Riyadh. It seemed Hailey also needed time to process the news and Ryan was grateful for it. He had always been an internal processor, and the dueling emotions that flooded his body would make it difficult to talk about it. Everything Ryan had experienced these last couple of weeks went beyond anything he had ever had to face before, and he needed the silence to try and find a place in his mind for the fact that Anna was alive. Currently, he found none.

It was a strange sensation. His core tightened with the ache of grief every time he thought about Anna's parents. Yet as soon as his thoughts went to them, his mind would divert to the fact that Anna was alive, bringing relief. Sorrow followed as he thought about Anna having to live in a world without her parents.

As the seconds ticked by, he wasn't making any progress in settling his mind. His palms were sweaty, and his throat was dry. He needed a diversion. Ryan turned to Hailey.

She was cradling the cell phone in both her hands and was looking at it. It seemed quite apparent that she was trying to will it to ring. *She could probably use a distraction as well,* he reckoned. *A watched pot and all that, won't do her any favors.*

"Hailey?"

She didn't even look up at him. "Yeah?"

"It will ring when it rings."

"I know. I just want her to call back. It's hard not knowing what to do."

"What do you mean what to do?" Ryan's confusion sparked his concern.

She finally looked up from the phone. Her brow was wrinkled with confusion lines.

"About our plans."

By her tone, she sounded like he should know what she was talking about, but he didn't. When he didn't respond, she continued.

"Well now that we know Anna's alive, it could change everything."

"How? We still need to get you out of the country." Ryan didn't like where this conversation was heading.

"Yeah, but Anna might need our help. I'm not going anywhere unless I know what's happening with her."

"OK. I get that, but–"

"Ryan, I'm serious. Anna has lost so much and I'm not leaving her. You have no idea what it's like to lose your family." With each sentence, Hailey's exasperation grew.

Ryan knew she was right. He couldn't fully understand, not the way that Hailey could. He took a breath before continuing so he could ensure his tone adequately conveyed his empathy.

"I know I don't understand, not like you do. And I understand the importance of you wanting to be there for her. But we still don't know how safe you are and I don't think you can understand how that affects me. I need to get you somewhere safe."

"I know." She smiled. "But what if Anna's injuries are worse than she let on? And what about her grief? She will need us with her, Ryan."

"So what are you thinking?"

"Well... I'm hoping she'll call back and we can make plans before we get to Buraydah. But if not..." Hailey dropped her eyes and bit her lip, "I want to stay in Buraydah until we know."

"Seriously?"

"Completely."

"Hailey, I don't know if–"

"Look, I'm sure we'll hear from her before we have to decide. Ryan, we're the only family she has left. We can't just leave her in Saudi all alone."

"Yeah, I guess you're right," Ryan sighed, relenting.

He wasn't thrilled about the possibility of leaving the tour, but there was no point in pushing the issue now. He just hoped that Anna would call back soon and he wouldn't have to fight Hailey about it further. He ran both his hands down his thighs to dry off his palms.

"I know you're worried." She reached out and took one of his hands. "But it's not like I'm planning on going back to Riyadh to get her. I was thinking, and this is worst case scenario, Anna meets us in Buraydah, and we use some of the money to pay someone to drive us up to the border, then we cross into Jordan, and fly home."

The plan concerned Ryan. Yet, he chose to let it go, at least for now. He pulled Hailey under his arm and kissed her forehead. She smelled like vanilla. It wasn't her usual scent but pleasant. He took in another breath of her. Hailey yawned and leaned against his chest, returning her eyes back to the phone.

"It will ring when it rings. Why don't you close your eyes and try and rest."

"Yeah, OK."

Hailey shifted to make room for her feet up on the seat as she curled in next to him. It surprised him but soon her full weight slumped against him, and she was breathing deeply. He kissed the top of her head again yet softer this time, so as not to wake her. He leaned back, trying to take his own advice. But sleep never came.

CHAPTER 7

She was huddled in an empty room. Large boots walked down the hallway towards her. Her skin was cold and clammy from the fear that grew with the sound of each step. She started counting the steps she imagined that it would take to reveal the intruder.

Five... Four... Three... Two...

It was at that moment that Ryan's gentle nudging pulled her from the dream. Her chest was rising and falling quickly with each panicked breath. Hailey closed her eyes as her brain tried to regulate her breathing.

"Sorry, but we're in Buraydah. Are you OK?" Ryan questioned, his concern held a bit of fear.

"Yeah, just having a bad dream."

Hailey leaned back into him. She knew his embrace would aid in steadying her. As he received her, she again felt safe.

Ryan's stomach growled. She laughed.

"Good thing we're here. I'm starving."

"Me too. I wonder where we're going to stop." Hailey sat up and stretched to look out the front of the bus. As if on cue, the driver's voice came on the speaker system.

"Well ladies and gentlemen, we have arrived in Buraydah." Joe's voice crackled. "I'm going to pull up to your hotel, The Blue Rose. It's a wonderful hotel, and I think you all will be very comfortable there. They have a few restaurants, pool, and a spa. You will have the full evening to rest and explore the hotel." Joe paused his instructions as he made a large turn. "I would ask that none of you leave the hotel until boarding the bus tomorrow morning. But if you have any questions let me know."

Minutes later the bus pulled up to a towering hotel. The front was covered with large, shiny, metal panels and cream columns held up a stone canopy with the hotel sign resting on top. The words The Blue Rose were written in dark, English, calligraphy lettering and sat under, what Hailey assumed, was the Arabic translation. A large blue crystal rose lay between the two.

As soon as Joe stopped the bus, Jack and Holly jumped from their seats. Resting on the backs of their seats, they anxiously stared at Ryan and Hailey.

"OK. It's been a few hours and we can't possibly wait any longer." Holly was practically bursting.

"Yeah, what happened to you two?" Jack's enthusiasm matched his girlfriend's.

Hailey looked at Ryan, then back at the two Aussies. The couple's kindness in vouching for two complete strangers had very possibly saved their lives. They needed to be told.

"It's a long, crazy story. And you probably won't believe it."

"That's OK," they both answered in unison.

Ryan leaned forward. "How about we get settled in our rooms and meet back in the foyer in twenty minutes. We can go grab some supper and tell you all about it."

They all agreed.

The check-in took a little longer than they had expected, but once in their room, Hailey still wasn't in a big rush to get down to the foyer. After plopping her bag by the front door, she went over to the king-sized bed and flopped down, face first.

"Ugh."

The mattress wasn't as luxurious as the one at Ehsan's but seeing that it was the first one she laid on since being a free woman, it was the best thing in the world.

"Tired?" Ryan laughed.

"Yeah." She turned her head to the side, so her voice wasn't muffled. "That nap on the bus wasn't at all helpful. I feel all groggy and weird now."

"Well, I'm sure having that big bed will help you get a better rest tonight. Bus seats aren't all that comfortable."

"You're sweet to give me the bed, by the way," she said as she raised up onto one elbow and looked at him. He grinned at her and it made her heart flutter.

A knock sounded at the door.

Hailey jumped as her muscles constricted with alarm.

"Hailey, it's OK. I'm sure it's just someone bringing up the cot."

"Right." She shook her head, feeling foolish. "I think I'm just on edge from not hearing from Anna yet."

Ryan crossed the room and opened the door. He was right. A small man struggled under the weight of a folded cot. After taking the cot from him, Ryan thanked the man and closed the door.

"Wow! I wish we had something like that in the prison," Hailey said as Ryan easily unfolded the bed and set it up by the window. But as the casualness of her words hung in the air, her stomach started to feel queasy.

"Are you alright?"

"Actually, I-I'm not sure." A feeling of vulnerability caught in her chest and constricted her throat. She decided to push past it. "Being at that prison was... terrifying." Hailey's body started to tremble as her mind began replaying scenes.

"Hey now. It's alright," Ryan said as he rushed over to her. He sat on the edge of the bed and started to rub her back.

Hailey pulled a pillow from the head of the bed and pushed it underneath her torso and turned to look at him. "Being paraded around naked like that was... was completely humiliating. And... and that woman..." Hailey's voice trailed off as more images flashed through her mind.

"Which one? The one who was shot?"

She nodded. "Ryan, there was so... so much blood. I see it whenever I close my eyes. Sometimes it mixes with sounds of Sarna's screams. I... I just wish they would let go of me."

"The memories?"

She nodded her head and buried her face into the pillow, trying to dislodge the images.

Ryan moved his hand up and started stroking her hair. The effect of his touch was soothing, and soon a sensation of safety returned. Hailey lay still allowing it to encircle her.

"Hon, you're safe now. I'll say it a billion times until it helps, OK? And the memories will fade with time. I promise."

Hailey turned her head and laid her cheek on the pillow. She smiled up at him. His support and empathy felt good.

"Thank you."

"Hey, anytime." He squeezed her shoulder and held her gaze. "Are you sure you're up for this?"

"Talking with Jack and Holly?"

Ryan nodded.

"Yeah, I think so."

"I can go fill them in if you like. You told me everything the day I found you, right?"

"Yeah, you know it all. But I think I'm OK. I just need a minute." Hailey sat up to stretch the tension in her back. "I still can't believe they covered for us. We owe them a lot. I'm not thrilled to talk about it all, but it's the least I can do."

He winked at her. "And I'll be with you the whole time."

"I know," she giggled.

Ryan smiled at her again and looked over at the cot. "Right then," he said as he slapped his palms on his knees and stood.

He walked back over to the cot. Hailey relaxed back onto the pillow. Having Ryan with her infused her with strength. She imagined there were innumerable ways God could have brought her back home, but she was incredibly grateful to Him that He had sent Ryan for her. She didn't even want to think about how much harder this all would be if Ryan weren't here.

"Yup, I think it will do quite nicely. It actually looks pretty comfortable," he said as he sat to test it out. "Yup, definitely better than the bus seat. But we probably shouldn't be too much longer. I think our Aussie friends will come hunting for us if we make them wait much more."

Ryan came over to the bed and held out his hands. Allowing him to pull her up off the bed, Hailey leaned in and gave him a quick kiss.

Exiting the elevator, Holly caught sight of them first. She raced over to her and grabbed both of Hailey's hands and pulled her forward.

"Jack found us a restaurant that sounds great. The man at the front desk told him that it's buffet style. So it should be quiet because we won't have a lot of interruptions from waiters. It sounds perfect for story time. Hurry on, mates."

Holly dropped one of Hailey's hands and continued to pull her along with the other. Hailey glanced back at Ryan. He shot her a quick wink as he started to follow, which she returned. Hailey gave Jack an amused smile as Holly dragged her past him.

Reaching the restaurant, they were greeted by a tall, slender man. He had a round, blue, embroidered cap perched on his head and was dressed in, what looked to Hailey like, blue satin pajamas. He nodded a hello and led them all to a rectangular table near the back of the room.

The walls were covered with blue and white fabric. It gave the room an elegant and oceanic feel to it. The way the material was gathered looked like flowing water. There were probably about twenty tables spread about the place. Each table had a sheer white tablecloth, white folded napkins, and silver dinnerware.

After they were all seated, the man gestured with his hand towards the buffet line and then back to each of their silver plates. They all nodded their understanding back to him. The man then pulled out two folded cards from behind his back and handed one to Ryan and one to Jack, nodded again and then left them.

Hailey and Holly leaned over to look at the card that each of the men was holding. Bright pictures displayed the drink selections.

"That's quite clever," Holly said.

Ryan nodded. "Yeah, I sure prefer this over charades."

After ordering their drinks, Holly and Jack leaned back in their chairs and looked from Hailey to Ryan, clearly waiting for one of them to start.

Hailey was about to break the silence when the man came back with some warm bread. Ryan practically leaped over the table to get to it. Both girls chuckled at the sight.

Hailey caught herself before reaching for a piece. She needed to wait until after the story. Her stomach wouldn't do well with food until she had finished.

"OK, first of all, I can't tell you how grateful we are to you for covering for us at the roadblock. Soon you will understand just how much." Hailey looked at Ryan who was bobbing his head in agreement, his mouth stuffed full of bread.

Hailey continued, "Well, honestly, the whole story is so ludicrous and... horrible. I still can't believe it myself. But I guess I'll just start from the beginning." She took a quick breath to clear her head. "We are both from New York. I was going to university and Ryan works for an oil company that has an office there. I had lost my parents a few years earlier and, I realize now, that I wasn't doing well with that. I guess I had never really processed it the way I should have and then when I had my heart broken..." Hailey paused and looked up from her cup.

When she saw Jack and Holly look simultaneously at Ryan, Hailey quickly spoke, "No, no, not by Ryan. We were just friends at the time. Actually, it seems all so stupid now so I won't bore you with the drama. Let's just say that with a broken heart and being betrayed by a different friend, I couldn't take it anymore. I made an extremely stupid decision. My old roommate was living back with her parents here in Saudi. They live... or lived... in Dammam in one of those westerner compounds."

"Yeah what are those?" Jack interjected.

Ryan answered for her, "They are pretty much like little mini walled cities. They have all the familiar amenities that you'd miss while traveling: similarly styled homes, shops, pharmacies, grocery stores, a few restaurants. You can dress as you wish and have a taste of home while living there."

"So..." Hailey continued, "with remembering all the stories my friend Anna had told me about Saudi, I thought it would be impossible to find a more different place to get away to. I was originally planning on visiting her after finals. But after all the crap going on in New York, I decided to leave early."

"Hailey had tried to get a hold of me before she left," Ryan added, "but we didn't connect. I had no idea she had left. My brother, Thomas, had driven her to the airport and I was trying to give her some space. It wasn't until weeks later that I knew anything had happened."

"What happened?" Holly asked with wide eyes. She was hooked.

Jack's face would have made Hailey laugh if it wasn't for the tension in her body from knowing what was coming next in the story.

"Apart from Thomas, I had left New York not telling anyone I was coming to Saudi. I thought it would be a good surprise for Anna. She's obsessed with surprises, and she had been so amazing with supporting me through so much. I thought it would be a nice gift for her. I made it through Germany with no hiccups, but when I got to Riyadh things fell apart." Hailey paused to keep her composure. "Part of it was definitely from my foolishness. I had changed into my abaya but had forgotten my headscarf in my checked baggage."

Jack shrugged. "What's the problem with that? Most people

would just leave you alone. It's obvious you're a foreigner."

"Yeah..." Hailey agreed, "But the key word is *most*. And I probably would have been fine until reaching my connection, but I got lost. There had been some changes in the airport, so the directions Anna had sent me didn't help. The airport had moved some of the flight boards to a different section. So when I tried to find them to check on my flight status they weren't there, neither was the attendant Anna said would be there to help if needed. I tried to retrace my steps and see where I went wrong but ended up getting all turned around. It was taking way too long, and I started to worry that I might miss my connection. I saw a group of businessmen and thought that there was no harm in asking for directions."

"Oh no!" Holly said.

"Yeah, but at the time, I didn't know that that wasn't a good idea. I had only been speaking to one of the men for a few minutes when one of the religious police, along with a few of his buddies, came up to me and started yelling. I was so confused. I tried to argue with them, but the man was just so, so angry. They took my papers and all my things, hauled me off through a security door, and put me in a holding room."

"You must have been terrified," Jack said.

"I was, but my confusion outweighed my fear. During the next few hours, I foolishly assumed that all this misunderstanding would be sorted out at any moment and then I could be on my way. But that's not what happened. Things just kept going from bad to worse, and I had no way of stopping it."

"So what happened next?" Holly asked.

"It seemed like the man who had approached me initially, wanted to make an example of me. They transferred me to the religious police holding office." Hailey's body gave a little shudder. "That is when I realized how much trouble I was really in." She paused for a moment, as her mind remembered what came next. "I was definitely scared when I arrived. I was placed in the hands of a horrible man. Faisal was the second in charge of the whole office, and he tried to blackmail me."

"How?" Jack and Holly said in unison.

"His buddies at the airport had given him the heads up about my situation and had sent all my paperwork to him. Faisal said that he would help me sort this all out, if and only if I let him process me."

Holly leaned further forward, "That... doesn't sound good."

"No, it wasn't. Faisal said that he needed to check to make sure I didn't have anything on me that could harm me. And that if I undressed for him, it would be payment enough for his help."

Ryan shifted in his seat. Hailey hated that he had to relive the story, but she needed to continue. Jack and Holly needed to know.

"I had never been faced with such a situation. I was completely trapped. My hesitancy didn't please him. He hit me and tore my clothes."

"Oh, Hailey!" Jack's concern filled his face.

"The next part is a bit of a blur. Thankfully we were interrupted, but he was angry that I had wasted so much time. He shoved me, and I fell to the ground. He kicked me and left. They transferred me to a different room, where I think I stayed for a day or two. I can't remember exactly. Then I was transferred to a prison."

"Wait! How did that happen?" Jack asked, shaking his head.

Ryan cut in. "Somehow that man at the airport got them to charge her with prostitution and a few other crazy charges."

Ryan rubbed Hailey's shoulder as he spoke and it gave her some strength, helping her to continue on.

"I tried to contest, but there wasn't anything I could do. No one would listen, and I was helpless. The prison was awful. A soldier shot a woman right in front of me." Hailey's eyes filled with tears as she spoke. "They stripped us down and paraded us to our cells. Thankfully we were given new abayas, but it was so embarrassing."

Hailey lowered her eyes to look at her hands, folded in her lap. Holly reached out and held her arm from across the table.

"Do you need to stop?" she asked.

"No, it's OK. It's just hard to think about. But it's not going to do me any good to avoid it." Hailey looked up and smiled at the couple. "There were two women in my cell. One was taken away and I never saw her again. The other woman, Sarna, was amazing. We gave each other so much support, and we got quite close. But the guards were horrid."

"I can't imagine," Jack said.

"Sarna had to endure unspeakable things while there."

"Just... Sarna?" Holly asked.

"Strangely, yes. The guards pretty much left me alone. I'm still not sure why though. But I'm grateful. A while later I was brought into another room where I met... a man." Hailey had trouble saying his name. It caught in her throat, so she didn't bother. "At first I thought he was my lawyer, so I trusted him. I was so stupid."

"It's not your fault, Hailey. How were you to know?" Ryan's words were meant to comfort her, but she still felt ridiculous for being so naive.

"But Ryan, that's the problem. There were so many things I should have known. And if I had, none of us would be in this mess."

Ryan didn't say anything, and she knew he agreed with her. It added to her regret and embarrassment, but she forced it aside and turned her attention back across the table to continue her story.

"The man, the one who I thought was my lawyer, arranged to take me to his house. At the time I was thrilled. I was so excited to be out of the prison. E-Ehsan, that's his name, gave me a tour of the house, introduced me to his wives, but then locked me in my room. He told me this stupid story about it being for my protection because some of his family wasn't happy with me being there. I believed him."

Hailey leaned forward and raked her hands through her hair. Telling the story again just showed her how absurd it all sounded now. No, not how it sounded: how stupid she had been.

How could I not have seen a problem with it all?

"So, what? You just sat locked in your room?" It was clear by Jack's tone that he was thinking the same thing.

"I know. I know," Hailey groaned. "Looking back, I can see how crazy it all was. But in the midst of everything going horribly wrong and being so terrified at what I witnessed at the prison, then to someone appearing to rescue me… I didn't even think to question it. I was just so… relieved."

"So what happened next?" Holly prodded.

"The next while was bizarre. I ate, slept, and signed papers that I thought were for my court appearance. Have either of you heard of sugaring?"

Jack and Holly shook their heads.

"Well, one day Ehsan's mother, aunts, and his wives came into my room. They literally ripped all my body hair off with a ball of wax. It was so painful. I asked Maya, Ehsan's first wife if this was somehow for my court appearance. I know, it's so stupid, but I thought I was going to be naked for it. After telling me I was ridiculous, which she wasn't wrong about, she told me..."

"That it was for her wedding. Can you believe that?" Ryan burst in.

"What?" Holly said, obviously shocked.

"How?" Jack asked.

"Ehsan is really high up in the government," Hailey explained. "And I guess... he pulled a lot of strings. He planned to make me his wife."

"Oh, crikey! What did you do when you found out?" Jack said, riveted, as he picked up his glass to take a sip.

Holly grabbed another piece of bread and started to nibble it nervously.

"What could I do? I was trapped in that house. But after the shock wore off, I knew I couldn't stay there. I tried to talk with Maya about things, but she refused to help. Maya didn't like the fact that Ehsan wanted me to join their family, but she didn't agree with going against Ehsan's wishes. I thought I was at a dead end. But then they held a ceremony in my room. All these women entered. If it weren't for the preposterous situation I was in, the scene would have been beautiful. They danced, sang, ate. They applied henna to my hands and feet."

Hailey pushed up her sleeves, stretched out her arms, and rested them on the table for them to see.

"But then I saw my chance. Everyone was distracted by the celebrations, and I noticed that no one was watching me. I was so scared, but I forced myself to move. Ever so slowly, I carefully made my way over to the door. I can't explain the feeling I had when the knob turned freely in my hand, and I was able to sneak out into the hallway."

"Hailey, it really is a miracle that no one saw you," Ryan said.

"I know." Hailey looked over at him, and they shared a knowing smile.

"OK, OK… so what happened next?" Holly flapped her hands to get their attention back.

"Well, once I was in the hall, the coast was clear, so I made my way down the stairs. I was hugging the wall as I kept scanning all directions. My heart was going nuts, and I was certain someone would spot me at any moment. I was looking behind me when I rounded a corner."

"Oh no!" Jack exclaimed.

"Yeah, I ran right into someone. But thankfully it was Ghada, Ehsan's second wife. She had always seemed a lot different than Maya. Maya seemed proud and confident. But Ghada looked like a meek servant in those surroundings. I was right in my assumption of her. It turned out that Ghada understood and wanted to help me escape.

"She got me out of the house and showed me where the cars were. I talked her into coming with me. We stole a set of keys, found the right car, and sped out of the garage. It was awkward getting around the grounds, but we had almost made it to the side gate."

Hailey paused to catch her breath. Jack and Holly both shifted in their seats.

"I could see the street through the gate, we were so close. But we weren't so fortunate. A car came screaming around the corner. I swerved to miss it but didn't see the tree. Then everything went black. I woke up back in the house, in a different room. My head was pounding, and my whole body hurt. We had almost made it."

Hailey looked away from the table, towards the windows, and out to the street beyond.

Ryan, as if on cue, picked up the story. Hailey was grateful. Thinking about Ghada made her heart hurt, and she couldn't continue speaking if she were to keep from crying.

"Soon Ghada came in, she told Hailey about Ehsan's third wife, whom he had killed for her disobedience to him. Ehsan had... ah... lent out his wife to a friend. When she had found a few men to stand with her to report the rape, they had changed their mind at the last minute and..." Ryan paused and looked at Hailey. "What was her name?"

"Fareefta."

"Right. Fareefta was then convicted of prostitution. Being a married woman, they gave Ehsan the choice of what happened to her. He shot her."

"That's awful," Jack said as Holly shook her head in disbelief.

"We thought we were alone in the room when Ghada was telling me all this. The room was quite dark, and we didn't see that Ehsan had been sitting in the corner the whole time. He used the lesson of that story as pull to keep Ghada and me in check. He said that if either of us were to disobey him again, then the other would receive the punishment. Ehsan never said what the punishment would be, but it kept us quiet and in line."

"So what did you do?" Jack asked.

"Nothing. We went through the wedding ceremony, and I said nothing. He led me back to his room, and I said nothing. He started to undress me, and I said nothing. It was horrible." Hailey started to cry.

Ryan reached his arm around her and pulled her protectively to his chest.

"Hailey, I'm so sorry."

Hailey sniffled back the tears as her mind remembered what was coming.

"I laid there thinking that the worst moment of my life was about to happen, but everything stopped. Ehsan got up unexpectedly, hit me, and left the room. I was shocked. I can't even remember if he said anything. He didn't return. I got up the next morning and there was still no sign of him."

"That's strange," Holly said.

Hailey shook her head. "Well... not in the big picture it isn't."

Holly and Jack both gave her perplexed looks.

"Do you guys believe in God?" Hailey wished it hadn't come out so tentatively.

"Yeah, I guess," Jack answered. "But we're not that religious."

"Hailey's story gets even more crazy from this point on. And then once you've heard my side of the story... you might be more certain... but maybe not. I have believed in God most of my life, and I'm still shocked by it all."

"OK..." Jack said cautiously. "Tell us."

Hailey listened while Ryan filled them in on what happened from his perspective. About the trouble he had with all the red tape, coming to Saudi, and meeting up with Anna. Hailey noticed that he skipped the part about the bombing. He moved on to tell them about being blackmailed by Faisal at the holding office, that he wanted money in exchange for Hailey's papers.

"Actually, it's funny. When I was at Anna's house, I was woken up from this crazy dream. Someone was about to hurt Hailey. I prayed for her all night. When Hailey and I were together again, we realized that it was that same night that Ehsan had left the room. You've got to admit that it's just too crazy to be a coincidence."

Hailey worried that Jack and Holly would feel uncomfortable by feeling like they had to answer, so she quickly continued with her story.

"So while Ryan was trying to track me down and get my papers back, I was at Ehsan's. After Ehsan didn't return that morning, I decided to get cleaned up. I got up and..." Hailey stopped.

At that moment she realized that she was about to share a very personal experience with two practical strangers. True, she had shared that particular experience with Ghada and Ryan, but she had still been in the thick of everything when she did so. Now that all the excitement had died down and she was safe, Hailey became aware of how vulnerable she was. Hailey's old self, the one who hid behind those walls for all those years, screamed at her to skip this part of the story.

Sharing her emotional state during the previous sections of the story had been more for dramatic effect than coming from a place of honesty and wanting to let people see her. But now, Hailey was fully aware that doing so for this part, wouldn't be possible. She felt extremely torn.

Hailey felt as though she was being compelled to be raw and vulnerable, with no masks, but she was scared. Hailey glanced at Ryan. He nodded to keep going. Hailey looked at Jack and Holly. They eagerly sat there, silently waiting for her to continue.

Taking a deep breath, she started.

"I got up and went to the bathroom. I felt so defeated It was like my life was over, and I was doomed to whatever Ehsan would choose for me. But then something happened. God met me. Right before my eyes, steam appeared on the huge bathroom mirror, and He started writing verses from the bible in it."

"Are you serious?" Jack's tone wasn't one of mocking but of disbelief.

"One hundred percent. It might sound corny to anyone not there, but it wasn't. It's what happened. As I kept reading what He wrote, He showed me how I had been so closed off to the world even before my parents died and how much worse it got after they were gone. I was a shell of a person, so dreadfully afraid of being not good enough and, because of that, scared that I wouldn't be accepted. I became a manipulator of my circumstances and never connected deeply with anyone. God opened up my eyes to see that it wasn't others who had pushed me in the dark-hole existence I was living, but that it was me who dug the hole and jumped in. When finally at the bottom, I then continued to rake the dirt over top of myself in hopes to be protected from pain. It was the first time I saw that I was suffocating from my own actions and running from Him was the opposite of what I needed.

"There is one verse that He wrote that has stuck in my head. 'Therefore I am now going to allure her; I will lead her into the wilderness and speak tenderly to her. There I will give her back her vineyards, and will make the Valley of Achor a door of hope.' Achor means trouble. I realized at that moment that this horrible situation I was in and all the events that led me here was actually an act of mercy."

"How?" Jack questioned.

"I had lost my way in life. Actually, I wasn't living at all really. The more I tried to keep all the plates spinning and balls in the air, the more that was added and the more I was destroying things. I tried to be better and do better. It was impossible, yet I didn't see it. I just kept getting angry with myself that I wasn't good enough yet and if I just pushed a little harder, then I could keep it together." Hailey paused so she could assess the situation.

Jack and Holly just looked at her.

"I'm sorry if that has made you feel uncomfortable."

"No." Holly cleared her throat. "Not uncomfortable at all. Please keep going."

Jack nodded slowly in agreement, so she continued.

"God asked if I would surrender it all to Him. I briefly thought of running away again and back to my safe place, but then realized that so-called safe place is what was actually destroying me. So instead of returning there, I went to Him. I can't explain really what all happened next, but He did something amazing. I believe that by Him allowing me to go so far off and using that to lead me to Saudi, it snapped me out of my delusion."

"I don't want this to come across rudely," Jack said with sincerity, "but if I'm honest, it sounds a bit.... ah... crazy."

"Believe me, I know. If you had told me the same story before it happened, I would have thought the same thing. But that's what happened, and I have to pay attention to it."

"So how did you find her?" Holly asked Ryan.

"That's another wild part to all this. While Hailey was planning another escape, I was running around trying to get money to give to Faisal at the holding office. I didn't want that man to have her information, but it was proving difficult to get my hands on it. Hailey came up with a brilliant plan to say she was going to cook them all a big dinner, and that she needed to get the ingredients for it. This gave her the freedom to get out of the house. She was still watched closely by her driver, but at least she was able to gather all the supplies she needed and plan to get away."

Hailey cut in, "After my poor attempt the first time, I knew that I needed to be better prepared this time and plan more. During one of my trips to the market, I overheard a man talking about tours. That's when I found out about this tour. The man and his brother were incredible. They got me a ticket, and the rest of the plan went smoothly. Well, except that Ghada refused to come with me. But I don't hold that against her. She has a daughter who is away at school, and she couldn't leave her. I admire her for it, but I was still scared to do it all alone."

"I can't believe you had the guts to do it at all," Holly said. "You must have been terrified that you would get caught again."

"Yeah, I was. But at the same time, I was confident that I'd get away. It's hard to explain."

"Weren't you worried that Ehsan would find out? Where was he in all this?" Jack questioned.

"That's the crazy thing." Hailey raised her hands up to show her gusto for how everything fit together. "This whole time that I was planning, he wasn't even at the house."

Hailey reached her hand over to Ryan and squeezed his.

"The part of the story Ryan didn't tell you was what happened to our friend Anna, the one I was coming to meet. Soon after Ryan had left the compound and headed to the airport, which was before all the mess with Faisal's blackmailing him, there was a bombing at the compound."

"Woah," the Aussies said in unison.

"You mean she was there?" Jack continued. "We heard about it. It was all over the news."

"Yeah. Ryan had left early in the morning to catch a flight to go meet a contact of Anna's father. But not long afterward a few suicide bombers drove into the compound and destroyed everything."

"Oh guys, I'm so sorry. Was your mate..." Holly said, trailing off.

"No, when we were on the bus, we got a call from her, if you can believe it. She's banged up but alive." Hailey glanced at Ryan before continuing. "We both are having trouble processing it all, but God must have stepped in."

Hailey was silent for a moment as the weight of that thought hit her.

"She's still in Dammam," Ryan added as he reached out and took her hand.

Hailey was thankful he took over. She was having difficulty speaking and keeping calm.

"But that's all we know. We're still waiting for her to call us back."

The emotion from the account and thinking about Anna and her parents crescendoed and threatened to break through. Hailey was losing control.

"I'm sorry," Hailey said as tears spilled into her eyes. "I think I need a break."

She pushed back from the table and weaved her way through the tables. She managed to get to the bathroom just as the sobs broke through. Hailey went to the far end and slid down the tiled wall, pulling her knees up to her chest. Her body fought to mourn the trauma she had lived through, yet she tried to contain it. It was futile. As even more cries broke through, she hoped no one was in there with her.

I just want to go home.

Maybe she should have taken Ryan up on his offer and stayed in their room. Her emotions apparently weren't ready to relive it, at least not all at once.

Anna, where are you? Hailey sobbed again as even more questions poured into her mind.

CHAPTER 8

Hailey didn't know how long she had huddled there, but the cold tiles were now warm from her body heat. The floor around her was littered with the tissues she had grabbed off the counter.

The sound of the bathroom door swinging open lifted her head. She quickly wiped the tears from her cheeks and dried her eyes as best she could as she waited to see who was entering.

It was Holly.

"Is it OK if I come in?"

"Yeah, of course," Hailey chuckled. It was a weak attempt to cover up her embarrassment.

"Ryan told us the rest of the story: about the square and getting away," Holly said as she lowered herself next to her. "Hailey, I'm so sorry you went through all of that. I'm so glad you made it out."

Hailey didn't respond for fear she would start crying again.

"Are you really thinking of leaving the tour?"

"Not if Anna calls. And she will."

An awkward air fell between them.

"How about we go back out there and join the guys? I think it might help if you get something to eat."

Hailey agreed. She quickly cleaned up the floor and followed

Holly back to their table.

"Are you alright?" Ryan asked as he rose and embraced her.

"Me? Yeah, I'm good." she lied, trying to lighten the mood. "Sorry about that."

"You have nothing to apologize for," Jack said as she took her seat. "I'm impressed you're still standing at all after what you've gone through."

Hailey smiled at him. In fact, she was surprised herself.

"Hey, everyone," a man's voice said, pulling their attention away.

James, the Englishman from the bus, was walking up to the table with his girlfriend next to him. Fabina was smiling, yet had a look of slight concern in her eyes.

"My girl and I were coming over to join you lot for a drink, but why all the grim faces?"

"Hailey and Ryan just told us the story of how they came to be with us," Jack answered him. "It's a ripper of a story."

"Really?" James said grabbing a chair and pulling it up beside Ryan. Once seated, he swung his large arm up and clapped it around Ryan's shoulders. "That's bloody brilliant. I love a good story."

Hailey smiled nervously when Fabina caught her eye. Fabina's face clearly showed that she noticed Hailey's red eyes.

"Ah... James dear?" she said leaning down as she touched his shoulder. "I don't think they've eaten yet. How about we let them go grab some food?" Fabina winked at Hailey.

Hailey sighed with relief.

"Great idea," Jack said.

Hailey rose from the table and fell in line with the others as they made their way over to the buffet.

"I think you're going to be OK," Jack said over his shoulder as they approached the long table of food. "You just need some time to recover."

"Thanks. Yeah... I think you're right."

As soon as he turned back around, Hailey pulled the phone out of her pocket and checked it.

Now if only Anna would call.

=======

As Jack led the way to their room after they had said goodnight to the rest of the group, he was still trying to sort out the story in his head. They had talked all throughout dinner and, even though Jack had a ton of his questions answered, he was still dumbfounded that such events were even possible.

He turned to check that Holly was still following him down the hall. Her face looked just as confused as his.

"Can you believe all that?" Jack asked her.

"Actually, no. I mean... I don't know why they would make any of it up. They seem to be pretty stand up people, but *come on*. Even setting all that God stuff aside, it seems a bit crazy for it to be even possible for someone to do that."

"You mean all that guy getting her from prison and the wedding stuff?"

"Yeah," Holly replied. "But then... you do hear some awful stories of things that happen in the world, even back at home. So maybe it is possible."

They walked down the rest of the hall in silence as they both contemplated the rest of what Hailey had told them. When Jack got to the door to their room, he got out the key card but paused.

"Do you think it's possible for God to really talk to someone like that?" he asked.

Holly shifted from one foot to the other. "I don't know. He's never done anything like that with me or anyone I know. Maybe it was in her head? But... Hailey doesn't seem like the crazy type."

"Well, I don't know what to make of it all."

=======

The night was filled with restless dreams. Scenes of her parents' faces mixed with sounds of explosions produced a fitful sleep. Anna finally jerked fully awake just moments before one of the other doctors came in the room.

"Are you alright? Do you have a fever?" With concern etched all over his face, her doctor approached and frantically started checking her vitals.

"No. I'm fine," Anna insisted. "I'm not sweating from a fever. I just had a bad dream is all." Anna briefly squeezed her eyes shut to clear the last images in her mind.

The doctor didn't seem to even hear her explanation, or maybe he didn't care. He went right on with his exam. Only after taking her temperature, checking her pupil response, and listening to her heart and breathing did he finally back away and relax.

"See, everything's alright."

"Yes, it does appear to be," he agreed as he made notes in her chart.

"So I guess that means that I can still leave..." her voice trailed off.

A man dressed in black military clothes entered the room. Seeing the handgun strapped to his hip caused Anna to tense. The doctor, noticing her recoil, looked up from the chart and followed her gaze to the door. Anna's breath caught in her throat as she waited for the doctor to respond. With any luck, he would tell the man to leave.

But he didn't.

The doctor nodded to the man and went back to making notes. She wasn't sure what was going on.

Am I in trouble for something? she wondered.

The soldier nodded and smiled at her.

OK… so probably not. He wouldn't look so pleasant if I was.

After a few more notations, the doctor closed her chart.

"I'm happy with the progress you've made, young one. Your MRI is clear and your vitals are good. I will be releasing you today. Do you need help making arrangements to leave?" he asked.

"Actually, I'm not sure," Anna said as she eyed the officer.

"No," answered the soldier. "I will be helping her with those. Is there anything she needs to do before leaving? Or may she leave now?"

"She only has to come and sign some paperwork for the records department before leaving the hospital. Her file needs to be complete before it's sent to…" the doctor looked down at the chart. "Oh yes, Entrata."

"Very well," the officer said.

Anna was confused. She seemed to be the only one in the dark as to what was going on. Her doctor made his way back to the door but turned before leaving the room.

"Anna, even though I am releasing you, I want you to be sure to get lots of rest. Do you understand?"

"Yes, but who–"

"I will make sure of it, Doctor," the soldier cut in.

Anna was now getting annoyed but forced herself to keep

calm.

"Very well. Take care of yourself," the doctor said with a nod and then left.

The room suddenly felt cold. The officer was still smiling at her, but Anna was always nervous around law enforcement. She shifted in her bed and wrung the top of the blanket in her hands.

"The councilman has asked that I assist you today in getting back in touch with your friend. So as soon–"

"Oh.... you're the man he left." Relief flooded Anna's core as she finally understood. "I was expecting an office bureaucrat or something. Sir, I gotta tell you, you had me scared there for a moment."

"My apologies, miss," he said as he moved closer to her bed. "I'm glad that we got that all sorted out because I have strict orders to get you back with your friend and aid the two of you in getting to wherever you would like to go. The councilman was hoping to return this morning, but he had some urgent matters to attend to. He does send his apologies."

"Nah, that's OK. No need to pull him away for little ol' me. I think between the two of us, we can figure it all out. Oh, wait! The other doc took my phone away last night." She motioned to the side table and shrugged.

"That's not a problem. Get dressed and packed up, then meet me in the hall. You can sign those papers and we can call your friend from my cell once we get out to my vehicle. It's parked right outside. Then once you know where you want to go, I'll personally take you directly there."

"Wow, my own bodyguard. Sounds perfect," Anna flirted.

The soldier blushed but nodded and then marched out of the room. Anna stifled the small chuckle that rose in her throat. The man was so official and serious and so… army like. But it only added to his charm. Once the door had been closed behind him, Anna let the chuckle escape. She shook her head at herself. She was such a sucker for a man in uniform. After it dissipated, she looked around the room. Seriousness pushed the last of the lightness away. She felt so alone.

All was silent, apart from footsteps in the hall and distant beeping from the medical equipment in one of the adjoining rooms. The machines in her room were turned off, leaving her room still. To most, hospitals were uncomfortable places to be but not to Anna. Strangely, she found solace being inside a hospital. She looked around the room as she let the comfort sink further in. Yes, there was the chaos of tragedy from people on their worst day, but seeing as there was tons of the same outside as well, she liked being here. At least in a hospital there were those that could help, and she felt safety in that.

Anna gave one more scan of the room as she came to terms with the fact, that in mere minutes, she would have to leave and enter a world that her parents were no longer a part of. She closed her eyes and took four deep breaths as tears stabbed her eyes.

Steady now, she told herself. *I need to focus on meeting up with Hailey and Ryan and find out what happened to them. And then we all need to focus on getting home. There will be time for more... more of that later.*

The thoughts helped to quell the desolation that was threatening to envelop her again. When the last of it inched away just far enough to where her body relaxed again, she opened her eyes. Not wanting to cause the officer to knock on her door from the delay, Anna swung her legs off the bed and stood. Her legs felt wobbly from not walking much in the last few days, but she moved slow enough for them to support her.

Her abaya had been cut away as the medical staff attended to her wounds, but graciously one of the nurses had brought her another one yesterday morning. Anna quickly changed into it. After scanning the room once more, she said goodbye to the safety of the room.

She gripped the doorknob, took a deep breath and turned it. Pulling it open, she moved to place herself in the hands of the handsome soldier waiting in the hall.

CHAPTER 9

When his cell rang and Daib saw the house number appear, his hand gripped the phone so tightly that the tension ran all the way up his arm and into his shoulder. Regret and fear stabbed in his gut. He had no clue what was going on at the house, and he was ashamed he couldn't bring himself to return.

The cell stopped ringing.

Daib continued to stare at it. Moments later it vibrated. Whoever had called had left a message.

Was it Taavi again? Was it Ehsan?

Daib wasn't up to hearing another tirade from Ehsan's head of security again, but his curiosity couldn't leave it unheard. He hit the button and punched in his code. His breath caught in his throat as the message started to play.

It was Ghada.

Relief was just starting to wash over him, but fear suddenly pushed it away. Something wasn't right. Ghada sounded hurt.

"… so I need you to come back to the house. Ehsan is furious, but he needs information I'm really hoping you have. I know this is asking a lot. I can't guarantee what will happen if you do. But I need you to come back anyway. I'm scared, Daib. Please call me back."

Daib ended the call. The hoarseness of her voice deeply concerned him.

What did he do to her?

He quickly dialed and prayed that Ghada would be the one to answer.

"Hello?" her timid voice rasped over the line.

"Ghada, I got your message. Are you alright?"

She sniffled. He could tell she was crying.

"What happened?"

"Never mind that now. Where are you?"

"I'm still in Riyadh. I saw that roadblocks had been set up, so I'm trying to lie low. I'm so sorry for leaving you. I am a coward." Daib felt a blanket of guilt wrapping his whole body in shame.

"Can you," Ghada stopped and coughed, "come back?"

Daib swallowed hard. He desperately needed to return and make sure Ghada was alright, but his fear fought against agreeing to it.

"Daib, please!" Ghada begged. "I don't know what he will do if I can't get you to come back."

Daib thought for a moment. He couldn't shake the overwhelming sense of responsibility he felt for Ghada and knew he needed to make amends for his cowardice.

"As you wish," he said as he shoved his fear aside. "But, Ghada, I need to know if you are alright?"

"I'll be even better when I see you again. Please hurry! And when you get here... you need to tell Ehsan everything you know."

"What about Hailey?" he asked tentatively, feeling torn.

"It's been two days since she ran from the square, so I'm hoping she's found another way out of the city. But the only possible way to get Ehsan to relent is if I can get you to come back and if you tell him everything. It's not a guarantee, but it's… the only chance I have."

"I will head back right away."

Daib hung up the phone and jumped in the car.

When the house came into view, the sick feeling about returning came flooding back, but he couldn't very well turn back and betray Ghada again.

Who know's what Ehsan might do to her. The thought quickly overtook the other, and so he kept his course and pushed harder on the gas.

He parked the car in front of the house and jogged up the front steps. After pausing for a quick breath, he clutched the handle and swung the front door open. Looking around the foyer, relief came to him as no one was in sight. He turned to close the door.

"Daib, finally!"

The deep voice behind him made his skin cold with dread. Daib slowly turned to see Ehsan approaching.

"My friend, I'm glad you called Ghada back and decided to return." Ehsan offered his hand. "You have nothing to fear. I'm glad you are back home. You are part of the family and to think that you should not return due to fear, is… is preposterous. You belong here."

Daib took his hand and forced a smile. Ehsan rarely was so friendly with the staff, and it wasn't sitting well.

"Now come. We have much to discuss."

"Yes, Councilman."

Daib followed Ehsan over to the library and entered after him.

"Please, sit," Ehsan offered as he motioned to one of the high-back, leather chairs along the far wall.

After Ehsan was seated on the other chair that faced his, Daib sat and tried to look comfortable. It was proving to be a difficult task.

"So we find ourselves in quite the predicament, don't we?"

"Y-yes, Councilman."

Ehsan remained silent for a moment and continued to look him over. It was uncomfortable sitting under Ehsan's gaze, but he managed to stay still and quiet.

"I am just sick that Hailey is out in the world alone," Ehsan finally said. "I know it was foolish of me to leave her so soon after the wedding. The poor thing had no time to settle in. But sadly, my presence was desperately needed, and so I had to go."

Ehsan paused again before continuing on. Daib didn't speak, he just nodded to try and convey his understanding.

"Ghada has told me all of what she knows, which has been very helpful. However, we are still missing one piece of the puzzle. But before I ask you to provide that last piece, I want you to think about Ghada's wellbeing before you answer."

And there it was. Ehsan's true colors finally showed and confirmed that Daib's uneasy feeling was not misplaced.

"I think you can attest to her frailty, can't you, Daib?"

The tone of the question troubled him. Did Ehsan know that he cared for her? Or was it just a subtle threat? He would have to be careful here in case it was a trap.

"I think you have made an excellent and wise choice to have her as your wife, Councilman." Daib hoped showing respect would distract Ehsan from any further suspicion.

"Why thank you, Daib. I think so too. And I think we understand each other. So now the only thing I need to know from you is simple. What is the name of the tour company Hailey was planning on taking?"

Daib's throat constricted and it was hard not to shudder from the shiver running up his spine. He had agreed with Ghada when she said that Hailey had probably not waited for the tour company.

But what if she had waited? What if she caught it this morning like she planned? Was the bus far enough away yet?

Daib tried to quickly calculate the odds, but he could see Ehsan was getting impatient. He had to answer and fast.

"Let me think," Daib stalled.

He couldn't lie and make up a name. Ehsan would surely look into it and find out. He couldn't refuse to tell him. Ehsan would surely punish Ghada until he told him. Daib realized there was no other choice.

"I believe it's called... Pat-Patetagi tours," Daib stumbled with his words as they stuck in his throat. Divulging the truth was proving difficult without knowing where Hailey was. "They are a small tour business in the city."

"And what was Hailey's plan? She has no passport or papers."

"I'm not rightly sure, Councilman. But she had talked with them on two different occasions. I wasn't present for either, but everything seemed to be sorted out."

Daib hoped that the information would appease Ehsan and he wouldn't ask any more questions.

"Very well. Now head back to your duties. We'll speak about the other issues later."

"Of course, Councilman. I will get right to work."

Leaving the library, Daib had to use his full willpower to not run back to the car and drive off. With Ehsan's last comment, it was now clear Ehsan wouldn't be trading the punishment for his insubordination for the name of the tour company. He chewed on the inside of his cheeks.

Please, let me, and only me, bear the consequences.

=======

Anna hadn't called.

Hailey's heart ached as she watched Ryan from behind the hotel's glass doors. He was helping to load up the last of the bags under the bus. And even though it was her idea to not stay with the tour group, she still hated the fact that Holly and Fabina were leaving.

Hailey knew staying was the right decision, at least she hoped so, but it didn't make the choice any easier. With not getting an update from Anna, Hailey didn't want to be on a bus for hours at a time and chance not having cell reception. There was also the chance that they would need to get over to Dammam if Anna's injuries were worse than she had let on.

Hailey had already said her tearful goodbyes to Holly and Fabina, who now sat on the bus and looked at her through the large bus windows. She hadn't known them long, but after telling them what had happened and seeing their empathy, Hailey felt intensely connected to them both. She waved to them again. Holly waved back, and Fabina blew her a couple of kisses.

When Ryan finished with the bags, he shook Jack and James' hands. When James pulled Ryan into a big bear hug, Hailey had to look away to keep from choking up.

Am I making the wrong decision? God... I hope You're still in all this.

After the men had boarded the bus, Ryan walked over to Joe

and started talking. Hailey looked back at the women. Holly had tears in her eyes, and Fabina was pressing her hand to the glass. Seeing their support pierced the last of Hailey's resolve. She blew them each a quick kiss, waved, and turned away to walk back to the elevator.

As she was passing the front desk, the knot in the pit of her stomach rose, pushing a sob into her throat. Hailey clamped her hand over her mouth just before it broke free. She broke into a run and headed for the stairwell. There was no time to wait for the elevator.

Bursting through the metal door, Hailey mounted the stairs two at a time. After five floors, her legs were burning and pushing for her to stop. She ignored them and mounted another three, but then collapsed on the next landing.

There were no additional sobs that came after the first one. The expelling of so much energy seemed to have dissipated them. Hailey swiveled around and sat on the top step of the eighth floor. She scooted over and pressed her shoulder against the wall. Her chest heaved as it tried to flood her body with fresh air. It took a few minutes, but soon her breathing slowed.

She took the phone out of her pocket and held it in both hands.

Anna, where are you? Call, damn it.

She leaned her head on the wall, pleading for the phone to ring.

Why isn't she calling? Something must have happened. It had to have, or she would have called by now. Oh, God, what if there was a complication from her injuries.

Hailey's stomached tightened. Images of Anna's unconscious body lying in a hospital bed, alone, flooded her mind.

She squeezed her eyes shut.

God, help her.

Hailey wasn't sure how long she sat there. But when Ryan's voice called out to her, resounding up from below, she finally opened her eyes.

"I'm up here," she answered back.

It took a few minutes for Ryan to reach her.

"Are you OK?" he asked as he took a seat beside her. "You weren't in our room. I had to ask the front desk if they had seen you."

"Yeah, sorry. I just couldn't watch them pull away."

"I don't blame you. I kinda wish I hadn't. But they're gone now. Do you want to head back up to-"

Ringing cut Ryan off as the phone in Hailey's hands jumped to life. The echo of it in the stairwell intensified the ring, startling Hailey. She jerked and almost dropped the phone.

"Anna?" Hailey asked as soon as she had managed to recover and get the phone to her ear. She couldn't even be bothered with a hello.

"Hailey, I'm so sorry I didn't get to call you back sooner."

"Is it Anna?" Ryan asked nudging her arm.

Hailey nodded to confirm that it was but said nothing.

"The stupid doctor took away my phone. But I'm out of the hospital now. Where are you?"

"So you're OK? They discharged you?" Hailey asked, ignoring Anna's question.

"Yeah, they released me this morning. Where are you?"

"Is she OK?" Ryan interrupted.

"Anna, hold on a sec." Hailey tilted the phone away from her ear. "Yeah, she's fine. The hospital discharged her this morning."

"So where is she now?"

"Anna, where are you now?"

"Funny story," Anna giggled. "You know the guy from the government that interrupted our call?"

"Yeah…"

"Well, he actually got kicked out by the doctor, but he left this soldier with me because he had to get back to Riyadh. They are going to help me get to you and then help in getting us out of the country."

"Wait… what?" Hailey's heart sunk. Something wasn't feeling right. But before she could ask Anna more questions to see if the feeling was from paranoia or if something was off, Anna kept talking excitedly about the plans.

"I know, crazy right? So if you would just tell me where you are already, we can all get home."

Hailey didn't know what to say. She didn't want to panic and alarm Anna. "Anna? Just a second OK? I'm just going to tell Ryan."

"Sure." Anna sounded so upbeat.

Maybe this is my paranoia. Hailey lowered the phone and covered the mic with her finger. For a second Hailey continued to look at the phone before raising her eyes to Ryan. When she did so, it was obvious he saw the fear in her eyes.

"What's wrong?"

"Anna said she's with a soldier and that the guy from the government had left him with her and he was to take her to us. She said that he was going to help us all get home."

Ryan slowly shook his head, "You don't think…"

"I don't know. I don't have a good feeling about this, Ryan."

"Is Anna with him now?"

"I don't know."

"OK, here's what to do. Take a deep breath," Ryan instructed. "You can't scare Anna until we know what exactly is going on.

After every answer, pause and tell me what she said. That way I can help you figure out what to say, and it will give you time to steady yourself before you respond."

"Yeah, OK. That should work."

Hailey was incredibly grateful Ryan had found her. If he hadn't she might have lost it right there and, very possibly, could have jeopardized Anna's safety.

"Ready?" Ryan asked.

"I think so."

"Deep breath," he reminded her. "And remember to keep your tone light."

"Right." Hailey took a deep breath to steady her voice.

"First, ask her if she's with the soldier now."

After one more breath, Hailey put the phone back up to her ear.

"Hey, are you with the soldier now?" With the speed of her heartbeat, Hailey was impressed she managed to sound so casual.

"Yeah, he's right here. We're just sitting outside the Dammam hospital. He lent me his cell phone. The councilman told him to get me to wherever I wanted to go."

"K... let me tell Ryan. Just a sec." Hailey repeated putting the phone in her lap and covered the mic, but it was nowhere near as smooth. Her hands were shaking.

"Oh, God!" Hailey prayed. She closed her eyes and tried to take a few deep breaths, but it didn't help. The wave of nausea continued to rise.

How could all of this be happening? I just want to go home with Ryan and Anna and get away from all this chaos. I can't lose Anna, not now. She doesn't deserve this.

You were made for such a time as this.

The words forcefully cleared her head. Hailey was about to ask how that could be and what He meant, but Ryan pulled her attention away.

"What!?! What happened?"

She looked up at him with terror in her eyes. "Ryan, he... he has her."

"What? How do you know? What did she say?"

Hailey relayed Anna's words to him. Ryan's face paled. He leaned forward and put his head between his knees. Both of his arms came up and covered his head.

"What are we going to do?" Her fear thickened, and it was hard to swallow. "Ryan?" Hailey urged him to answer.

Ryan raised his head and sat back up. "You have to alert her. But you have to prep her first, so she doesn't give anything away. Can you do that?"

"I... I... don't know. Ryan, I'm so scared." Hailey's hands were cold and clammy from the fear raging in her chest. They continued to shake, and she had to muster some effort to not drop the phone.

"Give me the phone," Ryan insisted.

Hailey moved the phone towards him, but he still had to pry it out of her fingers. Hailey listened intently as Ryan took over.

"Anna? It's Ryan... Yeah... Good... No, we're not... Anna, just hold on a sec, K? Don't ask any more questions. Just say 'OK' and then listen."

Hailey was impressed by how calm Ryan was able to act. It was hard not to hear Anna's side of the conversation, but she knew Ryan was doing a better job than she could have managed.

"In between what I'm going to tell you, I want you to say things like sure, yeah, sounds good. Keep your voice upbeat and happy, just like you were. Do you understand?"

Hailey reached out and touched his arm as she prayed that Anna would stay calm. Ryan's nod to her confirmed that Anna understood.

"Did you get the councilman's name? Just answer yes or no... Was it Ehsan?"

Hailey watched as Ryan closed his eyes and took a deep breath. It seemed like their fear was inescapable now. Ehsan had found Anna. Hailey had to bite her lip. She needed to keep quiet so she could hear what Ryan was saying.

"Anna, I need you to ask where we are again and pretend that I'm telling you. Can you do that? ... Good. Now I can't get into how, but Ehsan is the reason Hailey never made it to your place. He is a very dangerous man. I need to know if there is any way you can get away from that soldier. So if you think you can, say 'that sounds like a good plan.' If you're not sure, say 'I think that would work.'"

Hailey held her breath as she strained to read Ryan's facial expressions for any indication of what Anna might be saying. When she saw Ryan smile, a small moment of hope passed over her. Ryan didn't say anything for a while, and Hailey desperately wondered what Anna was saying. It was increasingly harder to be patient and wait.

"Good job. I think that sounded really convincing. Can you somehow tell me what your plan is? ... So you're not sure? ... Are you hinting that your uncle is Ehsan in this scenario? ... I think I get it. So we need to get out? ... OK, well as soon as you do, will you call us back? ... I will... Yup, take care." Ryan ended the call and handed the phone back to Hailey.

"So what was all that about?" Hailey asked. Everything sounded so odd with only being able to hear Ryan's side of the conversation.

"Anna did a good job," Ryan said, sounding impressed. "The ruse is that we have already left Saudi. She is going to fly to Riyadh and then to Paris and said that we should meet her there because she has an uncle that we can stay with. Then she went on for a while about her uncle."

"OK... but what's the real plan? And what's all that about Ehsan and her uncle?"

"It was quite coded, but she got her point across. She implied we need to get out of Saudi as soon as possible. I confirmed with her that the part about all the details about her uncle was to warn us. I think Ehsan is overseeing all the foreigners leaving the country because of the bombing. She wasn't able to tell me exactly what she had planned, but she said she'd call us when she was safe."

Hailey's head started to spin. Ryan reached over and grabbed her hand.

"Hailey, I think we need to try and meet up with the bus again. From how it was sounding, I don't think it's going to be safe trying to meet up with Anna. At least not right away. She said she had a plan and I think we need to trust her."

"How could you know that?" Hailey snapped. "What did she say exactly?" Her voice sounded harsher than she intended. "Ryan, I'm sorry. I don't mean to take this out on you. I know you're trying to help. But if we're not absolutely sure of what she meant..." she stopped to take a breath and level her emotions. "I just don't want to make a mistake is all."

"I know," Ryan said as he shifted closer and wrapped his arm around her.

The warmth of his embrace helped to steady her, so she let him hold her for a moment until her head cleared. She pulled back just enough to be able to look up at him.

"How confident are you that this is what she wants us to do?" she asked.

"Very."

Hailey laid back against his chest. The thudding of his heart and the woody smell of his shirt made her feel safe. Her fear still pushed her to feel uncertain about this new plan. It tried to coerce her to refuse to leave without her best friend, but she trusted Ryan and Anna. She needed to let go.

CHAPTER 10

When his man called telling him that he was about to take the girl to the airport and that she said Hailey had already left the country, Ehsan's displeasure started to boil.

"Where are you now?"

"In my vehicle outside the hospital."

"Step outside, but tell the girl to wait. I need to speak to you privately." Ehsan impatiently paced around his office as he waited for his man to complete the task. His mind raced with contingency plans.

"You may proceed, sir."

"Are you certain that she told you her friend had left Saudi?"

"Yes, sir."

"So what did she say her plans were?" Ehsan demanded.

"She is going to catch a flight to Riyadh and then fly to Paris to visit her uncle and that her friend would meet her there."

"Damn it, she's lying." Ehsan pinched the bridge of his nose. "Did you tell her who I was?"

"No, sir."

"Did something seem off when the girl was talking to her friend?"

"No, sir."

Nothing was making sense.

"Was there anything that seemed to distress the girl during the call?"

"No, sir. She seemed happy and excited."

Ehsan had no idea how, but it seemed they must have put the pieces together. If the lead with the tour bus was correct, there was no way that Hailey would be out of the country yet. He had to think of a new plan.

"OK, this is what you are to do. Tell her that she is free to go meet up with her friend, but that you need her to sign some papers first, so you're going to come to Riyadh with her. Tell her that a fellow officer will meet you at the Riyadh airport with the paperwork, so she won't be delayed in catching her next flight. Understand?"

"Yes, sir."

"And if she asks about me at all, just say that I'm busy with other matters and seeing how she is well, then she is free to go about her business. I need you to make it sound like I have no further interest in her."

Ehsan smiled. He was pleased with this new plan and even more pleased that this soldier would never dare ask questions or bug him to know the details surrounding the situation. He was a soldier and would just follow orders.

"Can you do that?"

"Yes, sir."

"Good man. My guess is that she isn't planning on going to Paris at all but will go wherever her friend is. I want you to have a third man at the airport ready to tail her. That way Anna should lead us right to her friend."

"Yes, sir. I will need some time to get that set up."

"That's fine, just get it done. You can stall if you have to…

even book a flight for tomorrow morning if needed."

"Yes, sir."

Ehsan leaned forward and hung up the phone. The chair creaked under his weight. He reached for the cup on the corner of the desk. The coffee was cold, so he decided against drinking the last few sips sloshing in the bottom. He raised the cup to his chin and sniffed in the earthy scent before replacing the cup back on the desk. He loved how it cleared his mind.

Leaning back in his chair, he interlaced his fingers behind his head and gazed at the ceiling of his office. Control slowly flowed back into his veins. He smiled and sighed.

Taavi was now on his way to the tour company to retrieve the tour's itinerary, and the soldier would ensure Anna is followed. Even if Anna doesn't lead him to Hailey, she would be excellent insurance if things went sideways.

He tilted forward and went back to his computer. Work would more easily occupy his mind now that he had two solid plans being implemented. As he punched the keys on the keyboard, thoughts of Hailey's return started to take shape. A small smile pulled at the left corner of his mouth.

=======

Taavi drove straight for the tour company after getting the update from Ehsan. He was glad that Daib had come through. With the imbecile at the roadblock, it would have been a tedious job trying to track down the correct tour company. Not to mention probably an utterly fruitless endeavor. The time it would take would most certainly close the small window, if any, they had remaining.

Pulling up to the building, it didn't look like much. Taavi

craned his neck and looked up the span of the facade as he turned off the car. The engine sputtered and fell silent. He jumped out, gently closed the car door, and jogged up to the door.

Taavi reached out his hand and pulled, but the door barely gave way.

Locked.

His eyes scanned the door and caught sight of a small sign taped to the inside, the message facing the street.

CLOSED UNTIL TOMORROW
SORRY FOR ANY INCONVENIENCE

Ehsan's not going to like that, Taavi thought as he returned to the car. He punched in the phone number. As it rang, he turned the air conditioning back on and waited for Eshan to answer.

"Taavi? That was quick."

"No, it's closed until tomorrow."

Ehsan swore.

"What would you like me to do in the meantime?" Taavi asked. He silently hoped it would be to take the rest of the day off.

"How many of the roadblocks did you interview yesterday?"

Taavi quickly counted them. "Uh... four."

"Well, you may as well go and talk to the rest of them. The chances are probably low, but I don't want to make any assumptions. Report back if you find anything. Even if you don't, it aids in confirming that it really was Hailey on that bus."

"I will get on it right away, Councilman. But..." his voice trailed off as he considered not asking the question.

"Was there something else?" Eshan sounded annoyed by his

delay.

"Do you think we may have lost our window?"

"Maybe, but I refuse to give up and let her get away. There are still many possibilities, so we're going to have to get more information. I have a man trailing Hailey's friend, which I'm sure will produce something. Now get going and check in when you're done."

Taavi hung up the phone and pulled away from the building. There was no question, he would obey Ehsan and check in with the other roadblocks. However, it seemed pretty clear to him that they had already found where Hailey was headed. Now it was just a matter of if they were too late.

CHAPTER 11

"Everybody off," Joe called out. "Please, ladies, remember to put on your head scarfs before getting off the bus."

James leaned down and retrieved the scarf from the bag under his seat and passed it to Fabina. He tracked her every movement as she draped it over her head and wrapped it around her neck. Even after three years, he found her just as striking. Typically he would have lost interest by this point, but he didn't see that happening with Fabina... not now, not ever.

Fabina smiled at him coyly when she caught him staring. She stood and waited patiently as he gathered his things. She was so sweet and gentle. He took another moment to admire her as he moved into the aisle to let her pass. As she moved ahead of him, he caught a trace of her perfume: rose and vanilla. Her choice of scent seemed fitting, gentle and soft, just as she was. But he also caught sight of a glimmer of sadness in her eyes.

"Love, are you alright?"

"Yes. I'm just sad for Hailey and what she went through."

"Ah, don't worry," Jack said, coming up behind James. "That girl's a ripper. She'll be alright."

Fabina turned away. "I hope so."

James followed her down the aisle with Jack in tow. He took

another moment to scan her small frame. She was such a vast contrast to his burly awkwardness. Fabina was graceful and elegant, and that variance had a crazy effect on him. It propelled him to be more of a stand-up guy, to protect her, even from himself and his old ways.

After all the passengers had exited outside, James and Fabina pooled with the others near the side of the bus. It was still early in the day, but his forehead was already beaded with sweat from the rising temperature. He pulled at his shirt sleeve and wiped his face dry. He was definitely built for colder climates.

A small stab of homesickness hit his heart. The feeling surprised him. This was the first time on one of his adventures that he longed for one of those rainy days in London: huddled under his umbrella as he crossed the cobbled street in front of his house and jogged to catch the Tube.

The slight moment of longing dissipated as James watched Joe walk a few yards from the bus and over to two waiting men. One man was tall and slender. The other, quite a bit shorter but had a more robust build. Both men wore long-sleeved, white robes, red and white checkered headdresses, and black sandals.

James couldn't hear them, but after a few minutes, Joe walked back to them. He smiled and got back on the bus without a word. The two men approached.

"Welcome! Welcome, my friends," the shorter one said. "My name is Ali. This is Hamza. We are happy to have you here and show you our ships."

James wasn't the only one confused by the comments as he looked around the group.

The men chuckled.

"To us, in great Saudi Arabia," He raised his hands in a grand display and beamed with pride, "camels are the ships of the desert."

Ali's unabashed enthusiasm and wild hand gestures were a bit much. James ground his teeth as he squeezed his jaw shut and managed to suppress his snicker.

"You will come to see today all that these magnificent creatures can offer," Ali continued, "and how uniquely magnificent they truly are."

Ali looked at each member of the group, eyes wide and filled with excitement.

"Now follow me," he instructed with a wave of his hand.

The other man, Hamza, never spoke but followed in step with Ali. The group walked in a clump behind the two men, kicking up dust as they went down the sandy driveway. At the end of the short road, they approached a brown and white clay building. The group followed Ali and Hamza around to the side of the building but didn't enter.

"If anyone needs to use the facilities, please do so now. They are located just through these doors," Ali motioned with his hand. "Men to the left and the women to the right."

James saw Fabina deflate beside him. He chuckled.

"Hey," Fabina whispered, leaning over to him. "It's not funny. My bladder is about to explode."

"I can see the hesitation," Ali said, "but don't fret. Here at Najma, we are fortunate to enjoy many luxuries. You will be happy to see that the toilets are similar to what you are accustomed to."

"Oh, yessss!" Fabina voiced, probably a little louder than she had intended.

James was amused when he saw color blush her cheeks. When he laughed again, she shuffled off towards the doors.

"You're never going to make a good world traveler, Fabina,"

James teased her.

"I'm OK with that," she called back without stopping.

Once the group was all together again, Ali led them up a slight incline to the top of a small hill. A thick, white guardrail spanned the length of the hill and went off in either direction farther than James could make out through the haze. Beyond the guardrail was a dirt track, and another guardrail lined the other side. It ran parallel to the first.

A few yards to their left was what James assumed was the starting line. There was a tall structure made from the same white metal as the guardrail. It rose from each of the rails and spanned across the track, about eight feet off the ground. But unlike the horse and dog tracks back home, there weren't any gates or shoots.

"This is the famous Najma Track," Ali announced to the group, his hands flailing about.

Ali was more dramatic than James usually appreciated, but the small man was starting to grow on him.

"Shortly, this whole site will be crawling with trainers, camels, and people that have come to watch the race. Yes, it will be exciting," Ali said, as he smiled and looked around at their surroundings. "Please, now follow me to some shade."

He led the way along the ridge of the hill towards a tall structure that enclosed rows of wooden bleachers. Cautiously, James helped Fabina climb a few rows and sat beside her. Ali remained standing at the bottom, with Hamza beside him.

"Before this place gets full, I would like to fill you in on some history and facts. This will be sure to enhance your experience today." Ali reached for a piece of paper that Hamza passed him, then continued. "Now, I'm going to ask you a series of questions. I know that adults can be... how do the American's say it?" He paused. "Ah yes, too cool for school?"

Ali leaned forwards as he said the expression, clearly hoping for a laugh. The group gave a pity chuckle, but Ali didn't seem to care and went right on talking. It amused James.

"But we aren't going to do such things. No... we aren't." He wagged a finger at them all. "We are going to have a competition, and we will have fun." Ali held up one arm and drew an invisible vertical line with his hand down the center of the bleachers. "The team on this side is the blue team. And this side is the red team. The only rule is that none of you can act like you're too cool to answer my questions."

"Hey Ali," Sam called out, "don't worry. James, the big black guy on the blue team over there, he's never been cool."

"Sam, you lazy sod, you're going down," James said as he stood up, playfully shaking his fist. James had only gone on a couple trips with Sam, but the big-brother rapport he had with him was entertaining and growing.

"Not a chance, you crazy Brit," Sam shot back.

James laughed and shot him a defiant glare, then sat back down. No longer annoyed with the proposition of the game, James was now committed and teetering on the edge of his seat. Determination to win flowed through him.

"Wonderful! Hamza will keep score."

For the next twenty minutes the game surged on as everyone's adrenaline infused the game with competitiveness. On the last question Fabina broke the tie, causing the blue team to erupt in boisterous taunting of the red team.

"Way to go, babe!" James said as he jumped up.

He pulled Fabina up into his arms. Fabina laughed as he spun her around with ease.

Abruptly, sounds of vehicles filled the air, diverting his attention away from the connection of the moment. James couldn't see them. His view was blocked by the back wall. James looked at Ali. He was glancing around the side towards the direction of the engine sounds.

"Splendid! Everyone, listen up. Please move over to the far-left side and relax." Ali waited until they had all shuffled over. "You are more than welcome to watch as everyone prepares and sets up for the race, but please don't get up and wander around. If you need to go to the toilets again, please let one of us know, and we will be happy to accompany you there. Hamza will be back soon with some refreshments."

James's gaze tracked Hamza until he disappeared around the other side of the bleachers, then drew his attention back to Ali.

"About twenty minutes before the race, we will all make our way to those vehicles over there," Ali said as he pointed off to his left.

James looked to see four white SUVs parked in a line along the white guardrail, all facing away from them.

"Please," Ali continued, "spread out between the vehicles and have only three or four people per vehicle. That will leave a spot for the driver and your instructor. Your instructor will explain the race to you as it happens. Does everyone understand?"

By the excitement in Ali's voice, James felt his own excitement grow.

"Wonderful! Now make way."

Ali started to climb clumsily over the people who were seated in the first couple rows. He finally stopped and wiggled his hips to insert himself into the middle of the group.

"It will get noisier as people start to arrive, so make sure each of you can hear me."

Ali was right. As people started to arrive, the volume rose exponentially. People were running all over. Some were calling out directions, others were yelling at the camels they were pulling, which caused bleating responses from the camels.

James leaned over to Fabina. "They sound like my uncle Greg when he burps."

She laughed.

Joy spread over him. Making her laugh was his favorite thing in the world.

=======

The warmth from the cup of coffee in her hands helped distract her slightly from the concern that Anna hadn't called back. Hailey knew it was absurd to feel anxious already, it hadn't even been an hour since Ryan got off the phone with her. Anna's plans, whatever they were, would obviously need more time. Still, she felt uneasy.

Ryan had generously offered to go pack up their things from their room and handle the checkout, giving her a chance to try and relax by the coffee cart in the foyer. She raised the small cup to her lips. The cart only offered Turkish coffee, something Hailey had never had before. As the coffee slipped through the thick dark foam and slid past her lips, it was a lot stronger than she was expecting. Hailey cleared her throat a couple times between a few more sips. She soon adjusted to the bold taste and was enjoying it.

Anna, hurry! she pleaded. *I just need to know you're alright.*

Hailey took another sip as she watched Ryan exit the elevator with their things and make his way over to the counter. He glanced over at her and she smiled.

I'm so glad he's here.

God... actually, I don't even know what to say. This has all been so... so crazy. I can't grasp the fact that Ehsan knows that Anna knows me. But she'll be fine. Nothing's going to happen, right? I mean, it can't... it just can't. Right?

CHAPTER 12

Hamza had come back with water and small bags of nuts and pita bread for each of them. Fabina nibbled on hers as she watched the bustle of the people.

"It will be a fairly small race today," Ali said after taking a long swig of his water bottle. "Some of the races can get very large. My dad took me to one when I was a kid and it had about seventy camels in one race. But today there should be only about twenty or so. But don't worry, it will still provide quite the show."

Fabina found it amusing how excited Ali looked as he smiled and looked around at each member of the group. It was evident he loved his job, his passion and joy were contagious.

The crowd was continuing to grow. Loads of people now lined the guardrails, camels were getting situated near the starting line, people were running here and there as they parked their vehicles and, either found seats in the bleachers or met up with friends along the hill.

"The camels will soon be in place and ready," Ali explained as he stood. "Everyone, please make your way to one of the vehicles. Remember, only three or four per vehicle please."

The group followed his lead and stood as well.

"You lady and gent want to ride with us?" James asked as he looked at Jack and Holly.

"Sure!" Holly responded as Jack nodded in agreement.

Fabina was glad. The race would be even more exhilarating with them in the car.

She followed James down the steps of the bleachers and over to one of the furthest parked vehicles. As they approached, she saw a small Filipino man standing by the driver's door. He was in the process of extinguishing his cigarette under his foot and waving away the smoke. The man nodded and smiled. Fabina returned the gesture before climbing into the back seat with Holly. Ryan followed her in, and James got in the front.

"Going to be a bit tight with you, big guy," the man commented. "Don't worry your driver is ill, so I'll be doing both jobs today." He moved around the car and got in behind the wheel. "Good thing too. I don't think we would have fit."

James shrugged and offered his hand. "I'm James."

"Crisanto."

Both men shook hands. The rest of the introductions went around as the car jumped to life.

"Are you all ready for a fun race today?" Crisanto questioned.

"Yeah!" the four said in unison.

"If you look behind us, you may catch sight of the start, but it is hard to see from here. Don't worry, I will tell you what is happening. First, the camels will all line up. They grunt and stamp. They get very excited to run. The trainers join the owners in their vehicles on the other side of the track. Everyone starts their engines."

Fabina smiled as she watched how animated Crisanto talked. He made it sound like a movie trailer.

"There are men on either side of the track who will raise the starting line. Once they are given the signal, they will pull on ropes and up the line will go. The camels will shoot off and will catch up to us quite quickly."

"How fast can they run?" Fabina asked.

"Because they are excited, they get up to about sixty or so kilometers per hour once the group thins out. However, they slow to a pace of about forty. It's a long ten-kilometer track, so they know to pace themselves," Crisanto explained. "Oh, I'm not sure what that is in miles."

"Not needed. Kilometers are good."

Fabina did a quick scan out each window. It seemed like everyone was now in their vehicles.

"This is more exciting than I expected," she said as she leaned forward to James.

"Agreed." He didn't look at her but continued staring towards the starting line.

Fabina smiled. He looked like an excited toddler.

"Everyone, get ready. It's almost time."

She looked out the back window of the vehicle. She could only see one of the men at the edge of the starting line. The man pulled the rope and up shot the line.

"Here they come!" Crisanto yelled out.

=======

When the cab pulled up to the track, Hailey peered out the window of the cab.

"Is this it?" she asked the driver. He didn't speak English, but she asked anyway.

The man didn't say anything or even nod. He jumped out of

the car and started to unload their bag.

"I guess so," Ryan said as he opened his door.

Hailey followed and got out. She scanned the grounds. Tons of cars were parked to their left, a large building sat just ahead of them to the right, and off in the distance shouts and yips emulated from a large crowd.

"Looks like the race has started." She wondered how difficult it would be to track down the tour group.

Ryan grabbed their bags and joined her after paying their fare.

"Ready?"

He didn't wait for a response and started walking towards the crowd. Hailey followed. As they drew closer, a scene to her left drew Hailey's attention away from the track. She slowed her pace. Ryan didn't notice.

Three young boys sat on a small sandy hill. Two of them must have been around ten years old, but the third, no more than four. Three camels were sitting just beyond them, each tied to a metal ring hanging from a white post that stuck out of the ground. One of the older boys was curled up and sleeping. The other two held long black sticks and were drawing with them in the sand. Hailey guessed they were playing a game.

She pulled her eyes away from the boys. Ryan hadn't slowed his pace and was now a few yards ahead of her. As she jogged to catch up to him, Hailey heard the boys giggle. Seeing their joy made her smile.

Hailey reached Ryan just as he was coming to the edge of the crowd. She scanned both directions to see if she could locate the group but saw no one they knew. Hailey's view moved further to the track. She couldn't see any camels, but a giant dust cloud to her left got her attention. Hailey gripped Ryan's elbow and rose onto her tippy toes but quickly decided against it and dropped her arm. She nervously glanced around. No one was paying attention.

As her immediate surroundings sunk in, Hailey's skin pricked with concern. She was the only woman. She frantically scanned around but saw only men. She instantly felt out of place. She started to slowly back away from the crowd.

=======

Crisanto stepped on the gas, and the vehicle leaped forward. Just as he leveled out their speed, the camels had reached them. The thundering of their feet could be heard over the engine.

"Whoohoo!" yelled James as he pumped his fist in the air.

"Yes, my friend. Whoohoo," Crisanto joined in. "It's very exciting. Camel racing is a great sport."

Fabina heard yips, shouts, and Arabic voices coming from the other side of the track.

"Look!" Crisanto pointed. "See how the trainers and operators try their best to stay beside their camel? The drivers have to be careful to stay with their master's racer but not crash into another vehicle." Crisanto shifted gears. "Wow! They are fast today. This will be a very exciting race." He gave a little more gas to keep in line with the head camel.

Fabina couldn't sit still. She twisted in her seat to look every which way to take it all in. Dust flew in all directions, car horns competed against each other, camels frothed at the mouth as their feet stamped over the sand, car engines revved, deep voices called out all around her, all of which set her senses ablaze with excitement.

=======

This time Ryan noticed she wasn't next to him. He turned and mouthed the words 'what's wrong?'. Hailey, being too timid to bring attention to them, didn't answer and just turned and walked farther from the crowd.

Ryan came up to her, confusion all over his face.

"There are no other women, Ryan."

"Oh!"

Ryan looked around, and Hailey did the same.

"Wait! Look!" Ryan said, pointing to the left side of the track.

Hailey's eyes followed his hand. There, about twenty yards away, was a covered section beside the track and inside sat rows of women.

"Why don't you go wait in there. When I locate the others, I'll send Holly and Fabina to come get you?"

"OK..." Hailey said hesitantly.

She didn't love the idea of separating, but she also knew it was best to be as inconspicuous as possible until they were safely back with the group. She gave a quick smile to Ryan before turning towards the other women.

Rounding the corner of the structure, Hailey slid in behind the back row and tried not to draw attention to herself. A few women noticed. Two of them smiled, but the third scrutinized her from head to toe before grimacing and looking away. Hailey slunk closer to the wall and turned her eyes back to the race.

The cloud of dust had now moved to the far side of the track and was about to round the last corner. Hailey rose herself up onto her toes and there, in the center of the cloud, was a large group of running camels in between two rows of racing vehicles.

The crowd continued to shout and cheer. The sound was so loud that it was almost painful. Minutes later, the racing horde came thundering around in front of them, moments from the finish line. Hailey squinted her eyes, she couldn't believe what she was seeing.

Beyond the line of vehicles that were racing outside the guardrail nearest to her, small children sat atop the towering beasts as they charged forward at an alarming speed. The children on the camels that were in the lead were shouting and smiling as they hit the flanks of their camels with black sticks. Hailey realized then that they were like riding crops. Her mind remembered the boys on the hill as her eyes moved throughout the group of riders. Upon reaching the children at the back of the pack, her shock increased. The sight broke her heart.

The four boys at the back of the group weren't smiling. Their hands clenched the reins. Tears ran from their terror-filled eyes, and their mouths contorted from their cries and gritted teeth.

Hailey looked at the watching crowd, but no one seemed concerned or disgusted by the sight. Were they really deeming this as normal? She returned her eyes to the youngest one. He was so small and currently in last place. He didn't have a stick and looked more scared than she had ever seen a child look. Hailey glanced at the finish line, then back again.

Hold on, little one. You're almost done. Hold on.

=======

"We're almost back to the finish line. Look!" Crisanto pointed ahead.

In James's excitement, he hadn't even realized they had made a full loop. He turned and looked through the front windshield as Crisanto pulled ahead of the pack.

As they passed the lead camel, James spun around to see it cross the finish line.

"Yeah!" he shouted, not able to contain the pure glee of the moment.

Crisanto drove a few yards further and then turned the SUV around, carefully avoiding the other cars racing past the finish line.

"That was awesome!" James said looking back at Fabina.

"Yeah, it was," Jack echoed. "I wish we could do it again."

=======

Hailey watched as the race ended. The crowd erupted, and all the women in front of her stood, blocking her view of the boys. Frustrated, Hailey walked along the back wall to the other side of the structure in hopes of getting her view of the boys back. It didn't help. There were just too many people. Hailey glanced back to the group of men that they had initially stood behind. She could undoubtedly see better from there.

Her curiosity about whether the little boy was OK thundered in her mind. Was her concern for the boy be worth leaving the group of women at this moment? Or should she wait for Fabina and Holly?

But they could be gone by then, she reasoned.

She bit her lip as she debated her choices.

=======

After piling out of the vehicle, the four of them jogged over to join the others. Everyone in their excitement started replaying the event. James readily joined in.

Soon Ali met them. He led them all back to the bleachers, where they sat and watched as people gathered around the center of the track. Official men came out and announced the winners and handed out prizes. The air filled with more yips and shouts.

Ali sat in silence, allowing them all to take in the sight. James watched with curiosity as he took occasional sips of water. The sun was rising higher now in the sky. Sweat was pouring from every pore, soaking his shirt.

They watched for another half hour as the people celebrated and packed up. Ali only broke his silence when most of the camels had been led off.

"Camel racing is a very prestigious event. Winning camels can sell for amazing amounts of money. The owners of the winning camels can receive large amounts of money and expensive gifts. They even get on T.V. at times." Ali paused as a few people passed by. "Alright, friends, up we go."

James shot up his hand. "Excuse me, Ali?"

"Yes?" Ali answered and lowered himself back down.

=======

Hailey's fear of what happened at the airport helped her make the decision and kept her feet from moving. The majority of the women cleared out of the structure quite quickly, so Hailey found a seat in the far corner and impatiently waited for the crowd to thin out. She hoped once they were gone, she would be able to see if the little racer was alright.

"Hailey!"

Jumping, she whipped around and looked behind her. Ryan's

head was peeking around the corner.

"What are you doing?" she demanded in a stern whisper. "You scared me!!"

"Sorry," he said dismissively. "I can't find the group anywhere. I ran the length of the track where the crowd was gathered, I searched the couple rows of benches on the far side, but I can't find them."

"That's strange." Hailey glanced back to the track. She still couldn't really see anything. "Do you think they left already?"

"No, I don't think so. I'm pretty sure this is the first race of the day."

"Did you try asking someone?"

"No, I didn't want you to be alone for too long."

Hailey was glad he came back for her.

"But yeah, that's a good idea," Ryan agreed. "Let's go up to the main building and ask."

Hailey looked around before moving. No one was watching. She slipped out of her seat and met Ryan behind the structure.

"You walk ahead, I'll follow. I don't want to draw any attention."

"OK."

Hailey followed Ryan along the back of the structure and back towards the main building they had passed on their way in. They were a few yards from the door when she heard cries that chilled her blood. The cries were followed by stern words that she couldn't understand.

Hailey looked at Ryan. He already had his hand on the door. Hailey stepped towards the corner of the building.

"What are you doing?" he called to her just loud enough for her to hear.

"Don't you hear that?"

"Yeah, but Hailey…"

"Sorry, I have to look."

As Hailey reached the corner of the building, she turned and pushed her back against the corrugated metal siding. The heat of it shocked her, but she managed to not yelp. She backed away. Holding her breath, she looked around the corner.

The first things she saw was the little boy from the race. He was crumpled on the ground, covering his head with both his arms. A fat man stood over him. The man held one of the black sticks high over his head. As the man brought the crop down and it connected with the boy's back, the child let out a painful cry.

Hailey saw blood dripping from the boy's shirt from the previous strikes. Her fury erupted as the man raised the crop, poised to hit the boy again. She took a step forward. Ryan's arm grabbed her elbow and pulled her forcefully back around the corner. He pressed her against the metal again, causing the heat to sting her back once more. Seeing her wince, he pulled back, dropping his hand from her arm.

"What are you doing?" he demanded.

"I'm going to stop him. Did you see what was happening? Did you see how little that child is?"

"Yeah, I did." Ryan's voice was angry. "But honestly, Hailey, what were you planning to do?"

"I don't know."

"Look around," Ryan shot at her. "We're not the first ones to see this happening. I am disgusted by it, but my main priority is to get you safe. There is absolutely nothing we can do for the boy that will actually help." He let out a heavy sigh. "Let's say we intervened. What then?"

Hailey's chest was heaving with anger. She was furious at

Ryan for stopping her and for how he was talking to her.

The boy cried out again.

"Ryannnn..."

Her eyes filled with tears. It was taking everything in her to stay put. She rocked her head back, slamming it against the building a few times.

"Ryan, he's so tiny. He was in the race, you know. I saw him. I think that man is punishing him for losing." Hailey thought about the stick. "Or maybe for dropping his crop. You should have seen how scared the boy was. He was just trying to not fall off and get trampled to death."

"But we can't just..." Ryan's voice trailed off as something caught his eye.

Hailey looked around. They were starting to draw some attention from the people leaving the track. Ryan backed away from her and stormed back towards the door.

=======

"Can you tell us what those things on top of the camels are?" James asked Ali as he pointed to a group of camels in the center of the track.

"Oh, they are robotic jockeys," Ali beamed. "I am personally thrilled to see so many races being moved to use them exclusively."

It was a funny little thing. The robot's body was bright yellow, as was its head. To James, it looked like a large, yellow tissue box. The robot didn't have any legs, but its yellow head was about the size of a baseball.

"Why is that?" Fabina asked.

"Those little robots are a solution to an unfortunate tradition in camel racing. In many countries, including Saudi, little boys are often sold into slavery to be jockeys. The boys come from all over: like Bangladesh, Sudan, and Pakistan. They are light, so the camels aren't weighed down like they are with adult jockeys, and they don't cost a lot to enslave." Ali paused, sadness etched on his face.

"How young are these boys?" James asked.

"I have heard rumors that some are as young as two. But I'm pretty sure they don't race when they are that young. So I think they are just sold that young. When the boys are bought, or kidnapped, they are forced to live in camps beside the racetrack. Many are not well treated."

"That's awful," Fabina protested.

Similar statements echoed throughout the group.

"Take heart, friends. Some countries are now banning the use of child jockeys and, with the invention of that little robot there, I hope more and more Saudi tracks will move towards stopping the use of child jockeys altogether. It will be a slow transition, but... progress takes time. But it is changing, and change is good."

James turned back to watch.

"If you look closely," Ali continued, "you'll notice that the robot's arm is quite unique. It is a whip. The operator, who was in one of the vehicles driving beside the camel, controls the robot remotely. This makes it possible for the operator to direct the camel as it runs. I've even heard that some of the newer models of the robots can detect the heart rate and speed of the camel. Most of the robots you saw today won't be quite that complex. But they do have audio so the trainer can speak to the camel."

James watched in fascination as the men removed the robots and packed them away in metal cases. Ali soon stood, and the group stood with him. James stretched and wiped his forehead once more with the edge of his shirt. The act didn't help much. His shirt was drenched in sweat. But at least it kept the beads from dripping into his eyes. After taking another sip of water, James fell in step with Fabina as the group walked after Ali.

Poor little chaps. James shook his head as they walked towards the group standing around the winning camel. The thought ignited a few images in his mind.

I can't imagine what those children must endure.

=======

Hailey watched as Ryan disappeared into the building.

Maybe Ryan is right, Hailey thought. *Even if we did get the man to stop this beating, it would probably just get us into trouble, and the boy would go right back to him.*

The realization grew her anger further. She resented how helpless she felt. But there was no point in standing there debating the issue with herself. The fact was, Ryan wouldn't help, and there was no way she could save this child alone.

Hailey peeked around the corner. The man and the boy were gone. With a quick defiant pounding to the wall with her clenched fist, Hailey stomped to the door and flung it open with an exasperated huff.

Entering the building, Hailey blinked a handful of times to get her eyes to adjust to the seemingly dim lit room. At first, she couldn't see Ryan or much of anything. She looked around. The corrugated siding loomed two stories above her. A handful of people walked about, and a few small groups dotted the foyer. There wasn't much else in the building, so it didn't take long to locate him.

Ryan was standing in front of a long counter at the far end of the building, speaking to a man. She didn't bother joining him. Instead, she found a deserted corner to the left of the door. Even if Ryan was right, Hailey couldn't shake off her anger at how cavalier he was about the whole thing and how he had spoken to her. Her eyes drilled into him as she watched him from across the room.

When Ryan finally turned to face her, she could see he was frustrated. She didn't know if his emotion was from their exchange outside or from the information the man had told him. Either way, a lump formed in her throat.

"We're at the wrong track," he snapped as he reached her.

"What?"

"We're at the wrong track." He gestured towards the counter. "The guy over there has no idea why the cab driver would have brought us here. Supposedly, this is the small track in Buraydah, mostly for locals, and there are never any tour groups here. Let's just get out of here."

Ryan didn't wait for a response. Charging back to the door, he half punched, half shoved it open and left. Hailey grunted her judgment at his tantrum. She continued to stand there, smoldering in her own anger at the sight of his immaturity. As it met with the full realization of their predicament, she felt oppressed by it all and stupid just standing there. Feeling justified in it, she followed suit and stormed out of the building.

When she reached him, Ryan had already walked back to where the cab had dropped them off. He was pacing back and forth with clenched fists, kicking dust as he went. A cab driver was loading their bags into the trunk of his cab a few yards in the distance.

"Why are you so upset with me?" she barked.

Ryan stopped in his tracks and looked at her. "What? I'm not."

"Could have fooled me."

"No, really." Ryan turned and walked away from her. "I'm mad at myself," he said as he pivoted away again.

Hailey eyed him suspiciously but waited for him to explain.

"Do you think I wanted to leave that boy?" his hand flew up as he motioned towards the building they had just left. "Damn it, Hailey." He continued to pace in front of her. "I can't believe I did that."

Hailey's whole demeanor changed. Her anger forgotten, she went to him. Hailey brought up her hand to stroke his face, but he pulled away.

"Ryan," Hailey said softly. She took a breath to fight off the last of her pride. "You were right. There wasn't anything we could have done. Nothing that would have helped anyway."

He didn't respond, and he didn't turn to look at her. Hailey glanced over to the cab. The driver had finished with their bags and had started to walk towards Ryan. Within a couple steps, Ryan noticed him. The man stopped his approach.

"Ready?" the man asked.

Ryan nodded and the man returned to his cab.

"Let's just go," Ryan said without turning.

He sounded defeated. Hailey decided not to push to try and reconnect with him. It was clear that he needed a moment to work through what he was struggling with. She was reasonably certain that any further words from her had a higher possibility of doing more harm than helping. She followed him silently to the cab.

=======

The silence remained during the twenty-minute drive to the other track. Ryan continued to stare out the window. He realized he wasn't being fair to her. She hadn't done anything wrong. Yet, with the embarrassment and guilt raging through him, he felt exposed and ashamed. He wanted to hide from her.

After thanking and paying the cab driver, Ryan stood and looked over the roof of the cab. He scanned the grounds.

"Actually, can you wait for us?" Ryan asked the driver.

The man nodded as Hailey joined him outside the cab. She looked confused.

"Look!" he said as he pointed towards the track.

Hailey's face fell as she saw what was before them. The grounds were almost completely deserted. A few men were cleaning off debris from the grass hill that ran down from the closest guardrail. Two men were raking the dirt underneath the large starting line off to the left. And, apart from a small group of people in the center of the track by a couple camels, the place was void of any activity.

"Oh no, Ryan..." The tone of Hailey's voice matched the dread rising in his throat.

"Wait here. I'll go ask around."

When there was no protest from her, Ryan jogged to the men on the hill. None of them spoke English, so he continued on to the right where there was a structure sitting close to the track. As he rounded the corner and looked inside, Ryan saw only empty wooden bleachers.

Spinning around, he made his way back towards a brown and white building beyond the structure. It was much larger than the building at the other track and was considerably more modern. Ryan could see why this was the track tourists came to.

He tried the handle. Relief pushed out the breath he had been holding when it turned freely in his hand. The air conditioning hit him as he stepped inside, causing tiny goosebumps to appear on his arms. He jogged past some washrooms and slowed to a walk as he approached the counter.

Three men were sorting through paperwork and laughing but stopped as they saw him.

"English?" Ryan asked with hopeful eyes.

"Yes, certainly, sir. How can we help you?" the man directly in front of him asked.

"I am trying to find my tour group. They were supposed to be watching a race here today, but I can't find them."

"Are you with Patetagi Tours?" the man on his right asked.

"Yes!" Hearing the familiar name and lightness in the man's voice sent relief through Ryan.

"I'm sorry, sir. They left quite some time ago."

The relief abandoned him just as quickly as it came.

"Are you sure? Maybe they are coming to a later race?"

"No, that is impossible. We only had one race today, and I know for a fact they were here. I personally gave them the tour. They came early this morning, watched the race, took their photos, and then–"

"So they're gone?" Ryan slumped backward one step. The last bit of hope fell out of him.

"Is there anything else we can help you with?" the first man said, his tone a bit pushy. He obviously wanted to get back to their work.

"Uh... no. Thank you."

Ryan turned away and plodded back to the exit. He hesitated as his hand grasped the cold door handle.

THE SAND BRIDE

How am I going to tell Hailey?

CHAPTER 13

The plan that swarmed in her mind when she had talked with Ryan, at the time, seemed so simple. But after the soldier got back in the jeep, everything changed.

"Well, can't your office just fax the forms here to the hospital?" Anna suggested. "I could sign them, and you can be on your way. Than you don't have to be troubled by coming with me to Riyadh."

"I'm sorry, miss. They must be the originals. But don't worry, it will only delay you mere moments. Then I'll leave you to catch your connecting flight."

"Alright," Anna lied.

It wasn't alright, but what choice did she have? She flopped back in her seat as he pulled away from the hospital.

Her mind hunted for contingency options. Initially, she was just going to get this guy to drive her to the airport, ditch him and go call Hailey. So simple. She'd be free to fly to meet up with them, regardless of where they were.

The sinking feeling in her gut made her nervous to stay with this man. His story sounded reasonably legit. Yet when he told her about Ehsan being too busy to make it, it seemed like he was trying too hard to convince her that she wouldn't see Ehsan again. Anna glared at the back of the soldier's head.

What are you planning? If Ehsan works in Riyadh, are you bringing me to him? Anna's stomach lurched at the thought. She had no idea what that man had done to Hailey. But with Ryan's warning still ringing in her mind, Anna had to figure out an alternative plan to get away.

Nothing was coming to mind.

=======

As soon as she saw him, Hailey knew what he was going to say. Hailey's knees buckled, and she slid down the door of the cab. Her body, despite the intense heat suffocating her, started to shake.

"We missed them, didn't we?" She stumbled over the words as the panic intensified.

Ryan didn't respond. He sat beside her, taking her hand and sandwiching it between his.

"Yeah, we did. But I–"

"Ryan, I'm so sorry. I should have listened to you. We should have stayed with the tour until we knew what Anna was doing." The sob in her throat distorted the last word. "Oh God," Hailey prayed as she looked up to the clear sky, "what have I done?"

"Hailey, it's going to be OK."

"How?" she challenged. "Ryan, we have no idea where they are. We are all alone with no way of knowing if Anna is OK or even where she is. Ehsan has her. What are we supposed to do?"

"We have to leave Anna in His hands. There is nothing we can do about that. But we can do something about us."

Hailey, confused, shot her head up to look at him. His calmness wasn't making any sense.

"When I was saying goodbye to Joe and the guys, he jokingly said that if we ever changed our mind, we could meet up with them. He mentioned the name of the hotel they were going to be staying at in Haql, the last city before the border."

"Really?" Hailey asked, hope flooded back in.

"Yeah, really! But if we are going to head there, it will be on our own. I don't know any other details... like when they'll get there or... what lies between here and there."

Hailey could hear the concern in Ryan's voice. She wiped her face with the edge of her headscarf.

"No, that's OK. I mean, I'm not thrilled with the idea, but what choice do we have?"

Ryan leaned over and kissed her forehead.

"Yeah and if it's our only option... He is going before us. Right?"

Ryan looked back towards the track. Hailey kept quiet to give him time to let his own words sink in.

"OK, I'll go talk to this cab driver and see if I can bribe him to drive us there. I have no idea how far it is, but let's hope he likes money," Ryan said as he winked at her.

Hailey rose and stood behind Ryan as he pleaded with the driver. She saddened her eyes and scrunched her forehead to try to aid Ryan's petition.

"Yes, I will go, but only on one condition," the man warned.

"Name it."

"I will only take you halfway. I will make a call and see if my cousin is interested in taking you the rest of the way. He lives in a town a bit off the route, but it shouldn't add that much time to the trip. Are you interested?"

Ryan turned and looked at her. Hailey's pulse quickened. The idea of not knowing how long the trip would take, or the exact route, made her nervous.

What if we take too long and miss the group? The possibility triggered her fear.

Hailey shrugged in response to Ryan's questioning eyes. She had already made a bad call to leave the group in the first place, and she didn't want to make this call. Ryan, seeing her hesitation, nodded to her. His confidence shone through.

"Deal," Ryan said as he turned to the man and offered his hand.

As Hailey climbed into the back seat after everything had been arranged, her heart wouldn't get out of her stomach.

God, please get Anna to call. If only we knew what was happening with her... it would make these choices so much easier.

What if this is the wrong choice?

CHAPTER 14

Pulling up to the airport seemed to bring a new level of anxiety. A million questions bounced around in Anna's mind.

Should I try and make a run for it once we're inside? Or should I wait until we get to Riyadh? Will I have a chance to even do so? What is this guy planning?

"Anna, wait here, please. I have to make a call to let my commanding officer know I'm being diverted momentarily to Riyadh. I'll only be a moment."

"Sure, no problem," she answered with a faked ease.

When the soldier exited the vehicle, he turned his back to her. Anna looked around. There were quite a few vehicles in the lot but not much else. Making a run for it now would be too risky. He likely would catch her quite quickly.

She resorted to see if she could catch some of the conversation. With any luck, she could confirm what was really going on... if anything. Reaching her hand out, she pressed the window control, and the window slid down a couple inches. The sound seemed abnormally loud, and she winced.

The soldier spun around. Anna shot him a sweet smile, then glanced around casually, so the action didn't look like an act of intrusion. The soldier walked a couple steps further from the car and returned his attention back to his call. She couldn't hear a word.

Damn it.

Anna sat unmoving until he finished the call.

"OK, let's head out," he instructed as he approached the jeep.

Anna gathered her things and joined him.

The foot traffic inside the airport was disappointing. It wouldn't help in giving her the cover she needed to run from him.

Dang it, what am I going to do? God, I need a window here.

She walked in step with the soldier as they passed the security desk and the bank of phones along the far wall. When they reached the luggage claim, Anna's chest started to ache. The last time she was here, Ryan was with her. They had been so worried about what had happened to Hailey, yet there was so much comfort in being together.

If only he were here now.

She glanced around again, urgently trying to assess if there was any way she could slip away. The ticket counter loomed closer and seemed to be lessening the possibility of escape with each step.

"Please, go stand in the family section over there," the soldier directed.

Anna looked hopefully towards where he was pointing. By family section, she knew he meant the women's section, and she prayed it was far enough from the ticket counter. Maybe it would provide the opportunity she was waiting for.

Sadly, it was not.

The section was just beyond the ticket counter and in his direct line of sight. The soldier would easily be able to keep an eye on her as he waited and bought tickets. Anna nodded and smiled her compliance. She walked away defeated and slunk into one of the empty chairs.

As the line in front of the officer dwindled, Anna racked her mind. With no way of knowing what might be waiting for her in Riyadh, she doubted she could wait until they landed to find an alternative plan.

Come on, Anna, think!

Four people.

Three people.

Two people.

Damn it!

The soldier was now at the front of the line, and Anna watched helplessly as he purchased their tickets. He started walking towards her. The act seemed to slam the last bit of her window shut. Her chest constricted.

There is no way I'm going to get a moment alone now. He is going to sit across from me in the men's section, probably as close as he can get. Yup, there he goes.

Anna watched as he walked over to the closest seat and set down his duffle bag.

"We're going to have to wait until tomorrow morning. The soonest flight I could get is at five o'clock, so there isn't any point in going to a hotel. Will you be OK here?"

"Sure, I guess so," she answered, looking around.

Not that you're leaving me much choice. Anna no longer had any fondness for this man.

Then it hit her.

The idea was a lame excuse. But it worked in movies, and at this point, she had no other option. It would have to do.

"Uh... I need to go to the bathroom."

Anna stood and started to leave the area. She turned to nod to the soldier but saw him grab his bag and take steps towards her.

"You don't need to come," she laughed awkwardly. "I actually know this airport quite well, and I know where the facilities are. I won't be long." Anna stopped walking to make sure he wasn't going to follow.

"Sorry, miss," he said as he caught up to her. "I have strict instructions to be your escort."

Yeah, I bet you do. Anna flashed him another fake smile.

"Really, I don't mind," he continued. "I will wait for you outside and walk you back."

Anna spun away from him and pushed herself to walk as casually as she could muster.

So much for that plan.

Once in the bathroom, she felt like a caged lion. Well, maybe that was a stretch. She was more like a bunny, small and frightened. She paced back and forth over the tiled floor. Every so often she caught sight of her reflection and each time she did so, she shook her head at herself.

The door to the bathroom opened.

Anna looked towards it. Seeing a woman come in, she stopped pacing and went to the sink to wash her hands. The cold water sent shivers up her arms.

The woman walked over to the other sink and placed her bag on the edge. She removed her veil. After splashing a few handfuls of water over her face, she dried off and looked at Anna. She smiled.

"Sure is a hot day," the woman said in Arabic.

"Yes," Anna replied, forcing herself to return the smile.

The woman replaced her veil. It covered everything but her eyes, which were now looking at Anna with concern. Anna looked away.

"Are you alright, dear?" she asked in English.

Anna remained staring at her reflection in the mirror, mouth open. She didn't know how to answer her.

"Do you need some help?"

She looked over at the woman, but still, no words came.

The woman gestured to the door. "Is there someone I can go get for you?"

"N-no. Thank you."

Anna bit her lip and looked at the sink. She hated crying in public.

"Are you sure?"

"I'm... alone." A shaky breath barely aided her in keeping control.

"There has to be at least one person you could call."

Anna looked back. "Yes... yes, there is. Do you happen to have a phone I could borrow?"

"Of course." The woman reached into her bag and removed a cell.

Anna took it and dialed the one number she knew by heart.

It rang, then rang again.

Answer, damn it. Answer!

=======

As the sun started to set over the An-Nafud desert, it seemed to ignite the sand. Their current location was not far from the city, but the terrain was drastically different in comparison. As far as Hailey could see, rolling dunes cascaded out in all directions.

The only time her eyes left the landscape was to momentarily glance at the phone in her lap. She kept her ears tuned to the small talk between Ryan and the cab driver, but she didn't look at either of them.

There still had been no word from Anna, and with each hour, Hailey became increasingly more concerned. After yet another look at the phone's black screen, she returned her attention back out the window, resuming her interest in what lay beyond.

The phone sounded two short beeps and vibrated.

Hailey's heart jumped. She looked down.

Ryan stopped talking and looked over. It was not an incoming call. Shining in bright letters, the low battery notification blinked on the screen.

Hailey's eyes shot to Ryan.

"It's almost dead."

Ryan's face reflected the concern in her voice.

"Do you have a charger?" Hailey asked the driver.

"No, sorry."

"Hailey, she'll call. Let's just pray it's before the phone dies."

"Yeah…"

Hailey cradled the phone in her hands, willing it to stay on. For the next hour, no one spoke, and Hailey didn't take her eyes off the battery icon.

Ten percent.

Nine percent.

Come on, Anna. Call me, please!

Eight percent.

Seven.

Hailey watched as it painfully dwindled down to three percent.

God, please. Step in here.

I know the plans I have.

But... can't it be this? Please!
Two percent.
One.
Please. No, no... no!

The call never came. The phone gave one small flash, and the screen went blank. Tears stung her eyes. Hailey hurled the phone onto the seat. She swore under her breath as she turned to the window and looked outside.

"Hailey–"

"Please don't."

She pressed herself against the door. She didn't want to be encouraged. She wanted to be left alone to wallow in her frustration.

What if Anna didn't get away?

CHAPTER 15

The rest of the drive, Hailey felt numb. She tried to sleep, but it was restless and disjointed. The random jolts from the car and the erratic dreams about Anna and Ehsan made it difficult to fully relax into a deep sleep.

It was late, but at least they were getting close to Haql now. The transfer between cabs went smoothly and, with Ryan giving her space, most of her frustration had diminished. The only emotion that remained was fear.

As they came into the city, there were practically no lights on in any of the buildings.

"What was the name of the hotel?" the driver asked.

"Tramarsha Resort," Ryan answered.

The cab only drove a few blocks into town before pulling over in front of a small shop. A few dim lights shone from somewhere deep inside. It didn't seem to be open. The driver parked the cab, jumped out, and walked over to the small building. He rapped his fist a couple times on the door, waited, then repeated the motion. Minutes later a figure's shadow darkened the glass panes in the door just before it opened.

"My apologies," their cab driver said, jumping back in the

driver's seat. "I'm not familiar with Haql, and I needed to check the directions."

The drive didn't last much longer.

Once the cab pulled into a parking lot next to the resort, Hailey threw the car door open and leaped out. She couldn't see the water, but the sound of waves lapping against the shore was unmistakable. She shouted a quick thank you over her shoulder as she ran for the front door.

Hailey burst through the double glass doors, causing the glass to rattle in the metal around it. She made her way to the front desk while she scanned the walls on either side of the foyer - relieved to see a few outlets lining one side.

"Do you... have... a phone charger?" she asked.

"Certainly. What kind?"

She handed the man the phone. "You don't know how much this means."

With a nod, he disappeared into the back. Hailey nervously tapped the counter as she waited. *Come on, come on.*

He returned moments later.

"Thank you!"

As she settled herself on the floor in front of the closest outlet, she heard Ryan coming through the doors. She kept her eyes on the task. Frantically, she plugged the cord into the wall but fumbled as she tried to insert the little end into the bottom of the phone. Her hands shook and made the typically menial task quite difficult. It finally cooperated. Hailey repetitively pushed the power button, waiting for it to respond.

"Hon, give it a second," Ryan said as he leaned down and kissed the top of her head.

It was the first thing he had said since her tantrum in the car. He was sweet to talk to her so kindly. She didn't deserve it.

Hailey took a deep breath and paused. She should say something.

But what?

"I'm going to go check us in."

Hailey lifted her head as he walked away. She sighed, then looked back at the phone.

Come on, little phone.

She pushed the power button. The phone's logo flashed on the screen. Hailey waited expectantly for a notification to appear. She knew the phone didn't have voicemail, but a missed call notification should pop up any moment. A breath caught in her chest. Nothing appeared, other than the time and date.

After the frustration had died down in the cab, she consoled herself with the fact that there would be a missed call and that, once the phone was charged, it would ring. When it didn't, fear crept back in.

When Ryan returned, Hailey hadn't moved from her spot on the floor.

"Ryan, she didn't call."

"How do you know?"

"There are no missed calls, no notifications at all."

"Hailey, if the phone is dead it won't log the calls. She could have called, and if she did, she'll call back."

Hope returned.

"Ryan, do you think she's OK? Are you sure she didn't mention anything about her plans or when she thought she could call us again?"

"No, she focused more on making sure we got out of the country. She seemed pretty adamant she had her stuff under control."

"So, I guess… we wait?"

"Yeah. It's all we can do."

"I'm going to go nuts. You know that, right?" Hailey huffed.

"I figured. You're pretty tightly wound these days," Ryan teased as he gave her a little nudge with his knee. "But I love that part of you."

"Oh, you do, do you?"

"Completely," he said grinning from ear to ear. "We should eat. It will help to pass the time."

She agreed. There was no point in sitting on the floor all night.

Hailey waited in the foyer to allow the phone to charge while Ryan ran their things to their room and checked with the front desk about a restaurant.

"What's it at now?" he asked, nodding towards the phone.

"Twenty percent."

"Good. That will last through dinner."

Hailey unplugged the cord and handed it to Ryan. He wound it around his hand and tucked it in his pocket. She kept the phone.

"So, where are we going?"

"The man said there is a great little place just through the garden. It's not part of the hotel, but there is a side entrance to it. It's just through there." Ryan pointed to a small wrought iron door a few feet away.

As Ryan pushed the gate open, it let out a loud creak as the rusted hinges groaned against each other. Just beyond the door sprawled an overgrown garden. A stone path cut its way from the door, through the center and forked off in a few directions. They kept straight and walked over to next building.

The restaurant was a sandy, two-story building with squares of mosaic-tiled panels decorating the front. Upon entering the side entrance, a soft light surrounded them. The smell of spices and dates filled Hailey's nose.

Roughly-cut, stone tiles showed from under the Persian rugs that laid intermittently throughout the entrance. For seating, long cushions covered in a rich red and gold fabric lay on the floor around the edge of the room. Similarly sized pillows rested on top for back support.

The ceiling was set low and added to the ambiance. Peeled-log beams were placed every few feet to support tightly laid strips of bamboo.

It felt secretive and romantic.

"Oh! Looks like we aren't eating together."

"What?" Hailey pulled her attention away from the ceiling and saw what Ryan was referring to.

Just beyond where they had entered, two signs stood before them. Below the Arabic script read women on one sign and men on the other. Each had an arrow pointing towards different doors on either side of the entryway.

Hailey was about to protest when a man appeared. He pushed through a curtain hanging at the back of the room. He chatted excitedly and waved his hands.

Reaching them, the man bowed, took Ryan by the arm and started pulling him towards the men's door. Over his shoulder, he chattered to Hailey in Arabic and waved her towards the other door. With his excitement and kind welcome, mixed with Ryan's smile, Hailey didn't bother to object. She shrugged to Ryan before he disappeared, then headed for the other door.

Pushing it open, Hailey peeked inside.

Sounds of chatting and laughing met her ears. Numerous women sat on benches about two feet off the ground. The benches were set in small groupings around the room, like little booths. A square table sat in the center of each set of seating, just slightly higher than the benches.

Hailey walked farther in. The door swung closed behind her. No one noticed.

The walls of the room looked to be made from compressed sand. The etched carvings - not of pictures but of patterns - were inset every few feet into walls. They were beautifully intricate. Hailey couldn't help tracing her fingers over the coarse texture of the one next to the door.

The lighting was electric, but each light had the look of an antique kerosene lamp. They were spread out over the entire ceiling and hung a few feet above her head from black chains. The women around the room all had their head coverings off. The cheerful sounds around the room reminded her of Sarna and Ghada. A lump caught in her throat. She missed them.

Hailey hesitated at the door. She wasn't sure what she should do. But when no one acknowledged her presence, she walked as casually as she could over to one of the empty tables and sat. She was in the midst of removing her head covering when an old woman came over to the table.

The woman said nothing but set a gold teapot in the center of the table. She bent down and opened two little doors under the table. Hailey hadn't focused on them before. A gold teacup was removed and placed in front of her. The women pushed on her knees and slowly stood with a grunt.

"Welcome, welcome." Her accent was thick but understandable. "Please sit, relax. I bring you wonderful food soon. Yes?"

"Yes, alright. Thank you."

Hailey watched the woman as she crossed the room and disappeared through another door set in the back wall.

I guess I don't get a menu. Ah well.

She looked at the phone as it lay on the table. Still nothing. She returned her attention back to the groups around her. It was quite interesting not having any men in the room. The women were so expressive and seemed so free. Hailey enjoyed watching them as she sipped her tea.

When the old woman returned, she placed a large platter on the table.

"This is kabsa. Best one in all of Saudi," the old woman beamed.

Hailey thanked her as she took in a deep whiff of the meal. It looked amazing and smelled even better. The dish consisted of chicken dripping in a yellowish-brown sauce, laid on a bed of rice. The whole thing was sprinkled with raisins and sliced almonds.

Again, the woman bent and went to retrieve something from under the table. After she set a small plate before Hailey, she bowed and left.

The rich depth of flavor pleased each of Hailey's taste buds. It didn't take her long to polish off most of the platter.

Agh. I'm so full, Hailey grunted as she leaned back from the table. *Definitely overate.*

The old woman, as if on cue, returned to the table and cleared everything away. She disappeared for only moments before she returned, carrying a round, silver tray with her. It was heaped with brown balls, about the size of golf balls.

"To finish your meal, these are called Qishd. Very, very good."

As soon as the woman was away from the table, Hailey, with her nose scrunched up, tentatively picked one up and smelled it. It smelled sweet. She sunk her teeth in and took a bite.

Oooohhh... that's good. Hailey licked her lips. She popped the rest into her mouth and grabbed another.

Hailey had never had anything like them before. The main part of the ball was finely chopped dates rolled in a wheat and butter mixture. She wasn't sure of the other ingredients, but she ended up having five of them.

Hailey sat back from the table after the dishes were all cleared and nervously waited. She wasn't sure if she should go back to the foyer or wait for the bill. She opted to sit a while longer.

"Your friend... he is at the door."

"Any word yet?" Ryan asked as she came through the door.

She shook her head.

"Did you like the food?"

"Yes, it was amazing."

"How many times did you check the phone," he chuckled.

"Only twice."

Ryan eyed her.

"OK, five. But eating did help to distract me. I could have been worse."

Ryan smiled. He took her hand and kissed her knuckles.

"A-hem..."

The man who had led Ryan away was standing back by the curtain with a disapproving look on his face. He cleared his throat again as he looked at their joined hands with raised eyebrows. They instantly let go of each other.

"Sorry," they said in unison.

Hailey put both her hands together and bowed, hoping it would ease the sting of their disrespect. The man smiled and nodded back. Ryan had already paid, so after another thanks to their host, they left the restaurant and headed back through the garden. Hailey rechecked the phone.

"You OK?" Ryan asked as he held the hotel door open for her.

"Sort of. It's just that... it's now... been twenty-four hours since we've heard from Anna. I'm worried, Ryan."

=======

He replaced the cell back in the pocket of his uniform after hanging up from the call. The councilman's new instructions didn't sit well with him. Yet he would comply if it came to that. He just hoped the tail he set up would do his job and that Anna wouldn't clue in.

He knew he had done a good job not alerting the girl of what was going to happen, but he was still nervous about the high fail potential of this mission. The councilman had been vague, at best, about the situation. Not having the whole picture always made things more difficult. Yet, it was something he was used to and, as usual, would proceed as circumstances allowed.

He shifted his weight yet again to the opposite foot and waited restlessly outside the bathroom. He placed his right palm on the backstrap of his handgun. Anna had been taking quite a long time, but it wasn't like there was anything he could do about it. He rubbed his eyes.

Why couldn't she be a man? I'd already be resting back in my seat if she were.

A moment later the girl emerged.

"All done," she announced as she passed him with a smile.

She seemed different. He couldn't quite put his finger on how, but something had changed. His instincts triggered as she walked away. The adrenaline caused each of his senses to be on

high alert.
 Something wasn't right.

CHAPTER 16

Anna barely slept. There were two things responsible for her not being able to relax enough. One: the soldier never closed his eyes and spent more time looking over at her then at anything else. And two: she had no idea if her Hail Mary plan would work. She shifted nervously in her chair, wishing there was a way to confirm what would happen once she reached Riyadh.

Tilting her head back to check the clock, she saw they still had two hours until their flight boarded. With each hour that passed, her uncertainty grew.

The possible alternatives started to burn at the edges of her confidence. She stole a sideways glance at the soldier. There was still the small chance this guy would let her go once she signed the paperwork. But it was more likely her circumstances would go from bad to worse. Anna hated that she was at the mercy of others and couldn't plan for contingencies.

She fidgeted incessantly in her seat until their flight was finally called.

Here we go. Lord, it's entirely out of my hands. What will be, will be... I guess. Anna took a deep breath and took her place in line with the other women to board the plane.

Despite that it was the first time she was out of the soldier's sight, her uneasiness continued during the flight. He sat rows ahead with the other men. But with nowhere to run, the privacy was no use to her now. It only mocked her.

The privacy was short lived once they landed. A short distance down the aisle, Anna caught sight of the soldier standing right outside the aircraft door. She tried to slow her breathing as she waited for the other women in front of her to exit. Her heart pounded. Her fate was about to be decided.

Either he is there waiting for me, or he isn't. Anna wished there was some way for her to be certain before she reached the solder.

"Did you have a good flight?" the soldier asked as she walked past him.

Anna didn't dare try and speak. Her fear would definitely show through, and she didn't want to alert him. She shrugged her shoulders and forced a smile.

"Exit into the terminal and then follow me," he instructed. "I will lead you to the meeting place where you can sign your paperwork before you head off."

He allowed her to walk ahead of him as they made their way to the terminal. Anna was grateful for the segregation rules of Saudi. It kept him at a slightly further distance from her.

The crowds were quite denser than they were in the smaller airport back in Dammam. For a brief second, she thought about running. But without knowing if her plan had worked, she quickly dismissed it. There was no choice but to see how it all played out.

Her pulse raced faster and faster with each step. Each glance over her shoulder to check on the soldier sped up her breathing. The doors to the terminal loomed ahead of her.

Here we go, she uttered under her breath as her hand touched the metal door.

Anna frantically scanned the crowd as she entered the terminal. People were hugging and greeting each other all around her. She saw no familiar faces.

Come on, come on, her mind demanded as she continued to look around.

Then something out of place caught her eye.

A man dressed in an expensive suit was standing a few yards to her left. He was holding a large sign that said: ANNA HARINGTON

The sight of her name confused her, and she stopped walking. The soldier came up behind her.

"What is it?"

"Look!" she said, pointing to the sign "My name."

"That's odd."

The soldier didn't hesitate for long, he walked towards the man. Anna's curiosity pushed her forward as she followed.

"Can I help you?" the soldier asked the man in the suit.

"I've been sent by the defense minister's office to come collect Anna. Is that you?" the suited man asked her.

"Y-y-yes," she stammered.

The soldier took a step forward, lowering his voice. "What are you talking about? That wasn't the plan."

Anna's blood ran cold. Something wasn't right, and now her fear was finally confirmed. The soldier did have alternative plans for her. But with the two men so close, there was no way she would get away now if she ran. Her legs froze.

The suited man pulled out his credentials and handed them to the soldier.

"Well, plans have changed. I have direct orders to collect her.

You are relieved of your assignment so you can make your way back to your previous post."

"Now hold on," the soldier ordered as he raised his hand. "I have to check this with my superiors."

"Do whatever you want," the man sneered as he snatched his credentials back. "But I'm not waiting. Miss, come with me."

Anna didn't know what to do. The man in the suit spoke with such authority. Her eyes dashed back and forth between the two men. She looked past them to the crowd around her. Her mind pleaded to catch sight of a familiar face.

"Now!" the man in the suit demanded.

The soldier took a step away from them as he glared at the man. He retrieved his phone out of his pocket.

"Miss, we have to go now!" the suited man repeated as he grabbed her elbow.

"Al-alright..."

The man practically dragged her through the crowd. His grip was firm, but he wasn't squeezing her tight enough to hurt her. Once they were through the group of people and into the open, Anna looked back to the soldier. Lines of anger carved on his forehead. He hung up his phone, then dialed again, listened, and hung up.

What is going on? she wondered. *Should I try and stay with the soldier? Or stay with this man?*

Stumbling, she faced forwards again so as not to fall.

Does it even matter? Anna's mind fought to decide as she tried to keep up with the man in the suit. Wherever he was taking her, he was in a hurry.

What if he's bringing me to Ehsan now? Anna realized the question had merit. The man said he was from the defense minister's office. Wasn't that the same place Ehsan worked?

Her heart was pounding so fast that it hurt to breathe. She made one last ditch effort to scan the passing faces. They were all strangers.

Anna hung her head in defeat.

My plan didn't work.

=======

His cell phone kept buzzing on the desk, but he couldn't possibly stop to answer it. Ehsan would never dare to try and put the minister on hold.

"Yes, Minister. I understand. I will get on it right away... Yes, very well... Alright."

He looked at his cell again as it vibrated for the fifth time and flashed the soldier's number. Ehsan wished the minister would finish already. He needed to answer that call.

"Yes, Minister... I will... Yes, thank you. Yes... goodbye."

Finally, Ehsan huffed as he slammed the phone down.

He grabbed his cell and answered the sixth call.

"What's wrong?"

"Councilman, I was under the impression from your call yesterday that the only change to the plan was that I was to bring Anna to you if she had become aware of her tail or if she made a run for it. And that I was permitted to use any force necessary."

"Yes, what about it?" This call was starting to annoy him. He didn't have time to repeat orders.

"So why did you send another man for her?"

"WHAT! I didn't."

"You... didn't send someone from your office to collect her?"

"No! Where is she? Please tell me she's with you."

"A-ah no, sir. She left with the man. I had no choice but to–"

"What man?" Ehsan screamed over the line.

"From the defense office. He had all the right credentials. I had no alternative, sir. I don't have that kind of jurisdiction to justify refusing or even delaying him."

"I don't care what credentials he had. Get her back!" Ehsan demanded. "Get her back, or it will be the last task you ever do." He didn't wait for another response or an excuse from the soldier. He threw his phone across the room.

Ehsan watched as it bounced on the carpet. Seeing it lying there in one piece erased the small release he felt from hurling it away. He let out a suppressed yell of rage as he swept his arms over the surface of his desk, sending everything crashing to the floor.

- - - - - - -

The man continued to pull her out of the airport and towards the parked cars just across the street. Anna turned and looked over her shoulder at the airport. Regret filled her as she longed to go back and try and run.

God, I don't know what to do. Help me!

When Anna turned back around, the man slowed as they approached a car. The far passenger door was opening. A man was getting out.

For a brief moment, Anna held her breath, expecting to see Ehsan's face.

George? her mind screamed as she recognized her dad's friend from Entrata.

"George!!"

The man in the suit had now dropped her arm and Anna ran

to the car. George opened his arms, and she fell hard against his chest. The force caused a small grunt to escape his mouth. Anna didn't apologize. She was too happy to see him. Sobs came from deep in her gut as she clung to safety.

"Are you alright?"

Anna couldn't speak. Once the first sob burst from her, the rest followed in a wild stream, one after the other.

"Shhh. It's OK," George consoled her as he stroked her hair. "You're safe now. I've got you."

George's words seemed to wrap her in a protective tower far away from the soldier, far away from Ehsan, yet closer to Hailey.

Hailey!

The thought of her friend acted like a barricade to the rest of her sobs. Anna choked on the last couple as she pulled back from George's chest. Still holding onto both his arms, Anna looked at him. She had to blink a few times to clear the tears.

"George, I need your phone!"

=======

The sound of the phone ringing beside her almost knocked her off the chair. Hailey had been sitting practically lifeless near the window in the hotel lobby for a couple hours now. She grabbed the phone and answered it before the second ring.

"Anna?"

"Hailey, thank God!"

Hearing Anna's voice thrust a wave of relief over her whole body. "Anna, thank God you are all right! Oh, I am so happy to be talking to you! What happened to you?"

"Me? Why weren't you answering your phone yesterday?"

"I'm sorry. It died, and we couldn't get it charged right away.

Are you OK?"

"Yeah, I am."

Hailey could hear happy tears through Anna's tone.

"Are you sure?" she asked again.

"Yes, Hailey. I'm safe. I'm with George."

"Wait, George?"

"Yeah, my dad's friend from Entrata. He's the guy who was going to help us find you. But when the bombing happened, and Ryan never showed, he had no way of knowing what had happened. He's glad you're OK."

"That's great," Hailey said dismissively. "But what happened to you? Why did it take you so long to call us back?"

"Hailey, things got a lot crazier when I got off the phone with Ryan. I had planned to ditch the soldier when I got to the airport and come meet you. But I don't think they bought my whole Paris story. I'm not sure what Ehsan was planning, but something wasn't right because the soldier wanted to fly with me to Riyadh. When we got to the airport in Dammam, I managed to borrow a phone from a woman in the washroom and called Entrata. My dad had made me memorize their emergency number when we first moved here, and after a few transfers, I got ahold of George."

"So you're in Dammam?"

"No, I'm in Riyadh. George needed time to call around to find someone to help. So I left things with him. He only knew I was in trouble and that I would be flying into Riyadh the next morning. Turns out he was able to get a friend from the defense minister's office to meet me. The man took me from the soldier and brought me to George."

"Anna, you have no idea how scared I was."

"Same here," Anna huffed. "Are you safe?"

"Yeah, Ryan and I are in Haql."

"Where's that?"

"Just south of Jordan, by the gulf. We're still waiting for the tour company to show up. The front desk just told us they are on schedule and should be here this afternoon. Oh wait, I guess you don't know about all that."

"No, none of it. All Thomas told me was that you had been taken, but that Ryan found you, and that you guys were trying to get out of the country."

Hailey spent the next twenty minutes telling Anna the quick version of her story. It was different than the last time she told it. The joy of knowing that Anna was alright helped keep her grief at bay.

"Do you think George can help us?" Hailey asked, hopeful.

"I don't see why not, but let me check. Do you want to hold on or should I call you back?"

"No, no! I'll wait." There was no way she'd let Anna get off the phone with her before she knew exactly what was happening.

"Hailey?"

"Yeah?"

"Did Ehsan have an actual marriage ceremony?"

"Yes. I had no choice, he was threatening Ghada. Why?"

"OK, just a sec."

Silence again. The delay wasn't doing anything for Hailey's nerves.

"Is there a way you can still get out of the country with the tour group?"

"Yeah... I don't see why not. why?"

"George is concerned about you waiting. He said that in the eyes of Saudi, you are Ehsan's wife. Ehsan doesn't seem like a stupid man, and George assumes he did things legit. He's worried that it could be a he-said-she-said situation and that it might take too long to sort out before he can get you home. And if that's the case, you might have to be returned to Ehsan until… and only if, George can even get it sorted out."

"Oh…" Hailey's voice trailed off. The thought of that possible reality pushed all other thoughts away.

"Hailey, I think you should stick with the tour group. I'm safe, and George can get me out of Saudi. So if you and Ryan can get to Jordan with the tour and get to the Embassy there, George thinks that's the safest plan for you."

"OK yeah, we can do that." Resorting to the original plan brought back a bit of comfort.

"And Hailey, I think you should still hide under the bus. With Ehsan being in charge of foreign restitution after the bombing, he might have more access to resources than we understand. And if he didn't believe me about Paris… he wouldn't have believed me that you were already out of the country. I don't want you getting stopped at the border. Haql is probably too far for him to bother with, but why chance it."

"Yeah, I agree."

"You sure?" Anna pressed.

"Yes, Anna, don't worry, I won't be stupid about it. I think I've used my life quota of dumb choices."

After a few more reassurances that she was fine and that Anna didn't have to worry anymore, Hailey saved George's number on her phone and said goodbye.

"Be sure to call me as soon as you are in Jordan, OK?" Anna added as Hailey was about to hang up.

"I will. Now stop worrying. Ryan's with me, and we'll be fine. I'll talk to you tomorrow." Relief flooded in. It felt so good

saying those words. "And, Anna?"
"Yeah?"
"I'm so glad you're OK."

Hailey leaned back in her seat, sliding the phone on the table. A long breath released and she closed her eyes to soak in the moment.

We're all finally safe.

CHAPTER 17

Hailey sat on the edge of the bed and watched Ryan's chest rise and fall. She couldn't remember the last time he had gotten any decent sleep.

He must be exhausted. I'm glad that he can relax now and get some rest. Hearing about Anna had to have helped.

After an hour, she rose to leave the room and go grab a drink. She was too wired to sleep.

As she rode the elevator, Hailey's mind wandered.

Poor guy. It couldn't have been easy not knowing where I was or if I was OK. And I can't even imagine being in the aftermath of that bombing. And losing Anna's parents? Wow! That's a lot to handle.

I wonder if he's processed any of that yet? It doesn't seem like it. He is holding himself together so well. It's impressive really.

I wish I was able to show that kind of strength.

Hailey lifted her head as the elevator doors opened. Her eyes focused past the foyer and front desk, to the sight outside.

The bus!

Hailey ran through the lobby and straight-armed it into the metal bar, sending the left door flying. The screech from the tires sounded as soon as Joe saw her. Confusion filled his eyes. Hailey beamed at him.

Joe set the bus in park and activated the door mechanism. He jumped from his seat and ran down the steps. James, Fabina, Jack, and Holly were close on his heels.

"What are you doing here?" Joe asked.

"Ah, I just missed you too much, Joe," she said, hugging him.

He laughed, awkwardly pushing back from her.

Before Joe had a chance to respond, James moved around him and swooped Hailey into a bear hug and swung her around. She felt like a tiny doll in his massive arms. A feeling of brotherly love surrounded her, causing a thin line of tears to gather along her eyelids.

"Hailey, I can't believe you're here," Holly said as James set her back on the ground.

"I know. I can't believe it either. It's so good to see you again. All of you."

Hailey hugged Jack and each of the girls.

"So what happened?" Fabina asked.

"When we finally heard back from Anna, she said we needed to get out of the country as soon as possible, so... here we are. She fell on Ehsan's radar for a moment, but she's safe now. We tried to meet up with you at the race track back in Buraydah but went to the wrong one. It was a big mess."

Memories flooded in. Hailey shook her head to dislodge them.

"Oh and, Joe? You have no idea how thankful I am that you told Ryan the name of this hotel. We would have never caught up with you, and we would have been... well, I don't know what we would have done."

"Well, I'm glad."

"So what's the plan now?" Jack asked.

"Same as before. Or at least I hope so. It's completely up to you guys, but we were hoping we could hide in the compartment under the bus as you cross the border into Jordan."

"It's alright with me," Joe said, and the others nodded.

"Are you sure? Would you guys be alright lieing for us again? If it came to that?"

Holly reached over and rubbed Hailey's arm. "It's not even a question."

"I-I don't know what to say. Thank you."

"Are you going to come with us to Egypt too?" James asked.

"No. We'll make our way up to the US Embassy in Amman. From there, Anna's friend from the oil company will help us get home."

"Hey, but at least you can join us diving today. So that's something," James beamed as he gave her a side hug.

It hurt a bit as he rocked her back and forth.

"Well, I don't know about that. I–"

"What's this about diving?" Ryan cut in.

"Ryan!" the group said in unison.

"Hailey tells us you're back with the tour?" Jack said as he pulled Ryan into a hug.

"Yup, looks like it. So... diving?"

"James is trying to get us to go scuba diving with them."

Ryan looked at her with a nervous look. "Uh, I'm not sure we're really up for all that."

"Oh, come on," Jack said. "It'll be fun."

Holly walked forward and stood in the middle of the group, just inches away from Ryan and Hailey. Smiling empathetically, she placed a hand on each of their shoulders.

"Look, you two. We all understand that you've been through a lot." Holly paused as she glanced over each of her shoulders.

The others nodded their agreement.

"You said that Anna is safe now. Right?" Holly looked at her.

"Yeah," Hailey said.

She looked at Ryan. "And now that you two are safely back with us, the crisis is over. Right?"

Ryan nodded.

"Have either of you dived before?" Holly asked.

Hailey shook her head. Ryan did the same.

"It is one of the most peaceful things I have ever done in my whole life. Think of it like... traveling to another world. Life above the surface seems to stop and, in a strange way, it's like it ceases to exist." Holly's eyes smiled as the corners of her mouth curled upwards.

"Trust me," Jack said as he walked up behind Holly. "You could use some of that."

Hailey looked over at Ryan again. He turned to meet her eyes.

"What do you think?" he asked. "She does paint a pretty great picture."

"Yeah, she does."

"I'm in if you are," Ryan said as nudged her.

Hailey wasn't sure this was the best timing, but on the other hand, it was on her bucket list.

She gave in. "Sure... why not," she said as she tilted her head back and shook her head.

"Brilliant!" James said as he slapped his hand against Ryan's back.

The force of it knocked Ryan forward a step. Hailey laughed. James definitely wasn't aware of his strength.

"Well if you're planning on going," Joe said, "you better get to it. Hailey, Fabina or Holly can fill you in on all the details. Won't you girls?"

It turned out that by details, Joe was talking about the dress code requirements. At Joe's instructions, they had to purchase something called a veilkini from the small boutique in the hotel.

As Hailey rummaged through the racks, sounds from Holly and Fabina's laughing in the changeroom created a lightness in her. She wished Anna was with them. Hearing Anna's antics over having to squeeze herself into so much fabric would have been hilarious.

I can't wait to see her tomorrow, Hailey thought as she grabbed two choices and made her way to the changeroom.

- - - - - - -

Hailey wasn't thrilled with the veilkini she chose, but the stretchy pants were comfortable, as was the long sleeve shirt. The piece of fabric that was attached to the back collar and stretched over her head like a swimming cap was another story. It was fussy. She had already adjusted the cap three times, and it still didn't feel like it was sitting right.

Hailey fiddled with it again as she made her way down the steps off the back patio of the hotel.

Ahh, whatever, she huffed, letting it sit where it liked and headed down to the beach.

Just beyond the stairs and a short distance over a section of sand, stood a wooden shack. A canvas awning protruded from the right side. It efficiently provided enough shade for the whole group. The barn-style doors underneath sat wide open and inside, lining each of the walls, rows of tanks, fins, and masks sat on waist-high shelves. Four men stood inside, attending to the equipment.

Not everyone had arrived yet, so Hailey joined Fabina under the awning.

"What's all that?" Fabina asked.

Hailey raised her hand to show her. "Oh, just, uh... our passports and cell phone."

Fabina's face scrunched into a perplexed look. "What's in the envelope?"

"Just... ah... a bit of money," Hailey lied. It was actually all their money. And it was a lot.

"Why not keep them in the safe in your room?"

"I just feel better having them with me."

"Yeah, that makes sense. I would too in your shoes."

"Have you gone diving before?" Hailey asked.

"No, never."

Hailey shifted her weight to the other foot. For years she had wanted to try scuba diving. Although, with the opportunity now right in front of her, tension gathered in her throat. Nervous excitement tingled through her arms.

"You and James are really great together. How long has it been?"

"Us? Uh... three? Yes, three years. He's really great. I love how awkwardly wonderful he is, and he practically has me in stitches all the time. I'm lucky to have him. And I can see you feel the same about Ryan."

"Yeah, I do."

Hailey looked around. Ryan was standing with James and Sam over by the entrance of the shack.

He's so cute, she thought, smiling at Ryan. *I love how strong his shoulders are. Actually... all of him. I like it all.*

Ryan caught her looking and winked. Her heart fluttered.

Hailey, you're a bit of a teenage mess, she teased herself as she forced her eyes to look away and return her attention back on Fabina. Any longer and she would lose track of what Fabina was saying.

As the last of the group ran up, Joe gave a nod to the four men in the shack. One man stepped forward. He looked to be in his early thirties, had dark spiky hair, and a well-kept goatee.

"Wow, you are gorgeous," a woman standing behind Hailey called out.

Fabina and Hailey snickered.

"Yes, well, ah… thank you for that," the man said.

Fabina leaned closer to her. "You've gotta love the single ladies on these trips."

Hailey had to use her hand to help stifle her laugh.

"Well, hello, everyone. My name is Armando," the man said. "I will be your dive instructor. These are your two divemasters, Moha and Omar."

Both men raised their hand and waved as Armando called each of their names.

"And that little guy inside… is Bobo."

Bobo waved.

"Bobo doesn't speak any English, but he's here to help with the equipment. We are from a little dive shop in Jordan and are excited to dive with you today. Now if everyone would like to take a seat where they are, we'll get started."

Armando waited while everyone settled themselves on the sand and the quiet murmurs of conversation to die down.

"It's a hot day, and I know you are all excited to get in the water as soon as possible, but there are some vital things we must go through before we start. First, I ask that everyone focus and listen well. Second, we need to know everyone's experience level. Whoever has their open water dive certificate, please raise your hand."

Hailey scanned the group. Jack, Holly, James, three of the other girls, and a few of the other men raised their hands.

"Wonderful. If you all would like to go into the shack with Omar and Bobo, they will get you set up and go through a quick swim test with you. The rest of you, please stay seated and we will go through your orientation. But don't worry, we'll have you in the water soon."

The orientation was a lot of information to take in all at once, but Hailey was hopeful she had retained the crucial parts.

"I'm going to hand out a quick medical questionnaire," Armando said as he took a stack of papers and a handful of pens from Omar. Handing out the sheets, he instructed them further, "Please fill it out and hand it back to Omar before you come gather your equipment from Bobo and me."

"And don't worry," Omar said. "If you forgot some of what Armando said, it's OK. We'll be there to remind you. The main thing is to *not* get distracted by swimming after a fish and leave the group. You have no idea how much of my time is spent chasing after newbies."

As she pictured Omar swimming in all directions after them, Hailey joined in laughing with the group. It felt good to laugh.

"Seriously," Omar snickered, "you wouldn't believe how common it is. It's like herding cats. So please, do me a favor and be aware of where we are at all times and stay close."

After Armando had finished handing out the questionnaires and pens, he went inside the shack. Omar remained at the entrance.

Hailey's hand shook from a mix of adrenaline and nerves but managed to fill out the form with somewhat legible information.

She walked over to Omar. He quickly scanned the page.

"Looks like you're all set," he said. "Go on in. Armando will help you with your equipment."

Hailey hesitated. The tingling in her arms returned.

"Omar, can I ask you a question?"

"Of course."

"Armando said that he was the dive instructor and you're the divemaster?"

"That's right."

"But you're going to be with us out there too, right? The whole time?"

"Yes, why do you ask?"

"I'm just a bit nervous is all. I'm guessing you're training Armando and that's why he's running the class?"

"Oh, sorry, no. It sounds confusing, but a dive instructor is actually more highly trained than a divemaster. Brilliant planning, don't you think?" He winked at her. "But don't worry, you're in good hands with any one of us."

Omar gave her shoulder a quick nudge then nodded for her to move along. She obliged, her nerves dwindling as she went. Excitement took over.

"Here ya go," Armando said as he held out what looked to Hailey like a cross between a harness and a lifejacket. It had a scuba tank attached to the back.

She turned, and Armando helped her slide into it. The weight of it was manageable but heavier than she expected.

"This vest is your buoyancy control device or BCD. First, we connect the cumberbun."

Armando connected a large piece of velcro together snugly around her waist.

"Then the chest strap."

He clipped a small strap across her chest and adjusted it to pull the shoulder straps closer together.

"Then the D-rings."

Grabbing two rings on either front of the shoulder straps, he pulled down. As he did so, the vest tightened down on Hailey's shoulders, making the load much more comfortable.

"This belt is called the belly band," Armando instructed as he connected a large fastex buckle over the velcro section around her waist. "You don't want to pull this too tight just yet. And here are your fins and mask."

As soon as Armando went to hand her the items, he noticed the things she was carrying. He chuckled as he turned to grab something off one of the hooks behind him.

"Here. This is a mini dry bag. You can put those inside and clip it to this strap here." He pointed to a small strap on her BCD. "That way they won't get wet."

"Thanks. I was hoping there would be a place for them."

A bit of color flooded her cheeks, but it was better than the anxiety she'd feel from leaving her things at the hotel. She thanked him again once the items were safely tucked inside.

"Now head down to the edge of the water," he said as she took the fins and mask. "But please don't go in any deeper than your knees. There's still some stuff to go over before you dive."

Hailey followed his instructions and headed for the water. Ryan was waiting for her halfway down.

"Everything alright?" he asked.

"Yup, all set."

After a few further instructions and some practice, Armando allowed them to submerge and descend deep into the water. At first, her body tried to panic. She closed her eyes and focused on taking slow, even breaths. When the fear seeped away, she opened her eyes. Omar was directly ahead and was leading a few of the other beginners deeper down. Hailey followed. When they hit about thirty feet, he stopped and motioned for them to explore.

The reef was stunning. As Hailey swam around, Holly was right. It did feel like she was on another planet. She felt safe like no one could touch her. There were no sounds to speak of, except for her breathing. Nothing to make her jump, no need to look over her shoulder, just calm blue water filled with vibrant sea life.

Something moved in her peripheral vision.

Hailey turned her head to see Ryan swimming a few yards from her. He stopped suddenly and started fiddling with his regulator. Hailey looked around to see if she could locate Armando or Omar. One was helping Fabina with her fin, and the other was pointing out a turtle to three others. Hailey kicked and swam over to Ryan to see what was up. As she approached, she saw panic in his eyes. He started to flail.

Something was wrong.

CHAPTER 18

Thankfully Ehsan didn't seem surprised yesterday that there weren't any leads from the other roadblocks. But having to call him today about what he learned from the tour company, would definitely get Ehsan upset. Taavi wasn't looking forward to it. Ehsan was a decent boss, but his patience was not one of his strong qualities.

"Get on with it. What did he say?" Ehsan interrupted. Annoyance coated each word.

"I didn't even get to talk to the owner. His nephew was in the shop today and said that Latif, the owner, had to go out of town suddenly. Something about an emergency."

"You've got to be kidding!"

Hearing Ehsan's anger rise over the line made Taavi all the more grateful not to be delivering this information in person. At times, seeing Ehsan's outbursts made him feel like he was working for an emotional toddler. Taavi rolled his eyes.

"I wish I was, Councilman. I had the boy call Latif, but there was no answer. I left him my number and told him to call me immediately when he heard from Latif or when Latif returned, whichever happens first."

Ehsan swore at the news. "Well, I guess we have no choice

but to wait again. Oh, hold on!"

The sound over the phone muffled. Taavi could faintly hear Ehsan talking to someone else.

"Taavi, I have to go. But until you hear from... what's his name... the owner of the tour company, I want you to call that computer guy you know and... ah... get him that photo and make the necessary adjustments."

Ehsan sounded vague. Clearly, whoever came into his office was still there.

"Do you understand?" Ehsan asked.

"Perfectly, Councilman. Consider it done."

"Oh and, Taavi? Don't let me down. The other lead got screwed up, so I'm counting on you."

"Understood, Councilman."

Taavi clicked off the phone.

What a relief, Taavi sighed. Having the full weight be placed on his shoulders again actually felt good. Taavi felt confident in his plan, and if it panned out the way he hoped, he'd have the full commendation of Ehsan for recovering the girl. An honor he didn't want to share or see go to someone else.

=======

When he went to take his next breath, nothing happened. Ryan's concern spiked. He tried to adjust the regulator in his mouth, but it did nothing. Ryan's lungs started to ache. He scanned the water around him. Hailey was only a short distance away, but she wasn't looking at him. He held his breath while he ran his hands along the hose to see if it was kinked anywhere but again found no issues.

He looked up as Hailey swam up to him. With as much

urgency as he could muster without letting go of the last of the air in his lungs, Ryan frantically pointed to his tank. He then moved his hand to his neck and slid his finger across it to signal that the tank was dead. Hailey nodded and started looking around for help.

His lungs were now burning for him to take a breath. Ryan's mind raced with the facts he heard at orientation.

Am I too far down to just swim to the surface without equalizing? How far down am I? How long is it that I have to pause to equalize?

The numbers swarmed in his head as the last of his breath left his lungs.

Ryan looked towards the surface.

Screw it.

He kicked forward. Hailey's hand grabbed his arm. Ryan shot her a look of panic.

What is she doing? I have to get air.

His face scrunched in pain. He tried to pull away, but she held tight.

With her other hand, Hailey took out her regulator and offered it to him. He quickly yanked out his. Thankfully the last lesson they had learned was still fresh in his mind.

Ryan pushed his tongue to the roof of his mouth and pressed the purge valve on the end of the regulator. Bubbles shot out all around his face. Taking a deep breath, Ryan's lungs stopped burning. He took another full breath from her regulator.

Hailey tapped him on the arm. He took one more breath and passed the regulator back to her. When she was on her second breath, the dive instructor approached. Armando signaled to Hailey to keep her regulator and offered his regulator to Ryan.

His heart stopped racing as he sucked in a few more breaths from Armando's regulator. Armando started to inspect his gear.

He signed something, but Ryan couldn't remember what it meant. Armando repeated the action. He put his hand flat out in front of him and moved it back and forth. Hailey got his attention. She repeated the action he had given to Hailey.

Yup, the tank was out of air.

Ryan nodded his understanding and offered Armando the regulator. Armando declined but gave them a thumbs up sign to signal that they were to start their ascent and another sign to say that they were to stay together.

Minutes later they were back up to the surface.

=======

Watching Ryan laying on the sand as he tried to calm himself, Hailey realized he wasn't as invincible as she would like to think. A pang of guilt hit her. It left an awful taste behind. She shouldn't have been so judgmental of him at the track. He had been through a lot.

I haven't been fair to him.

Thoughts of them running into each other as she fled the market hit her.

It was my doing that he was up on that pedestal. I put him up there. I shouldn't push him away. He deserves more grace from me.

Ryan coughed.

Hailey crawled over to where he lay and lightly placed her hand on his back.

"Are you OK?" she whispered.

"Yeah, I think so."

Hailey could hear a slight shakiness in his voice.

"Do you want to talk about it?" she asked.

Ryan took another few breaths before answering her. "I'm

not going to lie, that was scary. But I'm OK."

He turned over on his side to look at her. She reached over and swept a clump of wet hair from his forehead. Lowering her hand, she caressed his cheek with the back of her fingers.

"Actually, up until that point, it was the most peaceful thing I've ever experienced. It was beautiful." Awe surrounded each word as he spoke.

Hailey rested the weight of her torso on her elbow and listened as Ryan explained the dueling emotions of wonder and fear he felt. His openness impressed her. Vulnerability was a quality that rarely came naturally to her.

Armando interrupted them as he came up out of the water. His arms were full of the gear they had strewn behind them.

"Ryan, how are you?" Armando asked, kneeling near their feet.

"A little rattled but good."

Hailey smiled at seeing Ryan put on a brave face in front of Armando.

"I'm sorry for not checking on your earlier. But I have to say, I'm impressed with how quickly you sucked your tank dry."

"Did I? Is that unusual?"

"A little. But not unheard of."

"How long does your tank last?" Hailey asked.

"Mine? Well if I'm careful, I can go hours on a tank if I must. But first-time divers can usually last thirty to forty-five minutes. You blew through it in just under twenty. Were you scared or unsure down there?"

"I don't think so. I thought I was having a good time."

"Well don't worry about it. We just know from now on that either you need to take a bigger tank or, the better option, just try and regulate your breathing a bit more."

"Next time?" Hailey challenged. "I don't think he's going to want to do that again."

"Are you kidding? Of course I do!"

Ryan's answer surprised and impressed her.

"Are you sure?" she asked.

"Totally. I hated the last part, but I have to experience that first part again."

Armando laughed, "Yup, you're in trouble. You've got the bug now. I can see it in your eyes. I caught it when I was a teenager, and I've been in the water weekly, if not daily, ever since." Armando laughed again. "I'll go grab you both another tank. You guys still have time for a quick dive. But maybe not so deep this time, OK?"

Hailey looked at Ryan, who nodded emphatically back at her.

"OK, I guess it's a go."

During this dive, Hailey didn't leave Ryan's side. They swam, hand in hand fifteen to twenty feet down from the surface. The colors of the fish were so vibrant, they looked like they were glowing. As the sea life danced all around them, each of them intermittently pointed in a different direction as each new thing caught their eye.

Something moved in her peripheral vision. Just a few feet away swam a strange looking creature. She watched in awe at the creature's display while squeezing Ryan's hand to get his attention.

To Hailey, it looked like a cross between a strangely shaped stingray and a giant piece of arugula. The body was flat and mostly black but had an ombre effect that turned to a deep brown towards the center of its back. The outside inch of its body was bright white, as were the spots covering it's back. As the creature swam towards them, it swirled the outer rim of its body in waves like a flamenco dancer flicking her skirt.

The creature continued to approach. Hailey's pulse rose. She started to pull back as it got closer and closer, but Ryan held her in place. The creature swam a mere foot in front of them and then disappeared into the dark water beyond.

Breathtaking!!

After all the wild terror she had felt over the past few weeks, and all that Ryan must be feeling, Hailey couldn't find adequate words to thank God for this moment. The whole scene before them was perfect, a moment cut out just for them.

Her mind raced with images of more moments like this: more moments He'd set aside for them. Moments of getting back to their family and announcing their relationship. Moments of wedding plans and engagement parties.

Ryan gripped her hand tighter. He pointed to a school of fish emerging from around the section of reef right below them. She smiled at his excitement. There definitely was no other man meant for her. Ryan was the one. He had always been the one.

Once the group had gathered back on shore, they talked excitedly about all that they had seen. Hailey was less than impressed to find out that the creature was called a flatworm.

As the recounts continued, Armando, the two divemasters, and Bobo worked quickly retrieving all the equipment back from each diver and placed it back in the shack.

"Alright, everyone. Please, take a seat for a moment. I have a surprise for you." Armando waited till everyone complied. "I'm glad you all had a good time," he continued as he turned and winked at Hailey and Ryan. "Before I make my announcement, I have an award to hand out."

Everyone quieted down.

"Ryan, can you come up here please."

Ryan stood tentatively and made his way to the front. Armando put his arm around him. Hailey could see how uncomfortable Ryan was with everyone watching him. She gave him an encouraging smile.

"Our friend Ryan here accomplished quite the task today, and I'd like to present him with a sticker of honor." Armando handed Ryan a circular sticker.

Hailey couldn't see what it said, but it must have been funny because Ryan started to laugh.

"What's it say?" James yelled out from the back of the group.

Still laughing, Ryan lowered his head and pressed his thumb and forefinger against his closed eyes.

"Ryan managed to go through a whole tank and a half today. And..." Armando stopped and turned to look at Omar and Bobo. "... we call that..."

"An air hog," all three of them yelled out together.

Armando grabbed Ryan's hand that held the sticker and raised it in the air, facing it towards the group. The sticker was a profile of a plump pig wearing a white banner. Written in big black letters across the banner were the words AIR HOG.

"When you get home and get your own tank, as I know you will," Armando playfully punched Ryan in the arm, "you can stick it on your tank."

"Wear it proud, my friend," Omar said. "Wear it proud!"

Ryan's face went beet red. The group cheered and clapped as Ryan made his way back to her. Hailey was about to congratulate him when Armando started to speak, so she just rubbed Ryan's back instead.

"I hear," Armando said, "that you are all making your way

up to the border tomorrow?"

He looked around for nods of confirmation.

"Well, if you guys are up for an early morning, I'd like to offer you another dive opportunity. I know all you certified divers will be impressed. But I want to be clear, any of you newbies are more than welcome to join us. The boat ride is just under a half hour from shore, and the dive is about twice the depth as you did today. So does anyone want to see a sunken ship?"

The group immediately started chatting as shouts of 'I do's' flickered through the crowd.

Hailey looked at Ryan with hopeful eyes. "Do you want to go?"

Her heart sank a little when she saw the hesitation in Ryan's eyes.

"I don't know, Hailey. That's really deep."

Armando came over and squatted down beside Ryan.

"Ryan, this option is still open to you. I don't know if you checked your tank after your second dive, but you used a fraction of the air you did the first time. You can do this."

"You think?"

"Completely!"

Ryan looked at her. "What do you think?"

She desperately wanted to go but didn't want to push him. "Seeing the ship might be cool," she said as casually as she could muster. "But it's totally up to you."

Ryan bobbed his head as he took a second to mull it over.

"I'll be right with you both the whole time," Armando reassured him.

"Yeah, alright," Ryan smiled.

Yesss! Hailey's mind celebrated.

Armando stood and addressed the group again. "I need to see a show of hands of who would like to go."

Hailey shot her hand in the air. She looked around the group to see who would be joining them. All the women, except one, put up their hands, along with James, Jack, and three of the other guys.

Armando silently did a quick count. "Eleven! That's perfect. We'll split you into two groups and take one group out at a time."

The mix of excitement and nervous energy returned as Hailey thought about the dark caverns of the ship.

A chill ran through her, but she liked it.

CHAPTER 19

As the last of his supper slid down his throat, Taavi looked at the sprawling desert below. The lookout spot was one of Taavi's favorites and only minutes outside Riyadh.

The call could come at any moment, so there was no point starting another assignment. The trip to deliver the photo hadn't taken long and with nothing left to do, the day was passing by painfully slow. All he could do now was wait.

The sun started its descent. Most businesses would be closing soon, which meant that he'd have to wait until tomorrow to speak to Latif over at the tour company. Taavi's lungs expelled a deep sigh of frustration. If Hailey knew what was good for her, she would stay with the tour bus and not try and make it out of Saudi alone. However, with no guarantee of her intelligence, Taavi was finding it hard to be patient.

He leaned back and laid on the hood of the jeep, causing a few pops from the metal as it shifted under his weight. He interlaced his fingers behind his head and closed his eyes. He soon nodded off.

His restless dreams filled with a kaleidoscope of images where he chased Hailey.

He was a mere few feet behind her. His hand stretched out and grabbed her shoulder. Taavi felt the weight of his hand squeeze as tight as it could. Her scream felt good to hear. They both stopped running. He started to pull her towards himself and turn her. Her face was just coming into view when ringing filled his ears. It seemed out of place.

It took a few moments for Taavi to get his bearings and realize it was his phone waking him. A little disheveled, he jumped off the hood and rummaged in his pocket. He answered before even bothering to look at the number.

"Hello?"

"Taavi?" the voice asked.

"Who is this?"

"You... you asked that I should call to let you know when my uncle will be in."

"Yes, is he there now?"

"No, but he is on his way home. He asked that I give you his apologies and hopes that his absence didn't cause you any inconvenience." The boy paused.

By the speed of his voice, it was clear he was reading lines off a note.

"He is delighted to serve you in your travel needs and said that if you would like to stop by tonight, he can keep the shop open late just for you. Or he can open early if tomorrow would be more convenient."

The option had never occurred to Taavi until just that moment. His original plan of threats and force melted away.

"Tonight would be wonderful. What time will your uncle return?"

"He should be here fairly soon. Around seven or seven-thirty." The boy sounded happy.

He was probably just relieved that Taavi wasn't angry as he had been at their first meeting.

Taavi clicked off the phone after a few pleasantries, then dialed Ehsan to update him. There was no answer, so he left a quick message.

Taavi stole a quick glance at his watch as he jumped in the jeep. It wouldn't take him long to get there. The owner would still be almost an hour, but if there was any chance he might be early, Taavi needed to be waiting outside the shop when the owner returned. They couldn't afford to keep wasting time.

Taavi scanned each of the passing vehicles, but none of them slowed. It was now past seven-thirty. Taavi was getting restless. He had no clue how many days the tour was for, nor where they were headed. He wondered again if they were already too late to catch her.

Taavi got out of the jeep and started to pace the street, hands shoved deep into his pockets. Reaching the corner of the structure at the end of the block, he turned to make his way back to the other end. Upon turning, his eyes caught sight of a little man running into the shop.

Realizing that it must have been Latif, Taavi jogged to the door. His hand clasped the handle, but he paused to compose himself. Taking one deep breath then another, he needed to be calm for this plan to work. The door set off a few bells as Taavi pulled it open. Almost immediately the little man was at his side.

"Are you Taavi?" His smile looked as though it would split his face in two.

"Yes. Are you Latif?" Taavi tried to match the man's

enthusiasm.

The man nodded as he gestured towards the chairs behind him.

"Your nephew is a fine boy," Taavi said as he sat in one of the wicker chairs. "You should be proud of him for taking such great care of your customers."

Both men looked towards the counter where the boy was folding some papers. The boy blushed and bowed his head in response.

"Oh, yes. Very good boy. He does great work. I do apologize for the delay. From what my nephew tells me, you seemed quite urgent at your first visit. Is everything alright?"

"Perfectly. I merely need to plan a surprise trip for my wife. We haven't lived in Saudi long, and she has wanted to travel around." Taavi looked down and shook his head. "But sadly, my work has kept me quite busy."

"Yes, yes. I understand. What type of work are you in?"

Taavi didn't see the point in lying. "Private security mostly."

"What kind of trip were you thinking?"

"Do you happen to do any bus tours? Maybe ones that are longer than a day trip?"

"Certainly," Latif beamed. "That is what we specialize in."

"Wonderful! It's her birthday tomorrow. Would you have any leaving in the next day or two?"

"No, I'm sorry. We only have day trips over the next few days."

"When was the last multi-day tour? Did we just miss it?"

"Yes, it left yesterday morning. But I'm not sure that particular tour would be a good one for you. I'm sure your wife isn't as adventurous as you." Latif nudged him with his elbow. "But I may have another–"

"How adventurous?" Taavi cut him off. He couldn't give Latif time to divert the conversation.

"You see, that tour is more for the thrill seeker types. But I do have a lovely–"

"Actually, that may be just the thing. She married me didn't she?" Taavi laughed.

Latif joined in. "Yes, I guess she did. And if she doesn't like any of the activities, I am sure she'd still love to watch."

"Ah, you are a smart man, Latif. You have her pegged well. Now, tell me about this tour. I'm very intrigued."

Latif started to lay out the whole itinerary. Taavi found it painstaking to listen to it all but managed to keep his impatience at bay and not rush him. Raising suspicion now would not be wise, so he kept himself from fidgeting by jotting notes on the back of a brochure.

"And then you will cross into Jordan on Sunday morning around eleven o'clock, which gives you a chance to sleep in before you start making your way over to Egypt. In Jordan, you will enjoy a–"

"Wait!" Taavi jumped in. "The bus goes into Egypt?"

Taavi had to strain to keep up the act. Finding out that Hailey would be leaving Saudi the next morning made things even more urgent.

"Why, yes. Is that too far? Would you prefer to only stay in Saudi?"

"No. My wife will love it." Taavi checked his watch. "Oh, it's getting late. She will start to wonder where I am. Would it be alright if I return tomorrow to book the trip?"

"Yes, my friend, of course. I'm excited to serve you."

"Thank you." Taavi rose and shook Latif's hand, but made every effort to keep walking towards the door.

"I will look forward to your next visit to our humble-"
"Yes, me too. Goodbye." Taavi turned and left the shop.

It was already after eight, but with the fourteen-hour drive to Haql, they would be cutting things closer than he would have liked. Taavi jumped in the jeep, dialed Ehsan's number, and sped towards the house as the ringing filled the vehicle. Hailey would be out of Saudi soon, and they had to act fast.

CHAPTER 20

As Ryan jogged behind Hailey towards the beach, the first dive team pulled up to the dock. He still had a few knots in his stomach. Going down to sixty feet seemed a bit much after only two shallow dives.

The twin sisters, who they hadn't talked with much, jumped off the boat first and ran up to them.

"You both are in for a treat," one said.

"It's absolutely spectacular," the other added.

Hearing and seeing the women's excitement helped untie a few of the knots.

At least Armando will be next to us the whole time, Ryan consoled himself. The rest of the group disembarked and unloaded their equipment. As each of the group passed them, their comments resonated with the same air of thrill and awe as the first two girl's experience. It helped to ease him further.

Hailey squeezed his hand. "Are you still up for this?"

Ryan leaned over and kissed her cheek. "Definitely," he answered with some embellishment in his tone. No need to dampen her excitement.

=======

The calm water of the ocean looked like liquid glass. Hailey had never seen anything like it. With no waves, the speedboat cut through the water with ease.

Hailey watched as Fabina fought with her hair as it whipped about furiously. There was no wind, only a slight breeze, but the speed of the boat racing to their destination made Fabina's hair quite unruly. Hailey reached up and played with the short pieces of her hair near the base of her neck. At times, she missed the length, but there were definite perks to short hair.

"The place we'll be stopping," Armando yelled over the roar of the engine, "obviously doesn't look like much from the surface, but once you get down there... well, I won't ruin the surprise. But I can tell you a little about the history of the ship to perk your excitement."

They all gathered tighter to hear him better.

"It's a decommissioned Israeli warship they sunk back in the '80s. Actually, for her age, she was quite young, but because she was having some issues, they decided to retire her rather than fix her up. They organized a scuttling and down she went. Now she lays there in all her glory, creating a reef for the sea life and great diving for us."

Hailey could easily hear the joy in Armando 's voice, he obviously loved what he did.

"Hey, James?" Armando called over his shoulder. "Do me a favor and open the seat at the back on the left there."

James pointed to one of the seats.

Armando nodded. "Pull out the flashlights and make sure everyone gets one. You guys will be impressed how bright it is down there. It's not like you see in the movies where it's all dark and scary. It's..."

Armando trailed off as he steered around an approaching boat. The people on the passing boat waved. Hailey returned the gesture.

"Keep your flashlights handy. When we swim into parts of the ship, it's a bit dimmer and you'll be happy to have them."

After another few yards, Armando cut the engine and turned to face them. Hailey's heart sped up.

"Alright, team, gather up your stuff and let's get going. Joe gave me a stern talking to this morning about getting you back on time." Armando looked at his watch. "We're already pushing it, so we need to get moving. Joe seems like a nice man, but I don't want to piss him off."

Hailey chuckled to herself. She felt the same way.

"I'm going to split you into two groups. I want to make sure that Ryan, Hailey, and Fabina feel really comfortable down there, so I don't want to be distracted by too large of a group. The first group will be James, Fabina, and Holly and then I'll take Ryan, Hailey, and Jack after that."

Hailey was thankful for that division. With Jack being an excellent and experienced diver, she and Ryan would have Armando's full attention.

"Holly and James, can you help Fabina get ready? I'm just going to tie up to the mooring buoy and raise the dive flag."

Hailey didn't wait to watch Armando work or the others get ready. She made her way up to the bow of the boat to lay down.

The sun's heat caused almost a weightless feeling as her body temperature rose. Hailey placed her forearm over her eyes. Just before she dozed off, a sense of immense peace encircled her.

I am the vine. Remain in me, Hailey

"I will," she softly whispered as she drifted off.

"HEY! Sleeping beauty, you're going to miss something awesome!!" James's bellowing voice shot her back to reality. Hailey sat up.

"Are you guys back already?" Hailey asked, rubbing her eyes.

Holly hopped up on the bow and sat down next to her.

"How are you?" Holly's concerned tone erased any sense of the usual casualness of the rote question.

"We're good."

"No, really, how are *you*?" Holly asked again.

Hailey paused for a moment to think. She wasn't exactly sure how she was feeling. She did a quick inventory of her emotions.

"Honestly? A little overwhelmed."

Concern flashed in Holly's eyes.

"Don't get me wrong, I'm having a lot of fun with you all. But... I just want to get home."

"Yeah, I bet." Holly reached out and took Hailey's hand.

"Anna called again last night and we got a chance to chat more, which was nice. And... I'm glad Anna is safe."

"But?" Holly said.

Hailey smiled. "Well, I... I miss familiarity."

Holly didn't say anything but smiled a tight-lipped grin that showed her empathy. Hailey's eyes started to tear. Hailey raised her eyes to the sky to stop any more tears from gathering.

"Whew, I tell ya though, I'm excited to be so close to the border. I think I'll feel a whole lot better once I'm out of Saudi. And, Holly, thanks for... everything." Hailey placed her other hand on top of Holly's, sandwiching it between her's.

"Hailey, I'm glad you're back with us."

"Oh!" Hailey said as she reached beside her and grabbed the cell. "Can you keep this? If anything changes with Anna, I don't want to miss her."

Holly took the phone from her. "Definitely."

"You girls gonna talk all day?" Armando called from the back of the boat. "Or are we going to get some more diving in?"

Hailey's smirk mirrored Holly's.

"Coming," they both called out in unison.

Ryan was already in the water by the time Hailey had her wetsuit on. Jack remained onboard to help her with her tank.

"All set?" Armando called from below.

"I think so."

"Alright, just like you saw us do it. Sit on the side of the boat, put your regulator in, grab your mask with one hand and put your other arm across your tummy. Then lean back and gently fall into the water. Jack, can you help her?"

It looked simple enough when she watched Ryan and Armando do it. She waddled backwards in her flippers over to the side of the boat and sat on the edge. Jack silently stood next to her. He put his hands out as an offer of assistance if she wanted it. Hailey adjusted her mask once more, then picked up her regulator. Hesitating only a moment to take a deep breath, she popped it into her mouth.

She sat up straight, paused, and leaned back. Instinct kicked in as the feeling of falling caused the involuntary motion of her hand to shoot out and grab the side of the boat.

She broke out into a nervous laugh.

"Hailey, get in the water," Ryan teased from behind her.

"Yeah, yeah. I'm coming."

She tried again and forced herself to not repeat the action. This time succeeding in letting herself fall back.

The contrasting coolness of the water from that of the sun's rays took her breath away. Yet she managed to keep her breathing reasonably steady as she resurfaced and bobbed between Ryan and Armando.

"Ryan?" Armando said, "I was thinking about how quickly you went through your tank, and I realized that you might have had positive buoyancy last time. If that was the case, it probably caused you to fight too hard to get down, which can take up a lot of air. I'll watch you this time to make sure you have neutral buoyancy, OK?"

Ryan nodded.

"Jack, can you check Hailey's?"

They all lowered a few feet into the water to adjust their buoyancy. Jack made a few adjustments and gave a thumbs up sign to signal her to return to the surface.

"Good," Armando said, wiping the water from his face after taking out his regulator. "Ryan, that should make it easier for you. Oh, and before we head down, I brought this with me."

Armando pointed to a thin whiteboard clipped with a carabiner to his BCD. A pencil hung from it by a yellow string.

"Any of you are welcome to use this slate if you need to tell me anything or ask questions. I'll also use it to talk to you down there."

Hailey felt safer knowing she didn't need to rely on her memory of the hand signals.

After a wave to those still on the boat, they submerged themselves beneath the glassy surface.

=======

A few of his men had dozed off in the back of the jeep, but Taavi remained alert. His eyes stared so intently at the road they started to ache. He squeezed them closed a couple of times to release the tension.

A sign whizzed past. They were almost to Haql. Adrenaline shot through his core, causing it to be increasingly more difficult to sit still. He gripped the steering wheel tighter. The tour bus was scheduled to leave in about an hour, but they were still about thirty minutes out. A small bit of the frustration over how long it took to assemble his men and get on the road, crept back in and choked him.

Taavi pressed down harder on the gas pedal. This would be his last chance to catch Hailey, and he couldn't miss it. He wouldn't miss it.

CHAPTER 21

Armando had been right. The amount of light that shone through the water more than adequately illuminated their surroundings. Ryan followed the pace Armando set as they slowly descended, equalizing as they went. Ten feet, then twenty, thirty, then forty.

Jack stopped and pointed up to the surface. Ryan turned to look. The sight before Ryan was jaw-dropping.

Forty feet above them sat their boat. The surface of the water seemed to have disappeared, causing the boat to look like it was suspended in the air. The rays of the sunlight shone around the boat and extended down past where they had paused.

The bubbles from Ryan's breathing looked like growing jellyfish as they rose towards the boat. He felt like he was in a world where gravity didn't exist. He looked towards Hailey. She seemed just as enthralled. Hailey swam up a couple feet above Jack and started doing somersaults to catch his bubbles.

Armando swam closer and grabbed their attention. He tipped his head back, took out his regulator, and blew out while sticking his tongue out then in. A perfect bubble ring came from his mouth and grew as it rose.

Ryan returned his attention back to Armando, hoping to see

another. But he merely signaled that time was ticking. They continued their descent.

As Ryan looked down, he became confused. They should be almost down sixty feet by now, but he could only see the reef. There was no ship. Ryan looked over to Armando. He didn't notice Ryan's concern. Ryan caught Hailey's eye. She shrugged, echoing his confusion.

All around the reef Ryan saw different colored coral and schools of fish. The variety was more extensive than he had seen yesterday.

This is so beautiful, but where was the ship?

As they swam, they came to the edge of an outcropping of the reef. Drawing closer, Ryan saw the reef drop off dramatically. As his eyes scanned down a couple of feet over the drop, the ship came into view.

She was sitting on a large sandbar, fully upright, coral and sea plants coating most of her hull and deck. Large sections, the size of a patio door, had been cut out of the hull, allowing the sun to stream in.

Ryan started to swim forward, but Armando grabbed his leg.

WAIT HERE.
NEED TO CHECK FOR PREDATORS.

A paranoid feeling that he was being watched draped around Ryan. He jerked his head around, scanning in all directions. Seeing nothing didn't remove the sensation.

Ryan felt foolish for not thinking about sharks before that moment. Seeing how they were in open water, the possibility was so obvious. He shot a look at Hailey. Her eyes were huge and started looking around nervously. The same fact was clearly occurring to her.

Armando swam up to one of the patio-sized holes. Placing a hand on the edge of it, he poked his head inside, looked one way and then the other. Ryan's chest started to hurt. He slowly let out the held breath and tried to steady his breathing as he kept his eyes on Armando.

Armando turned and gave the OK sign, causing, what seemed to be, a collective release of tension. Large amounts of bubbles retreated from each of their regulators. As the bubbles rose upwards, the three of them all kicked forward and joined Armando next to the ship.

JACK WITH RYAN. HAILEY WITH ME.
ALL STAY CLOSE TOGETHER. HAVE FUN.

Ryan followed Hailey, being sure to stay back far enough to not be kicked by her fins. He snapped a quick glance over his shoulder to ensure Jack was with them, he was. In single file, they continued into the belly of the ship.

Once inside, the rhythm of Ryan's heart increased. The ship's engine room sprawled out before him. Numerous crevices and shadowy sections provided places for things to hide in. Was Armando sure they were alone?

Ryan scanned the room. Nothing of danger met his eyes. Six yellow fish, the size of frisbees, swam from behind a piece of machinery on his right. They seemed to barely notice their presence and swam right for Ryan. He leaned back to let them pass as they swam around him and left the ship.

Ryan closed his eyes. *I've got to get a grip. We're fine.* Calm returned.

They moved deeper into the ship, passing through the boiler

room, past the galley and through other rooms to which Ryan couldn't discern their use. His eyes barely paused for a moment as they tried to take in all they were seeing. Everything was covered with a moss-like coating. It gave a ghostly and historic feel to his surroundings, causing a strange sense of nostalgia.

Getting to the stern of the ship, Armando led them back outside through another cutout. They swam around the enormous propellers and past the rudder. Seeing the sheer size of them and the grand expanse of the ocean beyond, made Ryan feel incredibly small. He liked it.

A school of long, silver fish passed them and disappeared into the ship. Ryan looked at Armando. He was holding up a new message for them.

STAY CLOSE TOGETHER. SWIM FAST.
RUNNING OUT OF TIME.
NEED TO SEE BOW OF SHIP.

They swam straight up the stern of the ship and onto the deck. Armando weaved them around a turret, through the bridge, over two more turrets and around, what looked like, radio equipment. Ryan's imagination jumped to life as he looked over the deck and pictured the Israeli sailors operating such a large vessel.

Are they disappointed that this was her fate? I wonder if any of them have been down to see her since.

Reaching the bow, Armando kicked down over the edge of the deck. Ryan marveled at the sight as they swam in a downward spiral around the anchor's chain. Reaching the bottom, the crown of the anchor was buried in the sand but still sat upright. A small part of each fluke still showed.

Armando moved into the ship through a hole cut into the hull, about a quarter of the size of the others. They swam up a few companionways and past multiple cabins. Ryan turned to look inside one as they went and caught sight of a broken bunk sitting in the middle of the room.

He turned to look back just as Hailey's fin kicked his face. His forehead started to throb. A little dazed, Ryan raised his hand to check his face. No blood. That's good. Thinking about it, Ryan had visions of sharks looking for him if there was, sent shivers over his skin. Jack came around to check him. Ryan waved him off, he was fine.

Hailey hadn't turned around, she didn't seem to realize she had kicked him. Ryan's eyes focused past her, Armando was waving the slate at them.

TAKE A QUICK REST. NEED TO HEAD UP SOON. ALREADY LATE.

As Ryan tried to slow his breathing from the quick swim over the ship's deck, he looked around the place where they had stopped. It looked like a foyer with rooms branching off in each direction. The middle doorway was more substantial than those spanning out to either side.

Ryan looked at Jack. He didn't seem tired at all. His air bubbles were coming out slow and steady. Jack turned and disappeared through the middle doorway. Ryan looked back at Armando, but he hadn't noticed Jack's departure. He was helping Hailey adjust something on her mask.

Ryan turned his attention back to the door but saw no signs of Jack's return. He couldn't leave Jack alone, they were dive buddies. He swam forward to find him. Ryan was just getting to the door when Jack appeared out of nowhere, startling Ryan. Jack swam past and grabbed the slate.

ANYONE NEED TO USE THE HEAD?

Ryan had no clue what the message meant. Jack didn't wait long enough to see the confused look on Ryan's face. He swam back through the doorway and disappeared again. Ryan looked at Armando and shrugged. Armando laughed. It seemed he understood what Jack was up to and signaled for them to follow.

Upon coming into another room, Ryan spotted Jack near the back wall, perched on a cracked toilet. Jack looked ridiculous as he fought to reposition himself on the toilet. Ryan's laughter burst out of him so hard that he almost lost his regulator.

Armando nudged Ryan forward as he removed a camera from a pocket in his vest with his free hand.

There were two other toilets, one on either side of where Jack sat. The walls of the toilet stalls still stood, but the doors were nowhere in sight. Ryan took the one on the right. Settling himself on the toilet, he mimicked Jack's movements. Armando counted down from three on one hand, while steadying the camera with the other.

The flash filled up the whole room, as did the bubbles from their combined laughter. Ryan kept his eyes on Hailey. Seeing her enjoyment over the sight was more joyous to him then their silly antics. Once the laughter had dissipated, Armando put the camera away and checked his watch. His eyes widened and he waved each of them over. He tapped his watch. They needed to get back.

Giving one last look around the room, a soft chuckle vibrated in Ryan's chest. He kicked towards the doorway.

While swimming out into the open water, Ryan became overwhelmed with gratitude that he had gotten to see all this. He wished they could stay longer.

As they moved along in formation, they quickly swam back to where they had first entered the ship. Ryan took mental pictures of it all as he swam along. He was fairly certain he wouldn't experience something like this again, and he didn't want to forget any of it. The longing he knew he would feel when he looked back on this dive, made a short preview in his mind, sending another wave of nostalgia through him.

This is something I'll never forget.

Reaching the edge of the reef, Armando stopped.

REMEMBER 1 FT PER 30 SEC.
STAY WITH ME.

Ryan looked up to see if he could see the hull of their boat. He scanned the water above and located the small shadow far in the distance. He pulled his eyes away briefly, gave the OK sign to Armando, then turned his attention back to the boat's shadow.

A loud boom shook his eardrums. A flash of red light billowed out from either side of the boat's shadow. No one moved.

CHAPTER 22

Taavi checked his watch as they pulled into the city. It was 10:15 in the morning. They had made good time. He yelled at the men to wake up, as he scanned the parking lot.

It took a few moments for his eyes to settle on it, but at the far end of the lot sat a large tour bus. As far as Taavi could tell, the bus was empty. Only one man stood near the bus, probably the driver. The man circled the bus and looked to be inspecting it.

Taavi parked the jeep near the entrance to the lot, being sure to leave a clear line of sight to the bus.

"How would you like to play this?" one of his men asked from the back seat.

"Let's wait here until everyone has gotten their stuff on the bus. I don't want to alert anyone of our presence until we've had a chance to identify our targets."

Taavi rechecked his watch.

"They aren't scheduled to pull out for another forty to forty-five minutes, but I want everyone to scan the group for either of our targets. And remember, the woman is not to be harmed in any way so use minimal force if this goes south. Understood?" Taavi turned to look at his men.

The five men nodded.

Taavi returned his attention back to the bus and to the hotel. As he scanned from one to the other, both locations remained quiet. He surveyed the area. There was a lot of open space, and it made him nervous that Hailey might be alerted when they approached.

He did a quick tactical calculation and instructed his men to create a perimeter. He sent one man to the front of the hotel, one to the back, and the other three to separate lookout points around the parking lot. Taavi remained in the jeep, which closed in the circle around the bus.

He licked his lips. This was one of his favorite tasks in the world and something he missed since he was assigned to the councilman. The thrill of being a tactical officer never dulled and he reveled in the occasion. His prey was so close. He could practically feel the victory.

Taavi pulled out a pair of binoculars and surveyed each of his men's posts and around the perimeter. There was still no movement. After fifteen minutes had passed a few people exited the hotel and started across the parking lot. They all looked to be foreigners and each carried luggage. Taavi watched as the small group made their way to the bus, greeted the driver who helped load their bags under the bus, and then disappeared onboard. Hailey wasn't among them.

Soon after, more passengers trickled out of the hotel. Taavi watched intently. Three men and a set of twin girls made up the next group, but still, none of them resembled the woman he wanted. The radios of his men stayed silent, signaling that they also saw nothing of consequence.

During a lull in those exiting the hotel, the bus driver walked a few feet away from the bus and pulled out his phone. He dialed a number and then continued to walk towards the beach.

The driver raised up the phone to his ear, while simultaneously raising his other hand to shade his eyes. He hung up the phone moments later and then dialed again while repeating his lookout over the water. Taavi noticed that the driver didn't speak during either call.

"Now, what are you up to?"

Upon the second time the driver hung up, he moved back to the bus. Taavi returned his attention back to the hotel when he saw movement. Another three people exited and made their way to the bus. There was still no sign of Hailey.

Those three make fourteen. Taavi looked back towards the bus.

The driver made his way up the steps and closed the door. Alarms went off all over Taavi's body. He swore and reached for the door handle.

Was she already on board?

Slamming the jeep's door behind him, Taavi grabbed his radio off his belt and pushed the rectangular button on the side.

"Engage!" he yelled to his men.

Immediately all five men closed in around the bus.

CHAPTER 23

For a moment Ryan felt paralyzed. His brain wasn't comprehending what his other senses were relaying. His eyes saw splashes of things falling into the water. But there was no other boat, so there couldn't have been a crash.

Was that flash... fire? That would make sense if the boom were an explosion. But what could have exploded? What's going on?

Everything seemed to be moving in slow motion, but he managed to turn in time to see Jack surging forward. Armando reached out and tried to grab Jack, but he was a moment too late, and Jack swam away unencumbered.

Ryan was on the verge of kicking forward to follow, but Armando was quicker and grabbed him and emphatically shook his head. Ryan watched achingly as Jack shot up to the surface alone.

The ascent was painful, not physically, but emotionally. It was agonizing. Armando never let go of either Ryan or Hailey. He seemed determined to make sure they ascended at the proper rate.

It was hard to tell all that was going on above the water. From what Ryan could see by the random limbs, it looked like one of the girls had been thrown from the boat, and that James had jumped in after her. He was now floating a few feet from the boat and looked to be holding that person in his arms. There was no sign of the other woman.

When Jack reached the surface, he swam beside James for only a moment. Then left him and swam up to the boat and climbed aboard, disappearing out of Ryan's sight. James remained holding whoever was in his arms. But by Jack's departure, it must be Fabina.

When Armando stopped at the fifteen feet mark for the three-minute safety stop, Ryan's mind raced with frustration from the inability to go help. Something awful had happened, and their friends needed him up there. Ryan looked at Armando with pleading eyes. Armando tightened his grip and shook his head.

It wasn't until they reached the surface that the full weight of the situation hit his eyes. The back part of the boat was blown to shreds and was slowly taking on water. A thick, black cloud billowed out from the fire engulfing the engine compartment.

Ryan spotted Jack and Holly on board. They were both crouching on the undamaged bow. Jack was rummaging through a small medical kit, and Holly sobbed while she held her right arm tightly to her chest. Blood ran down her suit and pooled around her knees before dripping off the side of the boat and into the water.

"Holly, what happened?" Ryan yelled.

She looked up with pained eyes, "It... it was an accident. I... I didn't..."

Armando let go of Ryan's arm, pulling his attention away from Holly. He turned to see Armando swim over past the stern of the boat, towards James and Fabina. James had her cradled in his arms.

When Armando approached, James lifted his head.

"James, what happened to the boat?"

James ignored Armando's question.

"She won't wake up." James's words were difficult to hear over the crackling fire, but Ryan could hear the fear in his voice.

Armando reached his fingers to the side of Fabina's neck. The moment dragged, and Ryan's own fear rose as Armando readjusted his fingers, then pause again. When Armando slowly shook his head, the cry that emanated from James's soul almost destroyed Ryan.

"No, no, no," James moaned as he kissed Fabina's forehead and stroked her hair. "Love, wake up. Come on now, love, open your eyes."

Hailey started to whimper beside him. Ryan turned to hold her. Hearing James grief behind him and feeling Hailey's shoulders shuddering in his arms, broke Ryan's own resolve. He squeezed his eyes tightly, releasing the tears that had gathered there.

The moment didn't last long.

Hailey shoved him away. "No! She'll be OK."

Ryan tried to stop her, but she slipped from his grasp.

"James, hold her flat and keep her still. OK?"

James nodded and readjusted Fabina.

Armando grabbed Hailey's arm. "Hailey, she's gone. There's no point."

"You don't know that. No, she just needs air. She'll be OK."

Ryan's face crumpled with pain as Hailey tilted Fabina's head back and opened her mouth.

"Please, God, help me wake her up."

With each breath she blew into Fabina's mouth, Hailey became more frantic.

"No," Hailey blew in another breath. "Please, God." she blew another breath. "Don't do this."

Ryan had to stop her.

He swam up behind her and grabbed both her shoulders.

"Come on, Hailey, stop. It's OK, she's gone. You need to let her go."

"No, Ryan... please... she can't be..."

Hailey's whimpers mixed with James's moaning. Ryan pulled Hailey back and wrapped his arms in front of her. The back of her head touched his shoulder as she gave up the fight and slumped against him. Ryan tried to look at James to give him comfort, but seeing such a strong man at his weakest moment scattered his words.

"I'm so sorry, James," was all Ryan could manage.

Ryan's head shot around the instant the scream from the bow of their boat reached his ears.

"Help! Ryan, Armando, help!" Holly wailed.

Ryan gave Hailey a quick squeeze and then swam over to the edge of the boat to see what was wrong. Jack was now in Holly's arms, unconscious.

"What happened?"

Before Holly could answer him, Armando came up beside him. "He surfaced so fast that he has decompression sickness. We have to get him to the hospital."

"How?" Holly yelled at him as she flung one arm in the air. "Armando, you have to help him. Do you have oxygen on board?"

Armando looked towards the back of the boat. Ryan followed his gaze to the shredded stern.

"Not anymore."

"What are we going to do?" Holly's panic filled every word.

"I... I don't know."

=======

Ascending the stairs, Joe's body was tense with frustration. He had been clear with Armando that he needed to have the last group back to the beach by 10:30. The group was now fifteen minutes late, and there was still no sign of them.

Joe sat down hard in his seat with a heavy sigh. He hated being behind schedule.

They will get here when they get here, I guess. No use stressing over it.

His attempt to console himself didn't do much to reduce his annoyance.

To keep the heat of the outside air from choking out the A.C., Joe leaned over to activate the door closing mechanism. As it slammed shut and he returned his eyes forward. Joe's eyes met the terrifying sight just beyond the bus. Three men dressed in tactical clothing were approaching. With raised assault rifles pointed right at him, each of the men was swiftly closing the gap.

Joe shot a look over his shoulder and peered through the windows of the left side of the bus. Another man came from the east. Joe swiveled quickly to confirm his fear, another advanced from the west.

They were surrounded.

CHAPTER 24

When Ryan had left her to go help Holly and Jack, Hailey's eyes locked on James. He held Fabina in one arm and continued to stroke her forehead with his free hand. The moan emanating from his throat remained as he kept whispering to her, asking her to wake up.

As each tick of each moment passed, the sorrow in Hailey's stomach grew. It rose from deep in her and almost hurt as it reached her chest. Bottlenecking at her throat, the despair and fear could no longer be contained. It burst from her with great force.

"No!" she shouted.

Suddenly aware of the diving gear still attached to her, she felt suffocated. Panic took over as she fought to release the buckles of the dive vest. She couldn't breathe under their weight. The frustration in her grew as her fingers would not comply and accomplish the task fast enough.

"No, no. Come on," Hailey commanded them.

Finally, each buckle released and she pulled free of the vest and the tank. Not caring about their fate, she shoved them over the surface of the water. As soon as they slipped from her fingers, Hailey's hands went up to her head where they grabbed handfuls of her hair. Hailey looked up into the sky, and a deep despondent cry emerged from her lips.

"How can You let this happen?" she yelled into the sky. "What did they do? They don't deserve this." She made no attempt to contain her anger.

"Hailey?" Ryan's voice came from behind her as his hand rested on her shoulder.

His tone was empathetic, but his touch made her jump.

"Don't touch me," she warned as she jerked away.

Hailey surveyed the scene around her. Holly and Armando were still crouched over Jack, both of them were staring at her. Holly had tears in her eyes and wore a look on her face that mirrored Hailey's sorrow. She looked at Ryan. Both of his hands were raised, palms facing her as if she were a spooked horse that he was trying to approach. He kept his distance.

Hailey looked at James again. His attention was also on her, the pain on his face remained. Hailey did another sweep of all their faces. So much pain staring at her. Everything bowed and moved in on her. Her breathing quickened erratically.

The feeling of culpability for everything they were going through grew with each moment.

"I'm so sorry. I'm so sorry," Hailey sobbed to each of them.

You have to get out of here, Hailey's mind warned her. She jerked around and started swimming.

"Hailey! Stop!"

Hailey ignored Armando's instructions and pushed her arms and legs to move faster. All four limbs screamed out in pain for her to stop, but she ignored them all and continued to swim farther away from the boat and the smoke. She couldn't remain in these circumstances. The compulsion she felt to run and hide was too overwhelming.

The calm, glassy water that had been in view during the early morning was now gone. Choppy water swelled all around her. When her chest heaved with her sobs, it caused her mouth to periodically take in water. At first, Hailey ignored her coughing lungs, but soon it became too much and she was forced to stop. Floating on the surface as she tread water, her lungs were finally able to expel the last of the water and they relaxed. Hailey spun slowly to see how far she was from the boat. Bobbing in the vast expanse of water around her and seeing the distance she covered, made her feel so incredibly small and alone. Her body resumed its grief.

"Why bother leading me to this desert just to take more from me and to hurt others? I thought You were calling me back to Yourself to give me back hope. What do you call this?" Hailey yelled as she gestured to the burning boat. "Did you do this to them because of me?"

Hailey paused momentarily from her rant to listen. No words met her heart. She waited another moment. Still nothing.

"Great, so what, You're not here now? Is that it? Am I on my own now that You've gotten what you wanted, my devotion back?"

As soon as the words were out, a small twinge of guilt from her disrespect implored her to recant. She dismissed it and spun around to look behind her. Hailey didn't expect to see anyone, but it made her anger feel justified as her eyes confirmed her loneliness. With her back now to the boat, her rage surged and suddenly suppressed her grief. She stopped crying.

Hailey continued to tread water where she floated but made no more attempts to talk or demand answers. Her cold, raw emotions surrounded her, making her feel numb. She clenched her jaw and glared out across the water.

=======

Closing in on the bus in perfect formation, his team stopped a few feet out. Taavi walked up to the doors. He tapped the muzzle of his assault rifle on the glass.

"Open! Now!"

The driver looked nervously back to his passengers, then looked back to him. For a moment the man sat there motionless, but soon gave a small shake of his head. Taavi was in no mood for defiance. He raised his weapon from waist height, leveling it with his chin.

"I'm only going to ask one more time. Open the door now!"

The driver closed his eyes, and his shoulders slumped with a release of a defeated sigh.

Come on, friend. Don't be stupid. He gripped his rifle tighter.

The driver slowly stood and leaned over to release the doors. Taavi put up his fist to his men to signal that they were to hold where they were. After doing a quick visual check to each man, he mounted the stairs.

"What's... ah... going on?" the man asked.

"What's your name?"

"J-Joe."

Good, he's scared.

"Are you aware that you have an American fugitive on board?"

"No, sir."

Taavi looked to each of the seats, scanning all the faces. None of them belonged to Hailey.

"Everyone, get off and line up with your backs to the bus. If anyone tries to run or attempt to resist, you will be shot on site without warning."

Whimpers arose from a few of the passengers.

Taavi moved aside to let Joe get off first, then moved to stand in front of the driver's seat. As each passenger passed him, Taavi assessed them. None of them made eye contact. Once they all had exited the bus, Taavi made his way past each seat, scanning to ensure everyone was off and that Hailey wasn't hiding anywhere.

Nothing!

He swore and walked back to the front again and hurried down the steps. The gravel crunched beneath his boots as he exited the bus. He was happy to see that everyone had followed his instructions and were not being a bother. He was not in the mood to shoot anyone today and deal with the headaches it would cause.

"If any of you have information about a red-headed American girl that was on this bus, please raise your hand."

No one moved.

"She might have been traveling with a man," Taavi added.

Again nothing. The group stared at the ground. Some shifted nervously from one foot to the other. Taavi stretched his head to one side then the other, causing two loud cracks.

"If no one comes forward, each of you will be arrested and interrogated until someone tells me what I want to know. So, let's not make this difficult."

A few of the passengers glanced over at Joe. Taavi followed their gaze. Joe made no movement and stood silent, head down. Taavi looked back at those who had looked at Joe. When they saw that the driver wasn't speaking, they nervously turned their eyes downward again and copied Joe's posture.

"Alright, I guess a little persuasion is needed. Joe, step

forward."

Taavi walked down to the end of the line. Upon reaching Joe, Taavi smiled when Joe raised his eyes to his.

Taavi had seen it a thousand times: terrified men trying to stand their ground and hide their fear. Even though Taavi could see through the act, he had to give Joe credit. He was doing better than some.

"This will be my last attempt." Taavi put on his favorite tone. It was calm but eerie and one that always proved to be effective in persuasion. "Where is the American?"

Joe bit his lip. "I... I don't know."

Taavi took a full breath, filling his lungs. After blowing it out forcefully to show his frustration, he turned as if to start walking away. He then quickly swiveled back on his left foot, while raising up the butt of his rifle. The thud of the end of the rifle connecting with Joe's head reverberated up into Taavi's hands.

Joe dropped to his knees with a small grunt and whimper. Supporting himself with one hand, Joe raised the other to the deep gash on his forehead.

A few of the woman standing against the bus screamed, a couple men moaned, and two others gave a few words of protest. But one quick glare from Taavi silenced them all.

Taavi lowered his weapon back to his side and started walking up the line. Each slow and calculated step caused the group to flinch away from him, as if they were trying to sink into the metal of the bus and hide.

At about halfway back up the line, he stopped in front of two women, the twins. Taavi turned back towards Joe, who was still cowering on the ground.

"So, Joe. Who should be next? What about her?" he asked, pointing to the twin closest to Joe.

Joe raised his head and glared at him.

"Please... no one. I'll tell you. Just don't hurt anyone else."

"Fair enough. Stand up."

Joe tried but wavered and slumped back down. Taavi nodded to two of his men. Each slung their rifles back over one shoulder and moved towards the driver. With one of Joe's arms in each of their hands, they lifted him to his feet.

"Alright, Joe. Now talk. No more playing around."

"I was telling you the truth, I don't know where she is. They went out diving this morning and were supposed to be back by now. I don't know what happened. I tried calling them, but there's no answer."

Taavi thought back to the phone calls he had watched Joe make. The explanation seemed legit. Joe's compliance appeared to be intact now, so there was no reason to use more force. He softened his demeanor to encourage more transparency.

"I didn't know she was in this much trouble. I just thought she was a silly girl who got into a tight spot and wanted to get home... I swear."

Taavi narrowed his eyes. "Something has been bugging me about this plan of hers. How were you planning to get her over the border?"

Joe's face crumpled into a sorrowful state and tears gathered in his eyes.

"Oh, come on now. What is it?"

"I-I uh..."

The man seemed terrified of what might come from his answer. Taavi needed to ease off.

"I promise you, if you don't hesitate in answering my other questions and help in finding her, I won't direct any liability to you. You have my word."

Joe eyed him but didn't speak.

"Look," Taavi added, "my employer just wishes to have her stand to account for her crimes, and if you can aid me in doing that, I will consider us even. Deal?"

"A-alright."

Joe shook free of the men's support and moved past a few of the passengers. Taavi was about to stop him but hesitated as Joe started pushing a few of the passengers out of the way. Joe opened one of the luggage compartments. He leaned in and pointing inside for Taavi to look.

"I built a hidden compartment in this one," Joe said swallowing heavily as he straightened and turned to face him.

Taavi bent and took a look inside.

"Quite clever. And don't worry." Taavi said standing upright again. "I don't care about what you've done or will do with that thing. Just get me the girl, and I'll forget all about it."

Joe closed the compartment.

"So what time did they leave this morning?"

"Around 8:30 a.m."

"And when were they supposed to be back?"

"I told the instructor that they had to be back no later than 10:30 a.m."

Taavi checked his watch. "Hmmm... they're now over thirty minutes late."

Taav walked to the front of the bus and looked out over the water. There was barely any movement on the beach and no sign of the dive team returning.

"Which direction should they be coming from?"

"South."

"How many will be with her?"

"Five. Oh, and the dive instructor... so six."

"How far out did they go?"

"I'm not sure."

Taavi spun back to see if Joe was being uncooperative or if he really didn't know. Joe's face looked honest.

"Um... I can answer that." The sister of the twin he had threatened stepped forward. Taavi nodded his approval.

"We went out earlier today to the same dive site. The instructor drove the boat south and slightly west, near the center of the gulf. The whole trip took less than two hours, so they should be back by now."

Taavi paced in front of the group as he thought about what his next move should be. Spinning back around, Taavi walked up to one of his men.

"Go to the hotel and report there is a boat missing and that they aren't answering any attempts to contact, then–"

A man's voice, yelling from behind him, interrupted the last of Taavi's instructions. Two men were running towards them. Taavi readied his rifle.

Joe stepped forward. "Omar, what's wrong?"

Out of breath, the man Joe had called Omar, bent over and placed both hands on his knees. As he wheezed, his eyes did a once-over of Taavi and his men.

"There's... been an accident. I'm not sure the extent of it, but Moha is heading out with the rescue team, so we'll know more soon."

"I need to be on that boat. Have they left yet?" Taavi asked

"Wait, who are you?"

Taavi didn't have time for this. He raised his rifle to Omar's head.

"Tell me... NOW!"

"Hey man, calm down. I don't want any trouble. They're at the dock, north of the hotel. You might make it if you run."

"Don't get in our way," Taavi threatened as he nudged Omar with the barrel of his rifle. "And Joe, remember our deal. Don't interfere."

Joe emphatically shook his head.

"Good. You and you," Taavi nodded to two of his men, "stay with them until you hear from me. Don't let anyone leave."

Taavi took off running, the other three of his men in tow.

CHAPTER 25

"Hailey?" Ryan's soft words came from behind her, but she made no effort to turn and face him.

"Hailey, are you OK?"

"No, I'm not."

The calm hopelessness in her tone seemed to cause Ryan to pause, he didn't speak.

"Do you know what happened to the boat?" she asked.

"No, not yet. Holly won't talk about it. Hailey, I know you're angry right now and hurting, we all are. But you can't just run away."

Hailey turned towards him. "I know… it's stupid, isn't it? Where am I going to go?" Hailey said with a forced chuckle. "I can't very well swim home now can I." Seeing that the joke fell flat, Hailey looked away, embarrassed.

"That's not what I mean, and I think you know that. You can't just leave them, Hailey."

Remorse flooded her. Hailey hated herself for leaving. Seeing her selfishness blaring in a moment of other people's tragedy felt disgusting. She forced herself to glance at Ryan to see if the same disgust reflected on his face. She was surprised to see that it didn't.

"I don't want this to sound contrived," he said, "but I hope you see and understand that often a teacher is often silent during a test."

Hailey didn't respond to his suggestion. His words stabbed at her feelings of justification over her anger, and regret started to drip out. She closed her eyes to stop the leak and keep her rationalizations intact. Ryan continued.

"All of this is really overwhelming for me, so I can't imagine what it must be like for you after all you've gone through. But do you really think this is all happenstance?"

Hailey thought about it for a moment.

"I don't know. Yeah, how could it not." She knew there was no point in being anything less than honest.

"Well, I don't think it is. Take a step back from it all and just look at it as a whole."

Ryan stopped talking, so Hailey did just as he had asked and ran through the list of events in her head. An orphan New Yorker meeting a roommate whose parents lived in Saudi Arabia, deciding on a surprise trip to a foreign country she wasn't equipped to visit alone, getting kidnapped by a man to become his wife which led her back to a relationship with God, only now to be shipwrecked. Upon reaching up to the current moment of floating in the Gulf of Aqaba, Hailey's mind started to see the crazy unlikeness for all this to have happened by chance. However, because most of the events were shrouded in such tragedy, the realization didn't bring her any comfort.

If this isn't by chance, Hailey thought to herself, *then it wasn't that God didn't stop it from happening... it meant that God... allowed, maybe even caused it all? Is that possible?* The thought brought tears to her eyes.

"Hey, where are you right now?" Ryan asked.

"Honestly, I feel like I'm drowning. If this isn't all by chance, then that means that it was planned. But how can it be planned, Ryan? How could Anna's parents' death or Fabina's mean anything good?"

"Look, I can't say that I fully understand it all myself. But what I do know for sure is that He is love, that nothing happens without His knowledge or control, and that He can bring beauty from ashes." Ryan paused.

"OK..." Hailey wasn't sure where he was going with this.

"Think of Job's story," Ryan continued. "Everything that happened to him was still under God's authority."

Ryan looked at her to see if she was with him, but she wasn't.

"What do you mean?"

"Well, Satan was permitted to act, but God commanded to what extent. He set the parameters. Again, I don't claim to convey that it is easy to understand. But I do see how big God is, and so His plan is far bigger than we can grasp. I've experienced His love, as well as the crazy intricacies of parts of His plan. I know that His love and his control over everything are easily made to be opposites in our minds with our limited understanding and perspective... but I choose to hold onto what it says in Romans 8 - 'And we know that God causes all things to work together for good to those who love God, and are called according to His purpose.'"

Ryan stopped talking and smiled at her. Hailey didn't respond. Everything seemed so chaotic, so out of control. Hearing the familiar verse people often spouted during difficult times didn't bring her any solace. It annoyed her.

She wanted to snap at Ryan, to push him away. She stopped herself. He was just trying to help. She still wanted to run away from it all. Yet an unfamiliar feeling circled her: whatever lay at the end of that familiar road seemed more ominous than this path paved with Ryan's words. So she stayed put.

Hailey's muscles started to ache from treading water. She now regretted taking off her dive vest. She flipped onto her back and floated on the surface of the water to give her body a rest.

"Tired?"

"Yeah."

"Hailey, James and Holly need us."

Hailey knew he was right. She willed her mind to permit her empathy for her friends to push her into action. At first, the emotion threatened to overtake her, but with a few deep breaths, the compassion succeeded in scattering her confusion and fear.

"OK," she finally responded.

"Why don't you get on my back and I'll swim you-"

An enormous roar pricked their ears. Ryan stopped mid offer. They both snapped their head around to see a sixty-something foot yacht in the distance. It was coming right for their boat.

Without another word from either of them, they took off and headed back, swimming side by side as fast as they could. Yet again Hailey's body cried out for her to stop, but with the adrenaline surging through her, she was able to ignore the pain and push through.

Minutes later they were beside their boat, just as the yacht cut its engine.

=======

The boat was a futuristic-looking, double-decker vessel. Lines of people peered at them through the windows. Ryan swam up to Armando and Holly, who were now in the water, supporting Jack between them. Their own boat was still afloat, but the fire had now spread towards the bow.

"What's going on?" Ryan whispered to them.

"I don't know," Armando said.

Holly shrugged her shoulders.

Ryan looked around for James and spotted him a few yards off, still holding Fabina in his arms. He was no longer crying or trying to wake her up. A stone-cold blankness covered his face.

Someone on the boat called out to them in Arabic. The captain of the boat leaned over the side. Armando answered. Ryan listened to the exchange. The captain left and went back into the cabin.

"They're from Jordan. This is a passenger ferry from Jordan to Egypt. The captain is going to send out a distress call for us. Can you believe it?"

"Actually, yeah I think I can," Ryan said as he looked over at Hailey.

He reached over and squeezed her shoulder. Moments later the captain rejoined them.

"I put out the call," he said in English, "but it's going to take them a while to get here. You'll just have to wait and–"

"Armando, we can't wait," Holly cut in. "Jack…" Her words trailed off as she looked down at Jack, still unconscious.

"I know," Armando said. "Captain, our friend has DCS. We need to get him to a hospital as soon as possible."

"Get the oxygen." the captain called to one of his ship crew.

The man ran back inside.

"Where are you from?" the captain asked.

"Hailey and I are American. James, over there, is English."

"I'm from Australia," Holly said.

"What about the other girl?"

"She… didn't make it," Hailey answered as fresh tears

formed in her eyes. Hailey turned away but remained holding onto his arm.

"And you?" the captain asked Armando.

"Jordan, actually."

The crew member returned holding a canister of oxygen with a mask-style nozzle. Armando took it from him, and with Holly's help, they supported Jack's head so he could breathe in the oxygen.

The captain looked around at them all and squinted his eyes. "OK, well I can take him." He pointed to Jack. "We are headed to the port at Nuweibaa, and we can ensure he gets to the hospital. You can meet back with him there."

"I'm sorry, but I can't just leave him with you. Please, can I come?" Holly asked.

"What happened to you?" the captain asked her, nodding to her arm.

"I burnt my arm in the explosion. I-I need to get it looked at."

"Fine, I can take you both."

Holly looked over at Ryan and Hailey. "I couldn't possibly do this all on my own. Can they come too?" Holly begged.

The captain narrowed his eyes. "Fine, the four of you." He turned away and started talking to the crewman.

Holly looked at Ryan. "I know you want to get back, but–"

"No, whatever you need. We're here."

"No, that's not what I meant. Think about it. If you guys come with us, you can catch a plane from Egypt to wherever Anna wants to meet you. If you wait here, who knows how long it could take. You will be waiting for a flight either way. But if you stay, you'll have the wait for the rescue boat, and then you still have the drive to Jordan. Oh, and you can skip hiding under the bus."

THE SAND BRIDE

The option did sound more appealing. Getting out of Saudi was their ultimate goal and taking this ferry would probably get them to Anna sooner. There was also the added bonus of not needing to try to deal with what might or might not await them at the border.

Hailey squeezed his arm. "What about James? We can't just leave him."

Ryan looked over at James. Hailey was right.

"I'm sorry," the captain said, "but I can't take the... the body. The port won't allow it. And I can't take you," he pointed to Armando, "With you being from Jordan, you won't be allowed into Egypt. Unless you have an Egyptian visa by chance."

"No, I don't. But that's alright. I will stay with James and my boat until help arrives. My team is back in Saudi and can help us."

"Armando, are you sure?" Ryan asked.

"Yes, you guys should go if you need to. There is no chance James is going to leave Fabina with me and go with you. I'll take care of him."

Armando was right. Ryan would have never left Hailey.

Ryan nodded. "Yeah, alright."

"Armando, I can leave you with one of our life rafts." The captain left the deck and soon returned with a square bag.

"Do you know how to use this?" he asked Armando.

"Yes, sir, I do."

"Very well. Let's get the rest of you on board."

CHAPTER 26

Five of the deck crew assisted in their boarding. Jack was lifted on first via a backboard, ropes, and a couple pulleys. Hailey was quite impressed with their efficiency. Holly went next, and Hailey followed. Ryan came up last.

By the time Hailey had her feet on the deck, Armando had engaged the life raft and had climbed into it. He called out to James, trying to get his attention.

"James! James! Can you swim over here with Fabina? Do you want some help?"

Again there was no answer. James didn't even look over at him but continued to float where he was, staring blankly out over the water as he held Fabina.

"James?" Armando tried again with more empathy in his voice.

Again with no response. Armando slid back into the water and made his way over to James. Hailey couldn't stop herself. In one swift motion, she walked to the railing and dove in.

"Hailey!" Holly yelled. "What are you doing? We have to go!"

"Just a minute," Hailey called back without looking.

She would never forgive herself if she didn't say a proper

goodbye to him. Guilt still stabbed at her heart for swimming away from him earlier and for leaving Sarna in the prison the way she had. She couldn't make the same mistake again.

Hailey ignored Holly's protests and closed the gap between her and James.

Swimming up to them, Armando was working on taking Fabina. James didn't protest but looked at Armando with sad, accepting eyes. Fabina slipped from James's arms and flopped lifelessly against Armando's chest.

James's lip started to quiver. Hailey swam up right in front of him.

"James, I'm so sorry." Hailey's chin trembled as she spoke.

James didn't speak nor make any mournful cry. He just looked at her with a heartbreaking sadness. Hailey placed her hands on either of James's shoulders and pulled herself up so she could reach his cheek. She gave him a soft kiss, then moved her mouth to his ear and whispered to him.

"I'm so sorry that I have to leave you. But I will find you again, and I will be there for you in any way I can. You are not alone. This will not destroy you. You are loved."

As the last words exited her mouth, James's numb demeanor broke. His broad shoulders shook under Hailey's hand. She tried to hold on to them as tight as she could, but their sheer size made it difficult.

The sound of a boat drawing near drew Hailey's head up. The ferry was coming around them at idling speed.

"James, Hailey, I'm so sorry," Holly called out to them, "but we have to go. Jack's breathing is getting worse."

"Yes, of course," Hailey said. She gave James's shoulders another squeeze.

"James, I'm so sorry," Holly said again as Hailey climbed

back on board.

With Holly's words triggering more tears in James's eyes, he didn't reply. Instead, he turned and swam after Armando.

"Do you think he'll be OK?" Hailey asked Ryan as the ferry turned and picked up speed.

"I don't know. I don't think I would be if I ever lost you."

Hailey buried her face into his shoulder. She couldn't bear the thought.

=======

The boat was just pulling away from the dock when Taavi spotted it.

"Wait!"

A man at the stern looked up but made no attempt to move or alert the others on board.

"Wait!" Taavi screamed again as he pushed his body to run faster.

This time the man got the captain's attention. Following the pointing of the man at the stern, the captain saw them and cut the engine.

The ride out to the dive site was uncomfortable. Taavi's anticipation that his search was coming to an end made it hard to relax. He couldn't stop fidgeting. The boat bouncing on the tops of the white-capped waves added to the knots in his stomach.

The captain of the boat kept eyeing him and his men. Taavi ignored him and pretended not to notice.

Ten minutes ticked by, then another five. Taavi squinted towards the horizon to see if he could see anything. Nothing, except a dark oblong shape, standing vertically on the horizon. As they got closer, it came into focus - billowing smoke rising into the sky.

Oh, no!

Drawing nearer, the damage was evident. The entire boat smoldered and a few flames still crackled on the bow. A life raft floated close by. Taavi scanned the two faces peering at them. Hailey's wasn't among them.

Taavi swore under his breath.

What am I going to tell Ehsan?

His heart felt like a dead lump in his stomach. Taavi closed his eyes to think.

If she's dead, what will Ehsan do? I hope I don't get fired for this. But, it's not like there was anything else I could have done.

The boat slowed its approach.

"Is everyone OK?" the captain asked.

"No! We're not," snapped one man.

By his accent, Taavi could tell he was an Englishman. The man's eyes dropped to his lap. Taavi looked in the raft, following the man's gaze. The man's large frame supported the head and shoulders of a woman laying in the raft. It wasn't Hailey. The woman looked to be sleeping or unconscious. When the boat made its way up next to the raft, Taavi saw that neither was true. The woman was dead.

Taavi's fists tightened. "Where is the other woman?"

"Which one?" the other man asked.

"Are you kidding me?"

"Settle down!" the captain ordered. "Let's get them on board before the interrogations start."

Once all three people were on board, the Englishman, James, barely spoke. He sat near the dead girl and glared at them.

Armando, the dive instructor, was more helpful. Neither men knew the cause of the explosion, but something happened with or near the engine.

Taavi's phone buzzed in his pocket. He ignored it. He needed to find out more.

Apparently, the dead woman had been right near the explosion and had been thrown from the boat. The Englishman had been closer to the bow and wasn't harmed. The other woman on board suffered burns on one arm. There had been four people down diving when it occurred, one of whom was Hailey.

"So where are the Americans now?"

"What's it to you?" James said.

This man's snarky attitude was starting to grate on him. Taavi moved his rifle onto his lap. He wasn't in the mood for this.

A nervous laugh came from Armando. "Alright, let's take a breath. No need to get heated."

James leaned forward. "Armando, there is no reason he needs to know about those who aren't here."

"Sorry, James, but that's not really how things work over here. Whatever these men want to know, it's best we tell them. The reasons just don't matter." Armando looked at Taavi and gave an apologetic shrug. "The two Americans and the two Aussies went on the ferry over to Egypt. That's all we know."

"How long ago?"

"I'm not sure, maybe an hour?"

Damn!! Maybe it would have been better if Hailey was dead. If she's in Egypt, there is no way I can follow her. I don't have that kind of clearance.

The boat started back up and swung around to return to the

Saudi shoreline. Taavi watched helplessly as what remained of Hailey's boat finally succumbed to the waves and sunk below the surface. The sight angered him. The boat seemed to be mocking the end of his search with the end of its life. Taavi sneered and turned his back on the boat. He hated symbolism.

Taavi frantically combed through his options.

Hailey would most likely want to get out of Egypt and back home as soon as possible. So I really only have one option.

Taavi grabbed his phone. A voicemail notification blinked on the screen. He'd have to check that later. Taavi scanned his contact list and found the number, dialed, and held his breath.

Answer! Come on. Come on!

The call didn't last long, but the outcome proved fruitful. It was a last-ditch effort at best, but what other alternative did he have?

Taavi wasn't thrilled about owing that annoying little man multiple favors, but it would be worth it if it worked. Even if the man's help didn't amount to anything, reporting back to Ehsan that he had literally done everything he could to track the girl down, would make it worth it.

Satisfied, Taavi clicked on the voicemail icon.

"Taavi, it's Ehsan. I hope you've made some progress in Haql because our hands have been tied. You need to immediately remove all the roadblocks. The defense minister is furious. I don't see how he could know what we were up to, so my guess is that it's because of work. Considering I was put in charge of assisting the foreigners in getting back home, I can see how our roadblocks could portray the opposite. Anyways, they can't stay up, so take care of it. If you have any issues, contact me immediately."

Taavi hung up the phone, scowling.

"Trouble?" James asked in a cocky tone.

Taavi ignored him. He turned his back to the man and dialed the head office to clear the roadblocks. It only took minutes and went smoothly. Ehsan would be pleased. He phoned Ehsan. There was no answer. He tried again. Still nothing.

For a moment Taavi considered calling and canceling the deal he had made.

Nah, it's out of Saudi. There's no harm in it.

CHAPTER 27

Once Jack was being taken care of by the deck crew, Holly had fallen apart. She cried softly and rocked back and forth in a seat near the window. The movement made it difficult for the crew member trying to clean her burned arm. Holly's tears didn't seem to be from the pain of her wounds. She kept quietly repeating, it's all my fault, to herself.

Hailey wondered if the shock of the whole event was starting to hit her. Hailey went over to her and sat slowly, so not to startle her. The plastic seat was cold from the air conditioning blowing in the cabin. The few passengers in that section had moved over to give them space. Hailey was grateful. Holly looked like she could use the privacy.

Hailey reached out to Holly's shoulder.

"Holly, what do you mean? How is this your fault?"

Holly looked up at her with wet eyes. Her lip quivered again, and she dropped her head back down, squeezing her eyes shut.

"I shouldn't have touched it. I've never driven a boat before. What was I thinking?"

Holly's question seemed more directed at herself than to Hailey, but she still wanted to know what happened.

"What do you mean?"

"Ouch," Holly winced.

"Sorry," said the crewman, "I'm almost done. "

Holly looked up and with her free hand wiped her nose as she sniffed. "The lot of you were taking so long, longer than we did. I was worried we were going to miss the bus or at least delay the group. So I thought that I would start the boat to get your attention. We were already late. I didn't know what else to do."

Hailey was confused. "OK... but what does starting the boat have to do with anything?"

"I didn't think there was much to it. It's a vehicle, right? So I just turned the key." Holly paused and looked past the crewman's shoulder towards where Jack was laying, still unconscious. "Jack said that I forgot to clear the tanks. Whatever that means. He didn't get time to explain it before... he collapsed."

Hailey didn't know either.

"A second after I turned the key the whole back of the boat blew up. Fabina was..." Holly's eyes filled with fresh tears and her face crumbled with pain. "Hailey, what have I done?"

Holly dropped her head to her chest again and sobbed. Hailey's empathy ached for her. She put her arm around Holly, hoping to bring her a sliver of comfort.

"Are you almost finished?" Hailey asked the crewman.

He nodded with compassionate eyes.

With the placement of a few more pieces of tape on the gauze, he rose and left them. Hailey pulled Holly into her arms and held her as she cried. Hailey couldn't help but cry with her when Holly raised her arms and held on so tightly.

Minutes past as they held each other and mourned for Fabina, and for James, who would forever be changed by losing her.

Their sadness had dulled to silent tears and a few sniffles. Hailey heard someone approaching. It was Ryan.

"Jack's breathing is stronger, but he still won't wake up. The captain said that the doctors at the hospital are the only ones who can do more for him. The crew will still monitor him though and will make sure he's comfortable." Ryan looked at her and smiled, then looked at Holly. "Can you tell me what happened?"

Holly looked at her hands as they wrung themselves around each other. She said nothing.

Hailey shrugged. "There was something about starting the boat without clearing the tanks?"

"Oh... yeah. In the engine compartment fumes from the fuel can build up. There's a blower switch that needs to be turned on for a few minutes before starting the engine or the flumes can... explode. Oh, Holly, I'm so sorry."

"I can't believe I caused all this."

Ryan and Hailey exchanged an empathetic glance. Hailey wanted to offer Holly some supportive words, but what was there to say?

"Holly, it was a mistake and something that could have just as easily happened to me. I had no clue about that blower thing either."

Her words still sounded kind of lame, but it was all she had. Ryan shifted around and took the seat on the other side of Holly.

"Come here," he said.

Holly leaned into Ryan's arms.

"Shhh. We'll get through this."

As Ryan spoke and held Holly, he looked at Hailey and

raised his eyebrows, signaling that the words were meant for her as well. Hailey pursed her lips and nodded back.

"Sorry to interrupt," the captain whispered as he walked up.

"No, not at all. Please sit," Ryan said.

The captain lowered himself onto the bench directly in front of them.

"We're just a few minutes out, and we should go over some things. I can give you each a Sinai visa stamp. This is a fourteen-day pass to the Sinai region, but it should work for you. You have to understand that this will not give you access to places outside of the Sinai region."

"What's out of the Sinai region?" Hailey asked.

"Places like Luxor or Cairo. You need a whole different visa for those areas. I would suggest that you head to Taba as soon as you can. They have an airport. It's about ninety minutes from the port. You each have your passports, right?"

Hailey's hope deflated, she couldn't believe her foolishness. Her passport and Ryan's were still in the little bag attached to her dive vest, floating somewhere in the gulf. Her throat constricted.

"Yes, I have mine," Holly said.

"We have ours too."

"No, Ryan, we don't," Hailey moaned. "I took off my vest, remember?" Hailey bit her lip in anger at her stupidity.

The captain rubbed his neck, "Well that will be a–"

"No, Hailey, I have them," Ryan rose and walked over to where he had taken off his equipment. Turning back to face them, he held up the dry bag. "I took it off your vest when you swam away."

"Oh, you wonderful man."

Relief flooded all over her body.

"Alright then," the captain said. "Give them here, and I'll get you the stamp."

They all handed them over and watched him leave.

The three of them sat in silence. Hailey's mind raced to find something comforting to say to Holly. She dismissed each thought, they were weak. She resorted to holding Holly's hand and rubbing her back.

When the captain returned, a crewman was with him. The captain handed back their passports. They each gave him a thank you.

"It's my pleasure."

The captain turned to the crewman, who handed over a large garbage bag.

"When the other passengers saw what happened and heard you were coming with us, they all rummaged through their luggage and found each of you a change of clothes."

He handed the bag to Holly.

"I hope things start looking up for you," he told her, smiling. "Now hurry up and change. We will be docking shortly." Then he left.

Holly looked at her and Ryan, but this time with tears of thankfulness and an astonished smile. Holly put Jack's clothes on the bench. Hailey retreated to the bathroom with hers.

When she returned, the ferry was taking its place in line to dock. She took a seat, feeling much more comfortable in the new clothes. The last time she felt this familiarity and level of ease was on the flight to Germany before changing into the abaya.

The flowing, tan, cotton pants hung loosely around her legs. She could tell that even outside in the heat, they would be comfortable, as would the white long-sleeve top. Smoothing out the fabric of her pants with both hands, a young woman caught her eye from a few rows to her left. The woman smiled at her. Hailey smiled back.

She looked to be only a few years older than Hailey. The woman pointed down to the floor around Hailey. Hailey glanced down. Seeing nothing, she looked back up. The woman smiled and pointed to her own pants. Hailey noticed that she was wearing similar pants but in black.

Oh, the clothes are hers.

Hailey put both her hands together and mouthed thank you over and over as she bobbed her hands. The woman moved her hands into the shape of a heart. Warmth spread through Hailey. She nodded and mirrored the heart back to the woman.

Their gaze to the other broke as the boat pitched to one side as it nudged the dock, causing everyone to lurch to one side. Awkward laughter broke out all throughout the cabin.

"Aasif," the captain said. "Sorry."

The soft laughter continued for a couple more moments as the boat came to a full stop and the engines dulled to silence. Ryan, Hailey, and Holly stood to gather up their few belongings. Holly stopped a crewman as he passed.

"Can you see to it that these get back to the dive shop in Jordan? And see if any of the women who gave us clothes, would like these," Holly said as she handed him a bag with the veilkinis in it.

"Yes, ma'am."

"That was a nice thought," Hailey said.

"I think it's the least I could do for Armando after destroying his boat." Holly gave a nervous laugh. "See how I make jokes?" she gave another awkward laugh.

Hailey chuckled back. "It's nice seeing you smile. We'll all get through this, I promise."

Holly shifted her weight and looked away. "Let's get Jack off as soon as we can, OK? I have no idea how we're going to get him to the hospital. I hope it's not far."

It turned out that Holly didn't need to worry. The crewmen carried Jack out on his stretcher, and upon reaching the end of the dock, there was an ambulance there waiting for them.

"I took the liberty to arrange things for Jack," the captain said, coming up behind them.

Holly's eyes teared. She grabbed him into a bear hug. Hailey had to stifle a chuckle when the captain's face turned bright red. He stood there frozen, arms stiff and stretched out a foot from either side of Holly's waist. When the captain didn't return her hug, Holly pulled back.

"Oh, I'm sorry," she said, looking self-conscious. "But... I hope you know how thankful we are to you and each of your crew."

"We all are," Ryan said.

"Make sure you all get home safely, don't delay."

"We won't. Thank you again."

The captain left to assist his crew and the other passengers. A lump caught in Hailey's throat. She turned away. The medical team had already loaded and secured Jack in the rig. One of the medics approached them.

"We have done a quick assessment of your friend. The fact that he hasn't regained consciousness after being given oxygen from the boat crew does have us concerned. I would suggest that we transport him down to Sharm El-Sheikh. It's about two hours south from here. They have a state-of-the-art recompression chamber, and I think it's the best option for him at this point. But we should leave as soon as my team is ready."

"Yes, of course," Hailey said.

"No!" Holly shook her head.

"What do you mean, No?"

"I mean… yes, that's where he should go, but you guys aren't coming with us." Holly smiled at each of them. "You guys need to get home. If you go north, you can get to an airport in, what an hour and a half? Or maybe less?"

"Yeah. But Holly…"

"No, it's OK. If you come with us, there won't be anything for you to do and you'll just be waiting around. You won't be able to get to the airport for days maybe. Anna has been through a lot. She needs you, and I think you need her too."

Hailey felt sick. "But I hate to leave you. What if you need us?"

The paramedic cleared his throat, "We'll take good care of them."

"See? I'll be alright and so will Jack." Holly reached out and pulled Hailey into a hug. "We'll be fine. Now go."

Hailey held her tighter.

"You just make sure to find us later, OK?" Holly chuckled. "When everything calms down?"

"Definitely. Oh, wait, the cell phone!" Hailey pulled back and looked at her. "Do you have it with…" she trailed off, realizing there was little chance that Holly even thought about it. Even if she had, it would be soaked and ruined.

"I-I'm sorry, Hailey. I left it on the boat."

"No, no, forget it. It should have been the least of your worries."

"Wait a sec," Ryan said.

He jogged over to the medic in the ambulance. He returned with a pen and paper.

"Here," he said as he wrote. "Call us as soon as you can." He handed the paper to Holly, "This one here, is my brother's number. I'll be sure to get word to him as soon as I can. So if we each keep calling him with updates, we'll know where and how each other is. Deal?"

"Deal."

"OK, everyone, everything is all set. We need to get going."

After another hug, Holly jumped in the ambulance.

Seeing the ambulance speeding away with her friends inside, caused tears to gather in her eyes. Ryan's hand slipped into hers. Hailey only drew her eyes away once the ambulance disappeared around a corner.

"I hope Jack's OK," she said.

"I'm sure he will be. The medics seemed fairly confident he'll show improvement when they get him to Sharm El-Sheikh."

"Yeah, he'll be fine," she said. But it was more to convince herself than in agreement.

"Hey... you ready to get out of here?"

"So ready!"

Ryan cupped her head in his hands and gave her a kiss.

"Let's go find a ride to the airport."

As Ryan led the way to the port office, Hailey stole one more glance to the Ferry. The captain was nowhere in sight, but she offered a silent thank you to him and the crew as she followed Ryan.

Hold on, Anna. We're coming.

Hailey chewed on the inside of her cheek and hoped Anna wouldn't panic if she tried to call and they didn't answer.

God, give her peace... please... until we can get to a phone. And please, heal Jack. He needs you.

CHAPTER 28

The discussion with the harbor master was less than helpful. He seemed annoyed with them and merely waved them off. Exiting the port office out towards the main street, a long row of taxis sat waiting for passengers. The first cab refused, but the second cab driver agreed to take them north. He didn't speak much English, but they managed and climbed in.

Hailey rolled her window down farther. The warm wind felt better than the stale air inside the un-airconditioned cab.

"Ryan, I've been thinking about what you said," Hailey said once the port was out of sight.

"Oh, yeah?"

"But I'm having trouble with it." Hailey's honesty tasted bad in her mouth, but she refused to put on the old mask of pretending to agree when she didn't.

"Which part?"

"That God is in control of all this, like He caused it or something."

"Yeah. Honestly… I did too at first. Years ago, we were doing this study on the names of God, and I was faced with some pretty shocking verses from Deuteronomy and Isaiah. They were hard to swallow at first."

"Do you remember them?" she asked.

"The general gist of it, yeah. The one in Deuteronomy was about God telling us that He was the only one that puts to death and gives life. Also... there was something about Him wounding and healing."

"That doesn't sound like Him. It's not very loving," Hailey expressed. "What did the verse in Isaiah say?"

"Similar. That He was the one who does it all: causing well-being and creating calamity."

"What name were you studying?"

"El Elyon, which means God Most High. But after looking in the book of James and thinking it all through... it makes sense."

"How so?" Hailey was feeling incredibly uncomfortable with this new idea, but she was even more curious about Ryan's take on it.

"Well, I came to see that if I really do follow the one true God, if there really is no other, then I have to decide to follow Him or walk away. But regardless of my decision, it doesn't minimize His rule. I think for years I steered clear of some ideas that were challenging because if they didn't line up with what I understood, then I would be forced into a position of either ignoring the new information or admit that I was wrong. The latter was an option that scared me to no end. If I was wrong about something, then I used to worry that it could mean I was wrong about everything. So I fought to not really look at things that didn't fit with my overall understanding. But then I realized that I was missing a huge section of this all."

"What's that?"

"That my fear only exists because I don't really know Him. Regardless if I agree or understand all that He chooses to do, He doesn't cease to exist, and it is only my perception of Him that needs to change. So I had a choice to make: either I get to know Him and submit myself under His amazing love and higher wisdom or stay in this place of avoidance and allow my fear to cast this ugly shadow over my faith whenever circumstances didn't meet my expectations."

"Or you could just walk away."

"True. But with all that I've seen Him do, I couldn't possibly go back to thinking He doesn't exist. So if I am firm in the fact that He is... well, just is... and that I'm not willing to walk away, then I either get to know Him and let Him speak for Himself, or I push Him into a box that fits with my preconceived ideas. Ones like: how He should be and act, and how tragedies in my life are always ultimately bad and when I like or want something, it is always deemed good. But seeing how that would mean that God could never exist in that truth, that option is impossible."

"I don't understand?"

"Well, think about it. If I forced Him into a box, I wouldn't be worshiping Him. I would be worshiping an idol that I created, one that fits into my understanding. So if I shut myself off from my theology being challenged and allowing Him to correct or adjust my thinking, I am saying that I know and understand it all. Which... then kind of points to me being lord of my own life."

"But aren't you worried that you'll open yourself up to false teaching with that view? What about guarding yourself?"

Ryan smiled. "Yeah, I used to get quite anxious about all that. But then I realized that resulting anxiety is me leaning on my ability to discern and figure it all out - something I couldn't possibly do. So that is where I come back to look at Him as El Elyon. Like it says in Jude 1:24 'To Him who is able to keep you from stumbling, and to make you stand in the presence of His glory blameless with great joy,'" Ryan's eyes drifted off, and his lips curled. It looked like he remembered something. "El Elyon's got it, all of it, including me. I trust Him with it and bring it all to Him to correct, add to, and to teach."

Hailey's warning bells went off. Where was Ryan going with all this? She shifted in her seat. "But... how can we serve someone who causes all the horrid things?"

"I think I need to be clear that this world was not His desire. We were the ones that chose to walk away from perfect. He didn't create sin and doesn't cause it. But now that sin is here, it wasn't like it surprised Him. He foreknew it all, He still maintains His control, and nothing can thwart His will."

"I don't know, Ryan."

"Think about it. If God is truly El Elyon, God Most High, how could He not have control over it all? If something or someone else has more control over something and He merely turned it around for good, then He would cease to be God Most High. And that is an even more uncomfortable thought than serving a God of love who does things we don't understand. The latter can seem awful to us at the time in our limited understanding, but the former is terrifying. It would mean evil at times is ultimately in control. Remember Job."

"OK... yeah, I guess I see your point. But it kind of just solidifies my question. Are you really alright serving a god like that?"

"Definitely. If God is God Most High and if God is love, then I can fully trust that He is big enough to bring it all together and to act justly. Just think about it... this world is just temporal. Don't you see that there is so much more going on than what we see?"

He paused for a moment.

"Look," he continued. "I don't want to Sunday School this. But I do think there is something *huge* here. God is love, His creation is destroying themselves, He brings *everything* together to wake His creation up so that they will realize they were not meant to live apart from Him. To show them all that He made them to be and all that He is. He also sent His only son so that return to Him is possible. If you look at it as a whole, everything turns from being confusing to being beautiful."

Ryan stopped talking. Hailey rolled his words around in her mind. She had definitely seen that all play out since she left New York. She got to see God's hand moving her towards the scariest moments of her whole life, but she also saw such tenderness and love. Yet still, there was this nagging at the back of her mind that made it hard to accept what happened on the boat. She had come back to Him, so why did God cause all of that? What was the point?

Ryan grabbed her hand but didn't say anything. He looked at their hands. A look flashed in his eyes, causing his forehead to wrinkle. He looked concerned, but he remained silent, and the concern disappeared just as quickly as it came. She gave his hand a quick squeeze before turning to look out the window. She needed time to process it all before talking more.

She stretched in her seat.

Up until that point, before she left her faith after her family's death, she had always looked at God as staying just one step ahead of evil as it ran rampant around the world. But now she questioned if that stance left room for her to subconsciously think God wasn't ultimately in control. Had that been a large source of her fear? Ryan's words made sense in a theological sense but in experiential?

How can I serve someone who has such a hand in horrible things? Is

Ryan right? Or are we really off base on this idea?

Hailey's thoughts drifted to the death of her family.

Exactly, she thought to herself, *how could an accident that killed four people be good, or God ordained? How could my family's death be chosen by Him?*

Hailey allowed those thoughts to mull over in her mind. After their death, many people had tried to console her with words that this wasn't what God wanted, but that it happened for a reason, and that she should run to Him for comfort. But if she were honest, it just angered her. Their words seemed so contradictory. If it wasn't what God wanted, how was there any meaning in it?

Then Ryan's words returned to her.

So if God didn't cause that, then does that mean He isn't God Most High? If He didn't plan for and allow my family's death, then does that mean that something is above Him, outside His knowledge and control, making the tragedy possible? Was all this the reason there was no comfort in peoples words?

Hailey's mind jumped to Sarna.

Did God make those men rape her? Was He in charge of that as well? No! That was a sin. So that can't be true. But because He is God Most High, what is His role in that? My family's death was a circumstance, and Sarna's rape was sin, so does that make a difference?

Ugh, this hurts my head. I don't understand this.

Hailey rubbed her temples with her free hand and then rested her neck on the back of the seat, closing her eyes. Hailey hoped the ride wouldn't last much longer. She was anxious to get on a plane and get to Anna. She needed and longed for the distraction.

The trip took another half hour once she had laid back to rest, but her mind hadn't made any further progress in understanding. Hailey opened her eyes as they pulled up to the Taba airport. It loomed above the cab.

Horizontal burgundy stripes covered most of the exterior walls of the white building. Tall windows, containing differently shaped panes of glass rose from the ground, stopping a few feet short of the roof. Each of the three sections of the building attached to the other, yet the middle part rose another story above the other two. A yellow wood door sat slightly off center, looking a little out of place against the other colors.

Hailey followed Ryan inside.

"Ready?" he asked.

"You have no idea."

After waiting for a few groups to pass them, Ryan found a path up to the flight boards. Hailey glanced around as he scanned the board. A fair number of people bustled about for such a small airport.

"There," Ryan said getting her attention, "that flight leaves in an hour. But, if I'm reading this right, it looks like these are all charter flights. Maybe we can get a seat on one? Let's go ask."

They made their way over to the blue ropes that zigzagged out in front of the ticket desk and waited their turn. The man behind the counter on the far left waved them over.

"Do you speak English?" Ryan questioned.

"Yes," the man smiled. "How can I help you?"

"Is there any way we can get on one of those flights today?" Ryan asked.

"I'm sorry, no. That's not possible."

Hailey's shoulders slumped.

"Although, I could check with the pilots that are coming in and see if any of them are flying out to another destination for a pickup. It might be awhile, but it could work."

Hailey didn't like the idea of waiting. A spark of regret for leaving Holly burned the edges of this new plan, but they were committed now.

"Yes, please do that," Ryan said.

"Very well. Don't leave the airport. I will page you if I find something."

Ryan left his name and thanked the man. Hailey started to walk away.

"Is there somewhere we could buy a phone?" Ryan asked.

"No, I don't think so. But if you need to make a call, we have a courtesy phone next to the information desk," the man said, pointing to his left.

Across the terminal near the far wall, Hailey could see an oval counter. Illuminated letters hung above it said information with the Arabic translation above.

"What about for international calls?"

"Of course, sir."

"Really? For free?"

"Yes, sir."

"Wow, thank you."

Hailey started to walk towards the desk. When Ryan caught up with her, he increased his speed, passing her. She matched his speed, but he quickened his pace.

"Hey!"

"Sorry, babe. I've got a call to make." He broke into a run.

"Oh yeah, we'll see about that."

Hailey narrowed her eyes and propelled herself forward. She easily overtook him.

"Track star," she sang out in an operatic voice.

When she reached the desk, she located the phone on a thin

stand on the left side of the desk. A man held the receiver and chatted away on it in German. Hailey leaned on the counter to catch her breath.

"Dang, you're fast," Ryan said as he reached her.

The German man finished and moved away. Hailey took the receiver and held it out to Ryan.

"Hailey, I was just playing. Call your aunt."

"I know you were, but you deserve this. I don't know what I would have done if you hadn't come for me. Call Thomas. Really, I don't mind."

Ryan stole a quick peck and took the phone.

Hailey's joy soared as she listened to Ryan talk to his brother. Hearing his sarcasm and laughter warmed every part of her.

"Yes, I will... Yup, I'll tell her... I love you too. Bye."

Ryan set the receiver back on the base. He stood there for a moment looking at it. In one swift motion, his feet started stamping, and his fists started pumping the air.

"Ahhh... that felt so good."

Seeing Ryan's unbridled joy pushed soft rolls of laughter out of her. Tears of happiness tickled her nose and dampened her eyes. Hailey beamed at him.

"OK, your turn."

Hailey took a step towards the phone. She picked it up. Her hand started shaking.

Hold it together. You can do this.

Hearing her aunt's voicemail greeting come over the line caused her eyes to water.

"Hey, auntie, it's Hailey. We're safe. We are at an airport in Egypt. It's a long story. " Her emotion caught in her throat. "I love you. And... and I'm sorry for being so distant from you. That will change. I can't wait to see you. I have so much to tell you, and I'll call back soon. Love you. Bye."

Hailey reluctantly hung up the phone.

"You alright?"

Hailey nodded. "Just hard hearing her voice but not being able to talk to her."

A tear broke free. Ryan wiped it off her cheek.

"How about we get something to eat. It will help distract us while we wait."

Hailey took one last look at the phone. "Sure. I'm actually pretty hungry."

They made their way along the east wall to look at the few restaurants and shops. They chose a small cafe. Hailey scanned the menu. It was quite the international selection.

"I don't believe it."

"What?" Ryan spun around to look at Hailey.

"They have desserts from back home. Oh, my word, cinnamon buns! I can't believe they have them here."

"Huh." Ryan huffed.

"What do you mean, huh? Don't you like them?"

"Don't know, never had one."

"What! How is that possible?" Hailey was in total shock. "Go sit down. You won't be disappointed."

"Yes, ma'am."

While she waited, she looked towards the seating area. Ryan had found a table by the window. The look of concern covered his face again as he looked out the window.

"You OK?" she asked as she walked up.

Setting a cup of coffee down in front of each seat and the plate in the middle, she took her seat.

"Definitely," he smiled, the look vanished. "So… a cinnamon bun?" Ryan looked at her with one eyebrow raised.

"Hey don't underestimate it. They have to be by far, my favorite dessert." Hailey looked down at the plate. "And this looks like a good one. Just look at the way the icing oozes down the sides of the warm spiced bread, it truly is perfection," Hailey closed her eyes and took a deep whiff, "and don't get me started on the smell, it's simply intoxicating."

"Do you want me to leave the two of you alone?" He stifled a chuckle.

Hailey leaned over and gave him a playful shove.

"Just try it, smart aleck." Hailey took another deep whiff. "Come on, it smells like home."

Ryan grabbed a fork and slid it down to release a piece of the bun, speared it with the fork and mopped up some of the icing. Hailey's eyes widened as he popped it into his mouth.

He remained silent as he slowly chewed and swallowed.

"So? What do you think?"

"It's... wow, it's really good." Ryan dove in and grabbed another fork full.

Hailey giggled as she took a bite.

"What?" he asked, looking a little self-conscious.

"You're a walking cliché, you have some icing on your chin." She leaned over and wiped it with her little finger.

He smiled at her for just a moment before taking another bite.

"What did you just do!?!" Hailey didn't mean for her tone to come out so harshly.

Ryan froze, mouth full.

"What?" His voice muffled as he tried to speak around the large piece of bun taking up most of his mouth.

"What did you just do?" Hailey repeated the question, sitting there totally shocked but trying to sound lighter.

"I-I have no idea. What?"

"You just ate the center."

"Yeah, why? Are we not supposed to eat that part?"

"Do you not know anything about cinnamon bun etiquette?"

Ryan swallowed his bite. "Cinnamon bun what?" He laughed. "I didn't even know there was such a thing."

"Oh yeah buddy, and you just did the worst offense. Look, see?" Hailey shot him a smirk to let him know she was partially teasing. "Cinnamon bun etiquette is a method of conducting one's self when they are sharing a cinnamon bun, and you just made two dreadful errors."

"Only two?" Ryan mocked her.

"Hey buster, this is serious business if you wish to share one with me in the future. Now listen up."

Ryan cleared his throat. "Sorry, continue."

"Now firstly, there are still outer sections of cinnamon bun sitting on the plate. One does not eat the center until it is the only thing left. Secondly, one does not just take the center and shove it in their mouth in one haphazard bite. This is the essence of the cinnamon bun and is to be…"

A snicker escaped Ryan's lips. He stifled it and apologized.

Hailey eyed him. "It is meant to be split so each partaker may then be able to slowly enjoy its essence." Hailey winked at him and smiled. "Understand?"

"Yes, ma'am. Won't happen again."

They both laughed.

"Where are you going?" she asked as Ryan rose from his seat.

"To fix my dreadful error." He was gone before Hailey could protest.

Minutes later, he returned to the table with two boxes.

"This one is for you," he said as he placed one of the boxes in front of her, "and this one is for me."

He took his seat, a massive grin on his face. Hailey looked at him curiously as he opened up his box. She leaned forward to see its contents.

"What is that?"

"My attempt at an amends," he said with a small coy smile.

Inside his box was a pile of cinnamon bun pieces, which, sort of looked as if a tiny food grenade had gone off. Confused, Hailey opened her box and saw five perfect cinnamon bun centers sitting in a row. Her heart sang. It had to be one of the best presents she had ever received.

"Thank you."

"You're welcome."

Hailey wanted to lean over and kiss him thoroughly on the lips. She didn't care who was watching. But Ryan broke the gaze and grabbed his fork. He had another bite in his mouth before she could move a muscle. So instead, she just smiled and looked down at her own box again. After a moment she returned her eyes to soak in the view of this sweet man.

Hailey looked around and took in their surroundings. Everything still seemed so foreign around her, but at this moment, it felt like a piece of home emerged from the darkness, just around the two of them.

Confidence and peace flooded all around her.

"You OK?" Ryan asked.

Hailey turned back to look at him, "Perfectly!" she smiled.

=======

Ryan was happy that Hailey seemed to be enjoying the break. He kept stealing small glances at her enjoying her dessert. He savored seeing the sparkle return to her eyes.

After the buns were polished off and cups emptied, Ryan went and purchased a couple sandwiches and returned to the table. They chatted casually, and Ryan tried to keep their conversation light as they ate their lunch. He didn't want to see that sparkle in Hailey's eyes disappear. Soon only crumbs remained on their plates.

"Wow, I'm full," Ryan said as he leaned his chair away from the table.

Hailey's smile fell. "Do you think we should have stayed with James or maybe gone with Holly and Jack to Sharm El Sheikh?" The tone of Hailey's voice started to get heavier with each word and her eyes darkened. "Maybe it would have been easier to get a flight out from there. I'm pretty sure they have an actual airport, not just these charter flights."

"Hey, don't worry about that now. We're here, and we'll make the best of it. There's no use doing the what-ifs." Ryan hoped that he could steer their conversation back to a lighter air. He knew this intensity wasn't good for either of them.

"Yeah, I guess you're right," Hailey smiled as she shook her head a few times.

"I'm just going to go to the bathroom, OK? Then how about we take a walk to the other end of the airport? It will stretch our legs and help get your mind off things."

"Sure. That sounds good."

Ryan stood. He leaned over and kissed the top of her head, then left to find a bathroom. He wouldn't be gone long, but it still made him feel uneasy being away from her. He quickly washed his hands but didn't bother drying them. Wiping his hands on his pants as he came through the door, he rushed to get back to Hailey.

Upon turning the corner back towards the cafe, Ryan noticed

that he was about to pass a few officers. He knew that he had no reason to worry, but seeing them still made him feel uneasy.

There were three of them, each dressed in pristine white uniforms with black shoulder patches. None of them were paying him any attention, but seeing the handguns strapped to each of their hips increased Ryan's uneasiness.

Settle down, Ryan chided himself.

Ryan steadied his pace and moved to pass the officer who had his back to him. As he walked by, Ryan noticed the clipboard in the officer's hands. Casually Ryan glanced down, as he walked by.

Ice seemed to pour into every vein as his eyes met the page attached to the officer's clipboard. It took everything in him not to stop and almost more resolve than he had in him to not start running.

How? How is that possible? The questions pounded in his head as he increased the distance from the officers. Ryan couldn't steady his breathing as the adrenaline shot through him. All of his strength went into trying not to draw attention to himself.

You've got to be kidding me. Ryan tried to push the anger as it rose in his chest, but his attempt was pathetic at best.

He craned his neck around the approaching group of people to try and catch Hailey's eye. He was still a few yards off, but maybe he could casually nod for her to follow him towards the door. That way he wouldn't have to enter the cafe seating area, collect her and then show the officers their faces when they exited back out of the cafe.

"Damn," Ryan said between his uneven breaths.

His view was blocked. The group was too thick. When he managed to push past them and get a clear view of the cafe, Ryan's eyes darted about.

His mind filled with confusion as it tried to process what he wasn't seeing.

Hailey was gone.

CHAPTER 29

Ehsan couldn't believe that Taavi had disobeyed his direct orders. He paced the room. He squeezed the back of his neck with his free hand as the rings sounded over the line. Finally, Taavi answered.

"Hello?"

"Taavi, what have you done?"

"Councilman! What do you mean? I can assure you, I did as you asked. As soon as I got your message, I called to have the roadblocks removed. The commanding officer confirmed that they would be removed within the hour. Which," Taavi paused, "should all be gone by now."

"I'm not talking about the roadblocks. Why did you contact the Egyptian authorities? I never condoned such an action."

"I called in a favor, Ehsan. And I can assure you that I did it discreetly."

"I don't care how. I asked why."

"Because I confirmed that the girl got out of Saudi and is in Egypt. It was a last-ditch effort to get her back for you. I'm almost certain nothing will come of it."

"Well, I can assure you it wasn't done discreetly enough," Ehsan yelled over the phone. He didn't care about keeping his cool or who might hear him. "Apparently, an investigation has been opened. I have no idea how this happened. The defense minister personally knows about the roadblocks and about getting Egypt involved. He's furious. I don't know what he's going to do, but I can assure you, Taavi, that I won't be the only one held accountable for this."

"I-I'm sorry, Ehsan. Do you want me to call my contact and rescind the order?"

"I don't see the point, it's too late now. We have no choice now but wait to see how this plays out. I'm not sure how, but I'll try my best to spin this. If you hear anything and I mean anything, you need to call me immediately."

"Yes, of course. I will—"

A beep from an incoming call interrupted Ehsan's listening. He pulled the phone from his ear to check the source. Ehsan swore as soon as he saw the number.

"Our fate is about to be decided. I have to go."

Ehsan hung up. He took a deep breath and clicked on the other call.

"Hello?" he said tentatively.

"Ehsan, you were warned. Get to my office now!"

The call ended.

Ehsan's power puddled on the floor upon hearing the defense minister's voice. Seeing how he didn't pass the message through his secretary, could only mean the worst. Dread piled on thicker with each step as he walked out of his office to the waiting car outside.

After settling himself into the seat, the driver closed his door. Ehsan closed his eyes and put his head in his hands. His mind reeled with possible outcomes and countermeasures. With each thought, his anger grew. His whole being seethed towards the green-eyed woman who had destroyed everything for him.

=======

Ryan's eyes continued to frantically scan the cafe. Hailey wasn't in any of the seats, nor at the till. He looked down towards the ticket desk but couldn't make her out from among the crowd. Panic gripped each part of his body. His breath quickened, and his head started to spin.

Ryan spun around to look in all directions, the officers now forgotten. He looked back towards the washrooms, nothing. He looked across the walkway towards the other restaurant, nothing. She wasn't at the information desk. He looked past the cafe towards the two shops. The first one, nothing. The second... he saw a quick flash of red hair behind a rack of merchandise.

Hailey!

Ryan broke out into a run. Pushing past a few people blocking his route, he reached the shop.

"Hailey!" Relief upon seeing her almost knocked him over.

"What?" she looked shocked at his tone.

"We have to leave... now!"

Ryan grabbed her arm and pulled her towards the front door.

"Ryan, what's wrong? You're scaring me."

"No time. Just come,"

Ryan glanced over his shoulder towards the officers. They were quite far away, but it didn't seem like his running had caught their interest. He slowed their pace but kept ahold of Hailey's arm.

Reaching the blinding light outside, Ryan shaded his eyes to scan for a cab. Seeing the long line of them to the left of the exit, he pulled Hailey towards them.

"Ryan, what's going on?"

"They know you're here." Hearing the fact out loud tasted sour in his mouth, making it hard to swallow down the nausea threatening to spring up from his stomach.

"What? Who? Ehsan?" Hailey's tone mirrored Ryan's fear-filled confusion.

"I don't know how, but I have to get you out of here."

Ryan went up to the closest cab. "English?"

The man shook his head no. Ryan moved onto the next cab.

"English?"

"Yes."

"Jump in. We have to go right now!"

"Yes, no problem," the driver said, jumping into the front seat.

Ryan ran to the other side of the cab, reefed on the door and hurled himself inside. After slamming the door behind him, he turned to see if anyone was exiting the airport after them. Relief washed over him as he saw only passengers exiting and entering through the main doors.

"Whew!" Ryan exhaled.

The cab sped away from the curb.

"Ryan, what happened?"

"Sorry. I had to get you out of there. When I was coming back from the bathroom, I passed an officer. They had a picture of you, Hailey. I had no idea Ehsan would go this far to get you back. It doesn't make sense." Ryan ran his hands through his hair. "AHHHH!!," he yelled. "I should have never let my guard down."

"Ryan, there was no way we could have known." Hailey's words did little to comfort him. "What are we going to do now?" she asked.

"I don't know." Ryan looked at her, feeling defeated. "Hailey, we're in way over our heads here. It wasn't just a picture of you. They had an altered rendition that showed your new look."

"Oh..." Hailey reached up and touched the tips of some of her hair above her ear.

"How would they know?" Ryan's skin crawled at the thought of how Ehsan might have gotten that information.

"I-I'm not sure," Hailey said with tears in her eyes.

Ryan wondered if she feared the same.

"Ahem," the driver cleared his throat, getting their attention. "I can see you are in trouble, my friends, but I will need a destination."

Ryan and Hailey turned to look at each other. Ryan shrugged his shoulders. Hailey turned back to the front.

"Do you have a phone?" she asked the driver.

"Yes, yes. Here."

Taking the phone, Ryan watched as Hailey looked up the number for the US Embassy.

"Yeah, that's a good idea."

"It's the only thing I can think of," Hailey said as she dialed the number. "We need help, and they'd be our best bet."

Ryan couldn't hear the other side of the call over the hum of the cab's engine, but from what he could tell from Hailey's responses, things didn't seem to be going as Hailey had hoped.

"So you can't come get us? Why? ... We can't. People are looking for us at the airport... Israel? No, I don't think that would work. They could have people at the border waiting for us... Yeah, I guess we have no choice...OK, Thank you."

Hailey hung up and handed the phone back to the driver.

"So..." Ryan prodded.

"They said that because they only have jurisdiction on the

actual embassy grounds, that they can't authorize anyone to come get us." Hailey's eyes teared up again. "He thinks we should make our way to Cairo and if we can get to the embassy, they will get us out."

"Well, what's wrong with that plan?"

Hailey looked at her hands. "Ryan, they said that there is a ton of terrorist activity in North Sinai right now and that the only way we might have a chance is to bribe whoever we meet."

Her tears brimmed over and ran down her face, dripping onto her hands.

"Hey, it's OK." Ryan scooted closer to hold her. "You've been through worse, and we'll get through this." Ryan had to fight to keep his tone even. He wanted to reassure Hailey, but he was having trouble believing his own words.

"Seriously? Worse? It all sucks, Ryan. AHHH," she yelled, her eyes filled with anger and fear. "This is so ridiculous."

Hailey leaned forward. Putting her elbows on her knees, she covered her face with her hands. Her shoulders remained still, she wasn't crying. But Ryan could practically feel the hostility radiating off of her. Ryan found his own emotions threatening to take the same action. He gritted his teeth to try and keep calm.

Know that I am God.

Ryan squeezed his eyes shut and blew out a shaky breath.

"How far is it to Cairo?" he asked the driver.

"Oh, my friend, it is far. About five hours. But the lady is right. There is a lot of unrest in that region right now so with the military checkpoints it could take up to six or possibly more."

Hailey whimpered. Ryan's own heart sank. Hailey looked up at him. The pained expression in her eyes could have torn him apart.

"I don't think I can keep doing this," she moaned.

"If we pay you, would you take us there?" Ryan asked the driver.

"That is a very dangerous drive, and it would be a lot of money. How much do you have?"

Ryan opened the dry bag and did a quick count.

"Do you think we would need any money for the flights?" he asked Hailey. "Or do you think the embassy would fly us home?"

She sniffed. "They didn't mention cost, so I think they can get us home. Or, I imagine, at least cover it until we can pay."

Ryan thought for a moment to reason if he should divulge the full amount or not.

"We have a few thousand US dollars," Ryan lied, "and, apart from what we need for bribes, it's all yours if you can get us safely to the embassy in Cairo."

Ryan noticed that the man's eyes grew large at the information. The man didn't answer right away. Ryan held his breath.

"Please, sir. We need to get home," Hailey pleaded, her voice catching in her throat.

Ryan squeezed her shoulder.

"OK! I can take you. But you must trust me and do as I say if we run into any trouble. Understood?"

"Yes, of course. Thank you."

=======

Damari loved how life surprised him. When the couple approached his cab, he had no idea that his family's problem had been solved. He thought that it was just another wealthy couple arriving on a private jet who wanted a ride to one of the luxury hotels by the water. But now, he realized the true opportunity that this particular fare presented. These two foreigners could change everything.

Not in his wildest dreams could he have thought that the solution would come in such a way, but he was not about to let it slip by him just because of the perplexity of it.

"My name is Damari."

"I'm Ryan."

"Hailey."

"It will be a long trip, do either of you need anything before we leave Taba?" Damari asked, looking at them in the rearview mirror.

They both nodded.

Damari drove them to a small grocery store at the edge of the city. As he waited in the cab, bewilderment about the whole event covered him. He would have to play things as casual as possible for this to work, but at least the drive would give him enough time to plan things out before they arrived.

It was a good thing the couple didn't know their way around Egypt. If they had, not even the first step of the plan would work.

"Ready?" Damari asked as they came out of the store.

"Yes. Thanks again," Ryan said.

No, thank you! Damari thought to himself. *You have no idea just how thankful I am.*

The couple soon fell asleep and had not stirred. They were completely unaware when he turned off of the road to Cairo and headed north instead.

CHAPTER 30

When Hailey awoke, the car was still in motion. She had been using Ryan's shoulder as a pillow, but the angle had put a crick in her neck. She straightened up and tried stretching to release it. It helped, but only slightly.

Relaxing again against Ryan, Hailey studied Damari's face. It had a day's growth of stubble and a short mustache that spanned the length of his upper lip. He had bushy eyebrows that matched his short dark hair.

She hadn't noticed the scar before. It crossed most of his forehead. She wondered what had happened. The scar didn't give him a menacing look, by any means. Damari's eyes were soft and kind, so the scar almost gave him a wounded puppy look. He had the look of a hardworking man.

"Sleep well?" Damari asked, catching her eye in his mirror.

"Yes, actually. I didn't realize how exhausted I was."

"Well, stress can drain you of energy quite quickly," he said smiling.

Ryan stirred at the sound of their voices. He stretched and yawned. "How long were we out for?"

"Almost two hours."

"Is it strange that we haven't run into any stops yet?" Hailey asked as she looked nervously out each of the car windows. She saw nothing but desert and rocky hills.

"Not really. It's fortunate."

They rode for a while in silence. Hailey grabbed a water bottle and took a long drink, then wiped her forehead with the sleeve of her top. The air conditioning in the cab was on full blast, but it wasn't entirely winning the battle with the heat pressing in from outside.

She returned the water to their bag and rose to sit back up. As she did so, something caught her eye up ahead. It looked like shimmering water floating in the air. She squinted, but couldn't make out what it was.

"What's that?" Ryan asked.

"That is Hasna. It's my home."

She continued to look out the front windshield. Soon a few stone buildings took shape.

"Wow. You work far from home. I assumed you lived in Taba," Ryan said.

"One needs to go where the work is."

Two large oil trucks sped past, but most of the traffic was light to nonexistent. To Hailey, the small town looked like a cross between a truck stop and a ghost town. Though once they got closer to the center of town, more people and vehicles came into view.

The cab turned off the main street onto a dusty road. If Hailey had been driving she would have missed it. It barely looked like a road. The cab pitched from side to side sporadically as it hit a few holes and drove over random rocks.

Confused, Hailey looked out the back window. The town was practically invisible through the cloud of dust they left in their wake. The road didn't seem right.

"This doesn't seem like a road that would take us to Cairo. Are you sure we are going the right way?" she asked.

"Yeah, this doesn't seem right," Ryan said.

Damari didn't respond. He just stared straight ahead. The car's speed increased.

Her chest constricted. "Damari! What's going on?"

Ryan shot her a look of concern.

"Please, my friends. I will explain in a few moments."

"No! Damari, you will tell us now!" Ryan said.

"I'm sorry but... no. I will wait until we get there."

Hailey grabbed Ryan's hand. Her skin grew clammy, and her pulse quickened. The feeling of being out of control and having no idea where Damari was taking them, terrified her.

Don't fear, no one can deter My hand.

Hailey wasn't quite sure what His words meant, but they sounded similar to the verses that Ryan was saying earlier. She tried to relax but seeing Ryan's body just as tense made it difficult to ease away from the fear growing in her core.

She leaned into him. "Ryan? I'm scared," she whispered in his ear. "What have we gotten ourselves into?"

"I don't know."

Damari continued to snake his way down the road. Minutes later, at the base of a set of rocky hills, numerous crude structures came into view.

"This is my village."

Neither Ryan nor Hailey responded.

The cab pulled up to a tin, stone house. Three of the walls were unpainted, corrugated tin. The fourth wall was rough stones laid in concrete. A three-foot high firewood rack lined the north wall under the sloping tin roof.

Damari killed the engine and turned in his seat to face them.

"Please, don't be frightened. I need your help, and I can't take you to Cairo just yet."

"Are you kidding me?" Hailey didn't even try to attempt to curb her frustration or anger.

"Damari, we had a deal," Ryan said in a much calmer tone. "We need to get to Cairo."

If Ryan was frustrated, he did better at hiding it. Yet Hailey didn't let his calmness deter hers.

"Start the car now!" she yelled. The hot tears in her eyes surprised her, but she didn't make any effort to clear them. She was furious.

"Hailey, I'm sorry. I can't do that. Please, come inside and I will explain."

"No!"

"Hailey, calm down," Ryan said as he grabbed her shoulder.

"Are you serious? How can you be so calm?"

"Do we really have any other choice?" Ryan's sharp tone shocked her to silence. "Look around, Hailey. We're stuck in… only God knows where. And, I hate to say it, but he's all we've got."

Hailey's jaw tensed. She hated that their fate was in a stranger's hands yet again, but she hated even more that Ryan was being so forceful with her. His impatient frustration with her felt awful.

"If you come inside, I will tell you everything. Please, my friends, if you…"

"Stop calling us that," Hailey hissed at him.

"Hailey, enough!" Ryan ordered her.

Hailey slumped back in her seat with a huff. Crossing her arms, she pulled away from Ryan and glared outside.

"Damari, I won't lie," Ryan continued, "I'm not, in any way,

OK with this. Do you realize that you are our only hope to get home? You better have a damn good reason for... whatever this is."

Hailey turned her head to look at Damari, curious of what his response would be.

"I do, Ryan," Damari said. "Please come inside."

Damari got out of the cab and waited. Hailey turned away again and looked out over the landscape. The terrain looked desolate in all directions. There was no way she could run this time. There would be no point in it. She knew she was looking like a toddler in a tantrum, but she couldn't bring herself to get out of the car.

Over her shoulder, she heard Ryan open his door and get out. When the door slammed shut, she hated the loneliness that it brought with it. So with a last defiant huff, she opened her own door and joined the men in front of the house.

Damari dragged the tin door open. The grating sound it made as it moved stabbed at her ears. They ducked and entered the house. The soft light of the kitchen encircled them. A few kerosene lamps hung from beams above their heads. Ryan had to keep his head low to not bump the lamps as he passed them. Hailey walked comfortably underneath.

The kitchen was no more than a six or seven-foot square. There was a small metal sink set in a wooden table at one end, a two-burner cook stove rested on a similar table at the other end, and two chairs against the far wall.

A woman's voice called out from another room. Damari answered just as the owner of the voice came into view. The woman's eyes widened, and a small yelp of shock escaped her lips when she saw them. She quickly grabbed the light blue scarf hanging around her neck and flipped it twice over her head and neck, covering her braided hair.

The woman was strikingly beautiful. A few wisps of her hair fell softly over her flawless honey skin, and the coffee-color of her eyes matched the richness of her hair. She wore a red silk dress, patterned sparsely with different colored embroidered flowers.

The couple spoke for a few minutes. Hailey shifted nervously as she looked around the little kitchen, making sure not to catch Ryan's eye. The woman came over to Hailey and took both of Hailey's hands in hers. She wanted to pull away, her anger still surged through her. But something stopped her. There were tears in the woman's eyes.

The woman kissed Hailey's hands over and over again while saying, 'shukran, shukran'.

"This is my wife Eman. She is saying thank you. Eman doesn't speak English."

Hailey felt uncomfortable but let the woman continue. The woman's actions seemed to act like rain and washed most of her ill emotions away. The woman spoke a few Arabic words while looking from Ryan to Hailey and back again.

"She wants me to tell you that she is honored and extremely thankful you are here," Damari translated. "Oh, and this is my mother, Nada."

Another woman entered the room.

Hailey would be surprised if Damari's mother measured over five feet. She tried not to stare, but Nada's face was so eerily compelling. A maze of deeply set, tight wrinkles, black freckles and age spots covered her face. Her black lips parted into an inquisitive smile.

"Damari, what is happening?" Nada asked.

Hearing her speak in English shocked Hailey.

"Mother, this is Hailey and Ryan. They are from America."

"Damari... why are they here?" she said, not breaking her gaze with Hailey.

Hailey only briefly looked away when Damari's wife moved. Eman walked over to the small cook stove and put on a pot of water. Hailey looked back at Nada.

"To help us with Layla," Damari said.

Nada nodded a welcome to each of them as she shuffled over the dusty wood floor to stand beside her son. She placed a hand on his shoulder, giving it a little squeeze. She turned and moved to stand in front of Hailey.

Nada looked her over, then did the same to Ryan but said nothing. Nada's eyes looked black in the warm light, but a thin, white circle ran around the rim of the iris. The white part of her eye had a yellowish tinge. Hailey couldn't make out any eyelashes. Being under the watch of such intense eyes was unnerving, and she had to force herself not to look away.

"Has my son told you what has happened?"

Hailey nervously glanced at Ryan. "No, he hasn't yet."

She had to fight to keep calm, she couldn't handle another chiding from Ryan.

"I think he was just about to," Ryan said.

"Very well. Come... come."

Nada moved in between Ryan and Hailey, took each of their hands, and led them to another room. The old woman shuffled her feet quite slowly, and Hailey had to be careful to shorten her stride and not step on Nada's heels.

Turning a corner, they entered a room not much bigger than the kitchen. Three rolled sleeping mats rested against the far wall underneath a cracked, four-pane window. The setting sun poured through the small window and filled the room with a similar shade of light to the lamps in the kitchen, yet warmer with a reddish hue.

Hailey followed Nada over to the closest wall where four green, beanbag-looking ottomans sat, each with a small red pillow resting on top. A knee-high table sat in the center.

At Nada's request, Hailey and Ryan each took a seat. Hailey prepared herself to sink into it as she sat, but it was firm and barely gave way under her weight. Nada and Damari took the last two. Eman had remained in the kitchen.

After filling in his mother on how they had come to be there, Darmari seemed to wait with held breath for her response. Nada looked them all over with raised eyebrows.

"Damari is a good boy, he means well," Nada said as she leaned over and tapped her son's hand. She smiled at each of them with squinted eyes.

Nada had a riveting warmth to her. She oozed a mothering air, and Hailey strangely longed to be engulfed by it. Momentarily forgetting their predicament, Hailey wanted to leap across the space between them and hug her. She restrained herself and remained perched on her stool.

"Damari, you need to tell them."

Hailey's breath caught in her throat as Damari slowly filled his lungs and wiped his hands on his pants. He swallowed hard.

"I made a dreadful error a few months ago. As you can see," Damari waved his hand as he gestured to the room around them, "my people come from humble means. I am thankful for what we have, but I was struggling to provide for my family. I had been giving camel rides, but since the threat of terrorist activity has risen, there hasn't been enough work. The tourists have been remaining along the coast, staying close to the hotels. I knew I needed to find something different when I didn't have enough to feed my family. They were suffering."

Damari lowered his head. He seemed to be struggling to continue, but soon lifted his head and sighed.

"Some men came and visited our village not long ago. They told us that with a marriage of our daughter, which they could arrange, I would be given more than enough money in exchange. I admit I was foolish, but the amount would be enough to purchase a taxi. And a taxi would be a new start for our family. So I agreed."

Hailey tensed.

"The men returned a few days later. They had arranged a mut'a marriage for my daughter, and they said they would come to collect her soon."

"What do you mean by a... a mut'a marriage?" Hailey asked.

"Layla, our daughter, would only be gone a month. That is why I agreed. It seemed like such a small price to pay for a lifetime of security for us all. Of course, Layla was terrified. Eman was furious with me. But I saw no other way to survive, so I made the hard choice, the one that needed to be made." Damari seemed to force his shoulders back like he was trying to convince himself of what he was saying.

"Sorry, I'm confused," Hailey said. "Why would she be returned to you?"

"Oh, this arrangement wouldn't be for life. They called it a pleasure marriage. A man would marry her for a certain amount of time after he paid the dowry and then leave her shortly afterward. She'd then be permitted to come home."

"So... is that where Layla is now?" Ryan asked.

"Yes. They collected her seven weeks ago. I wasn't expecting her to be gone this long, but when I questioned the marriage brokers again, they said that her husband wanted more time with her. Normally this is forbidden. The marriage is supposed to be for a set amount of time, but they won't return her. They just gave me more money and wouldn't answer any further questions. I was foolish to agree to it. I see that now. But honestly, at the time I didn't know how I could have chosen not to."

"So what do you want from us?" Ryan asked.

"Well, my wife told me last week that she has been sneaking into Hasna for weeks now to watch Layla. She is a foolish woman. She could have been killed if spotted. We were warned not to interfere. During her trips, she saw that Layla has been…" Damari paused again to swallow, "… mistreated. Ever since, Eman has been demanding that I do something. But until today, there was nothing I could do."

"I'm sorry, I still don't understand. What could Hailey and I possibly do?"

"You have money."

Eman came into the room. She carried a tin tray with teacups and a pot of tea. They each thanked her and accepted a cup. As the hot, dark tea slipped down her throat, Hailey's fear returned as Damari's intentions took shape in her mind.

"Are you expecting us to go buy her back?" Ryan asked.

"No, that's impossible. We need to rescue her."

Hailey choked on her tea and almost spit it across the table.

"I know it sounds crazy," Damari said shaking his head, "but I have it all worked out. There is an organization in Cairo that helps young girls escape their marriages. It wouldn't be safe to bring her back here. So once you have her, you can carry on to Cairo. Your money will be used to pay off all the checkpoint guards and any terrorist cells you might run into, just like we planned. The only difference is now you will have Layla with you."

"Hold on," Ryan said, putting up his hands. "You're expecting us to do all that and you're not coming with us. Are you mad?"

"I couldn't possibly come with you. I have to stay here and protect Eman and my mother. Once the brokers find out Layla is gone, they will certainly come here looking for her. If I'm not here to keep up the ruse that we don't know anything, they will hurt them. I can't allow that."

Ryan stood and paced the room. Hailey would have joined him if her legs didn't feel like cement and there wasn't the rock in her stomach pinning her to her seat.

"God works in strange ways," Nada whispered, a quiet laugh followed.

Hailey's head snapped up.

"Don't start," Damari said, looking at his mother.

It was clear to Hailey that Damari wasn't happy with her comment.

"Pay no mind to my mother. Her beliefs are nonsense, and she shouldn't speak of such things." Damari shot her a glare.

"Damari, please give us a moment alone," Nada asked with a sweet smile.

Hailey watched Damari reluctantly leave the room to join Eman in the kitchen. Once out of sight, Nada asked Ryan to sit back down. He complied.

"I can only imagine how overwhelmed you both must feel. I'm sure you didn't think this would happen on your trip."

"Nada, you have no idea how true that is," Hailey said shaking her head. Her hands started wringing themselves together.

"You may not understand this, but I have been praying for

you. Of course, at the time I didn't know it would be you exactly... but for you nonetheless."

Hailey wanted to say something. Her mouth opened but nothing came out.

"When you say God..." Ryan started, "who do you mean?"

"The God of Abraham, Isaac, and Jacob. The Abba of Jesus of course."

Again, Hailey's words caught in her throat. She was left speechless as her mind fought to find understanding in what she was hearing.

"How do you...? How did you...?"

Dumbfounded, Hailey looked at Ryan as he struggled to speak, then back to Nada.

"I found a Bible when I was small."

"Where?" Hailey asked.

"My father is from a line of nomadic Bedouins. We were spending a few days in a small town, quite far from here. And on the first day, in the market, I saw a book sitting on a crate. I wanted to go look at it, but for fear that someone might see me, I left it alone. But on our last day, the book was still there, untouched. I smuggled it into my pouch and read it in our tent when no one was awake.

"I met someone within those pages, and it changed everything. I kept it a secret for fear of what my father would do if he found out. He was a devout Muslim and forbade anything that wasn't in line with the Quran. But despite my best efforts, one night he found me reading. He was furious. I was terrified. He destroyed the Bible but was gentle with me. I was devastated, yet something miraculous happened. My mind had memorized all that I had read. So late at night I would lie awake and recite what I had learned. Soon my father accepted the fact that his youngest daughter was not a follower of Muhammad, but of Jesus. I think the only reason he didn't shun me was that I was his favorite," Nada said with a small smile.

Nada looked down at her hands. Hailey wondered which memory had come to her mind.

"Since then, others have crossed my path over my many years, and I have come to learn and grow in all the Spirit showed me. I know, children, you must be confused. But I knew you were coming."

Hailey turned and looked at Ryan. He wore the same perplexed and wary look she did.

"I love my granddaughter very much. Layla is a sweet and gentle child. She doesn't belong where she is. God has heard her cries, and through my prayers, I was told of your arrival."

Suspicion climbed over her skin. "W-what do you mean?" she asked.

"God speaks to me in many wonderful ways. In a dream He showed me a man and a woman coming to our home and that I was meant to encourage you. He said that the woman would be fragile from the journey He brought her on to get here and that the man had questions he needed answered."

Hailey tried to keep them away, but the tears broke through her resolve. She intellectually knew God was with her, but being faced with the reality that He had gone before them like this, was too much to contain. A sob shook her as it forced its way out in an awkward gulping sound.

"It's OK to cry, my child. Holy tears are healing," Nada said softly as she leaned over and took one of Hailey's hands between hers. "Come over here, you two."

Nada rose up and went over towards the window. A few stacked blankets laid over the floor with a few pillows strew about. She groaned as she sat.

"Come, come," she beckoned.

Hailey rose and followed Ryan the few steps to where Nada sat. At Nada's direction, they sat on each side of her.

"Hailey, I have a word of the Lord for you. Close your eyes and listen to Him through my voice."

Hailey shakily followed Nada's directions.

"He wants you to know that you are deeply loved and that everything that has happened to you has passed through His hand."

Uhh, this sounds like what Ryan was telling me. The knee-jerk reaction to put an end to what Nada was saying hit her. Yet her curiosity managed to keep her quiet.

"Everything that you have experienced," Nada continued, "and the path that you have walked has now led you here. There was the individual purpose in each of those steps, but it also was meant to culminate to this very moment. Each day of your life was seen before the foundations of the world were set in place. There needs to be no devastation in it. It was all in His hand. For what others had meant for evil, God has meant for good. When you were on a long set of stairs,"

The stairwell at the hotel flashed in her mind.

"God told you that you were meant for such a time as this. You heard Him correctly, so trust Him. All that you have been told has been troubling you because you don't understand it. But don't fear, understanding isn't a requirement for peace. His peace surpasses understanding and can guard your heart."

Hailey opened her eyes. Her heart felt like it was going to burst out of her chest, as it thundered behind her ribcage. Her body was reluctant to accept that everything she had been terrified of after getting on the bus and after the boat exploded, was being answered with Nada's words right at this moment.

"H-how... how do you know all of that?"

"Child, you have much to learn," Nada said, with a soft laugh that bounced her shoulders. Her words were not mean or condescending. They were filled with compassion. "And He is excited to guide you. You both have yet to be faced with the most difficult steps. And so, I feel I need to tell you both what He says in John 16, verse 33," Nada looked into each of their faces, "'These things I have spoken to you, so that in Me you may have peace. In this world you have tribulation, but take courage; I have overcome the world.'" Nada smiled. "Remember, He delights in you and nothing can take you out of His hand."

Hailey nodded. "Yeah, we know those verses."

"Oh, do you?" Nada's words cut straight through her. Nada looked at her with a smile and a raised eyebrow. "Did your *knowing* have any benefit to you along the path that brought you here? Knowing has no profit, sweet one. Do you trust and believe?"

Her tone seemed gracious, yet Hailey felt awkward as Nada just stared at her.

Am I missing something?

Hailey recited the verses in her mind again. Nada smiled. Hailey repeated them again... then again, allowing each word to have its moment. After the third repeat of the verse, an indescribable peace washed over her. It was the same peace she felt after God had spoken to her back in Ehsan's room. Hailey felt safe and, against all logic, she felt like she was in a familiar place. And strangely Nada's words about what was yet to come suddenly didn't frighten her.

"Now, Ryan, close your eyes, please. He has a word for you

as well."

Ryan narrowed his eyes at first, but then closed them.

"God delights in you, child. You have been faithful to what He has called you to and have honored Him. You have a heart after His. He sees you struggling over troublesome questions about His providence. He is not angered by these and will clarify them for you before you reach home."

Ryan opened his eyes. He looked at Nada but didn't speak. Nada stayed silent, seemingly to allow him time to collect his thoughts. Hailey followed suit.

"This is... a bit overwhelming, Nada," Ryan said.

He seemed to be struggling to talk. Hailey was about to reach out to encourage him but decided against it.

"Hailey and I were... um... talking about this just a few hours ago."

Ryan turned and looked at her. He swallowed hard, and Hailey saw his adam's apple bob uncomfortably in his throat.

"I was trying to be strong for you... but..."

Ryan lowered his head, and Hailey could see a few tears drip onto his lap. She was confused by his sudden release of emotion.

"You need to be honest with her, Ryan. Pushing negative emotions down doesn't make them go away, it only stops you from feeling the positive ones."

Ryan nodded but kept his face down. It took him a few moments before breaking the silence.

"Hailey, I... I doubted how this all could have meaning. I didn't want to say anything about it at the time and add to your confusion or struggle." Ryan's shoulders shuddered, and it was obvious he felt too embarrassed to look at her as he cried. "I knew you needed my strength, so I jumped into my past experiences and spouted off doctrine I thought to be true. But... I am just as confused as you are, especially since the airport. I never had anything truly awful touch me before. Nothing even remotely close to what I saw on the boat or saw at the compound after the explosion."

He sniffed and wiped each of his eyes with the back of his right hand.

"Losing Anna's parents was the first time I've ever lost anyone I knew. I loved Chuck and Linda, and I can barely think about the fact that they're gone. So I ignored it and just preached at you."

"Ryan…" Hailey wanted to console him, but she couldn't find the right words. In her own struggle of faith colliding with her experience, she had no idea he had been wrestling in the same way.

"Ryan," Nada said softly, "your words to her were no less true, they just need some clarification is all, and that understanding will come."

"Hmm, maybe. But they were just words in light of what I was actually feeling. I wasn't ready to see the huge difference between doctrine and having that doctrine meet experience. My faith wavered."

Ryan looked up at her. Hailey hated seeing that kind of pain in his eyes.

"I'm sorry. I'm so sorry I wasn't honest with you. I just didn't want you to run from Him again because you saw me struggling. And I kind of thought if I could convince you to be confident in what I was saying then I, in turn, would have an easier time believing it myself. But I think my words might have done more harm than good."

He looked down at his hands again. Hailey didn't know what to say. His words had challenged her view of God, but she didn't blame him.

"Oh, child," Nada cut in. "Ryan, you will grow in your understanding of all that you talked about. You both will. When the Spirit reveals more to you, your heart will soar with joy when your eyes are opened. I want both of you to know, that you are fully known and that you are fully loved. Now come close, both of you, we need to pray."

Hailey and Ryan moved closer, and Nada laid a hand on each of their bowed heads. Words poured out of Nada unlike any prayer Hailey had ever heard before. Each word seemed to lift the darkness Hailey was feeling, raising her slightly off of the blanket to where warmth encased her. She felt detached from the terror and confusion she felt earlier and even a bit detached from the world itself. It was like entering another reality, but yet she felt more present in this moment than she had ever been before. It was an odd and beautiful sensation.

Hailey didn't know how long the prayer lasted, just that Nada's prayer was the most sincere and intimate expression of trust and faith she had ever witnessed. There were no words said in mindless rote, only ones of authentic connection. Hailey realized at that moment just how much of God she kept herself from knowing. She felt compelled to lean in and go deeper, so that she too may know God like Nada did.

Soon Nada's words trailed off, and the pressure of her hand lifted off Hailey's head. Hailey paused for a moment, keeping her eyes closed.

God, I still don't understand. But, I-I let go of my right to understand. I choose to trust and learn from You. I want to know You.

Hailey opened her eyes. When she raised her head, she saw Nada shuffling off towards the kitchen.

Nada laughed. "Let's eat."

Hailey looked over at Ryan. They both dried their eyes and went towards the other. They grasped desperately onto each other in a tight hug as they continued to kneel on the soft blankets.

"This was beyond anything I thought possible," Ryan whispered into her ear.

"Yeah...," she whispered back, fresh emotion catching in her throat.

Ryan chuckled, "I guess there's no point in saying no and fighting this path now."

"No," Hailey agreed and mimicked his laugh, "I think not. Seems like we're stuck with 'em."

CHAPTER 31

The girl had been one of the best investments that he had ever made. He never would have lasted so long on this dull business trip without her. The original arrangement had gone far too quickly, especially since he had to wait for her to heal after her procedure.

He had been so frustrated when the brokers denied the extension, but thankfully, his contacts within the Egyptian sex trade had proven to be quite useful. The pressure they inflicted on the brokers was more significant than his, and it put a fire under them. Not to mention that their forgery skills were impeccable. They would eventually help smooth things over with the brokers. The brokers would then placate her parents yet again, and all would be well.

Sure, going over the marriage broker's heads created a bit of a rift, but he just couldn't let Layla go. The temporary burnt bridge was worth it, and he was sure that after this meeting, when the brokers had their pockets lined yet again, all would be forgiven and they could move forward with the new arrangement.

As he looked over at his bride as she slept, his excitement for tomorrow grew. Layla would make an excellent wife and should fit in quite nicely back home. At tomorrow's meeting he would finally get to lay out his terms that the brokers could bring to present to her parents. He couldn't bear to leave her here in such a dusty and desolate place. Nor would he waste time bartering over a measly amount, so he made sure not to be frugal with his proposal. Everyone would certainly accept. The offer was far more than the previous two amounts.

The girl started to stir. Karim reached over and caressed the side of her face and cooed in her ear to calm her. She drifted back to sleep.

========

The samosas were delicious, but they didn't compare to the dessert, something called katayef. To Hailey, it looked like a pancake dumpling. It was filled with raisins, coconut, and hazelnuts, then deep-fried and drenched in syrup. Hailey had never had anything quite like it and had to restrain herself from having too many. She didn't want to be greedy and take advantage of their hospitality.

She had barely said two words over dinner, as her focus was primarily on the food. But she kept her ears open to the conversation, as she used her finger to mop up the last of the syrup on her plate.

"Once things broke tradition, I started to look into these types of marriages more. I talked to people in Hasna and in Taba. No one could help us, but I was able to get some more information about them."

Ryan rested his forearms on the table. "Like what."

"Some of these types of marriages can go for as little as eight hundred Egyptian pounds which... would be about forty-something US dollars."

Hailey had to quickly work up some saliva to clear the syrup from her mouth so she could speak, "Woah, wait. Some families sell their daughters for less than fifty bucks? That can't be right."

"Sadly, yes. The people I was talking with knew of a few instances where the families were so desperate, that the brokers were able to make the deal for so little. It is very sad."

"How old is Layla?" She was almost too scared to ask.

"She's twelve."

Hailey didn't know quite how to respond. There was no hesitation in Damari's answer. He said it with an air of pride.

"That... seems, ah... quite young."

It seemed Ryan didn't have trouble finding tactful words and Hailey was grateful. Hers wouldn't have been so gracious.

"A bit maybe. It isn't very common to be married that young. But definitely not unheard of. One in fifty girls are married by fifteen, and my Layla is, or at least if it were under better conditions, she'd be fortunate to be among them."

Hailey was speechless.

"And what about girls that are older?"

"I'm not sure, but I married Eman when she was seventeen, and all of her sisters were married at sixteen." Damari smiled over at Eman as he spoke.

Hailey smiled at their expression of love, but she felt sick imagining being married so young.

Ryan rubbed the back of his neck. "I would imagine that a traditional marriage dowry would be more than one of these arrangements, so why not just marry her off to someone she loved when she was older?"

"Yes, you are right. The payment is more, but that wasn't something the brokers were offering, and we needed the money."

Nada leaned forward. "The men that enter into these types of arrangements are usually away on business or would like to have relations with a woman, yet aren't able to take on the financial commitment of a having a wife. Prostitution is illegal, so these pleasure marriages make a way around that."

By the tone of Nada's voice, Hailey could tell she disagreed with these marriages. Although, there was a slight tenseness to it that made Hailey wonder if Nada was downplaying her disagreement to ease her son's mind.

"Everyone I have talked to," Damari continued, "has never heard of a broker breaking the contract. But I'm scared for Layla if we try going to the authorities. There is no guarantee that they could help and it might only make things worse for her."

"How are you expecting for Ryan and I to get Layla out? I would imagine that it would be impossible for us to simply walk out with her."

"Not as difficult as you might think. She isn't guarded or watched that closely. Remember this is... or at least was... an agreement between Layla's husband and us. There would be no reason for her to run, nor would there be anywhere she could escape to if she did."

"Eman has been able to figure out Layla's usual routine," Nada added.

"That's right. So we will find a window that will work for you to go get her. A friend has agreed to let you borrow his car. He has a brother in Cairo that can drive it back to him later."

It seemed like most of the details had been worked out, but it didn't do a whole lot to calm Hailey's nerves. She wouldn't let her mind even taste the potential of things that could go wrong.

"And what about Layla?" Ryan asked. "Will she even go with us? And what about this organization in Cairo, do they know we're coming? Is Layla just supposed to stay there for good? Will she ever get to see you again?"

"Well... I thought that Eman and I would write her a letter explaining it all. But I don't believe that it will be good to wait around for her to read it all. So I want to tell you my secret name for her. I only use it at bedtime when I say goodnight. No one outside our family knows it. It's an Egyptian blue water lily called the Nymphaea Caerulea. If you say that I sent you and call her by that name, she will know it's safe. Then, when you're on the road, you can give her the letter.

"As for the organization, no, they don't know you'll be coming. But they won't turn her away once she's there. I heard they are trying to work with international agencies to change the marriage ages. I'm not sure why exactly, but if they can help Layla, that's all I care about. Then, once I'm able to save up enough money from my fares, I will move our family to Cairo and collect her. It will be a brand-new start for us all."

Hailey bit her lip. "Um... what about the checkpoints? How are we supposed to navigate those without you? Isn't it going to look strange that two American's are traveling in remote areas with an Egyptian girl in the back seat? I kinda think that would stick out and draw some attention."

"Yes, you're right. It would look out of place. But here in the Sinai region, money covers over a lot of oddities. Just remember the word baksheesh. It means bribe and once anyone hears that, they will be quick to look the other way as soon as the money is in their hand. Even if you come across anyone official, like police, there are enough corrupt officers that you won't be delayed long."

"What about..." Hailey paused. She had to swallow hard before the words would leave her lips, "... the terrorist cells that the man at the embassy mentioned?"

"You won't need to worry about that. Most of that activity is farther up north and those that have been troublesome around here, haven't been heard from in a while." Damari stopped and smiled at her and Ryan. "I hope you know I'm not taking you or your safety for granted. I do understand the situation I have put you in. But…" his voice choked up with emotion.

Eman moved her hand over to hold his.

"But it's my daughter," Damari continued, "and there is no other way I can undo what I have done without your help."

Hailey's heart broke to see tears fill Damari's eyes. When they flowed over and spilled down each cheek, he suddenly got up from the table.

"I should help Eman clear dinner."

Hailey watched as he moved to the sink and turned his back to them. Eman nodded to them and grabbed a few plates before following him.

Nada stood. "Let's get you settled for sleep."

Soon, Ryan and Hailey each laid on one of the sleeping mats under a thin layer of cloth. Two freshly-lit lamps hung overhead.

Nada set a stack of three blankets in the small space between the two of them. "I will leave these here, in case you get cold."

Hailey thanked her.

Sounds of clanging dishes and soft foreign words sounded from the kitchen. Nada moved the green seats to the outside wall and then prepared three more mats. Soon the sound of dishes stopped. Damari and Eman came into the room, just as Nada had nestled onto her mat.

Damari went to his mat without a word, laid down, and turned towards the wall. Hailey wished she had a way to let him know he didn't need to be embarrassed.

It looked like Eman was about to follow suit, but she paused, then quickly walked over to Hailey. She bent down, grabbed Hailey's face with her hands and kissed each cheek twice. She stood and went to each lamp and turned the black metal knob to starve the flame. Darkness filled the room. Only a slight glow of light from the moon cascaded through the window. Eman walked over to her mat next to Damari and laid down.

Hailey looked at Ryan, who grinned back at her.

"Night," he mouthed silently.

"Night," Hailey mouthed back.

Ryan closed his eyes, and Hailey watched for a few minutes as he shuffled around to get comfortable. He turned away from her and soon the rise and fall of his shoulders from his breathing settled into a steady rhythm.

Asleep already, huh?

Hailey rolled onto on her back. She would probably be the last to sleep, if at all. Apart from the long nap in the car that took her due to sheer exhaustion, Hailey realized that life hadn't paused for a chance to stop and allow her to catch up. Any emotion that expelled itself previously was in the midst of the event that caused it. But laying there, warm and safe with Ryan just a few inches away, the day's events suddenly hit her.

Hailey had to put her hand over her mouth to keep her cries from sounding outside of her chest.

Fabina... Fabina.

James! I hope you're OK, but then how could you be?

Her mind raced with thoughts of Holly and Jack. Hailey prayed that Jack was able to get the treatment he needed and that he was OK. She hoped that Holly was doing alright handling it all alone.

I so wish I could have stayed with her… but… Anna has no idea where we are. I hope she calls Thomas.

Images of possibilities for her friends swarmed around her mind. So many things could have changed or gone wrong.

Did Jack's condition take a turn? Is Holly losing it by being alone? Is she scared? Did James and Armando make it back to Saudi safely? Saudi…

What if Ehsan set up roadblocks between here and Cairo? Is that even possible? But we thought we'd be safe in Taba, and we were wrong. What if he finds us… or… if the bribes don't work and we can't get to Cairo? What if something goes wrong with getting Layla out?

She clenched her jaw and tightened all the muscles in her face to keep from sobbing out loud.

Father… I need Your Spirit's power right now. I can't do this… I can't do any of this.

Hailey had never said those words before, and the honesty of them caught her off guard. But as soon as they were off the lips of her mind, the weight that was crushing her whole being lifted slightly. The sensation was unexpected, but she liked and welcomed it.

Father, I need Your Spirit's power.

The weight lifted even more. Hailey felt like she could breathe easier. The silent sobs stopped, and she was able to remove her hand from her mouth. Grabbing the top of the cloth, she pulled it up to her chin and listened.

I am Your God. Do not fear. It is My own peace that I give to you.

The rest of the tension in her body relaxed.

Please watch over them. May Your will be done with Layla, Ryan… and I. We are in your hands.

Hailey wasn't used to being so bold in letting go of control, but Nada's words to them were having a strange effect on her. Knowing that God had literally gone before them and met with Nada... there was no other option than for that fact to change everything.

What will be... will be.

=======

The man's touch made her cringe, but she pretended to go back to sleep. Maybe, just maybe he'd leave her alone tonight. Layla waited, forcing her breath to sound even. A few minutes went by. Still, he didn't pull her close. Her body relaxed allowing her to retreat back into her mind, into the only place where she felt safe.

Previously, that place of safety had been her home. But, with all these changes, she didn't understand her father anymore. He became a different man that day. The day he had told her what he had arranged.

What will happen when I go back home? Can I trust him again?

Still, no answer came to her. Would anything be the way it was? Would she even feel safe back in those small rooms? Half of her ached to be held by all three sets of her family's arms. To be held by someone and not worry about what they wanted, sounded alien now and she couldn't quite remember how it felt. And as more time went on, the distance from those memories only grew.

Over the last few weeks, Layla started to question whether her father told her the truth about how long she would be gone. When the days began to tick past the point he had said, her suspicion of his intentions swayed.

Did he just tell me that it would only last a month to keep me calmer? Is this going to last forever?

Why had Karim ignored her the other day when she asked when she would be able to go home? She had no idea why, but the question seemed to make him uncomfortable. She didn't try asking again.

Even with the uncertainty of what awaited her at home, Layla missed her mother desperately. Mama smelled good, like soap and cinnamon. Mama held her when she was scared, which made everything feel safe. Layla squeezed her eyes tighter, longingly trying to remember how her arms felt. She couldn't remember as well as before. She pushed her brain to remember. It was no use, Karim's scent of sweat beside her pulled her away from them.

Layla felt Karim shift. She held her breath. He stilled a moment later.

She hated having this man as her husband. The only thing she was thankful for was that Karim was kind to her. He didn't yell or hit her like Ruby's husband did. But he was old and smelled funny, like her neighbor back home who drank from those brown bottles. Most of her time with Karim was really confusing. He kept calling their evening time together special time. It didn't feel special. Thinking about it made her body want to recoil from his sleeping form. She bit the inside of her cheek to keep still.

Layla continued to lay there in silence. Soon Karim's snoring filled the room. She opened her eyes and looked around the large room without moving her head off the pillow. She felt numb, and the feeling seemed to be growing with each day. She didn't know how to stop it.

Apart from time with Karim in the evenings, she didn't mind spending the rest of her time alone in the house or shopping for groceries in the market. But on the rare occasion, when she ran into Ruby, those moments were her favorite. And even though she had to do all the talking, at least she wasn't alone. She smiled as she hoped tomorrow would be one of those days.

Layla looked over towards the wardrobe sitting against the wall directly across from her side of the bed. Her blue, silk robe hung off its left handle. Layla smiled. She liked the clothes she had been given, and that robe was her favorite.

I think I will wear it to the market tomorrow. Karim's meeting will be later in the morning, so I'll go after he gets back. That way I can have more time by myself. And maybe.... tomorrow is the day I get to go home. The thought brought some comfort, and she held onto it tightly as she drifted off to sleep.

CHAPTER 32

The sun shining on her face woke her before anyone else had stirred. Hailey stretched and turned over to look at Ryan. He was lying on his back, his head turned towards her. The scruff that had grown on his face over the last few days gave him a more rugged look. Usually, for work, Ryan had kept himself clean shaven, so she hadn't seen this look on him very often. She liked it.

Ryan's chest slowly rose and fell with each breath. She noticed how strong his shoulders and arms were. If it weren't for the possibility of offending their hosts, she would have shuffled over and cuddled up with him.

He looked so peaceful.

Sound rustled from near her feet. Hailey rose her head. Eman was up and folding her blanket. Noticing Hailey, she smiled, put down the blanket, and motioned for Hailey to follow her. Being sure not to wake Ryan, Hailey carefully followed Eman to the kitchen. Through a series of hand gestures, Eman conveyed how she could help with breakfast.

The dish consisted of mashed up fava beans mixed with cumin, lemon, salt and pepper, and a drizzle of olive oil. While the dish smelled good, Hailey wasn't excited about it. She didn't care much for fava beans. They tasted like what she imagined grass would taste like.

By the time everything was ready and the dishes set out, the others had risen and joined them at the table. Ryan winked at her as she sat. Eman made one more trip to the kitchen and retrieved a plate of the pita bread she had cut up.

"Did you sleep well?" Nada asked Hailey.

"Yes, thank you."

"And you, Ryan?"

He yawned. "Like a log."

"I'm glad. You both had quite the day yesterday, and you'll need your rest for today."

The conversation paused as they each scooped up their food and started eating. As the paste coated Hailey's tongue, it dashed her hope that the spices would hide the taste of the beans. She took a big bite of the pita to clear the flavor while smiling at Eman.

"Eman," Ryan called, turning Eman's attention away from Hailey.

Hailey sighed with relief, swallowing it was hard to act through. Hailey worked her tongue around her mouth and ate more bread to clear her mouth while Eman was distracted.

"When do you think would be a good time to go get Layla?"

Hailey smiled at Ryan's kind act to include her.

Eman looked at Damari and he translated. Eman looked thoughtful for a moment.

"She thinks that late morning would be best because Layla sometimes goes to the market in the morning. So we have about five hours to work things out."

"When can we get the car from your friend?" Hailey asked.

"It's just down the road, but it would be easiest to get it just before you head to Hasna."

He took a few bites of his breakfast. Hailey nibbled on the pita bread but couldn't stomach any more of the paste.

"Layla's house is about fifteen minutes through town, along a quiet street. There are three ways to it, but I think it is best to drive in on the north road and park at the house three houses before Layla's. There is a big tree down a small path beside it that you can park behind.

"Layla's husband won't be home. But the difficult part will be to make sure no one else sees you or at least no one that will care. There are at least five houses on that street that have been known to be used by the marriage brokers. So it would be best if you don't alert anyone. Try and stay hidden as best as you can and work fast."

Ryan and Hailey both nodded their understanding.

"Eman and I will write the letter after breakfast. We will also send a photo of us along with you. Seeing it should help Layla feel at ease. Once you have Layla, you need to hurry and get back to the car. When you leave, you will keep driving on the same road and head out the south exit. Get Layla to duck down in case anyone is watching."

"Is it usual for the marriage brokers to be around there? Or just the people who live there?" Hailey asked Eman.

Damari turned to Eman and relayed the question. Eman spoke while shaking her head.

"Eman has only seen a few of them in all the times she's gone to watch Layla. But she wants you to be careful just in case."

"How are we supposed to tell them apart from just regular people?" Ryan asked.

"You can identify them only by the car they drive. It's a large brown town car, and they always travel in pairs. But she also said to watch out for men in general. If any of the other husbands are home, they could alert the brokers. And..." Damari paused.

"And... what?" Hailey prodded. The way his voice trailed off didn't sound right.

"Well, there has been some other activity in Hasna recently."

"What... terrorists?" Hailey's heart raced as she spoke. "I thought you said that–"

"No, nothing like that. But there have been whispers of a local gang returning. They used to operate here quite often but moved to using marriage brokers for their human trafficking operations. They all drive big, black SUVs, so keep an eye out for them as well." He leaned forward. "I know how overwhelming all of this seems. I, myself, am a bit shocked that all of this has been happening in Hasna. My family has lived around here for three generations, and I knew nothing of this darkness."

"How did you find out?" Ryan asked.

"As I mentioned last night, when Eman found out that Layla was being mistreated and after the marriage brokers returned and threw more money at me, refusing to return Layla, I started asking more and more questions."

Hailey swallowed hard, not excited to ask the question. "How do you know Layla is being mistreated? Were there bruises?"

"No. Layla lost her joy. Eman said that at the market, she jumped whenever someone came near her. She keeps her head down, walks slowly, and rarely speaks to anyone."

Eman sniffed and wiped a few tears from her eyes.

Hailey gave her an empathetic smile. "I'm so sorry."

Nada patted Hailey's hand. "You both have a dark road ahead of you. But my granddaughter needs you. Please."

"We know." Hailey tried to sound supportive. "It's just a lot to take in."

Silence settled around the table. It seemed like everyone was taking a moment to play out what might lay ahead of them.

Damari clasped his hands in front of his lips. "We can't thank you enough for doing this. I mean, I know I put you in a difficult situation, but I'm grateful."

Hailey didn't know what to say. Damari wasn't wrong. But after their talk with Nada last night it wasn't like she could blame him. It seemed this plan was a lot larger than any of them.

Nada rose from the table. "We should get started."

Hailey was thankful that she didn't need to respond. Words weren't coming to her. She assisted in clearing the table, while Ryan helped Nada tidy up the rest of the sleeping mats and blankets. After everything was cleaned up and put away, Eman and Damari retreated back to the table to work on the letter, and Nada went outside to tend to a few chores. Hailey and Ryan settled down on the blanket, away from the green ottomans.

"Ryan?"

"Yeah?"

"Do you really think we can do this?"

"Honestly… no. But God must have a reason in it all. We just have to keep moving forward. But I'm hoping Nada is right… that I'll understand later on." Ryan sighed. "How are you holding up?"

"I can't seem to shake this feeling."

"Which one?"

"That I'm on the edge of something. It's strange. It's like I'm teetering on the side of a cliff and about to fall into something either amazing or… at least new… but good. At least I think it's good. It's hard to pinpoint. It's not a scary feeling. It's more of a compelling pull type thing."

"Hmm," was all Ryan said.

Hailey didn't know if he understood, she barely did. She didn't get the chance to ask.

"I need air," Ryan said, jumping up.

He headed for the door.

Maybe he doesn't want to understand.

When he disappeared into the kitchen, Hailey decided to follow him.

It was still relatively early, and the road was quiet: no cars nor people in sight. Hailey slid the door closed as she came out into the dry, hot air. She could hear Nada singing somewhere off to the right.

Ryan had walked over to the cab and now leaned against the trunk, his back to her. It was clear something was troubling him. She decided to give him some space to work it through. Maybe with some time, he'd come talk it over with her without her having to push him.

Hailey walked along the side of the house, following the sound of Nada's singing. She couldn't understand the words, but the sound was beautiful and happy. Rounding the back corner, Nada came into view. Two goats stood around her legs. A square of tightly-bound woven sticks made a pen around them. Nada laughed as the goats bumped and pushed her out of the way as they tried to reach the food she put down for them. She raised her head as she caught sight of Hailey.

"They certainly are hungry this morning," she said, laughing again.

"Do you need any help?"

"You're such a sweet girl. Hmm," Nada said, looking around her. "Yes. Can you grab that bucket over there?" Nada pointed.

"This one?" Hailey asked as she walked over and picked up the only bucket she saw, a blue, upturned bucket laying a few feet from the back of the house.

"Yes. Take it over to the pump and fill it for me, please. The goats are thirsty too." Nada turned back to tend to the goats and started singing again.

Hailey stayed still for a moment, but it was apparent Nada wasn't going to offer any further direction. Spinning in place, Hailey scanned around her.

Pump? What pump?

She saw the pen, the house, lots of dirt and sand, a small grassy hill that led away from the house, but no pump. Reaching the end of her spin, Hailey caught sight of a curved pipe peaking over the edge of the hill. She walked towards it. Getting closer she saw that it was a spout from a small pump. The base of the pump didn't run into the ground. Instead, it was connected to an extended section of pipe which ran down to a stream at the bottom of the hill.

A wooden platform sat under the spout. Hailey set the bucket on it and grasped the handle of the pump. She pushed down. Nothing happened. She raised the handle level again and pushed down. Still nothing. Hailey pumped it quickly three times, waited, but the bucket remained empty.

"Nada? It's not working," Hailey called out as she glared at the pump.

"You have to raise the arm all the way up before pushing it down."

The closeness of Nada's words startled her. Embarrassed, Hailey realized Nada must have been watching her first attempts. Hailey followed the instructions, and soon water poured from the spout and filled the bucket with only five pumps.

Hailey grabbed the full bucket and walked back over the crest of the hill.

Funny how different people's lives can be, Hailey thought as she reached the top. *Nada will never know such extravagances, and Ghada will know nothing of these beautiful simplicities. Then there's my life back home: somewhere in the middle.* Hailey chuckled to herself. *We all see the world so differently through our lenses.*

After the goats were watered, Hailey followed Nada back into the house. Ryan had already gone back inside and now sat with Damari at the table, and Eman was working in the kitchen.

"It's getting to be about that time," Ryan said as Hailey closed the door.

A little trepidation inched up her spine. "Alright."

Damari rose from the table. "I'll go pick up the car while you say your goodbyes."

After grabbing their bags, Ryan and Hailey followed him outside. Eman and Nada walked out after them. Hailey kept her eyes on Damari as he jogged down the road. She delayed looking back to Nada and Eman. She hated goodbyes, and this would be the last bit of familiarity and safety she would feel before getting to Anna. Hailey wasn't keen to let them go.

Hailey sighed, finally relenting to the situation. Her eyes met Eman's as she turned. They were already damp with emotion.

"Thh-ank y-you."

Hailey didn't have time to respond. Eman pulled her into a firm hug. It was a bit too tight, but she pulled back just enough to kiss each of Hailey's cheeks. She stepped back and stood close behind her mother-in-law, keeping her face to the ground.

Nada's face was filled with a huge grin, causing all her wrinkles to deepen and her eyes to squint.

"Ryan, remember my words. Understanding will come to you. And Hailey, remember to not let fear stop you. He made you for such a time as this."

Nada's words were still seeping into her heart when the sound of a car filled Hailey's ears. She turned to see Damari driving up.

"Nada, please thank Eman for us," Ryan said. "And, Nada, thank you for… for everything." He leaned over and squeezed each of their arms. "And don't worry. I'll make sure Layla is safe."

Ryan gave them each a big smile and went to the car. A large lump stuck in Hailey's throat, and again she delayed turning back. She bit her lip as Ryan threw the bags in the trunk and Damari got out of the car.

"Ready?" Damari asked as he walked up to her.

"Yes," she lied.

"Here are the directions to Cairo, and the letter for Layla. The photo is tucked inside."

Hailey took them from Damari, but couldn't make eye contact. Her resolve was too fragile.

Eman suddenly let out a small yelp and ran back into the house. When Eman emerged again, she was carrying a brown, cloth bag. She handed it to Hailey. Raising her hand to her mouth, all fingers together, Eman touched them to her lips three times, signaling that it was food.

Hailey nodded and thanked her.

"Let's get going, Hailey."

Hailey started towards the car but stopped. Spinning around, she ran back to Nada. Hailey leaned down, and Nada drew her into her arms.

"Ahh, my child. Your strength lies in God. Go in peace."

Nada reminded Hailey of her mother in that moment. Hailey said nothing, she couldn't. She pulled out of the hug, gave Nada a quick peck on the cheek, and ran to the car without looking back. She couldn't handle anything more. Once inside, Ryan pulled away after a wave out the window.

Dust from the road billowed out behind them, obscuring any possible view of the house or their three hosts. But Hailey didn't mind, she didn't think she could bear the feeling of seeing the distance from them grow.

=======

Hailey seemed distracted, but Ryan couldn't tell if it was from tiredness or from fear about what might be at the end of this road they drove on. The two possibilities battled each other, and he was unsure if he should break the silence or just let her be.

He glanced over at her. As she was looking outside, she rested her chin on her palm and her elbow on the car door.

What do you need? Ryan wondered.

His head buzzed not knowing if he should offer her words of comfort or if they would come across as patronizing. It was worth the risk.

"You OK?"

Hailey didn't turn towards him. "Um... yeah, I think so. I was just thinking about what Layla must have endured these last few weeks. I can't imagine."

Ryan remained silent. He wanted to give her some freedom to process all that must be raging around in her mind.

"I'm not going to lie. I am scared of what we might be walking into. But I'm glad we can get Layla out of there." Hailey finally turned away from the window and looked over at him. "Ryan..."

"Yeah?"

"She's only twelve. It makes me feel so stupid."

"Stupid? Why?"

Hailey shrugged. "I mean, I've heard of child marriages before, but in all honesty, I barely think about such things. Maybe when there is a news article about it, or I see a commercial asking for donations, I think about it for like... what... five minutes, at most."

Ryan looked over. He felt the same way.

She sighed. "Kind of hard to ignore it now that it's literally right in front of us."

"Yup."

"How long do you think it will take to get there?" she asked, handing him the directions Damari gave her.

"Um..."

He glanced from the road to the paper then back up, repeating the process until it was clear where they were headed.

"I think we should be at that tree in about twenty, thirty minutes."

"That seems really... fast." Hailey looked outside again as she ran her hands down her legs. She seemed so tense.

"Yeah, I guess it does. Do you need to pull over for a bit?"

Hailey's head turned back to him and smiled while biting her upper lip. She reached over and took his hand.

"How do you do that?" she asked.

"Do what?"

"Your insight. You seem to have a better grasp on what I'm feeling than I do sometimes."

"Really? I feel like I'm always running behind you trying to catch up."

"Well, you're not. Like when we were on the water, and you swam up to me after my little tantrum-freakout thing. You said that I hoped I knew that a teacher was often quiet during a test. I didn't want to hear it at the time, but it was exactly what I needed. I would never have thought of that on my own. Actually, it kind of bugged me at the time," she said half huffing, half giggling, "but it helped."

"Huh, I had no clue. I'm glad."

He squeezed her hand as he raised it to his lips, giving her knuckles a kiss. "So... can I assume that it's a yes to stop?"

"Yeah," she nodded. "If we have time, I think a moment would be good."

Ryan looked in the rearview mirror. He could see only dust, and there were no cars in front of them. He turned the wheel and brought the car to a stop just off the road, ensuring to miss a few bramble-looking bushes. Setting the car in park, he turned towards her.

"Anything I can do?" he asked as he turned the key, silencing the engine.

Hailey pursed her lips to one side of her mouth as she thought. "Can I ask you something first?"

"Of course."

"How are you doing with all of this? Are you in your strong-facade mode?"

Ryan lowered his head and looked at the console between them.

Looks like she has learned to have some insight into me as well.

He sighed and looked back at her. "Well... actually, I am a bit overwhelmed. Don't get me wrong, Nada's words were amazing and they helped calm me. But I'm scared to bring you into such an unknown and potentially dangerous situation."

Ryan had to bite the inside of his cheek to keep his composure. He looked back down. Hailey stayed quiet, which was Ok, he had more to say.

"I do have hope that Nada is right and I'll understand more about how everything fits together before we get home. But I kind of wish I could know now." He stopped for a moment to gather more thoughts. "And I know that we're not supposed to be afraid when we know He goes before us... but... I am."

Ryan looked up at her sheepishly, feeling embarrassed under the spotlight of his honesty. Hailey's eyes were filled with compassion.

She stroked his arm. "Is there anything I can say or do to help?"

Ryan thought for a moment. "Actually, yeah. Would you be able to stay in the car while I go get Layla?"

"Ryan..."

"I know it's a lot to ask, but I can't ensure to keep you safe when I have no idea what we might be walking into. This way if something goes wrong, you can drive off."

"You're joking, right?"

"Noooo," Ryan answered with a goofy tone as he dragged out the word. "Hailey, please. I'm not trying to be obnoxiously noble or anything. I just can't handle something else happening to you."

"I know," she smiled. "But I'm not leaving you. I can't. Just like you can't handle something happening to me, I can't handle something happening to you. I need you with me. Regardless of what happens, I'm staying with you. So if something happens... it will happen to us both."

"Yeah. I kind of thought it was a long shot. You're kind of

stubborn... but I had to at least try."

"Hey," she protested as she playfully punched his arm. Hailey rolled her eyes and shook her head at him.

A moment of stillness came between them as the gravity of the moment chased away the last of the playfulness.

He reached out his arm. "Come here."

Hailey shuffled to the edge of her seat and leaned towards him. He reached his hand around her shoulders, pulling her closer until her head rested on his chest. He stroked her hair, smoothing it down, then rested his cheek on the top of her head.

"We can do this."

"Totally."

Her tone matched his. It seemed like they both were trying to encourage the other while convincing themselves.

Ryan squeezed her shoulder. "If He brought us to it, there is a purpose."

Hailey pressed harder into him, and he gripped her tighter.

"Agreed," she whispered.

An eerie silence filled the car but holding onto her brought comfort. He hoped his embrace gave her the same feeling.

"Ryan, regardless of what our emotions are doing... He is in control. That is what's true."

He smiled and kissed her forehead. The memory of him asking her what is true when they were on the bus in Riyadh, dulled the edges of his worry.

"What about you?" He gave her shoulder a shake. "Is there anything I can do?"

"Can you kiss me?"

Ryan wasn't expecting that request, but it was an easy one.

"Definitely."

Hailey pulled away from his chest and sat up. The look she

gave him was intense, but not in an uncomfortable way. They held each other's gaze. Neither of them moved. Then slowly he moved to her. Using both hands, he cupped her face and gently pulled her to him as he leaned towards her. Her face felt so fragile and small in his hands. His thumbs caressed each of her cheeks.

As the distance between them lessened, his heart picked up its pace. He could tell Hailey's did the same. Her breathing quickened. With a mere inch between them, he only then broke the gaze. Closing his eyes, his lips met hers. Her lips were warm and soft. The touch caused tingles to run down each arm and into his legs.

The kiss started slow and sweet but soon turned hard and passionate. Not one that he had to put up guards against to keep them in check, but one of a deep desire to hold onto this moment, one that wanted to extract all that it could before necessity pulled them back onto the road.

The need for a full breath of air finally broke the connection.

"Wow," Hailey said breathlessly. "That was..."

"Amazing?" he offered.

"Yeah. It was exactly what I needed."

Ryan chuckled. "Same here."

Still holding onto her face, Ryan smiled and looked into her eyes.

"Hailey, I hope you're up for this because I want to marry you when we get home."

A huge grin took over her lips.

"Well..." Hailey answered, teasing him as she scrunched her face. "You'll just have to wait and see. Of course, you will have to ask properly to find out for sure."

"Done."

Ryan leaned forward and gave her a quick peck before letting her lean back in her seat.

"Ready?" Hailey asked him.

"Yeah, I really think we are. Oh, wait!"

"What?"

"I think we should separate the money. The thought occurred to me earlier, but with all the goodbyes I forgot to do it. If we do get stopped and pull out that huge stack of cash, there is no way they will let us go without taking it all."

"Good point."

Ryan leaned over and grabbed the bag sitting at her feet. He pulled out the money. Separating the bills, he placed each of the small piles into a different spot: the driver's door, the console, and under his seat. He handed two piles to Hailey and instructed her to put one in her door and the other in the glovebox. He split the last pile and gave her half.

"In case we get separated from the car, put this in your pocket."

Ryan put the last few bills in his pocket.

He straightened in his seat, stretched, and gripped the wheel. Taking one last deep breath, his eyes scanned the road and the desert that spanned out beyond.

What else is true? He asked himself as he started the car. He needed more truth if he was going to make it through this. He silently listed off things in his head:

He goes before us, He knows what's coming, and we are not here by accident because all of this was planned and known before I was even born.

Each realization further helped to pump him up. He looked in the rearview mirror. His trepidation seemed to slide off him and mix with the dust that flew up behind the car.

He pressed harder on the gas.
Hold on, Layla.

CHAPTER 33

The fact that she hadn't been able to reach Hailey concerned her. Anna dialed again. Each ring of the phone trying to connect caused more uneasiness to crawl over her.ABdejected, she hung up. It was now Monday morning, and the last time she had an update from Hailey was Saturday night - far too long for Anna's liking.

They should have been in Jordan yesterday. Why isn't she answering? Or calling me?

Anna thought through Hailey's words again. She was certain Hailey had told her that they would be heading to the border before noon yesterday. Things weren't making sense.

Anna looked down at the phone resting silently in her hands. Her mind tried to search for any possible explanations.

Could they have gotten in trouble at the border? The thought brought more worry with it. Anna pushed it away. It seemed unlikely now. With what George reported this morning, the investigation caused enough concern to alert the defense minister and remove the roadblocks, at least for the time being. So now that Ehsan's hands had been tied, there wasn't any reason for them to be delayed. Was there?

Did something happen to the tour bus?

That was definitely a possibility, the desert heat wasn't exactly kind on those big vehicles.

Could they have gotten lost? Nah, that's stupid. Hailey would have still called me. Maybe their phone died again?

She shifted uncomfortably in her seat. Anna hated not knowing the reason for the radio silence and hated even more that there was nothing she could do but wait.

=======

It had been a month now since he had been put in charge of this faction of the organization and Marco didn't want to disappoint. Yet his patience was wearing thin. The girl's husband, Karim, had already gotten them involved more than he would have ever chosen. And now Karim was late for the meeting. It also didn't help that the two brokers, who stood across from him, kept glaring at him.

Get over it, he thought to himself as he kicked some dirt with his foot and glared back at them. Marco made a slight lunge of challenge towards them. They both jumped backward. Marco chuckled as he reveled in the small victory.

The men glanced nervously at Marco's men sitting twenty feet away in the SUV.

"We don't appreciate you getting involved in this way," the man on the right said after composing himself. "It's just not... not how things are done. The arrangement was that you would bring us the clients and we would take care of all the contracts with the families. Do you know how unprofessional it was for us to just show up at the family's house in such a manner? There are rules for such arrangements."

"Aww, you poor, little rich men," Marco jeered them as he

looked from one to the other. "So what if Karim wanted her longer, if it gets us all a lot more money, then who cares. Her parents aren't going to protest. And if you hadn't refused, then I wouldn't have had to get involved. Trust me, whatever Karim's requests are, it's best to agree to them and then get the parents in line. You don't want to lose him as a client."

"Why not?" the other asked. "What's one client?"

"Do you even realize that one client isn't ever just one client? If Karim isn't happy, do you think he'll bother suggesting this little..." Marco looked around at the pathetic surroundings. "... hell hole? He's a nice man, but not that nice. If he's not happy, he'll never come back and who knows how many others will stay away because of it. Hasna isn't by any means a hot spot for travel or business."

The men looked at him, offense contorted each of their faces.

I can't believe this, Marco thought, *they really do believe they are kings in this pitiful dust heap.*

Screeching tires sounded in the distance.

Shading his eyes, Marco looked towards the street. Karim's car was speeding towards them, a Mercedes diamond silver metallic, AMG S65. Yet again, the sight of it put a smile on Marco's face.

"Sorry I'm late," Karim apologized as he exited the car.

"Not a problem," Marco lied.

"So..." Karim said as he looked at each of the men. "Is everything sorted out?"

One of the brokers took a step forward. "Of course. No harm done."

Marco was impressed, the man's lie came across even more sincere than his.

"I would prefer to wrap this matter up quickly for you,

Karim."

"Thank you, Marco. I appreciate that. Here are my terms."

Karim handed Marco the document. He quickly scanned it. It stated that Karim would like to move to making the girl his permanent wife and take her home with him. Marco was shocked. It was a bold move, bigger than he expected. He couldn't wait to see the reaction from the brokers.

He handed the document to the broker on the right. The other leaned over so they could both read it. He had to stifle his laugh when each of the men's eyes grew large as they read.

Karim cleared his throat. "Is there a problem?"

It seemed Karim had also noticed their response.

Marco clenched his jaw. *They better not ruin this deal.*

"No, no. This is fine. But I hope you know that because of the... unique nature of these changes, we will have to make sure everyone is... um... well compensated."

I'm impressed, these idiots do know how to close a deal delicately. Marco looked at Karim to see how it was being received. Karim laughed.

"That won't be a problem. I have a little with me now," Karim said as he moved towards his car.

Returning to them, he held a metal briefcase.

"Marco, could you hold this please."

Marco raised each of his hands to create a shelf. Karim placed the case onto his forearms, clicked the latches, and popped open the top of the case. Marco peered over the lid and down to the contents.

Karim looked at each of them. "This should cover each of your fees."

"More than cover," Marco said under his breath, quiet enough not to be heard when Karim turned to look at the brokers.

Marco had to force his excitement not to betray his nonchalant exterior. His cut looked to be about ten times that of what he made last time. Initially, putting the brokers in their place had helped satisfy some of his frustration from being called to Hasna. But, with this money soon to be in his hands, the trip was more than worth it now.

Karim closed the case. "So are we in agreement?"

"Yes," Marco answered.

The other broker stepped closer. "We are also satisfied and see no reason for further delay."

Funny, Marco thought, *when money is flashed in front of you, rules don't matter much now do they?* Marco glared at the broker on the right. *Fickle little man.*

"Wonderful," Karim said as he took the case from Marco's arms. "Let's head back to the house. I'll divide it up there and get you the amount for Layla's family."

Karim turned towards his car but stopped suddenly. He spun around and stepped quickly to face the brokers, stopping just inches from their face.

"I want to make myself clear on this point. Layla's parents are to be treated with respect, and they are to get the full dowry. I will be contacting them later to check up on you. And if I ever find out that you didn't use the utmost kindness and respect with them or that they didn't get the full dowry, you will regret it. Do you understand?"

The brokers shifted their weight nervously from one foot to the other.

"Of course," they replied in unison.

Well done, Karim, Marco smirked to himself. *You scared them more than I did. I didn't know you had it in you.*

"Good. Let's go." Karim spun back around. "Marco, leave your men here. You can ride with me. I don't want to alarm Layla. You two, follow in your own car."

If you can call it that, Marco teased them in his head. The brown boat of a car would never be something Marco would be caught dead in. He didn't care that the price tag was impressive, it had no class, no style.

Once Karim's back was turned, Marco signaled to his men to hold. He would happily trade a ride in that black SUV for a ride in a Benz AMG S65 any day. Before following Karim to his car, Marco couldn't help but give one more sneer to the brokers. It was just too satisfying giving them a hard time to let the opportunity go by.

Once inside the Benz, Marco admired the luxury interior: brown leather seats, a sleek middle console that swooped up to connect to the dash, the five air vents that sat under the large digital display panel and above the glossy button controls, the racing pedals near Karim's feet.

I'm so going to get one of these one day.

He didn't bother buckling in, Marco never saw the point in it. And it was a pain to adjust his shoulder holster to accommodate the strap. Without the seatbelt, he could sit comfortably with his .45 happily tucked in the holster right where it should be.

He felt like a little kid as the car cut its way through town. It hugged the corners of each turn and accelerated so effortlessly.

"Marco, when we get back to the house," Karim said without taking his eyes from the road, "I'd like you to stay outside with the brokers. I don't want those fools saying anything to Layla that could upset her. She isn't to know of the arrangement. I plan to tell her when we're heading back to Dubai, not a moment before."

"Certainly."

"And when I go into the house to sort out the money, I'd like you to make sure the proper documents will be prepared. I hate paperwork, so I don't need nor want to know what's needed. Just talk with the brokers to ensure they'll take care of everything. I only want to sign what I need to and be done with it. Understood?"

"Perfectly. I'll take care of it."

"Good."

Karim was definitely more pleasant than a lot of the men he dealt with in this job.

Lucky girl. Layla sure could do a lot worse.

=======

In the distance, Ryan could see the tree tucked back from the street. It was hard to miss, it was the only tree in sight. He slowed the car as they made their way down the top of the street. He wanted a moment to assess the area. Apart from two women dressed in long skirts and headscarves on the other side of the road walking away from them, everything looked clear.

"Looks good to me," Hailey said.

"Yeah, it does."

Ryan checked all the mirrors for the third time... still nothing. Then he spotted it.

A car down at the far end of the street made its way towards them. They were only a block away from the tree now, but the car was closing the gap fast. Ryan did a quick calculation, and he wasn't sure they could get to the tree before the vehicle passed them. But what choice did they have?

Taking a deep breath, he willed his body to not react and to keep a steady pressure on the gas pedal. Increasing speed now would only draw more attention. Ryan kept his eyes on the car as they reached the side road. The car reached Layla's house.

Please don't stop, please don't stop, Ryan's mind pleaded.

Just as he turned the wheel, Ryan raised his other hand to shield his face. The car sped past. Ryan turned in his seat to look out the back. The car didn't stop or even slow down. Sighing with relief, he pulled a quick U-turn and parked the car next to the tree.

He sighed and ran his fingers through his hair. "Whoa, I gotta chill out."

"It's OK. I'm freaking out too."

Ryan looked around him. "Let's not mess around. Let's go get her and get out of here. This place is giving me the creeps."

"Agreed."

Ryan opened his door and got out. Closing it softly behind him, he looked over the hood to Hailey.

"Ready?" he asked.

"Yup. Let's go."

=======

The amount of adrenaline running through her made her shake as she jogged behind Ryan to the street.

She'd better be home. Hailey couldn't believe that the thought hadn't occurred to her before. *Yikes, what if she isn't? What if she changed her routine today?*

Hailey's heart felt like it suddenly filled with ice. The questions quickened her pulse as they rattled in her mind. It was obviously too late for them to do anything about it. She shook the possibility from her mind, they were committed now.

Reaching the street after a handful of strides, Ryan slowed his pace. Hailey adjusted the scarf around her head to ensure that everything was covered. Ryan reached for her hand.

Hailey shook her head. "Better not."

"Right, sorry. Habit."

Hailey delayed her next step so she could walk a few steps behind him. She had no idea if similar rules applied in Egypt or not, but she didn't want to take the chance and stand out. At least this way, people might assume she was Ryan's wife.

Hailey kept her head lowered but kept her eyes on Ryan. He scanned around them, trying to casually survey each direction. She didn't dare look around. Two people looking around would look too suspicious. From Ryan's expression, everything seemed alright.

The distance to the house Layla was slowly diminishing, yet Hailey had to continually tell her feet to keep a slow pace. Each leg yearned to sprint towards the house and take cover. She counted the houses to distract her.

One!

Two!

Three!

The next house was Layla's. Hailey watched as Ryan slowed and looked around again.

"All clear."

She followed him up to the house: a soft yellow, stone mansion. Passing a terracotta planter and a few raised, stone flower beds, they speed walked over the brick driveway and up the three steps to the arched doorway. The black door nestled under the arch looked cold and uninviting.

"Do we knock?" she asked.

"I guess so."

Ryan grabbed the black door knocker that hung in the middle of the door. He paused.

"Do it!" The suspense was driving her mad.

Ryan gave the thing three knocks. They waited. Both of them nervously looked back towards the street: a measly twenty feet behind them. The women they saw earlier had disappeared into another house. Hailey wasn't sure which one, but it left the street quiet.

Footsteps!

They both swung their attention back to the door. Hailey's next breath caught in her lungs.

The door slowly opened.

Instantly, Hailey could tell this was Eman's daughter that stood before her. The girl's features: latte skin, wide eyes, high cheekbones, matched her mother almost exactly. The girl's dark, glossy hair poked out of her black headscarf which flowed down over a blue silk robe.

"Layla?" Hailey whispered so not to frighten her.

It didn't help. As soon as the girl heard her name, her eyes widened, and she tried to close the door. Ryan reached out his hand and easily stopped it. The poor girl, scared, started frantically yelling words they didn't understand and continued to try and push the door closed.

"Nymphaea Caerulea," Ryan said gently.

The girl stopped. Confused, she eyed them, desperately trying to sort out what was happening. Hailey didn't speak. Layla needed a moment to process.

Regrettably, the sound of another vehicle coming down the street thrust the moment aside.

CHAPTER 34

Upon hearing the sound of the vehicle, Ryan pushed all politeness aside and shoved the door open. Pulling Hailey inside, he slammed the door closed.

Layla again started yelling at them in Arabic. Ryan ignored her. He moved away from the door and towards one of the rooms at the front of the house. He needed to find a window to check to see if the car had stopped, or worse if it had turned to pull into the driveway.

Finding himself in what appeared to be some sort of sitting room, Ryan ran to the closest window. Pushing the velvet curtain an inch away from the window frame, he peeked out.

No cars.

He pulled back the curtain a bit further to look farther down the street. The car was nowhere in sight. Ryan sighed with relief. He spun around to make his way back to the door. He bashed right into Hailey.

"Ouch," she yelped as she bounced off of him. "Would you stop doing that?"

"Sorry," he said as he rubbed her arm. "What do you mean stop doing that? When have I ever done that?"

"At the market. I'm tired of running into you, you big tree."

Hailey playfully pushed him.

"Alright, alright. You OK?"

A small sound came from the direction of the door. Layla's small frame came into view. She held each of her arms protectively around herself and tentatively walked a couple steps into the room.

"Why... why did you call me Nymphaea Caerulea?"

Layla's voice was so soft, Ryan almost didn't make out what she had said. He slowly walked towards her. Fear flashed in her eyes and she backed away from him. He stopped and put up his hands to calm her. He took another step. This time Layla remained still.

"Your parents sent us," he said.

Layla narrowed her eyes. "Really?".

"Yes, honey. My name is Hailey, and this is Ryan. We've come to take you away from this place."

Layla looked with wide eyes from Hailey to him, then back to Hailey. Layla crumpled to the floor and started sobbing. Ryan's heart broke for her. He couldn't imagine what she had to endure within these walls.

Ryan took a step forward, but Hailey reached out and stopped him. She pushed past him and went over to Layla. Bending down beside the child, she gently reached out her hand. But she paused before it made contact with Layla's shoulder.

"Layla?" Hailey said, announcing her presence.

She then finished the movement. The feeling of Hailey's hand still startled the poor girl and caused her to jump. Layla's head shot up. Yet when she saw Hailey, the girl dove into her. The force made Hailey topple over, but it didn't deter the girl. Layla shrank into a ball in Hailey's lap and wrapped her arms around Hailey's waist.

"Shh. It's OK. You're safe now," Hailey whispered into Layla's ear as she held her and stroked her hair.

When Hailey raised her eyes to look at Ryan, they were filled with tears. Seeing Hailey cry always wreaked havoc on him. He went to them. Kneeling, he rubbed Hailey's back to offer his support. Ryan didn't want to startle Layla by assuming she would be OK with him touching her. She had been through enough and probably wouldn't trust him, for the simple fact that he was a man. So he kept a small distance from her and continued to offer his comfort through Hailey.

Another sound came from the direction of the street. It was faint, and he wasn't sure if it was a car or someone coming toward the house. Over Layla's whimpering, it was hard to make out. Ryan now wasn't even entirely sure he had heard anything.

He stood and went to the window. He peered out and scanned the street. Nothing. Maybe it was his imagination. But regardless they didn't have time for any more delays. He hated to push the girl, but they were too vulnerable just sitting here in the house.

Ryan turned back. Hailey's face filled with concern.

"False alarm," he whispered to reassure her. "But we should get going. Layla?"

The girl raised her head off Hailey and turned to him.

"What time does your... um..." Ryan struggled to know what to call him.

"Karim?" she said wiping her eyes.

"Yes. What time does he usually get home?"

"If he goes to do business, he's not home for a long time yet."

Ryan sighed with relief.

"But today he didn't go there."

"Where did he go?" Hailey asked her.

"A meeting close to here. I'm not sure when he is to come home."

Dread fired up the adrenaline in Ryan's bloodstream. He crossed the room and reached out one hand to each of them. Thankfully Layla accepted it, and he pulled both to their feet.

"We have to leave, now!"

"Are my parents with you?" Layla asked, her voice filled with hope as she followed him towards the front door.

"No, sweetheart. They didn't come," Hailey said.

"So I see them soon. I guess that's OK."

Ryan was about to correct her but stopped himself. He shook his head discreetly to Hailey so she wouldn't explain. Hailey nodded her agreement and kept quiet. They didn't have time to tell Layla everything in the house. They couldn't chance a bad response to the news that she wasn't going home. It was by far best to have that conversation take place in the safety of the car.

"We'll talk all about it when we get into the car, OK?" he said in hopes of precluding any further questions the girl might have.

Layla smiled and took Hailey's hand. "OK."

Ryan pulled the door open. He held his hand up behind his back, signaling for them to wait. Slowly stepping out from under the arch, he glanced down the street in both directions.

"All clear."

Leading the way, Ryan continually scanned around as casually as he could. Not a single vehicle or person caught his eye as they made their way back to the car. Opening the back door for Layla, she climbed in. A look of concern flashed on her face.

"What it is, Layla," he asked, door still open.

"Does Karim know I'm leaving? Will he be mad and come

looking for me? I don't want to get my parents in trouble."

Hailey leaned over the front seat and handed Layla her parent's letter. "Here, Layla, read this. It's from your parents."

Layla grabbed the paper and unfolded it. The photo fell into her lap. Seeing it, Layla grinned but left it where it was. Her eyes danced on the page. Within moments her excitement faded, her face fell. Layla's lip quivered. A tear dripped off the end of her nose. She rose her hand to wipe it away but kept reading. Soon the hand holding the letter fell to her lap, covering the photo.

"So… I'm not going home. Mama said I have to go with you. To somewhere safe. And that they will come for me soon."

Hailey reached over and put her hand on Layla's knee. "That's right."

"No!"

The force of the child's objection was startling and loud. Ryan's eyes lifted and darted around the area. He sighed. There was no one to be alerted.

He looked back in the car. "Layla, I'm sorry, but you must. You're not safe here, and Karim would just come looking for you at your house. You can't possibly go back there."

"No! No! No!" Layla repeated, obstinately. "I'm not leaving without Ruby."

Ryan was taken back. "What? Who's Ruby?"

"My friend."

"Like a toy?" Hailey asked.

Please don't be a stupid toy, Ryan thought as he used both hands to rub his eyes in frustration. *I don't want to go back to that house.*

"No, Ruby is not a toy. She's my friend. Ruby lives in that house over there."

Ryan looked but couldn't tell exactly which house she was

pointing to.

"Where?"

"The house just past Karim's house. Hailey?"

"Yes?"

"I can't leave Ruby. She's littler than me, and her husband is not nice. She needs me. I can't leave her. Please don't make me."

Hailey ducked her head and looked up at Ryan. He closed Layla's door and turned away from the car. Placing his hand over his mouth, his mind raced with obstacles that could arise from changing their plan. Each one would be reason enough to just drive away right now.

He sighed and closed his eyes. There was no way that they could leave that little girl here. The memory of the little jockey slammed into his mind. His regret over not being able to do anything for that boy only fueled his resolve. It was settled. Ruby was coming.

Ryan heard one of the car doors open. Hailey climbed out.

"Ryan, you know what we have to do, right?" she said softly.

"I know." He grabbed the back of his neck. "I'm just not sure how to go about it."

Hailey folded her arms on the roof of the car. Ryan opened Layla's door again and knelt, so he was at eye level with her.

"Layla? Does Ruby's husband work? Or is there a chance he could be home?"

"No, he is at work. He goes to the oil building every day, and I saw him leave this morning. He doesn't like Ruby to go out during the day. Except on some days, she is allowed to play in the yard. She's not allowed to go to the market like I am. There is a woman that comes to the house some days to bring groceries and watch Ruby while she is outside. So Ruby is home alone right now. I know she is."

"Could the woman be there now?"

"No. If she is coming today, it won't be until much later."

Ryan straightened and looked at Hailey. He shrugged. "OK, let's hurry. The longer this takes, the more worried I get."

Ryan closed his eyes and put his forehead on the roof of the car. It was hot from the sun, but he didn't move it off.

God, I couldn't possibly see how You could lead us here to just walk away. So I'm moving out in faith. Help us get these girls out.

Ryan led the way back past the three houses and past Layla's. He tried to keep his pace as slow as he had previously, but his feet kept betraying him. Hailey held Layla's hand and followed behind. He would have preferred for them to stay in the car but knew there was no way Ruby would go with him, she needed to see Layla. He didn't even bother trying to get Hailey to stay with the car. So, against Ryan's preference, here they were exposed and tramping out in the open again.

They had almost reached Ruby's house when Ryan spotted a few men exiting a house across the street. He held his breath but kept walking and used his peripheral vision to keep them in sight. The men didn't seem to notice them. Their conversation stayed even and constant.

When they reached the door, Layla moved past them and knocked. Soon two little eyes peaked out from behind the door. The girl didn't smile or show fear. She just stood there looking at Layla, then calmly looked past her to Ryan and Hailey.

Ruby was so small. Fuzzy, downturned little eyebrows sat above her brown almond eyes. She didn't look Egyptian, maybe Eastern European. Her hair was covered with a white cloth that tucked under her chin like a knitted neckwarmer pulled over her head. She wore a long-sleeved dress, patterned with yellow and orange geometric shapes and randomly-placed green flowers.

She held a raggedy doll in her chubby hands. Ruby looked like a sad cartoon character.

Ryan smiled at her. The girl didn't return it. Her sweetness and vulnerability overwhelmed him. He couldn't believe this precious little thing was forced to be someone's wife.

"Come with me, Ruby," Layla instructed.

The little girl said nothing in return. Ryan's eyes widened with surprise when Ruby turned around, closed the door behind her, and took Layla's hand without protest or question.

"OK, let's go," Layla said turning to face him.

"Well, that was easier than I thought it was going to be," Ryan whispered to Hailey as they turned to follow the girls.

Suddenly, sounds of squealing tires filled his ears. Ryan looked in the direction of where their car sat. At the far end of the street, a silver car came careening around the corner.

Layla whimpered, and Ryan snapped his head down to look at her.

"That's Karim's car!"

Instantly, Ryan felt foolish for being so cavalier. He grabbed Layla's hand and ran to the far side of Ruby's house. Hailey followed. Reaching the corner, Ryan tripped on a bucket of gardening tools, almost toppling to the ground and pulling Layla and Ruby down with him. Regaining his balance, he pushed the girls to stand against the house. Hailey went on the other side, keeping the girls between them. A twinge of pain throbbed in his left ankle.

"Are you OK?"

Ryan ignored Hailey's questions. He leaned his back on the wall and peeked around the corner. The silver car was getting closer, and just beyond it, a brown car came around the corner. Not quite as fast, but enough to imply they might be together.

"Damn it," Ryan said under his breath. He turned to Hailey. "There's another car."

"Ryan, what are we going to do? They're blocking our exit. How are we going to get past them?"

Hailey's voice wavered as she spoke. She seemed just as terrified as he was. He had to think quickly.

"OK, here's what we're going to do. We will only have a short window to do this. Layla, are there any fences out back separating the houses?"

"No."

"Ok, then once the cars stop next door, Hailey, when I tell you, I want you to run with the girls as fast as you can around back and get to the car. Here are the keys."

As she took them, she looked at him with concern. "But what about you? I'm not leaving you here."

"Hailey, we don't have time for this. I will keep a lookout. Take the girls and drive the car back up the road and out to the edge of town. Park by the first cream building we passed on the way in. Do you remember it?"

"Yes."

"Good. I promise I will meet you there." Ryan turned away before she had another chance to protest.

When his eyes met the street again, the vehicles were a lot closer than he expected. The silver car was already slowing to pull into the driveway.

Ryan signaled with his hand behind his back. "Get ready," he whispered.

He waited until the brown car had pulled up closer. He didn't want to chance that whoever was in the brown car would catch a glimpse of Hailey and the girls as they ran between the houses.

As soon as the brown car pulled around the silver car to park, Ryan turned and mouthed, "Go!"

The girls took off running and disappeared behind the house. Ryan stood motionless for a moment as he looked at the vacancy they left behind.

Please, hide them from their sight.

Turning back to the front, he peeked around the house again. There were now four men standing in the driveway, each taking turns talking. Their cars remained running, so it didn't seem like they were planning on heading into the house, at least not right away. Or maybe not at all.

Should I wait or run after the girls?

He looked again. Still talking.

Taking a deep breath, Ryan turned and took a step towards the back of the house.

STOP!!

The command almost knocked him over. He stopped in his tracks.

Father, why?

No answer came. A plan started to form in Ryan's mind. It was so complete and compelling that it was impossible to ignore. He pivoted back to the front corner of the house. Searching the ground, he spotted what he needed.

Damn!

The knife that had fallen out of the box of garden tools laid three feet past the corner of the house. He'd be seen for sure if he went for it now. He looked back at the men. There were only three of them now.

Where is the other one? Ryan's eyes frantically scanned around, but he couldn't see him anywhere.

He must have gone in. Ryan's pulse quickened. *If he went inside, he'd soon know Layla's not there. But I need that knife.*

Ryan let out a slow breath to steady his nerves as he continued to watch the other three men. Within seconds, the fourth man burst from the house.

"Layla's gone!"

"What?"

"I'm telling you. She's not here."

"Maybe she went to the market."

"No, she always leaves a note if she goes out. It's a rule I strictly enforce with her. She has never forgotten."

"Did you search the whole house?"

"No, not the whole thing. But she won't answer my calls."

All four men ran into the house.

This was his moment. Ryan went for the knife. As his hand tightened around the handle, he looked to make sure his path was clear. It was. Crouching low, he ran over to the brown car and ducked behind it.

At least it's not a black SUV. He stole a quick look over the hood of the car. All was still. *I bet the gang of sex traffickers are more hardcore than these marriage brokers.*

Over the hum of idling engines, Ryan could hear the faint voices of the men calling for Layla. He had to work fast. They could give up their search for Layla at any moment.

Ducking back down, he jammed the blade of the knife into the rubber of the front tire. It barely went in. It was harder to push through the rubber than he'd realized. He gave the butt of the knife a quick blow with the palm of his hand and gripped the handle tighter. The blade slid fully into the tire. Air rushed out as he removed the knife. He moved onto the others.

After the last tire of the brown car was slashed, Ryan kept his head down and crossed the four-foot distance to the silver

Mercedes. He jumped in and gently closed the door. Setting the car in reverse, he kept his eyes glued to the front door, looking for any signs of movement. Everything was still.

Being careful not to step on the gas too quickly and provoke a roar from the engine, Ryan slowly rolled the car out of the driveway. He glanced down to set the car into gear. When he raised his eyes back to the house, they met the eyes of one of the men. The man stood motionless in the doorway, stunned at the sight of Ryan.

Ryan yanked the steering wheel around. The man yelled at him while simultaneously reaching to his side. He pulled a gun. Fear shot through Ryan. Two shots rang out. Ryan slammed his foot on the gas, and the car jumped to life. As it leaped forward, the speed pressed his body into the seat.

Three more shots fired off, one of which connected with the back window, shattering it. Ryan ducked and looked in the side mirror. All four men ran into the street behind him.

"Ahhh-haha," Ryan laughed as he sped down the street. "Whoa, that was close. I can't believe that worked."

Jerking the wheel, the car spun around the corner at the end of the street with ease. Adrenaline pumped through him, his whole body shook from it. At the next intersection, Ryan barely bothered slowing down. The car glided effortlessly through the turn.

"I love this car," he yelled as he banged both of his palms on the steering wheel.

Ryan checked the rearview mirror. There was no way that they were going to catch up with him now, but he looked anyway. Nothing. Turning his attention back to the road, he allowed his body to relax. The instant he did, blinding pain shot through his shoulder. It was so intense that it made him buckle over, causing the car to almost veer off the road.

Narrowly managing to steady the wheel and straighten out the car, Ryan reached up to touch his shoulder. He was shocked that it was wet. He moved his hand into view.

It was covered in blood.

CHAPTER 35

Being away from the house removed some of her stress, yet Hailey felt uneasy leaving Ryan. She checked the rearview mirror. There was no sign of him yet, but then there wouldn't be so soon.

Help him do whatever it is he's doing, she prayed.

The car bumped over the lip of the driveway in front of the building at the edge of town. They drove into, what looked like, a dusty parking lot. Ensuring she still had a clear line of sight to the street, Hailey stopped the car in a spot facing the building. A handful of people milled about, but no one paid them any attention. Setting the car in park, she turned to look at the girls in the back seat. Layla had her arms protectively around Ruby.

"You girls OK?"

"Yes," Layla answered.

"And how about you, Ruby. Are you OK?"

Ruby didn't answer, her expression didn't change. She just looked at Hailey with this timid blank stare. Hailey frowned empathetically at her.

"Don't be sad," Layla said. "Ruby doesn't talk. Or... at least I've never heard her talk."

"Do you know if she understands English?"

"Yes, she does. I tried to speak to her in Arabic, but she doesn't seem to know what I'm saying when I do. So I speak to her in English."

"Thank you, Layla. That helps. Ruby, you don't have to speak if you don't want to."

Hailey turned to glance at the street. No sign of Ryan yet. Naturally, being on foot, he would be quite a bit behind them, yet Hailey chose to look anyway. She wished there had been time for him to tell her what he had planned. This waiting would be painful.

Looking back at the girls, Hailey smiled at Ruby again. "Hmmm, I wonder if I can guess how old you are. Are you twenty?"

Layla started to giggle as she turned and looked down at Ruby. Ruby remained still.

"Not twenty, hey? OK... what about nineteen?"

Again there was nothing from the little girl, not even a slight flicker or twitch.

"Silly lady, Ruby is eight."

"So... eight, wow," Hailey played up. "And Layla, you're twelve?"

"Yes, I just had my birthday not long ago."

"Ruby, honey, where are your parents?" Hailey made sure to address her directly, regardless if she would answer or not. It wasn't fair to talk like she wasn't there.

"Her family lives very far from here," Layla explained. "The lady who watches Ruby in the afternoons when we get to play said that you have to take a plane to get there. Hailey, have you ever been on a plane? I'd sure like to go on a plane one day. To be in the air like a bird is, I think, the best thing there could be."

Hailey chuckled. She looked back at Ruby.

"Well, don't worry. We will find a way to tell your parents and somehow get you back to them."

Tears formed in Ruby's eyes and dripped onto her cheeks, yet her expression didn't change, nor did she make any sound. She looked blankly at Hailey for a moment then turned her face into Layla's shoulder. Her little shoulders started to shudder.

"No, Hailey. You misunderstand. Ruby isn't allowed to go home. She was sold to the men in the big, black cars."

The traffickers, Hailey remembered. Her whole body cringed at the thought.

"I'm so sorry, Ruby. But that is all over now, I promise. You will be safe with us."

Ruby turned back around. Wiping her tears, she continued to look blankly at Hailey. Hailey paused a moment to see if Ruby would say anything. She didn't.

"How about some food? I bet that would help. Are you girls hungry?"

Layla said she was and Ruby gave the slightest head nod.

"Alright then," Hailey said as she turned around.

Hailey reached down to the floor of the front seat and retrieved the cloth bag. Pulling the handles apart, she looked inside. There were four cloth parcels tied with thin string, a bottle filled with a deep red liquid, and a jar of olives.

Hailey withdrew each of the four parcels and laid them on her lap. She grabbed one and untied it: dates and figs. She opened the next. Instantly her mouth watered. It was the dessert from last night. Hailey had already forgotten the name, but she was happy to see them. The other two bundles contained samosas. Hailey passed each of the parcels, one by one, back to the girls.

As Ruby saw what Hailey was giving them, her eyes

widened, her lips curled into a big grin, and a little, pink tongue popped out of her mouth. Hailey had to stifle a laugh.

Leaving the girls to eat, Hailey turned back to the bag and removed the bottle. It was made of glass and had a rubber cork: the kind that you could flip in and out easily because it was held in place by hinges and wire attached to the bottle.

Hailey popped out the cork and sniffed the contents. It smelled like a combination of honey, mint, and fruit. She brought it to her lips and tried a small sip. It had a good punch of sourness, but it was tasty. She took another sip, then turned to offer it to the girls.

Hailey couldn't stifle her laugh this time. Ruby had her cheeks stuffed full of the dessert. She looked like a little chipmunk. Crumbs covered her lips.

"Is that good?" Hailey asked.

The little girl gave a slight nod of her head.

"I'm glad. And you know what? I had those for the first time last night, and I love them too."

"You never had katayef before?" Layla asked.

"No, never." Hailey tried to add a lot of emphasis to each word to engage the girls more. "But they are now my favorite. Even more than cinnamon buns."

"Wow, katayef is my favorite too," Layla announced, delighted. "What's a cinnamon bun?"

Hailey smiled at each of them. "I'll show you one day."

Ruby raised her chubby little hands out towards Hailey. Moving her fingers in and out. She stared at the bottle Hailey held.

"Thirsty? Here ya go."

Ruby took the bottle and chugged a few good swallows before passing it to Layla. A couple red drips ran down Ruby's chin. She wiped them off with the back of her hand.

The girls finished eating and passed the rest of the food back to Hailey. She tucked it back into the bag and returned it to the floor on the passenger side. Turning her eyes back to the road once more to look for signs of Ryan, something caught her eye.

The vehicle, far in the distance, was acting strangely. It swerved and almost went off the road. Hailey squinted. The car smoothed out and sped down the road. Little hairs on her arms stood on end, and her breath quickened as the vehicle continued towards them. Hailey hadn't gotten a look at the cars that showed up to the house, but fear started to ask her if this car might be one of them.

"Girls, everything is OK. But I'd like you to duck down." Seeing fear rise in each of their eyes, Hailey switched tactics. "Let's play a game and surprise Ryan when he gets here. Let's hurry and hide."

The fear in their eyes didn't diminish, yet they both slid off their seats and onto the floor of the car. Hailey returned her attention to the approaching vehicle. It swerved again, but corrected and continued down the road.

The distance was closing fast. Hailey ducked and listened. She hugged the console between the front seats. Turning her head to face the back, she peeked through the gap in the seats to make sure the girls hadn't gotten up. Thankfully they remained huddled on the floor. Silent.

Hailey strained to listen to what was happening outside. It was silent at first, but soon the sound of an engine roaring closer filled the air, then a spray of gravel, then just the hum of an idling engine.

When Hailey heard the vehicle's door open, she realized just how close it was to their car. She squeezed her eyes shut and bit her lips. She prayed the men would leave before searching their car.

"H-AILE-YYY?"

The painful cry of her name caused her to shoot up from the seat. She looked out to her left and saw an expensive silver car parked about ten feet from theirs. The driver's door was open. As soon as Ryan's pained face came into view from behind the windshield, Hailey lept from the car.

"Ryan!"

Coming around the driver's side, she skidded in the dirt and almost wiped out. Grabbing the open door, she managed to stay upright. She looked inside.

At first, it took Hailey a few moments to process the scene. Ryan was moaning in pain. He was holding his left shoulder with his right hand. His hand, his whole left side, and the leather seat were covered in blood.

"Oh, God! Ryan, what happened?"

"I took... one of the cars." Ryan's words stumbled out of him, as he spoke through the pain. "But slashed the tires... of the other car... first."

Hailey removed her headscarf and pressed it to Ryan's shoulder, just next to his hand. He slid his hand over the top of the cloth. He winced. The quick change in pressure, caused a gush of blood to ooze out, but it slowed as soon as Ryan clamped down on it again.

"Why are you bleeding?" Hailey asked, panicked.

"Just as I was about... to pull away, a guy came out of the house... and pulled a gun. He got a few shots off. At first... I didn't even know... I was hit."

Hailey's stomach tilted, she had never seen so much blood.

"Hailey, we can't stay here. I assume they know... we have

Layla. Or at the very least... saw that I took their car. They won't be far behind me... once they find another car."

"Ryan, we need to get you to a hospital."

"Yeah... I think that that would be good. It really hurts. But we have to get away from... here. I gotta ditch this car. I'll... need your help to get to ours."

Hailey leaned down and reached between Ryan's torso and the seat. When he moved to raise his arm to put it around her shoulders, he screamed out in pain.

"Ow, ow, ow. That hurt. Just... just give me a minute."

By Ryan's breathing, she could tell how much pain he was in.

"OK, let's go," he said, winded.

This time Ryan pushed through. Again crying out, yet he didn't stop moving until he was out of the car. Hailey moved to his other side so that he could lower his hurt arm. She stayed next to him to help him over to the car, but he barely leaned on her.

When they reached the passenger side of their car, Hailey looked at his shoulder. Blood was still running down his arm.

"Ryan, we need to slow that bleeding down. That compress isn't working. Here, lean against the car."

Ryan obliged, wincing as he did so. Hailey pulled his hand away and peeled the scarf back. Bright red blood poured out. She would have to work fast. After wringing out the drench scarf, she looped it under his shoulder. She was just barely able to get it high enough around the upper part of his arm to clear the wound.

"Ready?" she asked, giving Ryan a chance to prepare.

"Yeah."

As Ryan took a deep breath, Hailey pulled each end as hard as she could. Ryan yelled out in pain, and his knees buckled. But he managed to stay standing.

"Oh, Ryan, I'm so sorry."

Pulling back, she surveyed the injury. Blood was still trickling out more than she would like.

"Ryan, that's not going to work. It's not stopping the bleeding."

Hailey turned away and looked around the ground. She wasn't exactly confident in what she was doing, but she had seen enough war movies to maybe come up with something that would hopefully help.

At least it should be better than just the scarf. She walked around while continuing to scan the ground. Finally locating what she needed, she bent down and picked up a small stick, then returned to Ryan.

"I'm sorry, but this is going to hurt even more."

Ryan grimaced. "Just do it."

Hailey slid the stick under the scarf, close to Ryan's armpit. Grasping each end of the stick, she gave it a swift clockwise turn and then another.

This time, Ryan didn't make a sound. Hailey looked at his face. It was so pale. Ryan's eyes fluttered and his head nodded forward. Hailey leaned into him, sandwiching him between her and the car, as his knees bent. She made sure not to let go of the stick so it didn't spin back around.

"No, no. Stay with me, babe."

Ryan snapped his head back up to look at her, alarm on his face.

"Whoa, that felt weird," he said blinking. "I think... I should sit down."

Hailey inspected the wound. The tourniquet was helping. The blood seemed to have stopped.

"Yeah, let's get you in the car. But here," Hailey raised Ryan's right hand and placed it on the stick, "hold this. Do not let it go!"

He nodded.

Gingerly, she helped support Ryan as he eased into the car and helped him buckle his seatbelt. Hailey ran around to the driver's side. Realizing she was entirely unprepared for help Ryan further, a nauseous fear gripped her as she jumped inside.

I need to get him to a doctor.

Whimpers sounded from the back seat.

Oh no, the girls.

Hailey turned to see two frightened faces staring up at her from the floor of the back seat.

"Girls, it's OK. You can get up now," she said as she started the car. "Ryan is hurt, but we're going to get him to the doctor. Can you get buckled?"

The girls jumped back in their seat and clicked themselves in.

"Good. Are you ready?"

Hailey didn't wait for a response, she slammed the car into reverse and peeled out of the parking lot.

Turning back onto the street, she slammed the wheel hard to the right. The car responded and turned. Ryan moaned. Hailey quickly straightened out the car, so not to aggravate his wound further. Moments later they were out of the city and speeding toward Cairo.

=======

Marco swore as the car sped away.

"What the hell was that?" he said, turning back to face the others.

Karim swore. "That jerk stole my car." Throwing up his

hands, he paced back and forth in the driveway. "I can't believe this."

Marco moved to the driver's door of the brown car. "Get in!"

As his hand grabbed the door handle, he saw the tire damage.

"You've got to be joking." He kicked the tire to let out some frustration.

Marco grabbed the phone from his pocket and dialed. One of his runners answered on the first ring.

"Where are you?" he demanded.

"Back at the house. Why?"

"Get to Karim's house now!"

"Why? What happened?"

"I'll explain later, just get here. Bring three others."

Marco hung up and shoved the phone back in his pocket. It was then that he noticed the watching eyes from across the street. Understandably, his gunfire had drawn some attention.

"Do you know any of them?" Marco asked Karim.

"Yeah, some. Why?"

"Go ask them if they saw anything else."

Karim crossed the street and chatted with one man. Marco couldn't hear what they were saying, but whatever the man was saying, angered Karim. Marco jogged over to see what was happening.

"What's going on?"

Karim turned away from the man and stepped into the street.

"He didn't just take my car, he took Layla." Karim let out a yell of frustration as they crossed back to the house.

"What? How? I didn't see her in the car."

"No, a woman was with him earlier and drove off with Layla and... a little girl named Ruby."

"What!! My Ruby?"

"Your Ruby?"

"Yes, she belongs to me. She was living in the house next to yours."

"You mean the little one?" Karim scowled at him. He obviously disapproved.

Marco didn't care, Karim knew very well what he did for a living.

Think whatever you want, old man, you're not much better. Marco would have loved to say the thought out loud, but seeing how he hadn't been paid yet, he couldn't risk offending Karim and lose the payout. He turned away with clenched fists.

While waiting for his men to arrive, Marco decided to make a few calls to see if anyone had spotted the silver Benz driving around. There wasn't much to go on, but at least they had a rough direction. The rest of the wait was agonizing. Thirty minutes later, his men arrived.

As the black SUV pulled up in front of the house, Marco spun around to Karim.

"If I can get her back for you, will you double what you owe me?"

It was a bold move but worth it. When Karim hesitated, Marco turned back to the car and walked to the passenger side. Before opening the door, he looked back at Karim.

"Last chance."

There isn't a chance that I wouldn't go after Ruby, but why not make a little extra cash while I'm at it. Marco had to concentrate so his thoughts didn't show on his face.

"Yes, yes." Karim conceded. "Just get her back. And my car."

"Done."

Marco jumped in and slammed the door.

"Go!" he yelled to his driver.

CHAPTER 36

With each jolt of the car sending shooting pain throughout his body, Ryan was finding it increasingly difficult to not cry out. He didn't want to scare the girls any further, but the pain was intensifying. His body was cold and sweaty. It was getting harder to think straight like his head was slowly filling with cotton. Ryan looked outside and hoped it would distract him.

Leaning his forehead on the glass, he watched the sand and rock whiz by. Abruptly, the cotton cleared, and everything seemed to move slower. He glanced over at Hailey. She didn't notice. She just drove on, staring straight ahead, occasionally glancing in each of the car's mirrors.

Ryan leaned his head back on the glass and looked back out his window. He felt something running down his arm. He looked down. Blood was trickling down his arm again. The jolt from the bumps along the road must have shifted the tourniquet.

Ryan suddenly realized that this... this was his last day alive. He felt scared and confused, and he tried to shake the thought away.

Didn't Nada say that I would understand things more before I got home? This doesn't make any sense. I'm supposed to get back home. I don't want to die yet.

I have gone before you to prepare a place for you.

Oh, not... that home.

Like a thundering waterfall, the understanding came crashing all around him. He saw everything so clearly. God had numbered each of their days and intricately worked all their stories together. Some were short, others longer. There was sadness in it, but not devastation. And that sadness was only one of short-term longing for what one had lost, not of something that had gone out of control and needed to be feared and fixed.

God held it all in His hands.

The clarity showed him the numerous things that God had orchestrated with just their stories: Chuck's, Linda's, Hailey's, Ruby's, Layla's, his. Each story came together in an intricate tapestry of events.

Couldn't You have chosen for it all to work out differently? Without all the tragedy? You could have still taught us and brought us together. Wasn't there another way to rescue these girls? What purpose was there is in Chuck and Linda's death? Or in Fabina's?

Remember what I showed you with Joseph's story? It was similar with him. I am about to complete the work I started in you.

Ryan hadn't thought about that lesson for a long time. He would have never dreamed that his life would mirror Joseph's. The comfort it brought erased all his questions, except one.

What about Hailey? She won't understand.

I will also show her what I taught you with Joseph's story. My word will not return to Me empty. She is in My hand, as are you. And today, you will be with Me in paradise.

As the last of God's words solidified Ryan's understanding, the pain crescendoed. Ryan tried to contain it, but the searing fire gripping his chest caused him to moan.

Hailey reached over and touched his leg. "Ryan, what's wrong?"

The concern in her voice broke his heart. He desperately wished he could shelter her from what was coming. His head started to spin, and everything was going in and out of focus.

"Ryan, answer me!"

It was hard to speak. "Hailey, pull over."

His words were barely more than a whisper. He tried to look at her, but the weight of his head was now too much for him to lift. He shifted his eyes to look at his shoulder. The trickle he saw earlier wasn't the only one. A small trail of blood ran from under the tourniquet. It disappeared under his armpit, making it barely visible. He slowly raised his arm as much as the pain would allow. The trail continued down his side and over the edge of the seat, then ran between the seat and the console to the floor.

His pulse started to race. His breathing came faster yet more shallow. Sweat gathered and dripped from his forehead.

Shock was setting in.

=======

"Ryan, we can't. There isn't anywhere to…"

In the distance, she saw a shimmering. Something was up ahead. Stepping on the gas, Hailey closed the gap. Two run-down buildings sat just off the road. She pulled off.

Setting the car in park, Hailey glanced around. There was no movement, no other vehicles, no other people. The place looked abandoned.

"We should really keep going." Hailey had to strain to add some compassion to her voice as she continued to look around, her desperation was coming through as irritation. "We need to get you to the next town or city and find a doctor."

When no answer came, Hailey turned her attention to Ryan. He looked paler, and he was sweating. His shirt was soaked, but he was shivering. Panic took over. She jumped out of the car, ran around to Ryan's door, and yanked it open.

She bent down beside him. "Ryan, what's wrong?"

His eyes were open, but his head was turned down and away from her. Ryan jerked his head towards her.

"I'm so sorry."

"For what?"

Sadness covered his face. "I'm so sorry."

He leaned over to her and went limp as soon as he touched her. His hand fell from the stick, and it spun undone.

"No!"

She lunged for the stick.

Making quick movements, Hailey tried to readjust the tourniquet, but it didn't seem to help. The blood running out of the wound didn't stop, only slowed. Hailey's eyes lowered and focused on Ryan's seat. A sizable pool of blood dripped over the side and down between the seats.

"Oh, no! Ryan, look at me."

Hailey rested her hip on his seat. She grabbed his face with her free hand. His head just flopped in her hand.

"Ryan!"

His eyes opened groggily and looked at her.

"Ryan, h-how long has it been bleeding like this?"

"Um... I... don't know."

His words were weak. Hailey had to stop this bleeding. She looked around and tried to readjust herself, but it was too cramped. She needed more room.

She reached down under her arm, ensuring to hold the stick

in place and awkwardly unclipped his seatbelt.

"Ryan, you're going to have to help me, OK?"

Hailey looked in the back seat. The girls' faces were ablaze with fear.

She forced a smile. "It's going to be OK."

Hailey wished her words had come out more confident. By their tone it was obvious she didn't believe what she was saying.

Ryan's effort was feeble, but they managed to slide him out of the car and onto the ground. Fear and adrenaline caused her to shake when she saw the blood flow increase. Hailey clamped both hands over the wound. The blood oozed between her fingers.

"No, No! Ryan... Ryan... I... I don't know what to do."

Hailey's eyes darted around their dusty surroundings, searching hopelessly for support.

She looked up into the sky. "Please don't do this. Please," Hailey pleaded. Her lungs hyperventilated with fear.

When Ryan's hand came up and grabbed her wrist, Hailey had to blink a few times to clear the tears in her eyes so she could see him.

"Hailey, it's going to be OK."

"But Ryan, there's so... so much blood. I don't know what to do."

Ryan started pulling on her hand. "It's OK, let me go. I understand now."

"Are you crazy? You'll bleed out. No, I just have to get this bleeding under control, and y-you'll be fine."

Hailey positioned her body further over her hands so she could use more of her weight to compress his shoulder. The sound of the blood squishing under hands made her skin writhe.

Ryan coughed. "Let go. Nada was right... I'm going home."

"No... please, no. Ryan..."

She dropped her eyes back to her hands. They were covered in blood. A pool was starting to form from under his shoulder. It had almost made its way to her knees. She looked back at Ryan, her mouth agape. No words came out.

"I-I love you, Hailey."

As soon as the words were off his lips, his body convulsed. The unnatural sensation of his body jolting under her hands was the vilest and most horrifying thing she had ever felt. It took everything in her not to pull away and vomit. She clenched her jaw and squeezed his shoulder with every last bit of strength she had.

Ryan's hand fell from her wrist and dropped into the dust.

"Ryan, no, no... don't let go."

His body convulsed again.

"Please, please, no, no."

Hailey waited for more movement. None came. He laid still. It was nearly impossible, but she forced herself to move her eyes back to Ryan's. He was still looking at her. However, she soon realized his eyes were no longer seeing her.

He was gone.

CHAPTER 37

At first, it seemed as though a pause button had been hit. Nothing moved. There was only silence. It was as if she and Ryan were in a little bubble.

Slowly, Hailey became aware of the wind. It swirled around them and picked up small grains of dirt. The grains stung her face. She felt the hard ground beneath her and small pebbles cutting into her knees. The sound of the idling car behind her seemed deafening, and the desolate surroundings seemed to press in on her.

Hailey eased the pressure off Ryan's shoulder, and her eyes scanned the length of him. This can't be happening. She lifted her head. Her gaze swept in a circle over the dirt around them. As her eyes made their way back towards her knees, she saw her hands. They rested in her lap coated in blood. Ryan's blood.

The play button was hit.

The bubble popped.

Ryan was dead. This was happening.

An immense cry of defeat and sorrow rose into her throat from the pit of her being. The force from which it thrust from her threatened to rip her apart. Her loneliness and heartbreak seemed to personify. Each one took a side of her and pulled, further helping her cries tear her in two.

Her chin dropped to her chest as she sobbed. She saw her hands. Seeing Ryan's blood again sent a wave of panic over her. She needed to get it off. Shoving her hands into the sand beside her, she grabbed handfuls of it and started to rub it vigorously against her skin.

Get off! Get off! she yelled in her mind.

The sand worked to remove most of the wet blood, leaving only the streaks of dried blood behind. Hailey sat there motionless as she looked at her hands. The scratches the sand had cut into her skin stung.

Her eyes moved back to Ryan. Her body rocked forward as another cry of grief racked her body. Her mind fought against accepting that the expectations for their future were now impossible. There would never be a wedding. He would never get to be her husband nor she his wife. There would never be a honeymoon or more diving. They would never get to raise their children together. Never get to grow old together. There were so many nevers and they all pressed down on her, crushing her.

"Noooo!"

Just as the next painful cry was about to reach the surface and burst from her, a soft little whimper sounded from behind her. The sound caused her cry to painfully catch in her throat and dissipate.

She turned to see Ruby standing near her. Hailey looked back to the car. Layla was still inside, leaning on the window and crying. Her face twisted in despair. Hailey turned her attention back to Ruby. Her little face had tears running through the dust on her cheeks. She was silent and, apart from the tears, Ruby's face still held the same numb expression.

Reaching out her plump little arm, Ruby held up her doll to Hailey. Hailey looked at it and then back to Ruby. The little girl was trying to comfort her by offering her doll. The act of kindness drove the loneliness to stop fighting over her torn soul for a moment. Hailey was able to finally take a full breath.

"Thank you, Ruby," she choked out as more tears gathered in her eyes.

It took an incredible amount of focus to keep the last fragment of her composure. She didn't want to squash Ruby's first attempt to connect with her. Hailey took the stained little doll and gave it a hug. After a kiss on the doll's cheek, she handed it back to Ruby.

"Your doll is very special. I feel a bit better." The truth in her words surprised Hailey. She actually did feel better. "Thank you."

It was barely noticeable, but Hailey caught sight of a smile tugging at the corners of Ruby's mouth.

"Head back to Layla, OK? I'll be there soon."

Ruby hugged her doll and made her way back around the car. Hailey hesitated to turn around. Taking a deep breath, she closed her eyes for a moment before forcing herself to do so.

The sight of Ryan caused bile to rise violently in her throat. Turning her head away from the girls, she leaned over just as it exited her body. Hailey remained hunched over until she was sure it cleared her system. Yet, surprisingly, the despair didn't return. Something told her that if it weren't for those two little girls, she wouldn't have been able to survive this moment.

Hailey sat there, unmoving. She wiped her mouth, unsure of what to do. The girls needed her, yet she couldn't just leave Ryan. Hailey reached out her hand. It shook as she leaned over and closed his eyes. She shifted her legs to the side and laid on his chest.

It was comforting to touch him but strange to not feel his chest rise and fall under her cheek, or hear the soft beating of his heart beneath his ribs.

Her heart ached for him to move his arms around her, for him to rub her back, for him to speak kind words to her, or tell her again that he loved her. But he didn't, and Hailey realized he never would again. Hailey thought about the kiss on the side of the road.

I wished I knew that that was the last time I'd kiss him. I would have made it last longer. Maybe this would be easier.

Her nose started to tingle with the threat of tears, and soft whimpers seeped over her lips.

This is all wrong. How could this have happened? How am I going to do this without you?

Loneliness sank itself further into the pit of her stomach.

God, I don't understand. Help me understand.

Silence.

Please, she pleaded. *I need help. I don't know what to do. Please… answer me.*

I'm here, Hailey. I'm always here.

What's happening? How does any of this make sense?

It is the same lesson I've been teaching you from the beginning.

What lesson? I don't understand. I can't do this without Ryan.

You can. My grace is sufficient for you.

His Spirit moved her heart, and she knew more understanding would soon come, but at that moment, she was meant to wait. Hailey was never any good at waiting, and her mind raged at her to ask for more answers. Yet her whole core was yearning for her to not fight against it.

OK. I'll wait.

Hailey continued to cry silently and hold onto Ryan as she grieved. She wasn't ready to leave him.

"Hailey?"

Layla's voice came from behind her. She sounded scared and timid. Hailey pushed back from Ryan and looked at her with concern. Layla was standing just outside the car, still holding onto the door.

Hailey wiped her cheeks dry. "What is it, honey?"

"What are we going to do?"

Hailey opened her arms to the girl. "Come here."

Layla didn't move. She nervously stared at Ryan's body. Hailey stood, walked over to Layla and picked her up. The girl wrapped her legs around Hailey's waist and hugged Hailey's neck with both arms. Hailey held her tightly. Layla started to cry.

"Shhh, it's OK," she said softly as she stroked Layla's back. "You don't need to be afraid. Ryan isn't here, he's safe."

"No... he's dead," she wailed.

"Nah. That's just his container." The metaphor started to form in her mind as she spoke. "Layla, were you sad when the olives and the katayef were gone?"

Layla leaned off of Hailey's shoulder and looked at her. She sniffed, confusion filled her face. Hailey bent and set Layla back on the ground but kept her hands on the girl's shoulders. Hailey checked to see if Ruby was listening. She was.

"You see... Ryan knew Jesus and Jesus made sure to come get him when his body broke. It's just like that cloth the katayef was in or the olive jar. You don't have to be scared of the cloth or the glass. It's just the container."

"Jesus? But I didn't see anyone come take Ryan."

"Jesus is God's son, and He came in a way we can't see."

Layla wiped her eyes. "Are you sad, Hailey?"

"Yes, Layla. I am sad." Hailey paused for a moment to try and keep the tears away, but soon changed her mind. She let them come. "I will miss him... so much. But... Ryan's actions saved the two of you." Hailey sniffed, "And I am so, so grateful for that."

Hailey leaned over and kissed Layla's cheek.

"And now, that job falls to me. So I need to get you two out of here, OK?"

"OK."

"Go sit with Ruby."

Once Layla was safely tucked back inside the car, Hailey looked over the hood of the car and out over the desert. She needed a minute to strengthen her resolve. Walking to the back of the car, she popped open the trunk and looked inside, hoping there was something in there she could use.

Pushing a few things aside: a few tools, a thin piece of cloth, and a few empty bags, Hailey located a tattered old blanket. Using it seemed disrespectful, but it was all she had. Hailey grabbed it and was about to slam the trunk back down but paused and looked at the cloth. She pursed her lips to one side as she debated with herself.

Probably best, she thought. *I can't very well use mine now.*

Reaching back into the trunk, she picked up the cloth. Hailey draped it quickly around her head and neck. After slamming the trunk down, she returned to Ryan.

Once the blanket was shaken out as best she could, Hailey gripped the edge of it tightly with both hands against her stomach.

"I'm sorry, my love. I know you don't care, but I wish I had something better."

Hailey gently laid it over him. The act stabbed her with regret and sobs threatened to take over. She turned away. She couldn't lose it, not again. The girls needed her, and it would scare them too much if she couldn't stay strong.

There will be time for that later, she consoled herself.

Opening her lips, she breathed out the building emotion in a long, controlled breath.

Hailey tried to look back at Ryan once she was back behind the wheel, but the car blocked her view. Hailey bit her lip. She couldn't possibly take more time. It was getting late.

Goodbye, my love.

CHAPTER 38

The search hadn't produced much, and Marco was starting to lose hope. He scanned each side of the road, peering down each street, hoping to see some sign of the man or Karim's car.

As they came to the south edge of town, one of the men in the back seat pointed up ahead.

"Look!"

In the distance, that beautiful Benz sat parked next to the Sidla building. Seeing it caused Marco's mood to lighten immensely. Once the SUV had come to a stop, he jumped out. The door was open. He looked inside and saw blood covering the seat.

Yessss! he hissed to himself. *At least I got a piece of you, you little punk.*

Marco scanned the area. The man wasn't in sight. More blood led away from the car. He followed the drops around the front of the car and over to where the trail stopped and pooled. A few feet away tire tracks cut deeply into the dirt.

"He's in a different car. Let's move."

=======

"Ready?" she asked the girls without turning around.

A quiet yes came from Layla

"Alright, let's get you out of here."

Hailey grabbed the gear shift to put the car into drive when steam started pouring from the hood.

"That's not supposed to happen, is it?" Layla asked.

"No, honey. It's not."

Defeated, Hailey turned off the car. Looking at the temperature gauge, she realized the problem. She chided herself for not thinking to turn off the car. This heat was too much for it to idle for so long.

She pushed the hood release and got out. Hailey reached underneath the hood.

"Ouch," she yelped, jumping back from the shock of how hot it was.

Hailey pulled the sleeve of her shirt over her hand and opened the hood, ensuring to lean back as she did so. A whoosh of steam billowed from the car. She propped the hood open and walked to the back door. She leaned down to look at the girls and opened the door.

"We're going to have to wait here for a bit I'm afraid. The car needs to cool down."

"Hailey, I'm hot too," Layla moaned.

Hailey straightened and looked at the buildings, being sure not to glance down at the covered form lying just beyond the car.

The first building, the smaller of the two, was made of corrugated tin, similar to Damari's house. Wood covered all the windows and doors, and it looked more like a large storage shed than anything.

The second had two floors but wasn't in any better shape.

Peeling paint covered the wood and brick exterior, and the front door hung off its hinges. Each of the picture windows on either side of the door was broken, one was completely shattered. Yet this building was definitely the better choice.

"OK, girls. Let's get inside and find some shade. Layla, can you bring the bottle? Maybe we can find a tap or pump to refill it."

Layla grabbed the bottle as asked and joined her outside of the car. After handing the bottle to her, Layla took Ruby's hand.

While holding Layla's hand in one hand and the bottle in the other, Hailey led the two girls up to the larger building. She only allowed herself one stolen glance at the blanket. She took a deep breath and looked away.

Hailey squeezed Layla's hand as they mounted the five concrete steps up to the broken door. With both hands, Hailey dragged the door open enough for them to squeeze inside.

The interior of the building was in better shape than the outside but not by much. The dim light coming in from the windows took Hailey's eyes a moment to adjust. The entryway sat before a long counter, and beyond that, two sets of doorways led to other rooms. Sand, leaves, and random sticks and debris covered the floor.

It looked like, at one time, it had been a place of business, yet Hailey had no idea what kind. A few sets of shelves and display cases lined the left wall, but they were empty. Three wooden chairs sat upturned and broken by the right wall under an unbroken window. None of which gave any clue to what the building had been used for.

The door creaked behind them, causing Hailey to jump. Layla let out a small yelp of surprise. Hailey spun around only to see the wind swinging the door back into place.

"It's OK. It's just the wind."

While working on steadying her breathing again, Hailey walked over to the closest picture window and looked outside. The wind was picking up. Dark clouds gathered in the distance. The darkening sky altered the landscape before her, changing the red of the sand to shaded browns. The sight gave her an eerie feeling.

"Hailey?"

"Yes?"

"I am really thirsty."

"OK, honey."

Taking one last look outside, she hoped that if a storm were headed their way, it would wait until they were farther down the road. Hailey turned back to the girls. They looked so little and vulnerable standing there, hand in hand in the middle of the room. Hailey reached out and took Layla's other hand.

"So... how about we go explore this place and see what we can find."

Layla nodded, but there was no response from Ruby. Hailey needed to try and find some way to reassure and calm her. These girls were her responsibility now, and she needed to try and get Ruby to trust her.

It would feel foreign to step up and provide what they needed when all Hailey wanted to do was to sit with Ryan and cry. But even though she hated the truth of it, she was the adult, and these girls didn't deserve to have another adult let them down. Hailey took a slow, deep breath as she pushed aside her discomfort and looked around the room.

"Ah-ha. Here we go."

She crossed the room and went over to one of the shelves behind the counter. A pile of little sticks laid in the corner. They were each the size of a thin piece of kindling: half an inch wide and about a foot long. There were six or seven of them, but she only needed two. Keeping her back to the girls she grabbed the two on top.

Popping each one under her lip, Hailey turned around to show the girls her newly acquired walrus teeth.

"Yes, I too, am so thirsty." Her cartoon voice made herself laugh, but she managed to stifle it. "Could either of you two be-e-eautiful girls help me find something to drink in this dusty place?"

Layla burst into rolls of laughter. Tears soon streamed down her face as she scrambled to catch her breath in between her laughs. Ruby just looked at her with a blank stare.

"I mean, yikes," Hailey continued. "Whoever is in charge of keeping this place clean, isn't doing a very good job. Call the government! Call his mom! He must do his job."

Hailey dramatically threw her hands up in the air and circled the room. This set Layla off again. The girl's unbridled joy lifted her own spirits. It impressed Hailey how Layla managed to retain her childlike wonder after all that had happened to her.

Hailey glanced down at Ruby: still nothing.

Determined to get Ruby to react, Hailey bent down in front of her. "Excuse me, sweetie... um... do I have something in my teeth? They feel kinda... funny."

Layla giggled beside her, but Ruby just looked at her.

Hailey smiled at Ruby. "Not funny, huh? Well, that's OK."

Straightening, she took the sticks out of her mouth and licked the inside of her lip to get the moisture back. After tossing the sticks on the ground, Hailey offered her hand to Ruby. Surprisingly, the little girl took it. Warmth flooded into every part of her. There was something so sweet and special about this little soul, and she could feel her love growing for her.

"Let's go exploring."

The three walked around the counter and through the open doorway on the right. The room beyond had, what looked to be, five stainless steel food-prep tables laid out in three rows. A few steel sinks protruded out from the wall just beyond the tables. Another counter sat in the closest corner of the room to their left. It reminded Hailey of what she'd seen at a convenience store back home. Yet it was void of a cash register or any merchandise.

As Hailey scanned the room, she saw more debris, broken chairs, peeling and cracked drywall, and smashed windows. But what really caught her eyes sat in the far-left corner.

An old-fashioned, turquoise fridge stood in the corner. The top bolt of the industrial handle had come loose and now hung from the bottom bolt. The front of the fridge curved, unlike the common ones. Hailey walked over to it and prayed that there was something inside.

Pulling on the handle, the door swung open. The smell that hit her almost knocked her off her feet. Hailey let go of Ruby's hand and covered her nose and mouth with the crook of her arm.

Most of the stuff in the fridge wasn't going to help them as it was now growing new stuff. The fridge clearly hadn't been working for some time. Yet near the back, on the bottom shelf, sat five unopened bottles of water. Hailey grabbed them and nudged the door closed with her foot. She handed a bottle to each of the girls, kept one for herself, and placed the other two on the closest prep table.

The water was warm but wonderfully thirst quenching. Hailey chugged down half of the bottle before replacing the lid.

She set it on the table beside the full ones. Layla took a few sips of hers and then helped Ruby open her bottle. Seeing the girls interact was precious.

After Ruby had taken a few sips, her fingers twisted the cap back in place. Layla walked over to the counter and slid her back down it until she was sitting on the floor. Ruby followed suit, then leaned against her. They seemed even smaller seated at the base of the big counter.

Layla put her arm around Ruby and Ruby rested her head on Layla's shoulder, closing her eyes. Layla rested her head on the top of Ruby's and also closed her eyes.

Hailey moved to one of the sinks and turned its handle. The pipes groaned, and a slow stream of brown-tinted water ran from the tap. The water didn't look safe enough to drink, but it would suffice in cleaning off her hands.

Hailey placed her hands under the tap. The small scratches stung, so she quickly worked the last of the blood off. She leaned over the sink and ran the bottom part of her shirt under the water and worked the blood stains out as best she could. The water only dulled the color of the blood and added a dingy hue to it. Hailey pursed her lips.

Oh, well. It's better than before and should look better when it dries.

She turned off the tap and glanced over at the girls. After a few moments, both girls opened their eyes and looked at her. Hailey walked over to the table as she dried her hands on her pants and grabbed a full bottle.

With a moan from her sore muscles, Hailey sat next to Ruby. She opened the fresh bottle and poured out a bit onto her sleeve. Hailey rose to her knees and leaned over to reach Ruby's face. She gently wiped off the tear-streaked dirt from Ruby's cheeks.

"Here, little one, this will feel better."

Hailey continued to clean the girl's face as Ruby looked at her. Ruby's almond eyes seemed so sad. Hailey's heart ached for her. She longed to bring the little girl comfort but wasn't exactly sure of how to do so.

"Ruby, you are safe now. I will do everything in my power to keep both of you safe." Hailey glanced over at Layla, who smiled at her in return. "As soon as the car cools down, we'll head to Cairo. The people there will help you, and I won't leave until both of you are taken care of by people you can trust."

Hailey thought against mentioning the possible difficulties that might be on the road ahead. Seeing how they were currently only manifestations of fear from her assumptions, she didn't see the point in preparing the girls for them. And there was always the chance that everything would be clear from here to Cairo, so Hailey prayed that would be their reality and kept the other possibilities to herself.

When Ruby was all cleaned up, Hailey lowered her head so that she was level with Ruby's eyes.

"How are you, Ruby? I'd really like you to tell me if you can. It might make you feel better."

Ruby just looked at her with wide eyes.

"Hailey?"

"Yes, Layla?" Hailey answered without moving her eyes from studying Ruby's face.

"Thank you."

Hailey looked at Layla. She had tears in her eyes.

"For what?"

"For coming to get us. I... I didn't like being there, and I know Ruby feels the same way, even if she can't say so."

"Layla, if you want to talk about what happened, I can listen."

Layla lowered her head, she seemed embarrassed.

"Layla, you have nothing to be embarrassed about." Hailey hoped it would give her courage.

Layla looked up at her with pained eyes. "Why did they have to do that?"

Her chin trembled. It was clear to Hailey she was having trouble understanding the betrayal of those she trusted.

"My father said it would be what is best for the family. But how can it be? Those people hurt me, Hailey. How can that be what was best for my family? Did I do something wrong and that was to correct me? Is that how it was what was best for my family?"

"No, Layla. You did absolutely nothing wrong. You are a sweet girl. None of this was your fault."

Layla sniffed. "When those men came and took me away, they took me to a building. Karim, my husband, was not there."

Layla stopped talking and looked down at the peeling flooring beneath her legs and started picking at it with her finger.

"They took me to a room inside the building. The room was big, with desks, and there were five women. One of the men brought me to them and then left. It was just the women and me. They smiled at me, and I thought that they would be nice. But they weren't. They weren't nice at all. They did give me two cookies and some goat's milk, and they seemed to be happy that I was there. One of the women took my milk away, I wasn't even finished. She told me to lay on one of the desks."

Hailey's skin grew cold for fear of where this story was going, yet she stayed quiet.

"I wished I hadn't obeyed. Father had always told me to obey my elders, but those women weren't nice, and maybe he wouldn't have been mad if I didn't listen… just this once." Layla sniffed back some tears. "When I was on the desk, another woman came over and told me that I was a lucky girl and that today I would show honor to my husband. I didn't understand… until I saw the scissors." Layla looked up at her with terror in her eyes.

"Scissors?"

Layla nodded. "I had heard the other girls in the village talking about their cutting. Their stories were so scary. I asked my mother about it, but she told me that it wasn't going to happen to me. She seemed mad when I asked why and wouldn't talk about it anymore. But I wanted to know more, so I asked another girl."

Layla paused and looked at her hand as it proceeded to pick at the floor again. Hailey stayed silent.

"She said that it needed to be done so that she could remain pure and… I can't remember the other words she said." Layla shook her head. "I didn't understand most of what she was talking about, but I didn't want to seem stupid, so I stopped asking. But I do remember the part about her saying how much it hurt. That is why I got so scared when I saw the scissors. I tried to tell them that my mother said I didn't have to do this. But they didn't care. One of the women said that's why I was lucky. She said that I would be an outcast if I didn't get it done and that my mother was foolish and didn't love me. I screamed at her for lying, but they all laughed and said I was a silly little girl. But Hailey, I'm not. I'm not a silly girl. My mother does love me."

Layla's eyes started to water as she tried to convince Hailey.

"Oh, honey, I know she does. She loves you very much."

Layla wiped her eyes with the back of her free hand. The

other still held onto Ruby. "I tried to fight them, but the women were strong, and they held me down. They... they..."

It was clear Layla was having trouble saying the words to describe what happened, but Hailey understood precisely what they had done to her. Sickening, vivid memories flashed into Hailey's mind.

A friend from back home posted a story last year about her time as a nurse. She had seen many cases of female genital mutilation and said that it was a massive worldwide epidemic. Hailey had been shocked to learn that the practice happened in North America but even more shocked to hear the stats from the countries where it was widely accepted. Hailey's brain strained to try and remember the details.

Was it eighty or ninety percent of girls underwent this procedure in three of the top countries on the list? Or was it the top five?

Hailey's stomach jolted realizing Layla was now one of the millions and millions of girls who had endured such a violation.

"Honey, I know what happened. You don't need to say it if it's too hard." Hailey scooted around to Layla's other side. "I am so sorry that happened to you." Hailey stroked Layla's hair as fresh tears gathered in Hailey's eyes. "Your mother was right, it shouldn't have happened to you. None of this should have happened."

"C-can I tell you the rest?" Layla asked.

Hailey swallowed hard. *What else could there be?* But obviously there was more, and the least she could do was listen.

"Of course. We can talk as long as you'd like."

"After... well that, they cleaned me up and put leaves with this stinky stuff between my legs. It stung, but it started to feel better. I was kept with the women for three days. They kept praising me and said I was a woman now and that my husband would be pleased. If I tell the truth, I didn't want to meet him. Father is a nice man, and he loves my mother, but if a man would be happy because they did that to me... I didn't want to meet him." Layla looked down at the floor again. "But once I was feeling better, Karim came for me and brought me to that house."

She stopped and looked back up at Hailey.

"Hailey," she said hesitantly, "do you also know... what happened with Karim?"

"Yes, Layla, I do."

At Hailey's admittance, relief seemed to cover Layla's whole body. Layla sighed and relaxed. She leaned over into Hailey and pulled Ruby with her. Hailey did her best to hold onto both of them.

"Girls, remember, nothing that has happened to you was your fault. And I want you both to know that I'm here and that you can tell me anything if you want to talk about it. You can even tell me over and over again if it will help you. Understand?"

"Yes, I do," Layla answered.

Hailey could feel Ruby's head nod against her forearm. The movement sent a shiver down Hailey's legs.

Maybe... or at least I hope... you will trust me soon, little one, Hailey thought to herself. She opened her mouth to offer more words of comfort, there was still so much to tell the girls and reassure them of. But the words caught in her throat.

The unmistakable sound of tires skidding in the dirt and slamming car doors, stabbed her ears. Hailey froze to listen. She felt both girls tense up in her arms. Hailey paused only a moment more until her mind screamed the confirmation to her.

They were no longer alone.

CHAPTER 39

"Stay here," Hailey whispered.

Ducking low, Hailey made her way to the front room. Using the counters at the back of the room as cover, she made her way to the end so she could look out the window. Hailey peeked up just enough to see above the windowsill and slowly enough so as not to draw the attention of whoever was outside.

There were five of them. Five men dressed in dark clothes and heavy army boots, all standing outside of a black SUV. Hailey's heart dropped. These men matched the description Eman gave of the traffickers. Hailey didn't even pause to question how they might have found them. It didn't matter. She needed to hide the girls.

Hailey crouched and made her way out of the room.

"Follow me."

She moved the girls to the other side of the counter they were leaning against. The back of the counter was hollow, and had one shelf that ran horizontally in the center.

"Layla, climb up here, honey."

Hailey helped her climb up on the shelf.

"Now lay as still as you can, OK? And don't make a sound."

She didn't wait for the girl to answer but moved to Ruby.

"Ruby, we have to squish into the bottom."

Hailey guided Ruby in first so that she was pressed up against the back of the counter. Hailey moved in to lay in front of her. She faced out, keeping her back to Ruby.

At least this way, if they find us, I'd be able to roll out towards them and... and... Hailey didn't know what exactly she would or could do in that scenario, but at least she'd be more ready than if she faced Ruby.

Squeeeeeek.

The sound of the front door opening chilled Hailey's blood. She could hear the muffled voices of men talking, but it didn't sound like they were entering the building. She held her breath and tried to listen. Layla's whimpers above her made it difficult to hear if any footsteps drew closer. Hailey strained her ears.

"Layla, shhh. Please, you have to be quiet. They'll hear you."

Layla's whimpers grew louder but soon muffled. She had probably clamped her hand over her mouth in the hopes of silencing them. It didn't last long. Her whimpers returned.

Hailey tilted her head to look at the end of the counter about a foot from her head. This spot was not going to work. It wasn't going to hide them for long. Her eyes refocused to just beyond the counter. There, she saw another wall that she hadn't noticed earlier. A thin stairwell tucked behind it. With Layla's whimpers, Hailey could no longer tell where the men were exactly. She could hear voices but no footsteps.

Her breathing quickened.

It's now or never, Hailey, she told herself, trying to push her body to move. But fear gripped her and held her in place. The window was closing quickly. But her body didn't seem to care.

GO NOW!!

The words of God's Spirit within her almost shook her whole

body. The instructions were so clear that Hailey didn't hesitate. Rolling from her spot, she lay for just a moment on her tummy, did a quick push up, helped each of the girls out of their spot, and pulled them over to the stairs. Refusing to look back, she pushed the girls ahead of her.

"Walk softly, but quickly."

They made their way, practically soundlessly, up to the top to a long hallway and three doors: one on the left and two on the right. Hailey doubted there would be time to check each of them. Biting her lip, she grabbed the handle of the one on the left and pushed it open. She guided the girls inside and closed the door softly behind her.

Regret jabbed her chest the moment she turned around. There was nothing in the room. No tables or desks, no beds or boxes. There was absolutely nothing to hide behind. Hailey turned back to the door. They needed to try another room. She turned the handle and cracked the door open. Sounds of voices near the bottom of the stairs stopped her. Hailey froze.

Father? We're trapped.

She closed the door and escorted the girls over to the one window. Looking down, it was too far to jump. There was nothing left to do but try and shield the girls. Pushing the girls to sit, Hailey did her best to wrap them in her arms and put herself between them and the door.

"I'm so sorry," she whispered to them.

Hailey's heart urged her to pray. She took a deep breath and released the words.

"El Elyon, God Most High, help us. I still don't understand Your plan in all of this, but I trust that You must have one."

Heavy boots sounded on the stairs.

Time had run out. They were coming.

"And if there is purpose in this," Hailey continued, "then it wouldn't make sense for it to end like this. Would it? So... Your will... be done."

The last part of her prayer felt thick in her throat as it exited her mouth and yet, surprisingly, it brought relief. Whatever was about to happen, it was just like Ryan had said. If it came to her, then it had to have passed through His hand first. It was not random, and it wasn't out of His control.

"I trust You."

Hailey turned her head to look towards the door. Her eyes bore into the handle, waiting for it to turn before her eyes. Hearing the footsteps stop and the floorboards creak in the hallway, her determination to face what was coming faltered. She squeezed her eyes shut. Hailey heard the opening of the door across the hall. Sounds of furniture being upturned echoed in the hall.

The men would most likely try their room next. Hailey hugged the girls and kept her eyes closed as she waited.

A giggle sounded... then another. It came from inside the room... their room.

Hailey's eyes flew open and looked to the corner of the room, left of the door. A soft light streamed into the room from an arched doorway. Hailey blinked her eyes a couple times.

How did I miss that?

A shadow emerged from the archway. Hailey tightened her grip on the girls. But when a hunched-over, old woman appeared, Hailey's confusion relaxed her hold on the girls. She stared wide-eyed at the woman. The woman shuffled her feet and took three steps into the room.

"Where? Who...?"

The woman smiled a toothless grin at Hailey, raised her

finger to her mouth and signaled for Hailey to remain quiet. Then with one more giggle, the woman moved towards the door. Hailey would have warned her, but sheer shock kept her speechless and still.

The woman swung the door opened and walked out. She turned left and disappeared towards the end of the hall. Hailey couldn't pull her eyes from the empty doorway. She strained her ears. The heavy footsteps resonated in the hall again. Only one man appeared in the doorway of their room.

Dread covered her body as she noticed a black handgun gripped in his hands. It was lowered, but both his arms were tense and prepared to raise it if needed. Hailey swallowed hard as he walked into the room.

Strangely, the man didn't make eye contact with her. He took another two steps forward, yet still didn't look directly at her. His eyes moved multiple times over them as he scanned the room, but they never settled on her and the girls.

It's like he doesn't even see us. How is that possible?

After a few moments, the man huffed in frustration and left the room. Following the direction the old woman went, he moved out of sight. Hailey again held her breath so she could hear every movement. At first, there was silence - just silence.

Pop.

Pop.

Pop.

Three gunshots rang out, violently shaking her eardrums. Hailey's heart raced, and her ears started to throb. Layla began to whimper softly.

Was the woman... dead? Hailey wondered. *Had the man killed her?*

She didn't want to get up and check, surprising the man

might get her shot as well. She remained where she was and continued to hold the girls.

Screams of terror filled the air… deep, manly screams. Hailey's mind raced as to what might be happening out of her view. Her eyes stayed glued to the doorway. The man's boots slammed on the floor as he ran right past their door. He didn't even pause. He thundered down the stairs, causing the whole room to shake as his weight impacted with each stair. He was yelling the entire way down. Then shouts from the other men joined in.

Car doors slammed.

An engine revved.

Tires spun.

Then silence.

=======

What the heck was that? Hailey's mind was void of any plausible explanation.

She relaxed her grip on the girls, and they lifted their heads. Hailey didn't move from being crouched next to them but kept her eyes on the door. She couldn't hear anything. When her legs started to protest, she slowly rose from her spot.

"Stay here. I'll be right back."

Hailey walked timidly towards the open door. She took a deep breath to steady herself, not sure of what she would find out there. Hailey looked down the hall. It was empty.

The last door… was open.

Hailey moved towards it cautiously, glancing behind her after each couple of steps. This would be the third dead body she had seen, but that fact didn't make it any less spine-chilling.

Getting to the door, Hailey peeked inside. The room was just as empty as the one she had chosen to hide the girls in. She took a few more steps forward and looked around.

Nothing.

No woman, no other doors, no closets.

What is going on?

Hailey pivoted on the ball of her back foot and went back to the girls.

They were still huddled under the window, and both jumped when Hailey came in the room.

"It's OK... just me. I want you both to stay here while I take a look downstairs."

The girls didn't say anything, they only looked back at her with fearful faces. Hailey hated to leave them, but, without knowing what she might find downstairs, they were safer where they were. After giving them a reassuring smile, she headed for the stairs.

A few of the stairs creaked under her weight, each causing her breath to catch in her throat. Reaching the bottom, she leaned against the wall of the stairway and poked her head out just enough to get a quick glance of the room. All was still. The room was empty.

Hailey moved around the wall, through the back room and out into the room at the front. She looked outside. The men were gone. She knew what her ears had told her when she was upstairs: that the men had left, but seeing the empty building was so bewildering.

Where did they go? And where is the woman? Hailey's logic was going wild without a clear explanation. Her mind replayed the events.

That arched doorway wasn't there before, was it? No, definitely not.

There's no way I missed it. But how is that possible? And w*here did the old woman go? It's like she vanished. But was that before the man freaked out? Or was it her that scared him so badly?*

Upon realizing the vast improbability of what just happened, her brain finally considered that the cause might be miraculous.

Had God done all this?

Hailey spun in a few circles as she scanned the front room again. The shock and astonishment of what she had just seen, bubbled up from deep within her. It rose and grew until she couldn't contain it. It burst forth from her in bouts of nervous laughter, punctuated by a few shouts of relief.

It was a miracle. An actual miracle. There was no door before. Whoever that woman was, she was sent to terrify the men.

The release of emotion was so invigorating that her body yearned for more. Hope rose in her and wrapped all around her. Hailey couldn't contain it. She fell to the floor.

Laying on her back, she stared up at the ceiling. Flapping her hands and legs she made dust angels in the debris around her, all the while continuing to yip, laugh, and shout. After a few minutes, she was out of breath. She laid still.

Indescribable peace surrounded her. It was similar to what she had felt on the floor in Ehsan's room after God had talked with her in the mirror. But this was more intense somehow. The hope was lighter, more joyful. Maybe it was because she knew she was getting closer to getting out of here, closer to home. Maybe it was because she was seeing how big God was and how she might be fitting into His plan. Maybe both.

Hailey didn't bother analyzing it further. She laid there in stillness and rest and reveled in the pureness of the moment.

The sound of little feet sounded by the door. Hailey turned her head. The counter was blocking her view.

"Hailey?" Layla said tentatively.

"I'm over here."

The two girls, hand in hand, peeked around the counter. Fear and confusion coated their faces.

"It's safe. You can come out."

"Are you... OK?" Layla asked in a shaky voice, still partially hidden behind the counter.

Hailey laughed. "Completely!"

"Where... did those people go?"

Hailey stood and ran over to them. She scooped them both into her arms and twirled them around. She almost dropped Layla but quickly readjusted and continued to spin them around.

Hailey shrieked with delight and kissed each girl on the cheek.

"They're gone! They are all gone. God has saved us."

"Why?" Ruby asked.

The shock of hearing the little girl's voice for the first time, made Hailey choke and almost drop them. She didn't want to make a big deal about Ruby breaking her silence and scare her back into her shell. She set them carefully back down.

"You want to know why God saved us?" Hailey asked with slow, soft words.

Ruby nodded.

"Well, it's because He loves you so much. He saw your hurt, and He wanted to heal it, so He sent me to you."

Hailey could see the confusion in Ruby's eyes. Hailey looked over at Layla and saw the same look.

"Come here, girls, sit down. I have a story I think you should hear."

The girls sat in front of her, so close they were touching her knees. She reached out and grabbed one of each of their hands. Looking to each, she gave them a comforting smile as she took a deep breath.

Hailey's mind was flashing with scenes from something she had read when she was a child. Realizing that the Spirit was bringing it to her mind, Hailey bowed her head. She needed a minute to calm the overwhelming reverence pouring over her.

It's OK, tell them.

"Long ago there was an Egyptian girl who was being mistreated, so she ran away. When God met with her in the desert and cared for her, she called Him: the God who sees. Ruby... Layla...," Hailey looked to each of them as she addressed them, "God sees you both, and He loves you more than you can imagine. He is kind and tender and holy, so He sent His son Jesus long ago to die for you so that you can be set free. Then He came alive again, so you can know Him and be with Him, and so He can take care of you."

Layla bit her lip. "But my father said that Allah doesn't need a son because Allah won't die, so Allah doesn't need someone to take his place."

"Your father is right. God doesn't need someone to take His place... but we needed Jesus." Hailey looked down at her hands as she put them into her lap. "I needed Him." A lump caught in her throat.

"Hmm, my grandmother says the same thing." Layla bit her lip again. "So do you follow the same God my grandmother does?"

"Yes, I do. And in a way... I guess Muslims and Christians kind of believe in the same God. But that belief split long ago and took two very different paths. God's promise came His way and in His timing, and He blessed everyone through Jesus.

Man's way of rushing God's plan led to Ishmael. The two sides have been in disagreement ever since."

Layla shook her head. "I don't understand."

"Well, you know what, maybe when we get to Cairo, we can find someone to help explain all of that to us better. I don't know a lot about Islam, and I don't want to say something that isn't correct. Would that be OK?"

The girls nodded.

"But what I can tell you, is that God had a huge plan to bring us together. I had run away from Him a long time ago because I didn't like something He chose to do. I live very far from here, but, just like that little Egyptian girl, He saw me, and He guided me to find Him again. Then He brought me to you."

Ruby squeezed Hailey's hand. "Hailey?"

"Yes, Ruby?"

Tears filled Ruby's eyes. "I'm happy He brought you."

Ruby crawled into her lap and wrapped her little arms around Hailey's neck. Hailey held her close as she wept.

"Me too, sweetheart," Hailey whispered softly, as she rubbed her back. "Me too."

Layla joined in on the hug and the three sat there in silence.

The sun had lowered just under the top of the window, filling the whole room with a warm light. Hailey raised her head and looked outside. The dark clouds seemed to have moved on.

Hailey didn't know how much daylight was left, but she didn't want to be caught in the middle of nowhere in the dark.

"Alright, you two. I think we should get going, it's getting late. The car should be cooled down enough now."

The girls ran to the car ahead of her and jumped in. Hailey paused on the steps. She looked down at the blanket covering Ryan. Hailey didn't really understand why, but she couldn't leave just yet. She knew he was gone, but regardless, she made her way over to his body.

Bending down, she grabbed the top edge of the blanket, braced herself, and pulled it down. Seeing Ryan's pale face sent a wave of longing sadness through her. She was grateful that God laid out this path before her, the girls needed her. But knowing that she wouldn't be spending her life with Ryan, filled her with grief and pain.

God, why does this have to be his path?

Because you have called out to Me, I will answer you. I will tell you great and mighty things, which you do not know.

Now?

Soon.

Hailey, suddenly remembering the verse in Lamentations, pushed her impatience aside. This abrupt recalling of scripture was surreal. It would take her some time to get used to it.

The Lord is good to those who wait for Him, she recited the verse again in her mind. She leaned down and kissed Ryan's cheek.

"I don't understand yet, but I will always love you."

Hailey sat there for a moment until she was able to stop the few tears that had welled up. She had her back to the girls, and she didn't want to sadden them by showing her grief again.

She pulled the blanket back over him.

"Goodbye, Ryan."

Father, please have someone find him and bring his body home.

Hailey dried off her face with her sleeve, stood, and walked slowly to the front of the car. With the back of her hand, she touched the engine. It was warm but not hot. The steam had dissipated long ago, so she closed the hood and climbed into the car.

She sighed and pulled the directions out of the console to

check them over. The road they were on should soon merge back onto the major highway. The next landmark Damari had marked down was Suez, a town two hours away. The highway would then turn off and cross a canal before continuing on to Cairo. She returned the directions back to the console. She turned the key and started the engine with ease.

Hailey gripped the steering wheel.

Here we go.

CHAPTER 40

"Hailey, what's that?"

Layla's question came just as Hailey noticed something in the distance. They had only been driving for about forty-five minutes, so it wasn't Suez.

"Um... I'm not sure."

After another mile, Hailey realized what it was. Three armored jeeps were barricading the road up ahead of them. There were two other jeeps pulled off to the side of the road - one facing each direction. Hailey couldn't count the exact number of men that milled about, but there was at least half a dozen.

The girls whimpered in the back seat as the scene registered with them. Hailey's own fear tried to ignite, but she extinguished it.

"Enough is enough," she mumbled under her breath.

After witnessing what happened at the abandoned building, there was no way she was going to freak out over this. Things were different now.

"It's OK. I was expecting that we might run into something like this. You don't need to be afraid."

Hailey slowed the car as they approached the barricade.

Three of the seven men that Hailey could see started walking towards them. All the men were dressed in brown army fatigues and had AK47s either in their hands or slung over their shoulder. They wore helmets and tactical vests covered in the same fabric as their fatigues and wore green plastic knee pads. Hailey wasn't sure if these men were police, army, or something else.

One of the approaching men held up his hand, signaling her to stop. Hailey kept both hands on the wheel and slowed the car to a stop. He came over to her window, while the other two walked around the car. One man went to the passenger side, and the other walked to the back and stood by the trunk.

Hearing tapping on the trunk, Hailey looked in the rearview mirror. The man at the back was tapping on the trunk with his gun. She popped the trunk release and looked at the man beside her window. He leaned down and looked at her, then glanced in the back seat at the girls.

With a confused look on his face, he motioned for her to lower the window. Hailey complied. The man said something to her in Arabic. Layla responded. Hailey didn't stop her.

"The little girl said you only speak English?"

"Yes."

The man shifted the nozzle of his rifle from Hailey to the girls. "What is going on here?"

Hailey froze. She didn't know how much she should tell this man. Was he safe?

"Baksheesh," she suddenly blurted out.

Hailey prayed that the sound of a bribe would silence any further questions.

"Baksheesh?" she repeated with more calm.

The man smiled, tilted his head while raising his eyebrows,

then backed away from the car. He gave a sharp whistle. The trunk slammed shut. The other two men walked away from the car and back to their original post. The man beside her bent down again and looked at her with pursed lips.

"How much?" he asked with a forward jerk of his chin.

Hailey swallowed and hoped that the first handful of money Ryan stashed in the driver's door would be enough. She pulled it from its hiding spot and held it out. The man took it and did a quick count. He licked his bottom lip and stared at her. Hailey smiled at him with hopeful eyes. The man looked at the money once more and then nodded to her.

"That will do. You may go through."

"Thank you."

Hailey's relief was almost audible, but she stifled her sigh as she waited for the other men to pull the jeeps out of the way. Hailey fought to not appear too shocked or happy. She wanted to keep her cool and not allow her inexperience with such situations to show and possibly change the man's mind.

Hailey glanced back at the girls as they pulled away. Seeing their smiles, she smiled at them.

"See, told ya. No problem."

- - - - - - -

The rest of the drive towards the Suez Canal was uneventful. The repetitious landscape blending with the melodic sounds of Layla's chatting, caused Hailey to struggle to stay awake. She stretched and fought it over the last twenty minutes, but the drowsiness was getting worse.

Hailey checked the clock. They should be getting to the canal soon, but beyond that, she wouldn't safely make the last hour and a half to Cairo. She needed to stop for a quick nap.

"Girl's we're going to find a place to pull over. I'm too tired to drive."

Up ahead Hailey saw a side road pulling off the highway and towards, what looked to be, some green crops. Slowing the car, she turned onto it as she looked in all directions for anyone who might be angered by them being there. Nothing sparked her concern, so she continued on.

A minute down the road, it veered to the right as it approached the crops. Four sugarcane fields spread out along the right side of the road. Three dirt roads separated each field. A water tank sat at the end of each one. Hailey pulled the car down the farthest one and parked just in front of the tank.

No one was in sight, and she could no longer see the main road. As long as no one drove down the road, this spot would work. Hailey turned off the car and twisted in her seat to look at the girls.

Ruby yawned.

"Tired too, huh?"

Ruby didn't respond. She laid towards the door, tucked her doll under her chin and closed her eyes.

"Layla, you should try and get some sleep too. Things might get pretty busy once we get to Cairo and some rest might help." Hailey smiled and nodded to persuade her.

Layla didn't respond but looked over at Ruby. Without looking at Hailey again, Layla turned and opened her door and got out. She softly closed her door behind her, walked to the front passenger side and climbed in.

"Can I sleep with you?" she asked.

"Of course, honey."

Hailey leaned her seat back, and Layla climbed onto her lap.

It was awkward at first, but the girl managed to maneuver herself to sit on Hailey's lap, rest her back on the door, nestle her head onto Hailey's shoulder and lay her feet over the console. Once situated, Hailey locked the doors and wrapped her arms around Layla.

"Can you sing to me? My mother sings me to sleep when I'm scared. It always helps."

"Sure. My mom used to sing me to sleep too."

Without even thinking about it Hailey started to sing Be Thou My Vision. Singing her mother's favorite song seemed fitting in this moment. A small, sad ache rose in her chest. The last time she heard her mother singing this song was the day she died. Hailey pushed past the pain and continued to sing.

> Be Thou my Vision, O Lord of my heart;
> Naught be all else to me, save that Thou art;
> Thou my best Thought, by day or by night,
> Waking or sleeping, Thy presence my light.
>
> Be Thou my Wisdom, and Thou my true Word;
> I ever with Thee and Thou with me, Lord;
> Thou my great Father, I Thy true son;
> Thou in me dwelling, and I with Thee one.
>
> Be Thou my battle Shield, Sword for the fight;
> Be Thou my Dignity, Thou my Delight;
> Thou my soul's Shelter, Thou my high Tow'r:
> Raise Thou me heav'nward, O Pow'r of my pow'r.
>
> Riches I heed not, nor man's empty praise,
> Thou mine Inheritance, now and always:

Thou and Thou only, first in my heart,
High King of Heaven, my Treasure Thou art.

High King of Heaven, my victory won,
May I reach Heaven's joys, O bright Heav'n's Sun!
Heart of my own heart, whate'er befall,
Still be my Vision, O Ruler of all.

The words now took on a whole new meaning at that moment. When Hailey's mom was alive, the song was so commonplace to her that the profound significance of the words hadn't registered. She wondered if God had used experiences in her mom's life to reveal the truth in the verses to her.

Was that why it was her favorite?

As Hailey got to the end of the song, she could feel Layla's breathing slow. Hailey kissed the top of her head.

Leaning her head against the headrest, Hailey closed her eyes and drifted off.

CHAPTER 41

Hailey shifted restlessly in her sleep.

The car sped over the canal bridge just past Suez, dark water stirred below them, wind from the open window whipped her scarf around. They were almost across. Hailey could see something up ahead. Another blockade blocked traffic, but it didn't concern her. Getting to the front of the line seemed unusually fast. Something seemed off. A man asked for her passport, and she handed it to him.

She smiled at the girls as he flipped through her passport. He suddenly started yelling at her. He shouted to the other men surrounding the car. Two men violently dragged her from the car. The girls screamed. Hailey spun her head around to see that they too were being pulled from the car. Their hands fought to get to her. The men who held Hailey pulled her in the opposite direction of where the other men were dragging the girls. Hailey tried to scream, but no sound came from her mouth. The girls screamed again.

Shooting awake, Hailey heard Layla yelp from her sudden movement. Hailey blinked wildly as she tried to regain her bearings in the dim light. Hailey had banged the girl into the steering wheel.

"Oh, Layla, I'm so sorry. Are you OK?"

"Yes, I'm OK. I'm not hurt. You just scared me."

"I'm sorry." Hailey shook her head. "I had a bad dream."

Hailey looked back at Ruby. Thankfully, she was still asleep. Hailey turned back and rubbed her face. Her pulse was racing.

"What was your dream about? When I tell my mother my bad dreams, it helps me feel better."

She placed her hands on each side of Layla's face. "Oh, you are so sweet. But it was just a silly dream. I'm OK now."

Hailey didn't feel OK, the dream was very unsettling. She checked the time. They had been sleeping for an hour and the sun had now set. There was only a bit of dim light left. Hailey had hoped to be across the bridge before dark.

"How about you hop in the back seat and we'll get going."

The girl complied and climbed over the seat.

Hailey hesitated for a moment, she couldn't shake the uneasy feeling the dream had left. She shook it off and reversed the car out and drove back towards the main road. Her mind replayed the dream. Halfway through, her mind stopped.

Oh no, my passport!

Hailey felt sick. The captain of the ferry had only given her a stamp for the Sinai region, which she was just about to leave. When Ryan had found her at the shop in the airport, there had been no time to go get another visa. Neither of them had even thought about it.

As she pulled onto the highway, Hailey looked at the girls in the rearview mirror. Both were asleep.

What am I supposed to do?

Go north.

The leading was quiet, yet clear. So when Hailey got to the bend in the road, she didn't take the exit for the bridge. She kept driving north, having no idea where they were headed.

Over an hour ticked by without any stops, nor anything else for that matter. The rest of the light that remained after the sun had set had now disappeared, and only the dark road spread out before her. The girls still slept soundly.

Road signs appeared announcing that they were coming up on Ismailia. Hailey had no idea where that was, or if it was somewhere they should go. She kept driving.

Thoughts of Ryan seeped in. The ache from missing him squeezed her heart. She looked over to the empty seat beside her.

This all would be so much easier if he were sitting there next to me.

A sad smile fell on her lips. Memories of diving with Ryan pushed the ache further into her heart. That was such a sweet moment. A sweet moment before such chaos. A gift. The realization hit her.

Thank you. Thank you for giving us that time.

Lights appeared up ahead. Hailey took a few deep breaths to calm herself. It was another barricade. She prayed her dream wasn't prophetic beyond the warning she was given about leaving the Sinai region.

Pulling up, she saw two jeeps and three men. Only one of

them approached when she stopped the car. The other two continued to lean against the hood of one of the jeeps. They didn't even pause their conversation or look at her.

The man who walked toward her was quite young, maybe only a few years older than she was. He wore the same getup as the men at the other barricade and had a short goatee. He gave her a big smile when he saw her.

He asked her a question.

She shrugged. "English?"

He held up a flashlight above the car so it illuminated her face but didn't shine directly on her face. He looked at her with wide eyes.

"Are you an American?"

"Yes," she answered shakily.

"Well well, aren't you a long way from home. Ah, miss? Things aren't exactly safe around here. There has been a lot of unrest and attacks from the terrorist cells. You're lucky you haven't run into any of them yet. What are you doing out here?"

Hailey didn't know what she should say, she just looked back at him while her mind raced with the possible choices. He seemed annoyed with the delay in response, but his eyes started to move past her as he noticed the cargo in the back seat.

He put one hand on the rifle hanging from the strap over his shoulder. "I need to see your passport."

Hailey gulped and turned to fetch it from the console. Her hand shook as she handed it to him.

"Where are you going?" he asked as he flipped it open.

"Honestly, I'm not sure. I'm just trying to get these girls someplace safe." Her honestly caught her off guard, but it was out of her mouth before she had a chance to stop it.

"Why? Where did they come from?"

When she heard his tone had softened she saw that she didn't have much to lose. There wasn't a believable lie she could quickly come up with, so she opted for the truth.

"Well... it's a long, sad story."

"Then you better start telling me."

"OK... well the older girl, Layla, her parents asked me to take her to Cairo. She had been sold into a short-term marriage, but the brokers changed the agreement and wouldn't bring her home."

The officer scowled but didn't say anything, so Hailey continued.

"The little one, Ruby, is Layla's friend. My guess is that she is from somewhere in Europe and was sold into the sex trade. She was living next door to the house Layla was staying in. When we came to get Layla, she refused to go without Ruby, so we took her too."

"We?"

"I-I had a friend with me. Some men found out and followed us. They shot him. He didn't make it." Hailey had to bite the inside of her cheek to keep the emotion away. It worked apart from her eyes watering a little.

"I'm sorry about your friend. Human trafficking in Egypt is getting out of hand, and the marriage brokers they use are vile men." The man glanced down at her passport again, then looked at her. "You said you're trying to get to Cairo? That's in the other direction."

"Uh, yeah I know."

"And you don't even have a visa to leave the Sinai Peninsula. If you're ever caught trying to pass into the other parts of Egypt, you'll be arrested. And I have no idea what would happen to the girls." The man's eyes saddened when he looked in the back seat. "I don't mean to scare you, miss, but I would get them out of Egypt as soon as you can. It's not safe for you here."

"Believe me, I understand. I... ah... just have no idea how to get out."

"Do you have any money?"

"Yes."

"A lot?"

Hailey suddenly realized how vulnerable she was sitting in the middle of a dark road with military men surrounding her.

"Yes," Hailey answered tentatively, her voice trembling.

The man exhaled forcefully, causing his cheeks to puff out. He handed her passport back to her and ran his hand over his goatee while he looked over at the other men.

"Sir? What's your name?"

"My name is Wadi."

"Wadi, can you help us? These girls have been through a lot and we need your compassion. Please?"

The officer let out another forced breath. Again, he looked towards the other officers. He rubbed the back of his neck.

"Wait here," he instructed.

Hailey's pulse quickened as she watched him walk over to the other men. They talked for a few moments before Wadi returned.

"How much do you have?" he asked.

Hailey hesitated.

"Look, lady, I'm not going to rob you. I just need to know how much I'm working with if I'm going to help you."

Hailey quickly did a rough calculation of how much she thought they might need to make it to an embassy once they were in another country.

"If I need to get out of Egypt, then I can give you around

fifteen hundred US dollars if you can help me. Is that enough?"

Wadi chuckled. "Yeah, that will be enough. Give me fifty for now."

Hailey opened the console and retrieved the amount.

"Oh, and a bit of advice, don't tell anyone else you have that much. If needed, just say you have a couple hundred. That will be more than enough to get you what you need at any given point."

Wadi took the bill from her and walked over to the other men. He talked for a few moments, then handed them the money and returned back to her.

"OK, you can go through. Head up north to Port Said. There's a commercial shipping port up there. You'll see signs for it once you get through the city. You'll only pass through a checkpoint before you get there, but I'll call ahead for you. If you give them another fifty, they'll let you through. Once you're at the port, ask for a man named Colson. If you give him... ohhh... say around five hundred, he should be able to get you and the girls on one of the container ships heading to Cyprus. Then you need to get you and the girls directly to an embassy. Understand?"

"OK..." Hailey said hesitantly. The plan sounded quite overwhelming.

"Oh, navigating Port Said can be a bit difficult until you get to the shipping yard. Uhh... I guess you'll just have to try and ask for directions as you go and pray you make it. I know it doesn't mean much, but I hope you do."

He flashed her an empathetic smile, but it didn't ease the tension that was building up in her. Hailey turned her head away and looked out the windshield. She wrung the steering wheel with both her hands.

"That is... uh... a lot to take in."

"Yeah, I guess it is."

"Wadi?"

"Yeah?"

"If I were to give you a thousand dollars right now, would you drive us to meet Colson?"

Wadi's eyes grew wide and he pursed his lips. "Um... wow. That is a nice offer. But look–"

"Don't dismiss us, please," Hailey cut him off. "These girls deserve better, and if I go alone, they will be frightened. So will I," she said with an awkward laugh. "I'd like to keep them from that if I can."

"Uh, I don't know."

"Please, Wadi."

"A thousand dollars?"

"A thousand and fifty if you can get us through the other checkpoint without paying."

Wadi chuckled. "Alright, fine. But we need to take my jeep. And we'll need to give that extra fifty to my men so they don't report me."

"Done," Hailey agreed as she grabbed another fifty and handed it to him.

"Wake up the girls and let them know what's happening. I'll go talk to my men and get my jeep. Stay in the car. I'll drive up to get you."

"Of course. Thank you."

Wadi huffed and shook his head as he smiled at her before walking away. Giving a little shriek of joy when he was out of earshot, Hailey turned to gently wake the girls. It only took moments to stir them. They jolted up thinking something was wrong. By the time Hailey had calmed them and explained what was happening, Wadi had the Jeep and was pulling up next to them.

"OK, girls. Time to go. Make sure you grab everything because we won't be coming back."

Hailey gathered up the rest of the money and shoved it in the cloth bag with the last bits of their food.

"What about my parents, Hailey? They won't know where to find me."

"Oh, Layla. I know this is scary. But we will find a way to tell them. I promise."

"We gotta get going," Wadi interrupted. He had gotten out of the jeep and was now opening Hailey's door. "I'd like to get up to the port as soon as possible before the shift change."

"OK. Girls let's go."

Wadi helped them all climb into the back seat of his armored jeep. The girls snuggled in on either side of her. Wadi swung the jeep around and headed for Port Said. Hailey put a protective arm around each of them, as she watched their car disappear from view.

"Wadi, thank you. I mean it."

"You're welcome."

They drove in silence for a few minutes. The girls fell back asleep.

"Miss?"

"Wadi, please call me Hailey."

"Alright... Hailey. It's just over an hour to the shipping port so you can get some rest if you want to."

"Thanks, but I don't think I'll be able to sleep till we get out of Egypt. My nerves are a bit on edge."

"You know you're safe now, right? I'll get you there, and Colson will take care of the rest."

Hailey's lip quivered. Hearing Wadi say she was safe felt

good. She leaned her head on the back of the seat.

"Are you alright?"

"Yes. It's just that it's been a long time since I've felt safe. It feels good to hear. So thanks."

"Anytime."

"You know, you're English is impressive."

Wadi laughed. "Well, I hope so. I studied in the States for four years."

"Really? Where?"

"Seattle. Where are you from?"

"New York."

"I went there once. That is one big city."

"Yeah, it is. I miss it."

"How long have you been gone?"

Hailey sighed. "Too long. How long have you been in the military?"

"Since I was fifteen. I volunteered early for the mandatory service, and I have no plans to leave. I love it."

As the girls slept, Wadi and Hailey continued to chat casually. Hailey welcomed it. The small talk was a nice break and helped keep her mind off of what could lay ahead.

When the checkpoint appeared down the road, Hailey tensed.

Wadi looked over his shoulder. "It's alright. I've got this."

He pulled the jeep up to the boom gate and rolled down his window. The man that walked up said something to Wadi, making him laugh. He noticed Hailey and nodded. She smiled and nodded back.

The men talked for a few minutes. Hailey looked around, trying not to seem nervous. But she was.

When the man finally walked away, Wadi rolled up his window.

"See? Nothing to worry about."

CHAPTER 41

Pulling up to the shipping yard, Wadi placed his arm on the back of the front seat and turned to look at her.

"Stay in the jeep while I go talk with Colson. I won't be long."

Hailey nodded.

She watched with held breath as he got out and went up to, what Hailey assumed, was the office. The structure had been converted from a shipping container. Three windows and a doorway had been cut into the side that faced her.

When Wadi disappeared inside, she looked around.

The shipping yard didn't seem any quieter for being so late at night. She eyed everyone that passed the jeep, but no one seemed to even notice the jeep or her sitting inside. Or maybe they didn't care. Everyone went about their business: loading and unloading cargo, driving around various vehicles or yelling at someone else.

Wadi had only been gone a few minutes. Hailey relaxed when she saw him. As he jogged back to her, he had a smile on his face.

That looks promising.

She smiled back.

"You're all set," he said as he opened his door and jumped in.

"Colson can be rough around the edges, so don't let him rattle you. I got him to agree to get you to Cyprus for four hundred. And..." Wadi checked his watch, "there is a container ship leaving in an hour that he can smuggle you onto."

"That sounds perfect."

Hailey leaned over the seat and held out the thousand dollars to Wadi.

"As agreed. You have more than earned it. You'll never understand how thankful I am for your help."

Wadi looked at the money and then over to the sleeping girls leaning against her. He pursed his lips and took the top two hundred-dollar bills off the top of the stack.

"You keep the rest." He chuckled. "This is just in case someone finds out what I did. It should help me smooth things over."

"I'm sure you could use the money. Please, take it."

"Ah, Hailey, my parents are actually quite wealthy. Really, I don't need your money. Spend it on them."

Hailey's face flushed with embarrassment. She had blatantly stereotyped him and equated Egypt, an African country, with poverty.

She closed her eyes and shook her head at herself. "I'm sorry. That was incredibly rude of me. Here you are doing this incredibly noble thing, and I go and insult you. Wadi, I'm sorry."

"Well, thanks, but don't give it another thought. We're good."

Wadi checked his watch. "It's time."

Tingles from jittery nerves ran down her spine. Hailey couldn't believe how the wait flew by. She nudged each of the girls to wake them. They moaned but barely moved.

"I'll carry Layla," Wadi offered.

Once Layla was in his arms, Hailey scooted out and picked up Ruby. She moaned again but nestled into her neck and stilled.

Wadi nodded towards the office. "That's Colson."

Hailey readjusted Ruby and looked over.

Colson's overweight frame leaned against the railing next to the office door. His unruly hair framed his clean-shaven face. His jaw was covered with smears of grease as were his hands. He eyed her as they approached.

"So... you need to get to Cyprus?" His accent was thick and European, but Hailey couldn't quite place it.

"Yes, sir."

"Don't call me sir," he snapped.

"Be nice, Colson. She's paying you enough, so you can at least be civil."

Colson snorted. "Fine, fine. Follow me."

They walked around the back of the office and along a row of stacked shipping containers. Passing three large cranes, they made their way over to the end of a dock, where a long metal gangway ran up to a fully-loaded container ship. The hull looked to have had a fresh red paint job, it glistened under the lamps on the dock. Block letters spelled out the name of the ship in white - Triumph Sol.

"Get on board and move to the top deck," Colson barked. "You can take those stairs over there once you're on board."

He pointed to a set of stairs looming above them. Hailey's eyes traced their way up the gangway and over to the stairs. Should be easy enough.

"When you get to the top, make your way to the front of the ship along the edge of the containers. It's hard to see from here, but there's a narrow walkway between the containers and the railing. You can either stay on the deck or climb down one of the three hatches. They all lead to a cargo hold just below deck, near the bow. Inside is an orange box bolted to the floor. Inside that are blankets. Feel free to use them... or not. I don't care."

Colson snorted and spit just beyond where she stood.

Wadi sneered at him. "Don't mind Colson here. He doesn't understand the concept of having a lady present."

Hailey smiled.

Colson ignored them. "The crew will stick to the navigation deck and the crew decks. Neither are anywhere near you, so you don't need to worry about anyone bothering you. If you need help, there's a radio in the cargo hold. Just press the black button and talk. I will be on the other end if I'm not busy. Do you have any questions?"

By the tone of Colson's voice, it sounded more like a rhetorical question than one of thoughtfulness.

"Nope, that's great."

He held out his hand "Good. Now, where's my money."

Hailey struggled to get it out of the bag while still holding onto Ruby, but she managed and placed the bills onto Colson's greasy hand.

"Happy sailing." He gave her a lackluster salute and a smug smile. "Wadi, pleasure as always."

Colson nodded to each of them and headed back to the office.

"Well, I guess this is it," Hailey said reluctantly.

"I guess so. Don't worry, you'll be fine."

Hailey looked at each of the girls. "Yeah, I actually think we will be."

Wadi tenderly woke Layla. "Time to go, little one."

He slid her to the ground once she had stirred enough to stand. Layla groggily rubbed her eyes. Hailey slipped the cloth bag over her other wrist. Being careful not to drop Ruby, she took Layla's hand.

A lump of emotion stuck in Hailey's throat. She didn't dare try and speak. She resorted to nodding her thank you to Wadi. He returned the gesture. Hailey walked over to the base of the gangway. After flashing him one more smile, she headed up.

Part way to the top she stopped.

"What's wrong?"

"I was wondering," she called down to him. "Would you do one more incredibly huge favor for me?"

"Name it."

"My friend. His body is lying outside an abandoned building south of Hasna. Could you see if there is some way to get him back to the states?"

Wadi smiled and nodded. "Consider it done. I'll look into it and make sure he makes it back to you."

Tears stung her eyes. "Thank you."

Layla waved. "Bye, Wadi."

Wadi waved back.

When she reached the top, he was still standing on the dock. She returned his wave.

It took a while for Hailey to maneuver up the stairwell and down the walkway with Ruby in her arms, but she found her way to the bow of the ship. Her arms burned under the weight of carrying Ruby so far. Hailey scanned the deck and spotted one of the hatches. Reaching it, she woke Ruby and set her down.

Ruby rubbed her eyes. "Where are we?"

"We're on the great big ship I told you about."

Ruby looked around and hugged her doll.

The handle of the hatch didn't budge. Hailey gave it a kick

with her foot, and it opened on the second try. The hatch lifted easily, and Hailey lowered her head inside as she gripped either edge of the hole with her hands. She peered down inside. The room was lit and empty apart from the orange box, a broom, and an old pair of boots. After jumping inside, Hailey helped each of the girls down.

The cargo hold was warm and stuffy. Hailey looked around. Next to the radio, four portholes looked out over the ocean. Each had a little latch on them. Hailey popped two of them. Fresh ocean air filled the room, making it much more tolerable.

She settled the girls under a couple blankets and sat with them as they drifted back to sleep. Hailey still felt wired. Maybe a quick walk on deck would help. She adjusted the blankets over the girls and returned to the deck.

The ship started pulling away from the dock. Hailey went to the railing and tried to look back down to the pier to see if she could see Wadi. The view was blocked. She walked to the bow of the ship, stepped up on the bottom rung of the railing, and looked down at the prow as it cut through the water.

The ship picked up speed. The ocean air whipped her headscarf off, and it floated behind her. Hailey didn't even bother to look back or try and catch it. It seemed kind of fitting that she was free from it, as if it somehow symbolized her leaving everything behind. She sighed as a weight lifted off her shoulders.

It's time, Hailey.

For what?

To understand.

About Ryan?

Yes, but also more than that.

Hailey stepped down onto the deck and leaned her forearms

on the top of the railing. She looked out over the blackness spanning out beyond the ship.

Do you remember Joseph's life?

Yes, well... parts of it.

Just as I have chosen to do in your life, it would be easy to question what I did in Joseph's life. If you look through man's eyes you could see an impulsive boy angering his jealous brothers, who then sold him into slavery. A false accusation that landed him in prison, forgetful friends who caused him, even more, years in prison, and a God who finally stepped in and brought good out of all the bad by positioning him in a place of power.

But... isn't that what happened? She must be missing something. He said, 'if you look through man's eyes,' which usually means not the best way to look at it.

Yet if you look through My eyes, you will see that there was a dreadful famine coming and that I took time to prepare Joseph to move from his humble life to the house of Pharaoh, so that many could be saved from starvation and know My love. You will also see a boy who honored Me through it all and came to be a man of restraint.

Hmm... yeah, I can see that. But couldn't you have just stopped the famine?

Hailey, who all came to know more about Me by this being Joseph's path?

Well, Joseph, all his brothers, his father, the cupbearer and the baker, Pharaoh, and... well, I guess most of the people of Egypt. If not all.

And if I had chosen to keep famine from the land, how many would have come to know Me better and know My love?

The realization hit her.

None, she answered. *At least no more than they did before.*

That is your answer to the questions you have been asking. I have completed what I wanted with Ryan's life while he was on earth. Yes, I can stop death, but you couldn't possibly fathom all that would cease or be altered if I had.

For My thoughts are not your thoughts, nor are your ways My ways. For as the heavens are higher than the earth, so are My ways higher than your ways and My thoughts than your thoughts.

Hailey stood there in silence for a moment to let His words sink in. The sound of the water crashing against the hull as the ship reached the open ocean, filled her ears. Millions of stars shone above her as the light from Port Said faded behind them.

El Elyon, I have no idea what I'm heading towards, but You do have great plans. I never realized it is You who accomplishes all things for me. I now see -

A scream from below deck interrupted Hailey's prayer. Alarm shot through her. She ran for the hatch. Jumping down into the cargo hold, Hailey landed wrong on her ankle. Wincing in pain, she looked around the room. Layla and Ruby huddled on top of the orange box screaming and pointing. Hailey followed their pointing fingers to a four-foot wide pipe protruding out of the wall in the corner and down into the floor.

"What? What's wrong?" She didn't see any possible threat.

"Look... look behind the pipe," Layla moaned then buried her head into Ruby.

Hailey swallowed hard and moved slowly towards the pipe.

Just as she was moving to look behind it, a hairy rat ran out and scurried between her legs. The movement scared her half to death, and she screamed. The rat ran under one of the blankets on the floor. The girls shrieked.

"Girls, settle down. It's just a rat. I'll get it."

Hailey grabbed the broom and wacked the moving bump under the blankets till it laid still. She couldn't bear to look at it or touch it. She scooped it up with the blanket and tossed it and the blanket, out the porthole.

Sorry, Carlson.

"Close it, close it!" the girls demanded in unison.

"But it's too hot in here with them closed."

"We don't care." Layla shook her head. "That's where the thing came in from, and it ran right across Ruby."

The girls looked terrified. Hailey went to them. They were shaking.

Ruby squeezed her tighter. "We woke up, and you weren't here. You weren't here. Where were you?"

"Shhh, now. It's alright. I'm here now. All the rats are gone. It's just us."

Ruby looked up at Hailey with sad eyes, "Promise you won't leave us... never again."

Pulling the girls into her, Hailey realized then and there that she was never going to go home. The vastness of God's plan for her started to take shape in her mind. She smiled.

"As the Lord wills it, I won't leave you... ever."

CHAPTER 42

– Six months later –

With arms full of bags, Hailey fumbled with the keys and got the door of the flat unlocked. She pushed it open with her foot. Setting the bags on the floor as quietly as she could, she turned and gently closed the door.

Tiptoeing to the sunroom, Hailey peeked inside.

Ruby's back faced her. Sunrays poured through the glass, encasing her in a warm light. She was playing on the floor with her doll and hadn't heard Hailey come in.

"Hello, Ruby," she whispered.

"Mama!" Ruby jumped up and ran into her arms.

"Hello, my darling. Did you have a good time with Anna?"

"Yes. We did a painting for you. I'll go get it."

Ruby wiggled out of her arms and ran into the house. Hailey watched her go but didn't follow. Instead, she turned and looked out over the garden. She smiled. It was wonderful seeing Ruby so happy. The struggles were still there, but Hailey was glad her nightmares were now few and far between.

"How was Cairo?" Anna said coming up behind her.

Hailey grinned. "Good. Layla is doing so well."

Anna handed her a cup of coffee.

"Oh, thanks." Hailey took a sip. "She misses you and Ruby, but she likes her new school. And you should hear her sing. I think those classes are really helping her heal."

Anna beamed. "I'm so glad."

"Look, mama! Look!"

"Now what do we have here?"

"It's our family. See here's you and me sitting by the tree. That's Layla and Anna playing at the park with gramma Nada. And that's Ryan reading with Jesus."

"That's beautiful, sweetheart. I love it. Could you go put it on my desk? I want to hang it up right away."

"OK." and off she went.

"I like how she still talks about Ryan."

Anna reached over and squeezed her shoulder. "Me too."

"Thanks for holding down the fort. Was she OK?"

"Don't worry. Ruby did fine. They were some of her good days."

"Still, I think I've finally decided. I want you to take over this next round of campaigning."

"Are you sure?"

"Yeah. I'm sure."

"What about the new safe house in Sudan?"

"It's mostly done. And the team is already up to speed with the others. It will be an easy transition for you."

Anna pulled out her phone. "Ok, well I get back from the Anti-Trafficking conference in Italy on Friday, so I can fly to Cairo on Monday and get started. What do you think you'll do now?"

Hailey took a sip of her coffee, pausing to let it warm her throat. "Work right here in Paris. It's our home. I think Ruby is tired of flying around with me so much. And honestly, I am too.

I'd really like to work more closely with the recovery center here."

"I think that's a great idea."

Ruby ran into the room. She hugged Hailey's legs.

Anna smiled at them. "I'm going to go check on supper."

"Sounds good. Thank you."

"How is Layla, mama?"

"Good."

"Does her family like their new home?"

"Yes, very much. Layla gave me a present for you."

"Really?"

Hailey set her cup down on the glass bistro table. She reached into her pocket and pulled out the beaded necklace Layla had made. Ruby's eyes grew wide. Hailey slipped it over Ruby's head and kneeled in front of her.

"What do you think?"

"It's beautiful. Can I call her and say thank you?"

"How about after supper?"

"OK."

Ruby ran the necklace through her fingers. A sadness fell over her face.

"What is it, honey?"

Ruby wrapped her arms around Hailey's neck. "Mama, promise you won't leave me... never ever."

It was a request Ruby still made often, and Hailey answered it the same way she always had.

She kissed Ruby's cheek and whispered in her ear.

"As the Lord wills it, I won't leave you... ever."

DID YOU ENJOY

VEILED

&

THE SAND BRIDE

SUBSCRIBE TO:

www.cyanagaffney.com

While you're there... check out the contest page for details about how to

ENTER & WIN

Be sure to follow Cyana on social media!

ACKNOWLEDGEMENTS

Colin, for all the brainstorming sessions and support.
Sister, for your insight & encouragement – they were vital.
Laura & Ken at Northwest Scuba, for your expertise.
Vanessa, for your help with editing.
Melissa, for your work on the cover.

Made in the USA
Columbia, SC
26 December 2017